"Join the delightfully clueless sleuth Barnabas and his resourceful sidekick, the winsome Wilfred, on their new adventure. Author Columbkill Noonan seamlessly blends cozy mystery with mythology, her clever humor and solid pace making this a whimsically engaging escape for readers."

Elizabeth Spann Craig,
author of the Myrtle Clover mysteries

"This is a charming book, well-crafted, and I love the characters. I highly recommend it to anyone who's looking for a good read!"

Dianne Harman,
USA Today and Amazon #1 Chart Bestselling Author.

"Sensational. A dazzling masterpiece of adventure and comedy. A fantastically fantasy-fueled ride from the first page to the last! Nobody writes like Columbkill Noonan..."

Isabella May
author of Oh! What a Pavlova, The Cocktail Bar, and Costa del Churros

Barnabas Tew and The Case of The Nine Worlds

Columbkill Noonan

Also available:
**Barnabas Tew and
The Case of The Missing Scarab**

CROOKED
CAT

Copyright © 2018 by Columbkill Noonan
Artwork: Adobe Stock © lynea
Design: soqoqo
Editors: Maureen Vincent-Northam
All rights reserved.

No part of this book may be used or reproduced in any manner whatsoever without written permission of the author or Crooked Cat Books except for brief quotations used for promotion or in reviews. This is a work of fiction. Names, characters, and incidents are used fictitiously.

First Black Line Edition, Crooked Cat, 2018

Discover us online:
www.crookedcatbooks.com

Join us on facebook:
www.facebook.com/crookedcat

Tweet a photo of yourself holding this book to **@crookedcatbooks** and something nice will happen.

*To all the amazing women
whom I am lucky to call friends,
who fearlessly take on the world
and show me over and over
the true meaning of bravery.*

*There's a
little piece
of all of you
in Brynhild.*

Acknowledgements

I'd like to thank, firstly, my wonderful editor, Maureen Vincent-Northam, who makes the editing process as painless as can be. Her attention to detail and remarkable insight make these "Barnabas" books much better than they would be without her! I'd also like to thank Laurence and Stephanie Patterson, the dynamic duo behind Crooked Cat Books, who took a chance on a crazy story and brought it to life. Another thanks goes to my husband, who patiently deals with me when I'm in the middle of an intense bout of writing and shush him relentlessly, and then serves as my first beta reader/initial editor without a word of protest. Last but not least, a huge thanks to Nichole Leavy, artist extraordinaire, who has worked up countless gorgeous flyers and promotional materials on the shortest of notice, and who lets me bounce all my weird ideas off of her and doesn't judge.

About the Author

Columbkill Noonan has a Master's of Science in Biology, and teaches Anatomy and Physiology. She also is an RYT-200 and teaches Aerial Yoga, Hatha Yoga, and Vinyasa.

Columbkill's writing has been featured on Female First UK, a British lifestyle webzine for women, and she has published over twenty short stories in various anthologies and literary magazines. Both novels, *Barnabas Tew and the Case of the Missing Scarab*, a humorous mystery/mythological caper, and her second novel, *Barnabas Tew and the Case of the Nine Worlds*, are published by Crooked Cat Books.

Columbkill lives with her husband and their three rescue cats. In her spare time, she can usually be found paddle boarding or spending time with her incredibly spoiled rescue horse, Mittens. As a yoga teacher, she can often be found doing yoga anywhere and everywhere, whether in a studio, in her living room, on a paddle board, or, sometimes, even, on Mittens (who does not mind, really, so long as there are apples involved).

Barnabas Tew and The Case of The Nine Worlds

Also available:
**Barnabas Tew and
The Case of The Missing Scarab**

Chapter One

The chariot bounced jauntily along, following roads of increasingly questionable maintenance that ran through lands of increasingly questionable civilization. Cold winds screamed down from the snow-capped mountains into the valley to buffet the passengers that rode inside the chariot.

One of the passengers (the driver, who hailed from Olavskirken, Norway) was unperturbed by the cold and the wind. The other two, Barnabas Tew and Wilfred Colby (late of Marylebone, London, and, until recently, quite ordinary subjects of the British Empire) were finding the weather to be extraordinarily uncomfortable.

"Really, I cannot tolerate much more of this cold," said Barnabas to Wilfred. He grasped at his robes, trying to keep them close to his slightly rounded and decidedly short little body to no avail: they billowed about most distressingly, so that his ankles and knees were entirely exposed to the biting wind.

"Indeed," replied Wilfred, who was suffering from the same travails, "these robes are, perhaps, not the most practical of attire in this climate."

"No, they most certainly are not," said Barnabas. He looked at the driver, who was wrapped in a thick fur cloak and who appeared to be completely comfortable. "You'd think that Anubis would have outfitted us properly, at the very least," he grumbled.

"He really could have been a bit more accommodating," agreed Wilfred. "Or perhaps Odin might have sent the appropriate attire."

"One would think," said Barnabas. "I must say, this oversight has left a bad taste in my mouth. I don't expect to be much impressed, from what I've seen so far."

"Well, perhaps it won't be as bad as all that. At least all of the Viking gods have proper heads," pointed out Wilfred.

Barnabas was a private detective, and Wilfred was his assistant. They had plied their trade, somewhat unsuccessfully, from their offices in Marylebone, until the Egyptian god Anubis had decided to fetch them to the land of the dead. They had solved Anubis' case quite successfully, but it was beyond Anubis' power to restore them to life which is why they were, just now, on their way to Asgard for an interview with Odin, the king of the Viking gods. And freezing, because they were still dressed in clothing that was more fitting for a hot Egyptian desert than for the bitterly cold mountains of Norway.

"Do they? Are you quite sure? It truly was tiresome, what with everyone having the heads of falcons and crocodiles and jackals and what-not," said Barnabas.

"And us, as well," said Wilfred. "Mustn't forget that!"

"How could I forget that?" said Barnabas. "One doesn't soon forget being turned into a mouse!"

Wilfred laughed. "At least we are restored to our proper forms," he said, trying to lighten the mood. But Barnabas merely scowled in return.

"It will do us no good to be proper people again, if we are naught but icicles by the time we get anywhere," he said petulantly. He looked at the driver again. "Ahem," he said, trying to get the man's attention. "Ahem, ahem!" he tried again, more loudly.

The man continued to drive, taking no notice of Barnabas. "Beastly manners!" hissed Barnabas to Wilfred, before peremptorily tapping the driver on the shoulder and issuing one last, "Ahem."

The driver, a man by the name of Vindr (which, coincidentally, meant *wind* in the language of the Norsemen; a fact that, of those in the chariot, only Vindr himself knew, and neither Barnabas nor Wilfred had either thought of or would ever think to ask, and thus would never know), turned his head and raised a questioning eyebrow.

"I say," said Barnabas, "might you have a spare cloak or two? My assistant and I are most uncomfortable." An unfortunate gust of wind lifted Barnabas robe all the way up above his waist, causing Vindr to guffaw loudly. Wilfred turned away and pretended to be incredibly interested in the passing scenery. "I say!" said Barnabas again, with a great deal more irritation. "Do you have a cloak or not?"

"Only what I've got on myself," replied Vindr.

"Perhaps we could share it?" suggested Barnabas hopefully.

"Then *I'd* be cold, wouldn't I?" said Vindr. He turned around and paid no more mind to the irate little detective shivering and fuming in the back of the chariot.

"Abominable!" huffed Barnabas to Wilfred. "I do believe the manners of these people may prove to be even more lacking than those of our former hosts!"

"Perhaps not," soothed Wilfred. "Perhaps they will be delightful. It will at least be very illuminating, to see Asgard and Valhalla for ourselves!"

"Hmph," said Barnabas. "I'd much prefer to see London once more, myself." He sniffed in Vindr's direction and wrinkled his nose in distaste. "And perhaps a bath would be in order, as well."

Just then, Vindr turned around to address his passengers. Barnabas quickly wiped the disdainful look off of his face and plastered an exceedingly unconvincing look of bemused innocence on instead. Luckily, Vindr either didn't see (or didn't care) what Barnabas' face was doing behind his back. The man merely pointed into the near distance and said, "We approach the Rainbow Bridge to Asgard. Hold on!"

"What? Which bridge?" asked Barnabas, trying to peer around Vindr so that he might see (which was, in truth, quite difficult, as Vindr was a rather large man, and his girth was added to by the immensity of his furs).

"*That* bridge. There!" said Vindr, leaning aside so that Barnabas and Wilfred might see.

There, just in front of them, was a very high, very thin bridge. It was, however, unlike any bridge either Barnabas or

Wilfred had ever seen.

It was made of a very strange metal, for one thing (if it was any sort of metal at all, that is) the color was neither grey, nor black, nor even a rusty brown, but was instead somehow a compilation of all colors at once so that it shimmered and glowed like the scales of a fish. It was quite beautiful to look at, but Barnabas immediately questioned the possible tensile strength of such a material.

The bridge rose high into the sky, with no apparent supports on either side, and no guardrail to speak of, besides. The arch was so high, and the span so long, that neither Barnabas nor Wilfred could see the other side.

"*That* thing?" gasped Barnabas. "You don't mean to actually drive the chariot onto *that*, do you?"

"Of course I do," replied Vindr. "There's no other way to Asgard, excepting for the Rainbow Bridge."

"I do believe I've rethought this. I don't wish to go to Asgard at all," said Barnabas. He looked quite green about the gills, and his eyes were wide as a cat's.

"Well, I suppose you could tell Odin that, once we've gotten there," said Vindr. "And look, we are almost on it, anyway." Barnabas looked and saw that the bridge was, indeed, quite close.

"Uh, well, no, that is to say, I think, let's not go over the bridge. You can just let me out here, if it's all the same," said Barnabas, clutching the sides of the chariot so tightly that his fingertips were quite purple from the pressure.

"I think it will be fine," whispered Wilfred.

"It does not look at all fine to me," said Barnabas. "No, really, I must insist. I'll be stepping out here, if you'd just be so kind as to slow down a bit…" The chariot picked up speed as Vindr flicked a whip at the horses.

"I'm sure Vindr here does this all the time," said Wilfred. Now the bridge so close that they would surely reach it in just a few seconds, if they continued on at their current pace.

"No," hissed Barnabas, shaking his head. "I do not wish to go over that bridge, not even if Vindr has driven across every day of his life, not even if Vindr can fly like a big fur-covered bird." But even as he said this, the chariot passed onto the bridge and they began ascending the steep incline at an alarming speed.

"Oh dear," said Barnabas, turning from green to ghostly white. He squinched his eyes shut as tightly as he could.

The chariot continued to pick up speed as it ascended ever higher into the air. The winds picked up speed and swirled around in all directions. A curious bird flew close to take a better look and inadvertently brushed Barnabas' face with its wingtips.

"Ahhh!" screeched Barnabas.

"Eeep!" screeched the bird, alarmed.

To hear the creature's cries so close to his face only heightened Barnabas' fear, of course (although if he had only opened his eyes he would have seen that the bird was nothing more than a tiny little swallow, and was indeed far more frightened than was Barnabas himself). Barnabas did not open his eyes, however, and therefore was convinced that the thing cheeping in his face was a terrible bird of great size and malicious intent.

"Ack!" he screamed once more, reaching desperately for Wilfred's arm. Unfortunately, he was quite turned around and grabbed Vindr's arm instead. The burly Viking glanced at the hand that clutched his arm with amused disdain and quickly plucked the prying fingers from his flesh.

"It's pecking me! Oh, I am being pecked!" cried Barnabas.

"Nothing is pecking you," pointed out Vindr. "If you'd just open your eyes…"

"It's just like the canary, Wilfred!" yelped Barnabas. "Is it the cursed canary come back to torment me?"

Wilfred, who had been with Barnabas on the repeated occasions of attacks upon Barnabas by said canary, put a consoling arm on Barnabas' shoulder. "It isn't the canary," he said. "And I do believe you've frightened it off."

Barnabas slitted one eye open, then the other. When he saw that his avian malefactor had indeed dispersed and, further, that the chariot was in no imminent danger of plummeting off of the precarious bridge, he opened them both fully and gasped.

"But it is beautiful!" he exclaimed, his fears forgotten. And it was, in truth, a glorious sight that opened up before them. The bridge was completely encased in clouds that glistened and sparkled with a diffuse light, so that the ground was quite hidden from view and therefore any sense of being up too high, or of falling to one's death, was removed.

Straight ahead of them was an arch, gloriously carved with all sorts of intricate figures of warriors, animals, and weapons. It was made of the same resplendent material as the bridge but seemed more *condensed* somehow, so that all of the colors were more intense.

Beyond the arch was a magnificent expanse of the greenest grass that Barnabas had ever seen, with graceful weeping willows framing the causeway on either side.

"Yes, it is beautiful, isn't it?" asked Vindr. He swept his arms wide with a flourish. "Welcome to Asgard!" he proclaimed.

"What a marvelous landscape!" said Barnabas admiringly. "See, Wilfred? This is what a true garden looks like. Nice orderly rows of trees, and everything in its place. Don't you agree?"

Wilfred, who liked all sorts of gardens, even the wild and unruly ones, nodded his agreement. "It is quite splendid," he said.

Vindr laughed. "Well, if it's order you're after, you'll certainly like the looks of Asgard. Although you may not find the rest of the realms as pleasing."

"The rest of the realms?" said Barnabas. "You mean we won't be staying here?" His voice held a hint of disappointment.

"That's not for me to say. Only Odin can tell you what needs to be done," said Vindr. His eyes turned up at the corners mischievously. "But I *can* promise that there probably won't be *too* many murderous canaries, at least."

Barnabas, seeing that the Norseman was poking fun of him, bristled. "Yes, well, it is easy to talk when one hasn't experienced such a thing. I'd like to see how well *you* would fare in the Egyptian desert."

"It truly was a vicious canary," added Wilfred helpfully.

"Wasn't it?" said Barnabas. "I wonder who would win in a fight: Bastet, or that canary?" he mused.

"Hmmm," said Wilfred, pondering. "Hard to say, as I haven't had the dubious pleasure of sparring with either."

"My money's on the canary," said Barnabas, nodding definitively.

Vindr smiled to himself and shook his head, wondering at the gods' choice of these two strange little men as he aimed the chariot beneath the arch and entered Asgard.

Barnabas looked from side to side as the horses' hooves clipped and clopped on the smooth stones of the causeway. Every moment brought some new wondrous sight, and his head turned to and fro so rapidly that he looked quite a bit like a curious canary himself.

"Oh, Wilfred! Do look at that!" he cried. He pointed at a beautiful, airy building that sat high atop a smooth white cliff, his fright (and his irritability at being dragged halfway across the world, and halfway into the sky, at that) forgotten in his delight.

"And that!" exclaimed Wilfred, directing his employer's attention to another hall, that had immense wooden doors of cherry wood that had been carved with intricate etchings and studded with a dazzling array of gemstones. "Isn't it is amazing?"

"And this!' gasped Barnabas. "Heavens, but I do believe this must be the most beautiful garden I have ever seen. He was staring, his mouth agape in wonderment, at a grove of trees with silvery bark.

But it was not a typical grove. The trunks of all the trees ranged in perfectly straight lines, as though they had been meticulously trained from germination; there was no variation whatsoever in their upright rigidity so that they looked like so many silver-clad soldiers standing at careful attention (an effect of which Barnabas wholeheartedly approved).

The most impressive aspect of the grove, however, was the

leaves of the trees. Wondrously uniform in size and shape, they were the color of the richest red-gold that one could imagine. So deeply hued that they appeared to be nearly metallic, they shimmered and glistened with a soft sheen in the sun.

Barnabas, moved by the beauty of the place, daubed surreptitiously at the corner of his eye. "But it is splendid," he whispered. "The most splendid place of all."

Vindr smiled proudly as he drove, clearly enjoying his passengers' admiration of his homeland.

"Quite so," agreed Wilfred. "The place takes one's breath away, does it not?"

"Indeed it does," said Barnabas, awestruck. Then his voice rose in pitch as a new sight excited him once more. "And look at this! What an amazing house!" He pointed towards the far end of the grove, where an immense hall with a roof of hammered silver stood framed at the end of a long avenue of the gold-leafed trees.

Vindr laughed heartily. "That *house*," he said, "that *house* is Valhalla. And it is where Odin lives."

"Valhalla?" queried Barnabas. "And Odin is our, ahem, *host* here, if I am not mistaken?"

"Yes, that is so," said Vindr.

"Well, Valhalla is a pretty name for a house, if a bit odd. What does it mean, do you know?" asked Barnabas.

"What does it mean!" exclaimed Vindr, astonished. "Have you never heard of Valhalla before?"

"It is the place where Viking warriors go when they die, is it not?" supplied Wilfred helpfully.

"Aye, that is so," said Vindr. "But only if they die while a-viking, you know."

Barnabas and Wilfred shuddered at Vindr's use of the word 'viking' as a verb. Neither had ever heard it used in that way before, precisely. Still, knowing enough about history to understand something of the warlike and marauding habits of the Vikings, it was easy enough to surmise that people who had died in the *doing* of 'viking' would not be the most amiable of fellows.

Vindr continued on, oblivious to the detectives' alarm. "And they'll only stay there until Ragnarok, of course," he said blithely.

"Ragnarok?" repeated Barnabas, frowning. "Is that some sort of tea?"

"It's no British tea, that's for certain," said Wilfred. "Perhaps a new sort, imported from China or India?"

"Well, I much prefer proper British tea," said Barnabas. "But then again, I am quite famished and in need of refreshment, so I suppose I will take whatever is on hand." He sighed and turned to Vindr. "Will Odin be serving this Ragnarok then? And will all those dead Vikings be joining us?"

"Serving Ragnarok?" boomed Vindr, confused and astonished. "What are you talking about?"

"The tea," said Barnabas patiently. "Will Ragnarok be the only sort of tea, or will there be some English types as well. A nice Earl Grey, perhaps?"

"Earl Grey would hit the spot," agreed Wilfred. "I cannot remember the last time I had a proper cup."

"Certainly not since we ended up in that dreadful Egyptian place," said Barnabas.

"No, there was most definitely no tea-time there," agreed Wilfred.

"And what I wouldn't give for a good old-fashioned watercress sandwich," added Barnabas. "Although that is not to disparage the marvelous cheese plates that Bindi served," he added quickly, reddening.

Wilfred nodded and politely pretended to examine his fingernails whilst Barnabas got hold of his emotions. Bindi was a mouse-person in the Egyptian underworld who was a hostess at a little roadside inn and for whom Barnabas had developed some ill-timed and ill-advised feelings (considering that she was a mouse person and he only temporarily so, at the time).

Vindr, of course, had no way of knowing any of this, and was completely flummoxed by the odd turn the conversation had taken.

"Why in Hel's name would the Viking warriors sit about drinking tea and eating watercrust sandwiches?" he sputtered.

"Water*cress*," said Barnabas, a bit smugly. "Being as there is no such thing as a water*crust* sandwich, of course."

"Bah!" exclaimed Vindr, annoyed. "I don't care what kind of sandwich…"

"Ah, so there *will* be sandwiches?" asked Barnabas.

"Ooh, a cucumber sandwich would be nice, too," said Wilfred.

"Quite so!" agreed Barnabas. "I hadn't realized how hungry I was, until all this talk of Ragnarok tea and water*cress* sandwiches."

"There will be no sandwiches!" yelled Vindr in frustration.

Barnabas and Wilfred, astounded at the sudden outburst, shut their mouths and shuffled their feet.

"Hmmph," muttered Barnabas at last. "I'm sure there was no need for *that*."

"No need? You were the ones going on about tea and sandwiches for no apparent reason," said Vindr, his temper cooling as quickly as it had flared.

"Well, you did say that the dead Vikings would be staying only until Ragnarok," pointed out Barnabas. "I was merely wondering if that meant they would be leaving just before it, or perhaps staying throughout it."

Vindr sighed. "Let's start over, shall we?" he said. "Ragnarok is not tea. It is…well, I think it's best if I leave it to Odin to tell you what it is, as it has everything to do with why you are here. Speaking of which, you really are here." He stopped the chariot directly in front of Odin's front doors. They had been so intent on their conversation that they hadn't noticed that they were quickly approaching their destination. "There you go. Time to get out and see what Odin wants with you. Go on, now." Vindr made shooing motions with his hands, as though he were eager to be rid of them.

Barnabas and Wilfred climbed stiffly from the carriage (they had been riding in it most bouncily for quite a long time). As soon as they had alighted, Vindr clucked to the horses and took off without another word.

"Well," said Barnabas, casting a disparaging glance at the retreating Viking's back. "What a rude fellow," he sniffed. "I do hope the other dead people here have better manners than he."

"I do believe we shall find out straightaway," observed Wilfred, nodding towards the hall. Two extremely large (and as hirsute as they were massive) men had emerged from the place and were striding quickly towards them. They carried enormous battle axes and were swathed in great cloaks of fur just as Vindr had been.

One of them coughed deeply and launched a gob of spit onto the ground beside him as he walked. He then gave a great, wet snort and wiped his forearm across his face.

Barnabas wrinkled his nose in distaste. "Oh dear," he murmured quietly from the side of his mouth. "I think we shan't have much luck, in terms of manners and what-not, after all."

"Perhaps it is better that they *don't* serve us tea, don't you think?" whispered Wilfred from the corner of his own mouth.

"Indeed," agreed Barnabas. "I think I have quite lost my appetite."

The men approached and the two detectives hastily arranged their faces so as to present polite expressions. Their efforts were to little or no avail, however, as the Vikings seemed disinclined to indulge in the pleasantries of civilized society.

"Come with us," barked the bigger one (whom Barnabas had already mentally named The Spitter, for obvious reasons). He turned and headed back to the hall without waiting for an answer. The second man, seeing that Barnabas and Wilfred made no move to follow, took hold of Barnabas' arm and forcibly led him along, with Wilfred in tow behind.

"I say!" cried Barnabas, flailing his arm about until it slipped from the man's grasp. "There's no need for man-handling, sir."

"You weren't coming," said the man simply. "Now you are. So looks like it worked."

"We are here at the explicit behest of Odin, you know," said Barnabas, drawing himself up as tall as his short frame could possibly go. "On important business."

"Ya, ya, we know who you are," said The Spitter over his shoulder.

"Then you have the advantage of me, sir," said Barnabas haughtily. "As I have no idea in the slightest who *you* are."

The Spitter whirled around and glowered at Barnabas beneath bristling eyebrows. "I am Thurm Thurmson, of Moster," he said in a voice that was much too loud for the occasion, considering that he stood only a meter away from the detectives and it was quite quiet in the grove, besides. "And this is Agar Jolafson of Avadnes. We both fell to the sharp swords of the Magyars."

"But we definitely took more than a few of them with us!" interrupted Agar, laughing.

"Aye, that we did!" agreed The Spitter.

"Huh," said Barnabas. "Well, that is quite nice, I suppose. I am…"

"We know who you are," said The Spitter brusquely. He stepped forward and bent down so that his face was just in front of Barnabas'. Barnabas could smell the ale on the man's breath; indeed, he was so close that he was certain that the slightest of breezes would cause the fellow's beard to blow forward and tickle his face. Alarmingly, Barnabas saw a drop of spit forming on the man's lip.

"Splendid," said Barnabas uncertainly. "Nice to meet you?"

"Ayuh," said The Spitter, "we know who you are." The drop of spit grew larger and heavier with each word. "But what we don't know is, why are you here?"

"We are here because Odin requires our services," said Barnabas.

"I don't care what Odin wants with you," said The Spitter menacingly. "I care how you got here." The spit droplet began to trail down one of his beard hairs, and wobbled precariously as the Spitter worked his lips around the words.

Despite his resolve to appear brave, Barnabas took a step

backwards. "I'm not sure I understand your meaning," he said, casting a nervous glance towards Wilfred.

"Are you simple?" boomed Agar. "Answer Thurm's question! How did you get here?"

"Uh, well, in a chariot, I suppose," stammered Barnabas. Wilfred leaned in and whispered in his ear.

"I do believe they wish to know how we died," he said. "Being as this is Valhalla, a place for warriors who die in battle…"

"What of it? We didn't come here on vacation, you know. We are only here because Odin sent for us," replied Barnabas.

"I'm not certain that means much to these fellows. I'm getting the feeling they think one should only be here if one died in battle," said Wilfred.

"So you think they are taking umbrage at our *mode* of becoming deceased?" hissed Barnabas.

"What are you two whispering about?" boomed The Spitter. "Are you men, or are you cowards?" He toyed with the hilt of a wicked-looking knife that stuck out from his belt.

"These two never saw a battle in their lives, I'd wager," said Agar scornfully.

"So you died in your beds, did you?" sneered The Spitter. "And you dare come here? Only warriors may come here!" He snarled, tightening his grip on the knife hilt. The spittle in his beard lost its battle with gravity and flew straight at Barnabas, striking him squarely between the eyes.

Barnabas closed his eyes and breathed in deeply. Then he deliberately wiped the spit from his face with a corner of his robe, and regarded Thurm with slitted eyes.

"Oh, but we *are* warriors," he said, his voice soft with menace. Wilfred looked at him with no small degree of surprise. This was not the nervous, gentle employer whom he knew so well. "We have fought the likes of which you could never dream."

"Like what?" asked Agar, interested.

"Bah," scoffed The Spitter. "They are no warriors. If they were, they would have just said so."

"I didn't wish to frighten you," said Barnabas, taking a step forwards and staring The Spitter in the eye. Wilfred gasped and fluttered a hand up to cover his mouth, shocked (and a tad alarmed) at Barnabas' unprecedented audacity.

"Frighten us? Like the likes of you could ever scare the likes of us," retorted The Spitter. However, there was a new tone of doubt in his voice.

"No?" said Barnabas. He deepened his voice, as one does when one is telling spooky ghost stories. "Would it not frighten you to know that we were killed battling a great mummy king? Have you ever seen a mummy? Hmmm? Have you?" While it was true that Barnabas and Wilfred had, of course, been killed by a mummy in a London museum (sent by Anubis), it was somewhat less true that either of their deaths had been due to a battle of any kind; indeed, the entire affair had been quite one-sided, with all advantage going to the mummy.

"Well, no," mumbled The Spitter, shuffling his feet. "Is it some kind of Slav?"

"We wouldn't be here if a mummy was just a Slav!" shouted Barnabas, somewhat crazily. (Indeed, he had no idea what a Slav was, or how a Slav might compare in terms of frightfulness to a mummy, but he thought it prudent to press his point as far as was possible.) "Indeed, mummies eat Slavs for breakfast!"

"For breakfast?" asked Agar doubtfully.

"Yes, for breakfast," said Barnabas.

"Huh," said The Spitter, still not entirely convinced. "And what was this mummy king's name?"

"Uh," said Barnabas, who had quite forgotten the name of the mummy.

"Ginger," supplied Wilfred.

"Yes, King Ginger, the Mummy King," said Barnabas.

"Huh," said The Spitter again, scratching his beard. Then he shrugged. "Well, all right then. I suppose that's good enough." He turned and waved for them to follow. Agar shrugged and walked beside The Spitter.

Barnabas and Wilfred stayed behind for a moment.

"Did you see how splendidly I handled that!" whispered Barnabas proudly.

"Quite splendid, indeed!" agreed Wilfred. "You even had me quite convinced."

"I didn't go too far, did I?" asked Barnabas. "I didn't sound too maniacal?"

"Not in the slightest," said Wilfred. "You were just the right amount of maniacal."

"I thought it best to sound at least a little crazy," said Barnabas. "I think I did quite well at it."

"Exceedingly well," said Wilfred.

"Well, I suppose we'd best follow them," said Barnabas. The two Vikings had reached the doors, and were waiting for the detectives with impatient looks on their faces. "Best not to push our luck. They are certainly *unpleasant* fellows, are they not?"

"Most definitely," agreed Wilfred. "I do hope that Odin himself is more amiable."

"He *must* be," insisted Barnabas. "His hall is terribly splendid, so it follows that he himself must be civilized as well. And he is a king, is he not?"

With that, Barnabas strode eagerly past Agar and Thurm and disappeared into the shadows beneath the immense doorway. Wilfred, trailing behind, prudently refrained to point out that they had met quite a few kings in the past months who were not as amiable as one could have wished.

He heaved a deep breath for courage, and followed his employer into the hall of Odin.

Chapter Two

Wilfred promptly collided into the back of Barnabas, who had abruptly stopped walking after taking only a few steps into the hall.

Barnabas stood as if frozen, although a dozen or more fires blazing in the hearths that lined each wall made the place quite warm. "Wilfred!" he whispered. "I do believe I've changed my mind. I don't think Odin is amiable at all. In fact, I think he may be entirely *un*-amiable!"

Barnabas' eyes were wide as he stared towards the front of the hall. His first few seconds in Valhalla had told him all that he needed to know about the place, as far as he was concerned.

Because of all the fireplaces (not to mention the hundreds, if not thousands, of torches that hung on the walls) the hall was not only warm but also brightly lit. The flickering light of the flames, however, offered no comfort, as it merely highlighted the spectacle laid before them.

The room that they found themselves in was ridiculously long; indeed, the front of the room looked to be nearly a mile away from where they stood. A narrow aisle ran between twin rows of innumerable long wooden tables, at which sat an even more innumerable number of bearded, fur-cloaked men.

Great flasks of ale sloshed atop the tables, and many of the men looked to be in the advanced stages of drunkenness. Some were slouched down in their seats, turning bleary, reddened eyes upon the detectives. Others lurched from side to side, struggling to maintain balance as though they were aboard a ship in heavy seas, not in a completely stationary hall firmly affixed to land.

All of them carried battle axes, or swords, or enormous war hammers, and nearly all wore decidedly *un*friendly expressions on their faces as they turned to stare at the two detectives.

"There are two empty seats at that table, just over there," whispered Barnabas, leaning in close to Wilfred. "If we could just slip in over there, perhaps they'll forget about us."

Wilfred looked pointedly at the light, airy robes that they wore (having just come from the Egyptian desert and not having an opportunity to change, much less more weather-appropriate clothing to change *into*, to boot), then jerked his head in the direction of the thick furs worn by the Viking nearest them (which just happened to be Thurm, who was currently in the process of scowling most alarmingly at them).

Barnabas took Wilfred's meaning immediately. "Yes, I *know*," he said. "But there's nothing for it. We shall just sidle over here, and perhaps they'll start drinking again and forget all about us." He began to edge sideways towards the nearest table, where there was a small gap on the benches just wide enough for himself and Wilfred to sit.

"Welcome to my hall!" boomed a voice from the front of the hall. A wide, raised dais ran crosswise along the front wall, and a large table was situated crosswise across it. A great throne sat at the middle of the table, and atop the great throne sat a giant of a man (or god, Barnabas supposed; for surely this was no ordinary Viking). The man-god was bigger, and gruffer, and *hairy-er* than the others, and therefore much more frightening.

Barnabas quickened his crab-steps towards the corner. "Blend, Wilfred! Blend!" he cried, panicked. "Look inconspicuous!"

Wilfred tried to comply, but a rough hand grabbed both him and Barnabas by the necks of their robes. They were lifted an inch off the ground and plunked down right back where they had started from.

The big man on the throne scowled at the detectives. "Is this what Anubis sends me?" he bellowed. "*Men* who hide at the sight of a few warriors?"

"Well!" huffed Barnabas, insulted. He wriggled against the hand that still held the nape of his robe (a hand which belonged, of course, to The Spitter) to no avail. "We were merely moving out of the way. There was no *hiding* involved, you see."

"Looked like hiding to me," said the big hairy man. "Am I wrong? Am I mistaken? Were they bravely trying to be like little mice there in the corner?" He looked around the hall, feigning honest confusion, to the amusement of all.

Barnabas looked about at the drunken warriors, all laughing at his expense, and narrowed his eyes. Wilfred, who knew his employer better than anyone, and knew the sorts of rash acts of which Barnabas was capable when irked, nudged Barnabas with his elbow.

"Barnabas!" he whispered urgently. "I do believe that is Odin himself up there…"

"And look how they struggle to and fro," continued the man on the throne (who was, indeed, Odin), his voice pitched high like a girl's. "When, oh when, shall our brave guests free themselves from Thurm's mighty grip?" He put the back of his hand to his forehead, excellently miming a damsel in distress. The warriors howled with laughter.

"We thought merely to take a seat and partake of the feast," lied Barnabas through gritted teeth. "When one has forced someone to travel a long way, then one should, of course, feed that someone straight away, is what I always say," he continued, although he had never said such a thing in his life, having never had occasion to.

"Really," hissed Wilfred, "I don't think it's wise to provoke him…"

"Oh, is *that* what one should do?" said Odin. His voice no longer sounded mocking, but instead dripped with menace. "Please, little man, tell me what else you think I should do?"

"Tell your man to unhand us," said Barnabas pertly, blithely unaware of the sarcasm of Odin's words. "At once, if you please. And we should like some tea."

"Barnabas, please!" said Wilfred. "I think it unwise to

annoy him any further!"

"Some tea, you say?" said Odin. He turned to address his warriors. "Should I give him tea, or should I give him a taste of *this*?" He pulled out a wicked looking sword and hefted it threateningly.

"Some tea!" yelled one man (who presumably didn't know exactly what tea was, and wanted to find out). He was promptly punched by his neighbor, and fell off his seat to the ground. "The sword!" yelled the rest of the men.

"Oh dear," said Wilfred.

"Hah!" yelled Barnabas. To Wilfred's horror, his employer had gone quite red in the face. His features were all squinched up, and he was clearly highly irate.

Barnabas flailed his body so quickly that Thurm was unable to maintain his grip on his robe. Freed from captivity, Barnabas whirled about and kicked Thurm repeatedly in the shins. "I. Was. Promised. Tea!" he yelled, punctuating each word with a swift kick.

The warriors' laughter intensified, but their calls to give the detectives the sword soon turned to calls for tea, though none of them knew what that was. Even Odin laughed at the display, and watched as Thurm unsuccessfully tried to dodge Barnabas' quick footwork.

"Enough, enough," Odin said at last. "Desist, little warrior man in the silly robe." Barnabas, running out of energy, obeyed and turned to face his host. "You have proven your mettle," said Odin, still smiling. "Come up here, both of you, and sit at my table."

"Yes, well, thank you," muttered Barnabas. Now that his anger was spent he felt more than a little embarrassed at his outburst. "Very sorry about that. It's just, well, Vindr *did* say something about tea, you see…"

"Ragnarok, he called it," added Wilfred helpfully.

"Ah, well, I don't know anything about tea, but I can tell you a great deal about Ragnarok. Come join me, and I shall give you meat and ale and tell you what you need to know."

Barnabas and Wilfred shared a glance, then walked nervously down the long aisle towards the dais.

"Are you quite recovered?" murmured Wilfred as they walked.

"I think so," answered Barnabas, patting himself down as though searching for signs of physical injury. "But I do think it best to be careful. This Odin fellow is quite mercurial."

"Hmm," said Wilfred, privately thinking that Barnabas himself could be a bit mercurial at times, as well.

They reached the dais. The table where Odin sat had no empty seats, but Odin rather rudely dismissed two of the warriors seated to his left to make room for the detectives.

"Magni, Modi, move," he said. The warriors grumbled, but Odin waved their protests brusquely away. "Go train or something. How do you expect to wield your father's hammer with puny little arms like that?"

The two warriors in question rose, and Barnabas shrank back a bit. They were huge men, bigger than any of the other warriors in the hall (who all appeared quite enormous to the little detective). Indeed, they were larger even than Odin. Their arms bulged with muscles and it looked to Barnabas as though the biceps of either one could crack a man's head like a walnut.

"Go!" Odin yelled, gesturing for the giants to leave. "Sit!" he bellowed at the two detectives. Barnabas and Wilfred quickly sat in the newly empty seats with nervous smiles of apology.

"And Magni, leave that here!" continued Odin. He slapped at the nearest giant's hand, which held a knife upon which was speared a half-chewed chunk of meat. "My guests are hungry."

"But, Grandfather," whined Magni petulantly, "*I'm* hungry too."

"You're always hungry, the both of you," retorted Odin. "Drop it!"

Magni put the knife with the meat back on the trencher that was in front of Barnabas, but not before rebelliously taking a great slobbery bite.

"Darned sons of a giantess," grumbled Odin as Magni and the other giant left the hall. "Eat me out of hearth and home, they will," he added, though he watched them go with an indulgent smile.

"Giantess?" asked Barnabas. "And the one is your grandson?"

"They both are," said Odin. "Magni and Modi. Sons of my favorite son, Thor. Jarnsaxa the giantess is their mother." He glanced at the abandoned piece of meat on Barnabas' trencher. "Eat!" he commanded.

Barnabas eyed the slobbery, ragged meat on his plate with distaste. Then he looked at Odin, who was beginning to scowl anew as he waited for Barnabas to take a bite. Seeing no way to avoid it, Barnabas closed his eyes, screwed up his face and took a hearty bite of the disgusting meat.

He swallowed with effort and opened one eye to see Odin still watching him. "Mmm?" he said. "Delicious?"

Odin clapped him on the back and laughed. Wilfred dutifully continued to nibble on his own already-gnawed-upon meat while Barnabas politely inquired about Odin's grandsons.

"So," he said, "they are strapping lads. What is this hammer you speak of, that they must train so much in order to wield it? It must be bigger than a tree!"

"The hammer is not so big, but it is immensely heavy. It is called Mjollnir, and at the moment Thor is the only one who can heft it. But after Ragnarok, it will be left to Magni and Modi."

"After Ragnarok?" asked Barnabas. "I think I must have the wrong idea entirely about what that is, since I can't figure for the life of me what tea has to do with a hammer."

"What is this 'tea' that you keep going on about?" asked Odin, shaking his head. "I am talking about Ragnarok, the end of the world."

"The end of the world!" yelped Barnabas and Wilfred in unison. Wilfred had just taken a rather large bite of food (hunger had quickly won out over squeamishness) so that it sounded more like, "Da ermd ub da wurd," but everyone could tell what he meant to say, regardless.

"What are you yelping about?" chided Odin. "Everyone

knows the end of the world is coming. No need to sound so surprised!"

"I'm quite certain *we've* never heard about this," said Barnabas, his eyes wide with alarm. "Have we, Wilfred?"

Wilfred, still chewing, shook his head.

"And I do believe I'd remember if I had heard that the world would end, and what-not," added Barnabas.

"Ah, yes, well, the world is going to end. There. Now you've heard it," said Odin.

"When?" asked Barnabas. "Not soon, I hope?"

"And how?" chimed in Wilfred, who had finally swallowed his food.

"Sooner rather than later," answered Odin. "It seems that the prophecies about Ragnarok are already starting to happen."

"The prophecies?" asked Barnabas. "What prophecies?"

"Why, the prophecies about Ragnarok, of course," answered Odin obtusely.

"Which are…" prompted Barnabas.

"That Loki will escape his bonds, and there will be lots of earthquakes, which is already starting to happen."

"Loki?" asked Barnabas.

"Yes, Loki. The trickster god? We used to use him to trick each other, and to start mischief, and to find out things about each other, but we had to imprison him after he tricked Hod into killing Balder, of course."

"Of course," said Barnabas, though he had no idea who either of those people were. Still, tricking someone into killing someone else seemed a deplorable thing to do, so Barnabas felt certain that it was best that such a nasty fellow remain locked up. "Has Loki broken free, then?"

"Not yet," said Odin. "But it looks like he might soon. He's thrashing so hard that his bonds are sure to break any day now. And it's causing all the earthquakes. It's giving me a headache, what with all the shaking and the rumbling."

"Why is he thrashing?" asked Barnabas, thoroughly confused.

"Because someone took the bowl that catches the serpent's

poison before it falls on his face," said Odin, as though this were the most obvious thing in the world.

Barnabas and Wilfred shared a flummoxed glance. "Uh," said Barnabas. "Terribly sorry, but…the serpent? Poison? A bowl?"

"Don't you know anything?" sniped Odin. "When we imprisoned Loki we set a serpent to watch over him. The serpent drops venom from its teeth every day, right onto Loki's face."

Barnabas tightened his lips disapprovingly and shot Wilfred an alarmed glance. He and Wilfred had had a most dreadful encounter with a snake-god in the Egyptian underworld, and therefore neither was kindly disposed towards snakes in the slightest.

"So," Barnabas said to Odin, "what do this serpent and its venom have to do with the end of the world?"

"Loki doesn't like it, so it makes him flail and thrash and that is what makes the earthquakes, of course." said Odin.

"Of course," nodded Barnabas sagely, as though he understood perfectly (when, of course, he did not understand in the slightest). "But what is the significance of the bowl?"

"Loki's wife, Sigyn, took up a bowl to catch the poison before it can land on her husband's face," explained Odin. "She sits there with him every day and catches the poison in that bowl. And good thing she does, too. *That's* what keeps the earthquakes from happening."

"Perhaps, then, if you merely removed the serpent?" asked Barnabas.

"No, no," said Odin dismissively. "We can't do that."

"Why not?" asked Wilfred.

"Because the serpent is fated to be there," replied Odin, maddeningly.

Barnabas snorted. "So, why not just make sure that Loki *doesn't* get free?" he suggested.

"Because it's prophesied that he *will* get free," said Odin.

"But if he doesn't get free, then the world won't end?" said Barnabas.

"Exactly," said Odin.

"So keep him locked up then!" exclaimed Barnabas, frustrated.

Odin shook his head. "The prophecy says he's to get free, so get free he will."

"I'm sure I don't understand this at all," sighed Barnabas.

"What's to understand?" said Odin. "Ragnarok is coming and Loki's getting free will be the start of it. That's why you're here."

"To keep Loki from getting free," repeated Barnabas.

"No!" said Odin impatiently. "Aren't you listening?" He shook his head. "*Loki* never needed this much explaining, when I asked *him* to do things for me."

Barnabas sighed again. "Perhaps if you'd just tell me precisely what it is you want us to do."

"Find out who stole the bowl," answered Odin. "And bring it back to Sigyn."

"So as to stop the earthquakes, and therefore stop Ragnarok?" said Barnabas.

"No, no no," said Odin. "You can't stop Ragnarok. What will be will be. It is fated."

"So, why do you want us to find the bowl, then?" asked Barnabas.

"Because I'd rather the end of the world waited a bit," said Odin. "Plus all these earthquakes are annoying. But since they've already happened I don't think it would ruin the prophecy if you put a stop to *them*, at least."

"I see," said Barnabas, considering. "Tell me, what did Sigyn have to say about this affair?"

"What do you mean?" asked Odin.

"I am merely wondering if Sigyn had any useful information to divulge about the theft?" replied Barnabas.

"How should I know?" said Odin.

"I simply supposed Sigyn would be the first person to ask about it, since *she's* the one from whom the bowl was stolen. Unless I am mistaken and it was stolen while under someone else's watch?"

"No, you're right. Only Sigyn was there. And Loki, of course, but since I'm sure he doesn't have much to say, being as there's a snake wrapped around his head and all," said Odin, as though this were the most commonplace thing in the world to say.

"So no one talked to Sigyn at all?" persisted Barnabas.

"Why would they?" said Odin.

"To find out who took the bowl!" said Barnabas.

"Well, that's what you're here for, isn't it?" retorted Odin. He smiled smugly, and looked quite pleased with his own cleverness. Barnabas opened his mouth to utter an indignant retort, but a quick jab from Wilfred's elbow stopped him.

"Ow!" yelped Barnabas.

"We'll go speak to Sigyn ourselves, then," interjected Wilfred before Barnabas could complain any further. "Splendid idea, Barnabas."

"A very good plan," said Odin approvingly. "I knew Anubis would send me a clever detective."

Barnabas beamed, his fears about the end of the world forgotten as he enjoyed the praise (even if that praise did, in fact, rightly belong to Wilfred).

"I'd still like to know exactly how the world would end," said Wilfred. "Just so we understand the stakes, if you will."

"Well, as for *how*," said Odin blithely, as though he were discussing the happenings in a knitting circle rather than the end of the world, "Jormungand will come free and devour everything and we'll all die. Well, most of us, anyway. Some of us will return, just like last time."

"Jormungand?" asked Wilfred, swallowing audibly.

"*You* know," said Odin. "The giant snake that circles the world."

Barnabas whitened. "Ahhh," he said through clenched teeth. "*That* snake." He turned wild eyes towards Wilfred. He had never heard of a snake called Jormungand in particular, but he was quite certain that he had no desire to meet a snake large enough to wrap itself around the entire world.

"No need to look so anxious," said Odin brightly. "It's fated, so nothing you do will prevent you from being eaten by Jormungand along with everyone else." He clapped his hands together as if brushing dirt from them. "See? Nothing to worry about!"

"Oh dear," said Barnabas, looking terribly green about the gills.

"We'll be off then," said Wilfred, eager to end the conversation before it got any worse. "We'll question Sigyn straightaway." He grabbed hold of Barnabas (who was nearly petrified with fear at the thought of the great snake that was destined to gobble them up) and began to lead him out of the hall. He stopped after a few steps, and turned back around. "Could you, ah, tell us *where*, exactly, Sigyn might be?"

"Of course," said Odin beneficently. "In fact, I'll do even better than that!" Odin clapped his hands, and a very tall, armor-clad Viking lady strode into the hall, leading a large grey horse. "Meet Brynhild," he said. "Your guide."

Chapter Three

Everyone stopped to look at the lady warrior. She coolly stared back, unperturbed by the attention. Barnabas stepped forward and bowed (most gracefully, he thought) deeply over an extended knee.

"Greetings, Ms. Brynhild," he said gallantly. "I am Mr. Barnabas Tew of Marylebone. And may I present my assistant, Mr. Wilfred Colby?"

The great grey horse chose that moment to lift its tail and drop a steaming pile of manure onto the floor. Barnabas and Wilfred crinkled their noses in distaste as the hall erupted in raucous laughter. No one made a move to clean up the mess.

"Don't mind Hynder here," said Brynhild, affectionately patting the horse's face. "He does what he wants when he wants."

"Admirable," said Barnabas, trying and failing to keep the sarcasm from his voice.

Brynhild laughed. "Very much so," she said. "I strive to be more like him, every day. Now, come along. Hynder and I will take you to see Sigyn."

Barnabas and Wilfred looked at each other and shrugged. Then, stepping gingerly over Hynder's mess, they followed Brynhild out of the hall. Instead of continuing on straight, down the avenue between the beautiful trees through which they had passed on their way in, Brynhild took a smaller path to the left.

"Thank you very much for your assistance, Miss Brynhild," remarked Barnabas politely. "I'm sure having a guide will prove to make all the difference in the success of our case. Being as how we don't know our way around in the slightest."

"I am not simply a guide," replied Brynhild. "I am a skald, as well. And there's no need to call me 'Miss'. Just 'Brynhild' will do. And I will call you Barney!" Her eyes glinted mischievously.

Barnabas reddened. "Oh, please don't," he sputtered uncomfortably. "'Barnabas' will do fine, if you *really* insist on such informality, although I suppose if we shall be working together so closely on this case that *some* degree of informality is natural, and must be assumed, although it *does* seem a bit premature to…"

"So, Brynhild," said Wilfred, interrupting his employer's ramble (which was threatening to go on for some time). "A skald, you say? Forgive my ignorance, but I'm not entirely certain what that is."

"A skald is someone who knows the histories. I know all of the stories about all of the gods. I know their personalities, what they want…sometimes I even know what they *will* do." She winked at Wilfred and grinned.

"Like a seer? Or a sorceress?" asked Wilfred.

"Not quite," said Brynhild. "A seer can see into the future. I just understand the gods' motivations. If you know someone's motivations it's not a trick at all to guess what they'll do."

"Quite right," agreed Wilfred admiringly. "Don't you think so, Barnabas?"

"Yes, that is quite foresighted for someone as obtuse as Odin seems to be," said Barnabas (a bit petulantly, if truth be told; indeed, he was a bit put out at having been interrupted and was feeling a bit peevish).

"Do not underestimate him," warned Brynhild. "He is more canny than he lets on."

"Harrumph," said Barnabas.

"Well," said Wilfred, trying to steer the conversation back to a more pleasant tone. "This is a fine horse, as well."

"Thank you," said Brynhild. "But Hynder is no mere horse, either. He is magical."

"Magical?" asked Wilfred.

"He can take us wherever we need to go, in the blink of an

eye. Well, maybe not *exactly* where we need to go, but he can at least take us to the right *world*."

"The right world?" said Wilfred perplexed.

"Of course," said Brynhild. "You do know about the worlds, don't you?"

"I must confess that I don't," admitted Wilfred.

"You've never heard of the nine worlds?" exclaimed Brynhild, astounded.

"Where we come from there is only one world. We discovered the Egyptian underworld rather suddenly, and entirely against our will. I suppose we are still trying to get used to all of this, as it's still quite new to us." Wilfred flashed her an embarrassed smile.

Brynhild patted him kindly on the shoulder. "No matter," she said reassuringly. "I'll tell you everything you need to know. That is why Odin gave you my services, no?"

While Wilfred and Brynhild talked, the path had taken them into a side yard of sorts, filled with all sorts of delightful distractions. To Barnabas' eye, it was even more splendid than the pristine rows of trees in the front, and he quickly fell behind as he marveled at the sights.

A pretty labyrinth made entirely of rosebushes (Barnabas did so love rosebushes!) had been laid out in a circular pattern on the middle of the lawn. Flanking the entrance to it were two intricately crafted topiaries. One was of a horse. The other looked quite a lot like a troll, or a giant. Barnabas could not approve entirely of the subject of the thing, of course, but he still quite admired the obvious skill of the trimmings.

Farther off across the neatly trimmed lawn was a great stone fountain. A large statue of a woman stood in the middle, bearing a sword in one hand and a pitcher in the other. Water flowed out of the pitcher to splash into the basin below.

In the basin lounged two men. They were apparently engaged in a conversation that looked to be exceedingly intense, and paid no mind to Barnabas and his companions as they passed by. Barnabas squinted his eyes in order to see better in the distance and saw that the two men were none other than Magni and Modi, Odin's grandsons.

Barnabas had just begun to shake his head at the sight of the two disobedient young men (who were supposed to be training with a hammer of some sort, Barnabas recalled) when he was distracted by the sight of that very hammer lying discarded and forgotten, for the time being at least, on the grass beside the path.

"Ohhhh," said Barnabas to himself, "but this is *beautiful*!" He looked about and, seeing that no one was paying him any attention whatsoever, tip-toed off the path to get a better look at the hammer.

It was wrought of silver, and had been hammered until the surface was dotted with a myriad of facets that reflected the light every which way. The hammering end was unadorned, but the handle was studded with gemstones of every color so that it looked like a veritable rainbow.

Barnabas glanced about again. Magni and Modi were still in the fountain and completely engrossed in their conversation, and Wilfred and Brynhild were likewise occupied up ahead. Furtively Barnabas bent down and picked up the hammer.

Immediately the vestiges of annoyance he had been feeling intensified. He thought about how hard he worked at being a detective and how little respect he was accorded. He thought of all of the indignities he had suffered over the years. But, perhaps because it was the most recent memory, thoughts of the rough treatment he had received at the Viking guard Thurm's hands quickly rose to the surface and drowned out all else.

"The Spitter," spat Barnabas. "Grrr." He gripped the hammer tightly as his face turned red with rage.

Meanwhile, Wilfred and Brynhild had gone along quite far ahead before Wilfred noticed that Barnabas was no longer beside them. "Barnabas?" he called. When there was no answer, he called again more loudly. "Barnabas! Where are you?" He turned around and was astonished by what he saw.

His employer stood, just to the side of the path. He was

holding an enormous hammer high up above his head. But, most alarmingly, he was *snarling*.

"Barnabas!" yelped Wilfred once more. "Oh, damn!" exclaimed Brynhild. Together they began to run back towards Barnabas.

Even as they came close to the little detective, however, Barnabas began to circle the hammer ferociously through the air. He spun on his heels and began racing back towards the hall.

"Die, Spitter, die!" yelled Barnabas. The hammer was so heavy that with each arc of its swing it threw Barnabas to the side, so that he weaved and stumbled like an angry drunken sailor.

"Barnabas, wait!" called Wilfred, to no avail.

"Who's the big Viking now, Spitter?" cried Barnabas, waving the hammer even more wildly.

"Hynder, help!" screamed Brynhild. Immediately, the grey horse charged past Wilfred and Brynhild and quickly overtook Barnabas as well. Stopping abruptly in front of him, the stallion raised his back legs and planted a kick squarely on Barnabas' wrist.

Barnabas squealed as the hammer flew out of his hand. Both he and it dropped harmlessly (and separately) to the ground. Barnabas landed with his face in the grass and stayed there as Wilfred and Brynhild rushed up to him.

"Ouch," said Barnabas into the grass. "Your horse kicked me. I am horse-kicked!"

"And good thing he did!" chided Brynhild. "What were you *thinking*?"

"I was thinking that horrible gasbag The Spitter needed a good whacking in the head with a hammer, and as I just happened to have a hammer…" While he was speaking Barnabas sat up and saw the look on Brynhild's face and suddenly realized that her question had been rhetorical, and that she hadn't really wanted an answer at all.

Brynhild's eyes were narrowed with suspicion and her jaw was clenched so tightly that Barnabas could see the muscles there bunching up. But it was her pallor that was most alarming. All the color had gone out of her already pale face (with the exception of her cheeks, which flamed hotly pink), so that she looked a bit like a chunk of wet concrete that someone had smushed two large raspberries on top of.

He looked to Wilfred for clarification, but his assistant merely looked surprised and confused. Even Hynder the horse was staring at him intensely. He turned back to Brynhild, who was still glaring at him with that odd look.

"What?" he said. "Why are you all staring at me?"

No one answered, but just continued to stare. He clambered to his feet and brushed at the grass stains on his robes self-consciously. "It's not polite to just *look* at someone without explanation," he huffed. "Have I done something outrageous?" He said this last with no small degree of sarcasm, as he was certainly not the type to do things of the outrageous variety and he was sure that he had done nothing of the sort now. The red rage against The Spitter had disappeared as quickly as it had come on, and he didn't quite understand what everyone was carrying on about. In fact, he was having a hard time remembering exactly what had happened before the horse kicked him.

To his surprise Brynhild barked out a harsh, shocked laugh. "I'd say!" she exclaimed. "*Outrageous* is not a strong enough word for what you just did."

"I only picked up a hammer," grumbled Barnabas. "It's not as if *that's* a crime, is it?" Both Wilfred and Brynhild looked even more shocked than they had before.

"He only picked up a hammer," repeated Brynhild, shaking her head in disbelief. "He lifts Mjollnir up over his head and tries to go all Viking on Thurm, and he says 'I only picked up a hammer.'"

"Going Viking?" protested Barnabas. "I was only just going to bash his head in, it wouldn't have taken but a moment..." He broke off abruptly, suddenly seeing her point. "Oh," he concluded sadly.

"How about if you just start from the beginning, and tell us what happened," suggested Brynhild.

"Well, let's see," said Barnabas, scratching his chin. "We

crossed over a bridge, it was a terribly high one, too, so high, in fact, that one could see birds beneath you (beneath you!)..."

"No, no," interrupted Brynhild. "Not *that* beginning. I mean starting from when you saw Mjollnir."

"Mjollnir?" asked Barnabas.

"Thor's hammer," said Brynhild, quickly losing patience.

"Oh, *that* hammer," said Barnabas. "Why didn't you say so, then?"

Brynhild shot him a warning glance, and he hurried on with his story. "So, the bridge, and the hall, and then we met you..."

Brynhild made a waving motion with her hand to hurry him along.

"...and then we were walking, and I saw Modi and Magni over there in the fountain." He gestured to where Modi and Magni were still deep in conversation, oblivious to all that had gone on just yards away from them. "Anyway," continued Barnabas, "then I saw the hammer. It was so beautiful that I, of course, picked it up, as anyone would..."

"*Anyone* would not have picked it up," said Brynhild.

"Well, *I* did, and that's that," said Barnabas. "I had only just done so, and had the thought that perhaps The Spitter could do with a bit of retribution, before your horse so rudely kicked me. You really should train him better."

Brynhild huffed in exasperation. "You threatened to bonk Thurm over the head. *Somebody* had to stop you."

"I did not!" exclaimed Barnabas. He looked from Wilfred's concerned face, to Brynhild's still-angry one, then back again. "I couldn't have. No, I most certainly did not. Did I?"

Wilfred and Brynhild both nodded (Wilfred kindly, and Brynhild a bit *less* kindly). "Yes, you did," she said. "And Hynder kept you from making a terrible mistake. You should thank him for only kicking your wrist, and not your head. Although it seems that your head is pretty hard, as stubborn as you are."

"I say!" said Barnabas. "I am not stubborn in the slightest.

And I'm sure you must have misinterpreted what I was doing. I am not the violent sort, as Wilfred could tell you."

"Well, you *did* kick Thurm in the shins," pointed out Wilfred. "Before we left, there in the hall."

"He deserved that!" sputtered Barnabas. "I am much aggrieved that you would think I would actually bonk someone in the head with a hammer." He pouted and turned away.

"You said that's what you wanted to do," said Brynhild. "You were yelling, 'die, Spitter, die!'."

"I never!" gasped Barnabas, aghast.

"Uh," said Wilfred hesitantly. "Do you not remember running about with it, and waving it over your head?"

"Of course not!" said Barnabas, his entire face as red as Brynhild's cheeks had been. "Well, that is to say, I suppose that I felt a bit irritable, after picking up the hammer. And I remember *thinking* about The Spitter, and feeling quite put out by him. But I'm sure I never would have actually hit him with a hammer. That's barbarous!"

Brynhild (whose face had softened during the telling of the story) put a comforting hand on Barnabas' shoulder. "I'm sure it's something you wouldn't normally do," she said. Both Barnabas and Wilfred nodded in agreement. Such violent behavior was entirely out of character for the affable detective. He was capable of irritability, and moodiness, and the occasional petulance, but nothing more.

"It's the hammer, you see," continued Brynhild. "It's Thor's hammer. When someone picks it up, they become invincible."

"And, a bit crazed," added Wilfred. Barnabas shot him a betrayed look.

"Yes, and a *lot* crazed. It's supposed to bring on berserker behavior," said Brynhild.

"There, see?" said Barnabas smugly. "I couldn't help it. I was berserk, is all."

"But what worries me," said Brynhild, as though Barnabas hadn't spoken at all, "is that you picked it up at all. Only Thor is supposed to be able to do that."

"And Magni and Modi," said Barnabas. "Odin told them to go train with it."

"They are training to be able to pick it up at all," corrected Brynhild. "See where they are?" She pointed over to the fountain. "See where the hammer is?" she pointed at the hammer, lying in the grass only a few feet away. "Were they holding it? No. Because they can't yet. And they gave up."

"*I* picked it up, and *they* can't?" said Barnabas, marveling at the strong young gods who sat talking in the fountain. He looked at his arm and made a muscle. "Perhaps I should try again?" So saying he began to walk over to the hammer.

Brynhild grabbed his arm just as he started to reach out for it. "I think not," she said, laughing. "You've caused enough trouble for one day."

"But if I can wield it, perhaps it will come in handy!" said Barnabas.

"And have you running around like a crazy person, swinging it at everyone you see?" said Brynhild. "I don't think so."

"I'm sure I wouldn't act like that again," said Barnabas primly.

"And besides," continued Brynhild, "It wouldn't be good if anyone found out you can lift it. There are lots of gods who might either try to use you, or others might be jealous enough to try to kill you."

Barnabas gasped. "You don't *really* think so, do you?"

"I *know* so," answered Brynhild firmly. "So no word of this to anyone. Understood?"

Wilfred nodded and Barnabas pressed his lips tightly together to mime silence.

"Good," said Brynhild. "Now, if we're done talking about it, we've got a goddess to interview. So climb up on Hynder and we'll be off."

After much ado (and with a great deal of help from both Brynhild and Hynder herself), both Barnabas and Wilfred were seated on Hynder's back. Brynhild leapt up in front of them easily and took hold of the horse's mane.

"To Midgard!" she commanded and, to Barnabas' and

Wilfred's great astonishment, the horse jumped straight up into the air and began to fly.

Barnabas, who was behind Wilfred, let out a yelp as Hynder ascended sharply into the sky at an astonishing speed. He wrapped his arms around Wilfred and clutched tightly onto him. He emitted a series of soft whimpers as he buried his face into Wilfred's back.

Wilfred, who was seated directly behind Brynhild (and only slightly less afraid of heights than was Barnabas, besides), felt that it would be terribly improper for him to grab hold of her in the same way that his employer had done to him. Therefore, he sat stiffly behind her, with his hands politely at his sides. Unfortunately, Barnabas' wild clinging set him quite off-balance, so that he began to slip slowly off the side of the horse, with Barnabas following suit.

"Wilfred," mumbled Barnabas into the folds of Wilfred's cloak. "I feel that we are sideways. Is the horse flying sideways? Please tell me the horse isn't flying sideways."

"It's quite all right,' said Wilfred (although it was very clearly not all right at all, as the two of them were now tilting off Hynder's back at an alarming angle. "I just need to scooch a bit to the right and we'll be right as rain."

Barnabas peeped open one eye. He saw the world arrayed below him an astonishing distance away. He saw the great rainbow bridge stretching out into the mists just ahead of them. And he saw that while Brynhild was sitting up entirely straight, he and Wilfred were tilted off the left side of the horse at such a rakish angle that they were in imminent danger of slipping right off of Hynder and down into the midst of it all.

"Ahhh!" he yelled, jerking his torso sharply to the right. Of course, this only served to throw both his own body and that of Wilfred even further off balance, so that their shoulders were directly above Hynder's spine but their bottoms slid even further to the left. This resulted in the two of them performing a very odd-looking (and exceedingly dangerous) type of half-split, with their right legs stretched precariously over the horse's back and their left legs dangling straight down. Slowly they began to slide.

"Oh dear!" cried Wilfred, trying to anchor his right foot into Hynder's side to no avail.

"We are falling!" yelled Barnabas. "We are falling from the sky horse!"

"You *could* put your arms around my waist," suggested Brynhild calmly.

"Are you certain?" asked Wilfred. "I don't want to insult…"

"You'd rather plummet off the horse?" said Brynhild. "Here. I'll make it easy for you." So saying she reached behind her, grabbed hold of Wilfred's robe, and pulled him and Barnabas as a unit back into the upright position. "Now hold on from now on," she chided. Wilfred shyly obeyed.

"I feel I might be ill," said Barnabas miserably from behind.

"Don't be ill," said Brynhild. "At least, not while we're on Hynder."

"I feel that I do not like this *flying* in the slightest," continued Barnabas. "In fact, I am certain that I rather dislike it, and a great deal at that."

"Would you rather *walk* to Midgard then?" asked Brynhild. "Walk straight over Bifrost in those silly robes of yours, in the freezing cold? I'm sure it'll only take you a month or so, and of course you'll be completely frozen by then…"

"Midgard? Bifrost?" asked Barnabas.

"Midgard is the land of the living," supplied Wilfred. "And Bifrost is the rainbow bridge that Vindr drove us across. It connects Asgard, the home of the high gods, to Midgard."

"And how do you suddenly know all of this?" asked Barnabas suspiciously.

Wilfred coughed discreetly. "Yes, well, you see, Brynhild told me all about it whilst you were, well, *involved* with that hammer," he said at last.

"At least Vindr took us across in a proper sort of vehicle," grumbled Barnabas. "One that stayed on the ground and that didn't threaten to simply dump one into the sky every time one loses his balance."

"This isn't so bad," said Wilfred, "now that we've got ourselves situated. Look at all the things we can see!" He pointed down to a large complex of enormous halls, each with a roof made of some precious material of another.

"There are twelve halls," said Brynhild proudly. "Each belonging to a different god. There's Valhalla, over there in the distance, where we just left. And there's Thor's hall, Thrudheim, and Himinbjorg, Heimdall's home on the cliffs up there." She pointed out first one, then another.

"Perhaps we could, uh, *land* at one of them," suggested Barnabas. He paused for a moment, trying to think of a good reason to do this. "We really are in need of some weather-appropriate clothing, you know." He looked at Himinbjorg, which was perched rather precariously on the side of an extraordinarily high cliff. Then he looked at Thrudheim, which was nicely situated safely on the ground. "Might I suggest Thor's house?"

Brynhild laughed. "You do need some warmer clothes, that is true," she said. "But we are nearly to Bifrost now, so we might as well wait until we are in Midgard. There's a town close to Loki's cave, near Fanang Falls. They will have supplies there."

"And once in Midgard we shall stay in Midgard?" asked Barnabas. "No more need to go flying back and forth from Midgard to Asgard again?"

"Oh no, we will be traveling via Hynder quite a bit. It's not just Asgard and Midgard, you see."

"There are nine worlds," proclaimed Wilfred proudly. He had listened carefully during his conversation with Brynhild in the gardens. "Three are above ground, three are of the earth, and three are below."

"Very good!" praised Brynhild. "And I suspect we'll have to go to most, if not all, of them."

"I assume there are other ways to travel between them?" said Barnabas.

"But Hynder is the fastest by far," said Brynhild firmly.

"Well, still," said Barnabas stubbornly. "When one has only a flying horse for transportation one should walk as often as possible, is what I always say." Of course, he had never said such a thing, but no one was willing to point that out.

"Uh," said Brynhild. "Anyway." Then she brightened. "Look! We are on Bifrost now..."

"Not precisely *on* Bifrost," muttered Barnabas. "We are quite a good ways *above* it, I should say."

"...and I can see Fanang Falls already," continued Brynhild, ignoring Barnabas entirely. "See the village? We'll stop there first and get you some decent clothes, and then it's on to see Sigyn!"

So saying, she cued Hynder to descend, and they swooped down towards the village. They dropped so quickly that everyone's stomach felt as if it were in their throats (a feeling that Brynhild obviously enjoyed, as she lifted her face up towards the sky and let out great whoops of delight).

Barnabas and Wilfred, on the other hand, did not enjoy it nearly so much. Wilfred clamped his lips tightly shut and looked as though he might be sick, whilst Barnabas smashed his face as closely into Wilfred's back as it would go and repeatedly groaned something that sounded like, "Urgh. Urrrgh."

The landing was little better, as Hynder hit the ground hard and came to an abrupt stop, nearly unseating everyone. Luckily, however, everyone managed to stay atop the horse, and Barnabas and Wilfred breathed sighs of relief.

"Urgh," repeated Barnabas. "I feel as if my outsides have left my insides entirely behind."

Brynhild laughed gaily. "Fun, isn't it?" she said.

"Hmmm," murmured Barnabas noncommittally, thinking that the experience had been anything *but* fun. Wilfred turned his head around to nod in sympathetic agreement.

"Anyway," said Brynhild, opening her arms expansively. "Here we are! Welcome to Fanang Falls."

Chapter Four

"Ahem," said Barnabas, after everyone had safely dismounted (a process which had taken far longer than one might expect, since Brynhild couldn't swing her leg over to jump down with Wilfred and Barnabas behind her, and Barnabas had proven to be somewhat unwilling to let go his grasp of Wilfred's back. Indeed, he had clutched even tighter to Wilfred and yelped, "Too high! Too high!" when a helpful villager tried to offer a helping hand, forcing the villager to grab hold of him and forcibly extricate him from the horse).

"Ahem," repeated Barnabas. "Fanny Falls seems a strange name for a town. Are you quite certain that this is where Loki and Sigyn are?" He looked dubiously at the rather motley collection of ramshackle buildings that comprised the village.

"Fanang Falls," corrected Brynhild.

"Fang Fang Falls?" said Barnabas. "That hardly sounds any more promising. In fact, it sounds quite a bit worse, I think. Puts one in mind of snakes and lizards and, and..."

"Bears?" suggested Wilfred.

"Yes, bears!" said Barnabas. "All sorts of unsavory creatures with great big teeth, is what I mean."

"Well, there *is* the serpent that drips the poison on Loki," said Brynhild.

Barnabas sighed and shook his head. "I do so hate serpents," he said mournfully. "Why does it always have to be serpents?"

"There's nothing to fear," said Brynhild. "The serpent is only there to torment Loki. No one else."

"Oh, well *that* makes it better," said Barnabas sarcastically.

Brynhild ignored his tone. "And besides, it's *Fanang*

Falls. Not Fang Fang Falls."

"As I said," replied Barnabas. "Anyway, you said we'd be able to procure some new clothes for Wilfred and myself. But I don't see anything that even resembles a proper tailor, so perhaps we should carry on to a more, well, a place that is a bit more, ah, how *do* I put this..."

"Nicer?" supplied Wilfred.

"Yes, that's it," said Barnabas. "We ought to find a nicer town, perhaps one with real buildings made of bricks and stones instead of these dilapidated wooden huts. And one that doesn't smell so much like wet sheep. Then we can find some clothes, and perhaps a nice supper. I suppose it must be getting close to suppertime?"

Brynhild sniffed. "I don't know where you expect to find a nicer *place*," she retorted, "or *nicer* buildings, or *nicer* smells. This is Midgard, not Valhalla, and these *huts* are our homes, and these sheep keep us fed. You'll be glad enough of their fleece once the wind starts to blow."

"Oh dear," said Barnabas, looking chagrined. "I'm terribly sorry. I didn't mean any insult."

"Well," said Brynhild. "Just remember that not everyone lives in these *nicer* places you speak of. I, for one, grew up in a village just like this one." She sounded quite a bit put out despite Barnabas' apology, which made him feel even worse.

"I really do apologize," he tried again. "I spoke too hastily, I'm sure." He looked about, frantically trying to think of something nice to say about the place. "Why, look over there! What lovely cloaks!" he said at last, pointing to a building that had a row of what looked to be roughly sewn cloaks of uncarded (and, judging by the smell) unwashed wool. All were a dirty brown color and had such uneven hems that Barnabas felt sure that the tailor who made them must certainly be crosseyed, but he was eager to appease Brynhild, who had, after all, been quite kind to him after the incident with the hammer.

"Oh," said Brynhild, "you really think so?" She smiled proudly when Barnabas nodded his agreement. "See, my people really are very skilled at a great many things," she said. "Everyone thinks we just go around pillaging and fighting, but our craftsmen are the best in the world. Let's go get you both one of those cloaks."

Barnabas and Wilfred smiled politely and followed her as she led the way to the shop with the smelly wool cloaks. As soon as her back was turned, Wilfred shot Barnabas a sardonic look. "Lovely cloaks?" he asked, raising one eyebrow.

"Well, I had to say *something*," said Barnabas.

"Hurry along," called Brynhild. She had got a bit ahead of them, and was even now speaking to the owner of the shop. She held up a big expanse of fleece in a roughly ovoid shape, with a great mud stain in the middle. "How do you like this one? It'll be nice and warm, which is good since it's going to get cold soon."

"And here I thought it already *was* cold," Barnabas said.

Wilfred nodded. "As did I," he said, pulling his flimsy robe closer about himself. "I think we really *shall* be glad of some fleece, funny smell or no."

Just then a great gust of wind blew, billowing up under their robes and freezing their legs and underparts with its icy breath. Both quickened their steps towards the shop, where Brynhild was standing with a lady whom Barnabas presumed to be the shopkeeper. She was holding up another robe. This one was a very large, particularly hideous fleece.

"What do you think of this one, Barnabas?" she said, looking the raggedy thing up and down and nodding approvingly. "I think it will fit you perfectly."

The thing *did* look warm, Barnabas thought, but warmth was just about the only positive attribute he could find about it. Like all the other robes displayed, it was made of a rough wool that looked as though it hadn't even been properly washed, much less combed or carded. It was a mottled brown color (though whether the speckles on it were the natural colors of the wool or dirt stains, Barnabas could not tell). Flecks and strands of green that looked quite a bit like rotted, dried algae were scattered about all over.

The worst part, though, was the stench. It smelled both

mouldy and musty, as though it had been thoroughly wetted in mud (probably with a particularly *slimy* mud, of course, thought Barnabas), then dried, then wetted and dried again. Barnabas wondered if the sheep from which this wool came from had been possessed of the habit of wallowing about in the rankest smelling mud bogs he could find.

Wilfred quickly averted his eyes and stepped off a few steps to inspect a collection of slightly smaller robes hanging from another post, leaving Barnabas alone with Brynhild, the shopkeeper, and the dreadful fleece.

"Oh. My. Well. Quite lovely," said Barnabas politely, trying very hard not to wrinkle his nose in distaste. "But I was thinking a jacket and overcoat would do better, don't you agree? And perhaps a nice pair of trousers?"

The shopkeeper narrowed her eyes as she looked critically at Barnabas' form. She reached out and fingered the flimsy fabric of the lightweight Egyptian robe he was wearing and frowned. "Too thin," she proclaimed. "Going to freeze to death." She took the fleece from Brynhild and held it up, ready to wrap it around Barnabas' shoulders. "Put it on before you do. And why are you wearing a dress?" she finished, frowning.

"It is *not* a dress," said Barnabas indignantly. "It is a robe of the finest Egyptian cotton, given me by..."

"Doesn't matter who gave you the dress. Freeze to death anyway. Put on the wool," the shopkeeper said simply.

"It's only going to get colder," agreed Brynhild.

"Uh, yes, well," said Barnabas, stalling. He was cold, but still reluctant to don the smelly, horrid fleece. "Perhaps one in a different color?" he suggested. "Something other than algae, er, that is to say, not quite so green? A nice blue, maybe?"

"No blue," said the shopkeeper peremptorily. "Just this."

"Better put it on," said Brynhild. "We've got to get going. Sigyn will be waiting." She pulled out a bag of coins and handed a few to the lady.

"All right," sighed Barnabas. "I suppose this one will do." He turned around so the shopkeeper could wrap the cloak around him, and saw Wilfred emerging from inside the shop. He was wearing a cloak that was rather well-stitched (in comparison to Barnabas', at least). It even seemed to be quite clean. The worst thing, though, was that it was a very pretty blue.

"Why, Wilfred's is blue!" complained Barnabas. "I thought you said there were no blue ones!"

The shopkeeper reached out and prodded Barnabas' belly (which, though it was a bit round, didn't protrude *that* much). "Blue too small for you. Brown and green are just as nice, though."

Brynhild let out a loud guffaw, whilst Wilfred averted his eyes politely. Barnabas turned a bit red in the face, mortified, then sighed again in resignation. His new cloak *did* smell abominably, but it was also quite cozy and warm. In fact, if it wasn't for the smell, the thing would be extraordinarily comfortable. Perhaps, he thought, the smell would go away after a while.

He shrugged, pulling his nasty, smelly cloak closer about his shoulders against the cold. "Fine," he said. "Splendid. Shall we go find Sigyn then?"

Brynhild passed a few more coins to the shopkeeper and left Hynder in the woman's care before leading the way out of the village and onto a small dirt path that led into the trees that surrounded the village. Barnabas wondered that she had elected to leave the horse behind, but as they walked farther along the path he quickly realized why she had done so.

As the path wove its way deeper into the forest, the trees quickly changed from the slim birches with narrow trunks that skirted the village into massive oaks with dark, mouldering bark and trunks thicker than any Barnabas had ever seen. Indeed, he doubted that his hands would meet were he to try to wrap his arms round them.

Their leaves were so dense as to form a heavy canopy that dimmed the light, creating a false twilight. The path twisted and turned around the tree trunks in ever more convoluted contortions as it found its way through the ever-tighter spaces between them. It was easy to see that a horse would have had a great deal of trouble navigating the path.

"Is it much farther to the cave?" asked Barnabas grumpily, after banging his hip painfully onto a protruding knot of a particularly massive tree.

"Not at all," said Brynhild. "It's right there. See?" She stopped and pointed straight up.

Barnabas and Wilfred bumped into each other a bit as they emerged from the path behind Brynhild and strained to see where she was pointing.

"Why are you pointing up like that...oh. Oh dear." said Wilfred, who had managed to come out of the woods a step ahead of Barnabas. His words broke off as his eyes followed Brynhild's finger and he saw the cave.

"What? What is it? What's the matter?" asked Barnabas anxiously, jostling everyone as he tried to see. Then he, too, saw the cave, and opened and closed his mouth repeatedly, as though he were trying to speak but no sound would come out. "Oh dear, indeed," he managed to squeak at last.

The cave sat at the top of a high, rocky cliff. The path made no pretense at being easily walkable, or safe, or anything that could even remotely be considered a civilized trail, but instead simply ascended in the steepest, most direct line straight up the cliff to the cave. Indeed, there were places where large boulders stood directly in the way, so that it looked as if one would have to clamber up them like a billy goat in order to continue on.

A tall, thin waterfall snaked its way down the cliff on one side of the path, tumbling and bouncing this way and that as it bounced off the rocks. On the other side was a sheer, unforgiving cliff face that was certainly impassible.

Barnabas looked up and swallowed audibly. There would be nothing to cling to on the cliff side of the path, and a fall off of the waterfall side would almost certainly result in death.

"Mightn't we call to Sigyn?" he suggested hopefully. "Perhaps *she'll* come *down* to *us*, instead of *us* going up to *her*?"

"She can't," answered Brynhild. "She can only leave the

cave when it's time to empty Loki's bowl."

"But the bowl was stolen," said Barnabas.

"Right," said Brynhild. "So she's not going to have to empty it, is she?"

"Which means that she should be free to come and go whenever she chooses," pointed out Wilfred reasonably. He, too, did not like the looks of that path, nor did he think highly of their chances of making it to the top unscathed. "Being as she's not tied to the bowl anymore," he added.

Brynhild shook her head and made a face. "So she'll have no cause to go empty the bowl, since it's not there anymore. Meaning that she can't very well empty a bowl that isn't full, and that she doesn't even have in the first place,' she said slowly, as though this were the most obvious thing in the world.

"But…" began Wilfred. He was stopped by Barnabas, who held up a restraining hand. The little detective was quickly learning that it was useless to argue with a Viking who had made up her mind about a thing. He realized that it would probably be easier to climb the path than it would be to unravel the convoluted logic of being bound to emptying a bowl that was no longer present and therefore no longer required emptying.

"If Brynhild says Sigyn won't come down," he sighed, "it's clear that we, then, must needs go up. There's nothing for it, so up, up, up we go!" So saying, he stepped purposefully up onto the first rock and turned to look back at Wilfred and Brynhild.

He stood stiffly erect and held his head as high as he might, clearly trying to portray an image of an intrepid explorer who feared nothing. However, even his thick furry cloak could not conceal the tremble of his legs (which shook like an undercooked soufflé) nor could it hide the paleness of his face (save for two strawberry colored blotches on his cheeks) or the wild look in his eyes.

Barnabas was, of course, terrified, but as Wilfred was technically his employee and Brynhild was a lady (a frightfully strong lady, to be sure, and one who could probably clamber up a cliff like this far more easily than Barnabas ever could), still he felt that he had a certain responsibility towards them.

"My dear lady Brynhild," he began. His voice quavered a good deal, causing him to cough loudly to cover his nervousness. "Lady Brynhild," he began once more, nodding his head towards her. "My dear lady Brynhild. Fear not! Ahem, ahem!" (His lip had begun to quiver, necessitating a fresh coughing fit.) Anyway," he continued, once he had collected himself, "fear not! I will go up first, so that I may show you the easiest way, and point out to you any dangers that may arise."

"Maybe I should go first," suggested Brynhild. "Since I've done this be…"

"Nay!" interrupted Barnabas. "As an employer, and a man of the Great British Empire besides, it is my duty to lead the way, to be first into danger, to go down with the ship so that the crew might survive!" He bowed gallantly (which was quite remarkable considering how badly his legs were shaking) and began to climb.

Unfortunately, he slipped almost immediately, and fell back down to where he had begun, barking his shins most painfully in the process. Brynhild caught him before he could tumble off the path entirely (although, in truth, he wouldn't have fallen far since he had only taken three steps at the most).

"Carefully, now," said Brynhild, trying not to smile as Barnabas reddened in embarrassment. Wilfred tactfully feigned an extreme interest in arranging the folds of his cloak, and pretended not to notice what had happened.

"Yes, well," he said. "Quite slippery there on that first rock. Do watch your step. Good thing I went first, or else someone could have been terribly hurt!" He began to climb again, more carefully now, and successfully got himself atop the first slippery rock. "See?" he said proudly. "Easy as can be, once you have the hang of it."

Barnabas continued clumsily up the path, his feet sliding out from under him with every other step as he grunted and yelped by turns. Still, he managed to hang on, and soon was making good progress despite his less-than-graceful efforts.

Brynhild, trying hard to stifle a laugh, gestured for Wilfred to follow him as she brought up the rear, which was the best position from which to catch any falling British detectives. However, they made it to the top with only a few minor slips and stumbles (although each time either Barnabas or Wilfred slipped, their hearts would flip-flop and their stomachs would clench most uncomfortably, so high were they by the end).

At last, they all stood at the cave mouth, safely away from the cliff's edge. "And here we are," proclaimed Barnabas proudly. "You're welcome," he added, though no one had said 'thank you' yet.

"Much thanks indeed," said Wilfred. He saw that, whilst the color had returned to Barnabas' face, the wild, slightly crazed look in his eyes remained. Barnabas was clearly overexcited. "I would have surely fallen, had you not shown me the way around those tricky spots," continued Wilfred soothingly.

"Yes, well, of course," stammered Barnabas, pleased yet embarrassed by the praise. "All in a day's work to keep your employees from falling to their deaths, is what I always say!"

"*Does* he always say that?" whispered Brynhild to Wilfred as Barnabas moved to look inside the cave.

"He *does* say it quite a bit," admitted Wilfred.

"Do people fall to their deaths a lot around him then?" she asked with a frown.

"No, not at all," said Wilfred. "I mean he says 'something or other is what I always say', all the time. Not the bit about 'falling to their deaths'."

"So why did he say he always says that?" pressed Brynhild, confused. "If he doesn't actually always say that?"

"It's just a figure of speech, I suppose," said Wilfred. "He doesn't really *mean* it."

"I don't think I understand...," began Brynhild, then stopped abruptly as a dreadful screech came from within the cave. "Sounds like Barnabas has met Loki's snake."

Wilfred quickly followed Brynhild into the cave. Yelps

and hisses and, oddly, laughter reverberated from the cave's walls, so that it was impossible to tell from whence they came, or what, exactly was going on.

Once Wilfred's eyes had adjusted to the dark, he saw the most astonishing tableau, one that explained the strange sounds that he heard.

A man lay tied up upon an altar made of rock. He seemed to be unconscious, but he thrashed and moaned as if in great pain. Above him hovered a giant snake. Its fangs were the size of a man's forearm, and a slimy substance dripped from them onto the man's face. The man's thrashing redoubled each time a drop fell on him.

Fluttering about the man and the snake was Barnabas. He threw rocks at it and darted in and out to swat at it, yelling, "Back, you foul beast! Get back, I say!" Each time he landed a blow the snake would hiss and snarl and its fangs would drip even faster.

The laughter came from a very beautiful woman of middle age, who watched Barnabas' struggle with the snake. She clapped her hands and giggled with delight as Barnabas smacked the snake right on the snout, making it cross its eyes even as a great droplet fell from its teeth onto the man below, who groaned and writhed in apparent pain.

"Wilfred! Brynhild!" cried Barnabas, seeing his friends. "Oh, do help! The snake is tormenting this poor, captive man. And I do believe it has driven this woman completely insane." He looked askance at the laughing, clapping, woman, then ducked as the snake swung the tip of its tail at him.

Wilfred moved forward to aid his beleaguered friend, but Brynhild laid a restraining hand upon his arm. "Barnabas, stand down!" she commanded. "You're going to cause an earthquake!"

"Huh?" asked Barnabas.

"If you don't stop smacking that snake, there will be an earthquake," said Sigyn, as though that explained everything.

"How will I cause an earthquake by hitting a snake?" asked Barnabas (quite reasonably, thought Wilfred, who was as confused as his employer).

"Because," said the pretty, crazy woman, "when you hit it, it drops more venom onto Loki, which makes him flail about. And when Loki flails the earth trembles with him. So please, do keep hitting the snake. Another good one on the snout should do it!"

"Sigyn!" admonished Brynhild. "Stop inciting him." She turned to Barnabas, who was looking from Brynhild to Sigyn and back again. "Barnabas, the man on the table is Loki. And this here is Sigyn, his wife."

"Oh!" said Barnabas. "Well, shouldn't we untie him, at least? I don't want to start earthquakes and whatnot, but we cannot simply leave him there with that, that...*thing* hovering over him!" He began to fumble with the ropes that bound Loki to the altar.

"Yes, yes, untie him," said Sigyn happily. "Quickly now, before the snake bites you."

"Barnabas, stop it!" commanded Brynhild.

"I can't!" protested Barnabas, ducking as the snake snapped at his head. "We must get him away from the snake!"

"Go on, do it!" said Sigyn. "The ropes are tough, since they are made of my son's intestines, of course, but perhaps you'll be able to work it out."

"Barnabas, if you free Loki it will start Ragnarok. The world will end!"

Barnabas quickly pulled away from the ropes. "The world will end?" he said. "Intestines?" He looked down at his hands and wiped them on his cloak, making a disgusted face. "*Intestines*?" he repeated.

"Yes, *intestines,*" said Brynhild. "And Sigyn, why would you want him set free? He killed your lover, the father of your son!"

"Technically, he didn't," said Sigyn. "It was Hod who drew the bow and sent the arrow through Balder's heart."

"Because Loki tricked him!" said Brynhild. "You know as well as anyone that Hod loved Balder, and is as blind as a bat besides. It never would have happened if not for Loki."

"And then the rest of the gods punish him by using Narfi's intestines to bind Loki here forever?" spat Sigyn bitterly. "How is that justice? Narfi was my son, mine and Balder's. Is it justice that Balder's own son was murdered in order to carry out Loki's sentence."

"Of course not," said Brynhild. "But still, you can't possibly want Loki freed. After all he's done!"

"Wait a moment, if you please," interrupted Barnabas. "I just want to be clear. You're saying that this man here…"

"Loki," said Brynhild. "Sigyn's husband."

"Yes, fine, Loki," continued Barnabas. "Loki tricked a blind man into killing his wife's, um, well, I suppose I can't seem to find a decent word for this…"

"Special friend?" suggested Wilfred helpfully.

"Precisely!" said Barnabas. "Thank you, Wilfred. So Loki got Sigyn's *special friend* killed, so, to punish him, Odin murdered her son, who was fathered by the murdered, ah, *friend*, and used his intestines to tie up Loki here?"

"Right," said Brynhild. "And put the snake there to drip venom on his face."

"Which makes him thrash about and it is this thrashing that causes earthquakes?" asked Barnabas.

"Yes. Which is why Sigyn holds a bowl over his face."

"To catch the poison," added Sigyn. "So there are no earthquakes."

Barnabas cast her a doleful look. "Obviously," he said. "But it is this bowl that has been stolen?"

"It is," said Brynhild.

"Which means more earthquakes," concluded Barnabas. "So why don't we simply cut Loki loose?"

"Because once Loki gets loose, Ragnarok will begin," said Brynhild.

"The end of the world," supplied Wilfred. "But why, then, did Sigyn want Barnabas to untie Loki?"

"Why indeed?" said Barnabas. He looked suspiciously at Sigyn. "Perhaps it was she who stole the bowl, hoping that Loki might thrash himself free. But why?"

"Because Balder will be set free from the realm of the

dead after Ragnarok," said Brynhild.

"Aha!" cried Barnabas, pointing to Sigyn. "J'accuse! J'accuse you of stealing the bowl and plotting to cause the end of the world." He slapped his hands across each other as though dusting them off, satisfied that the case was solved.

"Except," said Brynhild, "that Sigyn knows no one can untie those bonds."

"So when she told Barnabas to untie them…" began Wilfred.

"…she knew it was impossible," finished Brynhild.

"Did you or did you not want me to free Loki?" snapped Barnabas to Sigyn.

Sigyn sighed. "I did not," she said. "I was merely bored. I've been sitting in this cave for ages, with only Freya to come visit me."

"You were bored?" sputtered Barnabas, outraged. "You risked causing earthquakes, which could have hurt people, you know, not to mention the end of the world, because you were *bored*?"

"Well, one passes the time the best one can," said Sigyn.

"Abominable," muttered Barnabas.

"*You* try sitting in a cave for a thousand years with a husband you loathe, holding a bowl and catching poison with it day in and day out," retorted Sigyn.

"It is true," said Brynhild. "Sigyn has most faithfully guarded us all against Ragnarok for a millennium. In her defense."

"I still think she might have stolen the bowl," grumbled Barnabas. "She seems entirely deranged. And she certainly has motive."

"There's one way to know for sure," said Wilfred. "Didn't Odin say the bowl was stolen whilst Freya was visiting Sigyn?"

"He did," said Brynhild.

"And he was right," said Sigyn. "Freya came to see me, and we stepped out to sit by the waterfall together for a time. When we returned, the bowl was gone."

"And how do we know this Freya isn't in collusion with

you, to steal the bowl and end the world?" said Barnabas.

"Because Freya is one of the most respected goddesses of the Vanir," said Brynhild. "She is completely trustworthy, as far as goddesses go."

"Perhaps we should interview her?" suggested Wilfred.

"Hmmph," said Barnabas, annoyed at having his easy solution to the case stolen from him so quickly. "I suppose. As long as Sigyn has nothing further to add? No visits from anyone else? No suspicious people lurking about or plotting with you?"

"Only Freya," said Sigyn. "I wish there were some suspicious people lurking about to plot with. Then at least I'd have some fun." She pouted prettily, and Barnabas glared at her.

"Very well then," said Wilfred. "Thank you for your time, Mrs. Sigyn." He bowed politely.

"You're welcome," said Sigyn. "And feel free to come back any time. It really was entertaining watching your friend swat at the snake."

"Time to go!" said Brynhild brightly as Barnabas harrumphed with indignation. "Come then," said Brynhild, tugging at Barnabas' arm when he tarried. Indeed, she had to forcibly pull him out of the cave, so intent was he on continuing to glare at Sigyn. "Time to go see Freya."

Chapter Five

Barnabas was at last convinced to leave the cave and head back down the path, though he protested the whole way. He kept muttering about how terrible Sigyn was, and how they shouldn't abandon her as a suspect so quickly, until Brynhild shushed him and told him that Freya would be terribly displeased if she heard that Barnabas doubted her word.

"And, besides," she added, "why would Sigyn steal the bowl, after sitting there for untold years doing her duty? She doesn't want the world to end any more than the rest of us do."

Even Barnabas had to admit the sense of this, and reluctantly followed Brynhild down the path back to the village.

The way down was far easier than the way up had been, as is usually the case, and they arrived at the village in good time. Hynder was still tied up to the post where they left him, eating potatoes out of the shopkeeper's open palm.

"The cloaks are good, yes?" she said as they approached, nodding with approval at the sight of Barnabas and Wilfred bundled snugly into their cloaks. "Keep you warm?"

Barnabas had entirely forgotten about his dislike for the cloak, and had long since ceased to notice the smell. Indeed, now that the shopkeeper drew his attention to it, he realized that an icy wind was blowing quite cruelly. He should have been horribly cold, but instead was as warm as a bug in a rug.

Not one to withhold credit where credit was due, Barnabas smiled and graciously nodded his agreement. "Quite warm," he said. "Indeed, I could be sitting in front of the fire in my study in Marylebone, I am so cozy."

"Don't know about Marylebone," said the shopkeeper.

"But the green cloak is good for you."

"I do believe I agree," said Barnabas (and, surprisingly, he found that he actually did). "The cloak is most satisfactory."

During the exchange Brynhild had untied Hynder from the post, adjusted his reins, and otherwise made him ready for travel. She effortlessly leaped up onto his back and reached out a helping hand to the two detectives. "Ready?" she said.

Barnabas and Wilfred looked at each other and sighed. Neither was eager to climb back up onto Hynder, not if it meant another wild ride like the one that had brought them here.

"Is Freya's house, er, mansion, ah, *palace*, I suppose," said Barnabas. "Is it far? I feel my legs could use a good stretch, you see."

Brynhild laughed. "You cannot walk to Freya's palace. It's in Vanaheim."

"One mile?" suggested Barnabas hopefully. "Two?"

"It's another world," replied Brynhild. "Although it's on the same plane as Midgard, at least, in that they are both Earthbound, so I suppose it's relatively close. As close as one world can be to another, that is."

"Of course," said Barnabas sardonically, as he reluctantly accepted Brynhild's hand and clambered aboard (a process that was a good deal less graceful than Brynhild's had been). He, in turn, reached out to help Wilfred climb up behind him. Brynhild clucked to Hynder, and they were off.

As soon as they left the village of Fanang Falls they began to ascend. "Mightn't we travel by land?" asked Barnabas. "The flying makes my stomach queasy, it seems."

"Sorry," said Brynhild. "To travel between worlds one must fly. Which is why Odin sent me and Hynder with you. I suspect that he knew you'd have to go to all nine worlds, by the end."

"Nine worlds!" exclaimed Barnabas. "And we must go to them all?"

"Perhaps," said Brynhild. "I guess we will see, won't we?"

"I suppose," said Barnabas. "But perhaps we might solve the case in Vanaheim. Perhaps Freya saw something. Or knows something." He waggled his eyebrows suggestively. "Perhaps she is the culprit."

"Maybe," said Brynhild. "But it seems likely that we'll need to investigate further than just Sigyn and Freya. There are all sorts of people who would benefit from Ragnarok."

"Who on earth would benefit from the end of the world?" said Barnabas.

"No one on earth, really," said Brynhild, taking him literally. "But people in the other worlds, definitely."

"Like who?" asked Barnabas.

"Anyone who is destined to survive Ragnarok," said Brynhild.

"How is anyone to survive the end of the world?" asked Barnabas.

"Well, it's not the *end*, exactly, so much as a new beginning," said Brynhild. "Most will die, of course, but there are plenty who will live, and who will even benefit from it. Like Balder, for example."

"But Balder is dead, is he not?" said Barnabas.

"Only until after Ragnarok," replied Brynhild. "Afterwards, he'll come back to life."

"So anyone who wants Balder back might be to blame?" said Barnabas.

"Exactly," said Brynhild.

"Or," suggested Wilfred, "perhaps it's someone who might benefit in a different sort of way. Didn't Odin say that Thor's sons would inherit his hammer after Ragnarok?"

"He did, and they will," said Brynhild. "So you can see that we have many suspects to think of, and very little information as of yet."

"You mentioned that Vanaheim was earthbound, just like Midgard," said Wilfred. "What does that mean?"

"There are three realms," said Brynhild. "There is the earthbound realm, and the realm above, and the realm below. Each of the realms has three worlds within. Asgard, Muspelheim, and Alfheimer are above. Midgard, Vanaheim, and Jutunheim are the earthbound realms. And the worlds below are Svortalfheim, Nidavellier, and Niflheim."

"Midgard is the realm of the mortals?" said Barnabas. "Which is where we just were?"

"Yes," said Brynhild. "And Vanaheim is the home of the Vanir gods, like Freya. And look!" She pointed down to a spectacular palace that they could just barely glimpse through breaks in the clouds below them. "Speak of the goddess. That's Freya's palace."

They all looked down to where an enormous white castle sat in the midst of an equally enormous field. The castle had innumerable spires that reached high up towards the clouds, dotted by dainty windows that were flanked by pretty shutters of the palest blue.

The field, likewise, was covered entirely in blue and white flowers. From the vantage point of flying horse, it looked to be like a canvas painted in dreamy pastel watercolors. The only thing that marred the pristine beauty of the place was the large number of figures, small in the distance, clad in rough brown cloaks, much like Barnabas' own. If he squinted hard enough Barnabas could just make out details of the tiny people. Shields and swords, axes and pikes were slung, forgotten, over shoulders, or held loosely in left hands, as their owners frolicked and cavorted about in the field below.

"Are those...They look like...well, what are they, exactly?" he asked.

"Warriors," replied Brynhild. "The field is called Folkvanger, and it's ruled by Freya. Freya gets half of those killed in battle, while Odin gets the other half."

"But they seem to be playing," observed Barnabas, laughing as he watched a group of them engaged in what appeared to be a game of tag. "Is that a maypole?" he cried, astonished to see grown men dancing around a tall pole, weaving brightly colored ribbons around and about each other as their weapons dangled, forgotten, on their backs.

"Looks like it," said Brynhild, pressing her lips together.

"In Odin's hall the warriors seemed much more, ah, warrior-like," said Barnabas.

"The Vanir are much less warlike than the Aesir gods," said Brynhild. "And there is a magic in Folkvanger. Anyone who lingers here becomes like that." She wrinkled her nose at the happy warriors, and Barnabas realized that she was disgusted by them. He thought about it for a moment. He could see that the carefree, childlike behavior of the warriors below seemed a bit unnatural, as though there was something *wrong* with them that made them act this way. Then again, he hadn't much cared for the rough ways of the warriors in Odin's hall, either.

"The Aesir?" he asked, to change the subject.

"The major gods," explained Brynhild. "Like Odin, and Thor. All the gods who live in Asgard. But that's enough about the gods. Let's go down and talk to a goddess."

Brynhild cued Hynder to descend (which the horse did sharply and nauseatingly, affirming Barnabas' fears that this was simply the usual way in which Hynder landed). Once safely down on the ground, Brynhild left Barnabas and Wilfred to hold Hynder while she found someone to escort them into the palace.

"*Someone* has to keep an eye on Hynder," she said. "And since I know the etiquette of approaching the Vanir, well…" she trailed off, giving them a knowing look.

"I assure you," said Barnabas primly, "that Wilfred and I are quite able in terms of anything having to do with etiquette. Indeed, I do believe etiquette is what we are best at."

"Be that as it may," said Brynhild, "it's probably best if I talk to her steward first myself. So that things go smoothly."

"Are you implying that I cannot conduct things smoothly?" exclaimed Barnabas indignantly. "Have I done anything to give one the merest suspicion that I might conduct myself in anything less than a manner of utmost professionalism? Well, have I?" he demanded, giving Wilfred a pointed look.

Wilfred thought of Barnabas maniacally flailing about with Thor's hammer across Odin's lawn, and then of him unwisely (if also impressively bravely) attempting to do battle with Loki's massive snake whilst calling Sigyn a madwoman and accusing her of starting the end of the world.

"Of course not," he said. "I can't think of one thing."

Brynhild choked back a small laugh. "I'm not saying that you don't *mean* well," she said, biting her cheeks. "I'm just saying that I'm obviously the best choice when it comes to actually *talking* to the gods."

"Poppycock!" said Barnabas. "I'll simply state that we are here on important business of Odin's, and…"

"Best not to mention Odin," interrupted Brynhild. "Freya's father Nord is a hostage of the Aesir, you see. There was a big falling out between the Vanir and the Aesir."

"Ohhh," said Barnabas, rolling his eyes. "All right, then we'll say that we are here to prevent Loki from escaping and starting the end of the world. Anyone would want to help with that!"

"Maybe," said Brynhild. "Her brother Freyr is destined to die during Ragnarok. But then again, Nord is fated to return to Vanaheim after Ragnarok, so she might want that. Plus, her husband Od is missing, and if anyone can find him it's Loki. So you can see that she could possibly have some mixed feelings on the subject."

"Very well," snapped Barnabas irritably. "Go on then. Clearly *you* are the only one who can do *any*thing."

"I meant no offense,' protested Brynhild. "Merely that I know Freya's mind better than you."

"Of course, of course," said Barnabas. "Carry on. And good day to you!" So saying, he crossed his arms and turned his back on Brynhild.

"Really," said Brynhild, "I can't see why you're so…"

"It's no use," said Wilfred. "He won't talk to you anymore once he's said 'good day'."

"At least hold the horse," said Brynhild as she tried unsuccessfully to hand the reins over to the recalcitrant detective. He looked away, pretending great interest in the clouds above. Brynhild, meanwhile, tried to fold the reins over his elbow.

"I said 'good day'!" said Barnabas tersely over his shoulder as he folded his elbow in so that the reins fell to the ground. He turned his body this way and that so as to further avoid the proffered reins. Brynhild picked up the reins and attempted to sling them over his other arm. Her efforts were to no avail, however, as Barnabas merely kept twisting away and flapping his elbows in and out.

Wilfred saw the situation devolving into a fruitless quagmire of futility. He stepped forward, smiling apologetically, and took Hynder's reins from Brynhild. "We'll wait here," he said. "Go on and talk to Freya, and we'll be ready when you send for us."

Brynhild shook her head, perplexed, and headed off into the interior of the castle.

"Barnabas," began Wilfred, "I'm not certain that Brynhild deserved that."

"Maybe it is *I* who didn't deserve what she said to *me*," said Barnabas. "Acting as though we don't know how to do our own jobs. Preposterous!"

"I don't think she meant it that way," said Wilfred.

"Then why did she say that we wouldn't know what to say to Freya, or that we couldn't help but offend her?"

"I don't think she said exactly that," said Wilfred.

"No, but that's what she meant!" said Barnabas. "I'm a detective, you know, and I can tell what people are *really* saying, underneath all of the things that they *actually* say."

"She's only trying to be helpful, I think," said Wilfred. "I think perhaps the problem is simply that these Vikings are much more direct than we are accustomed to."

"They are blunt to the point of rudeness, don't you think?" said Barnabas. "Like that shopkeeper, who as good as called me fat."

"It is just their way, it seems," said Wilfred diplomatically. "If we are to solve this case we shall have to get used to it. Or at least learn to abide it."

Barnabas sighed and uncrossed his arms. "So you really don't think she meant to insult me?" he asked.

Wilfred, unsure if his employer was referring to Brynhild taking charge of the investigation, or the shopkeeper calling attention to Barnabas' extra girth, replied simply, "I'm sure not."

"And the way she flapped those reins at me!" exclaimed Barnabas. "She's a bit of a gobermouch, don't you think?"

"I'm certain that she doesn't mean to overstep," said Wilfred. "Indeed, I'm sure that her intention is merely to help us."

"But you must admit that her help *is* somewhat intrusive," insisted Barnabas. He saw the sense of Wilfred's words but was unwilling to be done with his righteous anger just yet.

"Perhaps," said Wilfred. "But remember how it was in Egypt, when we had no help? We wished many times for a guide such as this."

"Well," grumbled Barnabas, "maybe not one entirely like this."

"On the whole, however, I'm sure that you'd admit that her assistance, brusque as it may be, has served us quite handily," said Wilfred.

Barnabas shuffled his feet and mumbled incoherently.

"Pardon?" said Wilfred, leaning closer in an attempt to hear. His motion unintentionally brought Hynder closer as well. The horse stuck his snout into Barnabas neck and gave him a wet nuzzle.

Barnabas reluctantly let out a small giggle as Hynder's whiskers gave him a tickle. Then he sighed and turned to face Wilfred. "I suppose I've overreacted a bit, haven't I?" he asked sheepishly.

"It is completely understandable," soothed Wilfred.

"Still, I shall have to apologize."

"Perhaps it might be best to simply not mention it again. Indeed, I'm sure Brynhild hardly noticed a thing."

"Really?" said Barnabas hopefully. "It's not as if I berated her, or called her names. I was merely the slightest bit sarcastic, really." Then his face darkened with doubt. "But I did say 'good day' in a terribly nasty way."

"Did you?" asked Wilfred. "You must have said it so softly that I didn't hear it," he said, although he had, of course, heard it, as had Brynhild.

"Splendid!" said Barnabas, brightening. "Then we shall pretend as if it never happened, and that will be that.

Although, you must admit she could do very well with being less of a know-it-all."

"Well," said Wilfred, "I think we shall find her knowledge quite useful, don't you?"

"I suppose," Barnabas admitted. "This place is so complicated, I'm not certain that we could feasibly untangle all of the threads without *some* assistance."

"Nine worlds!" said Wilfred, shaking his head. "Can you believe it? It's even more complex than the Egyptian underworld."

"Yes," said Barnabas, "and since there are nine worlds to visit and no telling how many trips between them, that means we shall have to get used to Hynder's, ah, less-than-smooth descents."

"Ugh," said Wilfred. They both rubbed their bellies, thinking of the discomforts to come.

"Anyway," continued Barnabas, "it is good to have someone who knows where they're going, and what the gods are about, and all of that sort of thing. Even if it *is* terribly annoying."

"Quite so," agreed Wilfred.

"And," added Barnabas, still rubbing his belly, "I am most certainly not fat. I merely have a healthy roundness about me."

"So," said Brynhild, coming up behind them and startling them both out of their skins so that they screeched and jumped up like corn kernels on a hot griddle. Brynhild gave them a quizzical look, then shook her head. "Freya will see us now." She took Hynder's reins and handed them to a boy who walked behind her, then turned on her heels and headed back into the palace, clearly expecting the two detectives to follow her.

"See?" whispered Barnabas to Wilfred as they did so. "No manners whatsoever. An *astonishing* lack of manners, even." He put on a beleaguered expression. "Still," he continued melodramatically, "I shall try to be more patient, although it does wear my nerves so. Oh, what I wouldn't give for a day in London, where everyone behaves precisely as one expects them to, and...oh my, look at this!" His mild diatribe was cut off abruptly as he beheld the interior of the great white palace.

Inside, the walls were as pristinely white as they were without. The floors were comprised of tiles that were made of some sort of remarkable material that gleamed and glowed like the inside of a seashell. Alternating squares of blue and white tiles, outlined in a shimmering silver trim, made a soothing chess-board pattern. Vases of hammered silver filled with bouquets of blue and white flowers (presumably plucked from the fields outside) were placed at regular intervals on ornately carved white pedastals.

The beauty of it took Barnabas' breath away, but he was most impressed with the sheer orderliness of things. Everything was in its proper place, and arranged in pleasing rows of precise straightness and perfectly measured right angles.

Barnabas, who valued order and predictability above all else (like any good Englishman), was most impressed. "But this is fabulous!" he cried happily, looking about with approval. "Absolutely splendid!"

"It's is something to see," said Brynhild, winking at him. Baranbas, his ire completely forgotten, agreed wholeheartedly.

Brynhild led them up a wide curving staircase (that remarkably somehow managed to maintain the straight lines and regularity of pattern of the white and blue tiles, despite the concavity of the steps). They followed a wide balcony that overlooked the reception hall through which they had just passed, and came to a set of silvery double doors.

"This is it," said Brynhild. "Remember, try not to mention Odin too much. We don't want to annoy Freya."

"She's the goddess of love, is she not?" asked Wilfred.

"She is," said Brynhild. "But also of gold and beauty..."

"All very nice things," said Barnabas, eager to meet the owner of this wonderful palace.

"...and war and death," finished Brynhild. Barnabas and Wilfred both popped their mouths open in some alarm at this statement, but were unable to question her further as she rapped immediately upon the doors. A youth, dressed in blue and white, of course, promptly opened the doors and motioned for them to enter.

Brynhild did so without hesitation. Barnabas and Wilfred glanced at each other, more than a little concerned about the revelation that their hostess was also the goddess of war and death. Still, if their investigation were to proceed they must question Freya.

"There's nothing for it. We must go in," said Barnabas, though he made no move to follow Brynhild.

"Indeed we must," agreed Wilfred, whose own feet were likewise rooted to the spot upon which he stood.

"Together then?" suggested Barnabas.

Wilfred nodded. They both took a deep breath, and entered Freya's chamber.

Chapter Six

It was not at all what either of them had expected. Gone were the white walls and the blue and white tiles. Likewise not to be found was even a hint of silver. Indeed, the entire room was entirely devoid of the pleasant orderliness of the rest of the palace.

The walls were painted in a myriad of colors, each swirling around the other in decidedly chaotic patterns. The floor was covered in thick furs. The furniture was made of heavy wood and decorated with large hunks of raw gold.

"Please, have a seat," said a small, dark woman. She was seated on a large, plush cushion that was set into an alcove of a small open window, and was enveloped in a wide cape made of feathers. She indicated a pair of hard wooden benches that sat opposite her own perch. Brynhild was already seated upon one, so Barnabas and Wilfred took the other.

"Falcon's feathers," whispered Barnabas to Wilfred, referring to Freya's cloak (for that was quite obviously who the woman was). Indeed, the detectives had cause to know the difference between a falcon's feathers and that of other birds, as they had quite recently apprehended not one but two falcon gods in the Egyptian underworld.

"Thank you, Madam Freya," said Barnabas politely, trying not to look at the distracting and somewhat unsettling array of objects in the room. Statues and amulets of clearly pagan origin were scattered haphazardly throughout the chamber, with no apparent thought of design or order. Colors and fabrics and textures were all mismatched, so that the eye was drawn in every direction. Barnabas found it all far too over-stimulating, and yearned for the delicate beauty of the reception hall.

Freya noticed Barnabas' discomfiture and smiled. "You prefer the sweet prettiness of the entrance over the wild abandon of my inner chambers, do you?" she said.

"Ah, well, no," stammered Barnabas, unsure of how to frame a polite response to such a question. "That is to say, of course I like very much the blue and white, but I'm sure that this mode of, um, ah, *decoration* has a beauty of its own, as well."

Freya laughed and clapped her hands. "Answered like a true gentleman," she said approvingly. Barnabas let out the breath he had been unknowingly holding. "You see," said Freya, "the outer rooms reflect my position as the goddess of love and beauty. But the inner rooms..." She paused, her eyes twinkling mischievously. "The inner rooms are like my inner nature. Sex, and war, and death."

"Oh my!" exclaimed Barnabas nervously. Wilfred glanced at him and saw that he had gone quite red in the face. "Oh my, indeed!" repeated Barnabas. He was spared the need for further comment as a giant pig chose that moment to come out from behind a fur-covered sofa. It waddled over to Freya, turned in a circle a few times, then settled with a grunt on the furs at her feet.

"Meet Hildisvini," said Freya, affectionately rubbing the creature on its neck. Barnabas and Wilfred wondered that her hand didn't come away bleeding, so course did its bristles appear. "He is my pet boar."

"Ah, yes," said Barnabas. He looked askance at the animal, which probably weighed over 40 stone, at the least. Seeing that it meant no harm (at the moment, anyway; who could tell what such a beast might decide to do in the future?) but was intended only to take a nap at its mistress's feet, Barnabas offered a polite smile. "Quite nice," he said to Freya, who was looking at him as though expecting him to say more. "A very fine-looking, ah, pig," he concluded, looking to Wilfred for help.

"The finest pig I've seen, I'm sure," said Wilfred uncertainly.

"Thank you," said Freya, beaming with pride at her bristly, snoring giant of a pet. "Now. Brynhild says you have some questions for me?"

"Oh," said Barnabas, momentarily flustered by the rapid progression of the conversation. "Of course. Odin sent us…" A sharp hiss of breath from Brynhild stopped him. He coughed to cover his faux pas. "That is to say, we are here straight from Asg… What I mean is, we've come from, well, ah…"

"Fanang Falls," interrupted Brynhild, rolling her eyes in annoyance. She pulled a face at Barnabas, which he pointedly ignored. Freya, however, held up a hand. "Relax," she said. "It doesn't matter to me if you come from Asgard or Helheim itself. My ill will towards Odin has nothing to do with you, or your business here. You are my guests, and are welcome here."

"Hah!" said Barnabas, shooting Brynhild a triumphant look. Then, recovering his manners, he looked back at Freya. "You are most gracious, my good lady," he said with a humble bow of his head.

Freya laughed softly. To Barnabas' ears it was a pleasantly melodious chuckle that sounded like the singing of a thousand birds. "To tell the truth, I'm simply not in the mood for the 'war and death' side of me just now. No, I'm definitely more in a 'love and sex' kind of mood." She aimed a lascivious wink at Barnabas, who reddened with mortal embarrassment. He immediately amended his original assessment of the sound of her laughter to 'a thousand *predatory* birds', instead.

"Well then," he said uncomfortably. "Good, I suppose. Anyway. We've come to ask you some questions about Loki's bowl."

"Loki's bowl?" asked Freya with an exceedingly innocent look on her face. Barnabas and Wilfred shared a warning glance. This goddess was turning out to be more wily than expected.

"The bowl that Sigyn uses to catch the venom of the snake before it falls onto Loki's forehead," said Barnabas. "It has been stolen."

"Why come here, then? Why come to me?" Freya's question was posed reasonably enough, but Barnabas fancied that he heard an undercurrent of threat in her voice. Immediately, his suspicions were aroused. Still, he was not eager to repeat the mistake he had made in Loki's cave. He would not unleash his accusations directly at Freya as he had done with Sigyn. He resolved to try a more subtle approach.

"So," he said as casually as he could, "what are your feelings about Ragnarok?"

"The end of the world?" asked Freya, confused. "My feelings? What do you mean?"

"Oh, I'm just trying to make sense of the whole affair," said Barnabas, feigning ignorance. He ignored a warning glance from Brynhild and pressed on. "It seems as though some people are for it, whilst yet others are against. Get as many opinions as you can on a thing before forming opinions of your own, is what I always say!" he continued, despite never having said such a thing in all his life.

"And why," said Freya softly, "would someone be *for* Ragnarok?"

Wilfred sensed the growing menace in Freya's tone and delivered a none-too-subtle kick to Barnabas' shin, which Barnabas, oblivious to his danger, ignored.

"Oh, there are many reasons," he said. "Some will survive and inherit valuable goods."

"Like Modi and Magni," supplied Freya.

"Precisely!" said Barnabas. "Whilst others might have loved ones returned to them." He waggled his eyebrows suggestively.

"Like Sigyn and Balder," said Wilfred, trying to steer the conversation to safer waters.

"I don't think that is the relationship to which your friend here refers," said Freya, never taking her gaze away from Barnabas. Barnabas, realizing that the goddess saw through his attempt at subterfuge, felt his heart begin to speed up in trepidation. Still, duty required him to explore all possibilities, and he could not (would not!) back down in fear.

"No, my lady," he said politely. "It is not. I refer, as I believe you know, to the restoration of your father from his imprisonment in Asgard."

"And you accuse me of orchestrating the theft of Loki's bowl so as to bring about Ragnarok in order to effect that restoration?" said Freya.

"No, I'm sure that's not at all what he's saying," said Brynhild. "He has a tendency to prattle on sometimes, is all."

"I'm certain there is a reasonable way to work through this," said Wilfred at the same time, flapping his hands wildly as though to attract Freya's attention from Barnabas to himself.

Freya, however, never took her eyes from Barnabas as the others fluttered and flustered around them. To his credit, the little detective met her gaze boldly (though, in truth, his face was as red as a beet and his hands were trembling visibly with the distress of it all).

"I do apologize for any offense my question has caused, my lady," said Barnabas, his voice shaking only just a little. He held his head up as high as it could go, trying to affect an air of confidence (although he succeeded mainly in appearing somewhat uncomfortably *stretched*, instead). "Still," he continued, peering over the tip of his upraised nose, "I have taken on this case, and as a detective my duty compels me to explore all avenues. So I will speak plainly: did you abscond with Loki's bowl, or collude with others in the theft of said bowl, in order to bring about Ragnarok and the return of your father?"

There was a taut silence. Everyone, shocked by Barnabas words, froze. Even Barnabas himself could scarcely believe he had had the nerve to say such a thing. Wilfred, usually so adept at rescuing his employer from a well-intentioned faux-pas, was at a loss for words. Brynhild, for her part, was torn between being incredibly impressed by Barnabas' timid bravery and wanting to cuff him on the head for endangering all of their lives by offending Freya so.

Freya, accustomed to people fawning over her and

agreeing to her every word, was equally taken aback. She stared at Barnabas for a long moment, her mouth and eyes all wide open with shock.

Then, surprisingly, she laughed. Gone was the soft, tinkling sound of birds. In its place was a real laugh; a deep, gleeful sound that bubbled up out of her belly. It was a deep laugh; a hearty one; and a contagious one. Wilfred soon found that he could not help but laugh himself, and was quickly followed by a relieved (if somewhat confused) Barnabas. Even Brynhild found herself giggling alongside everyone despite herself. Only Hildisvini the pet boar was immune to the hilarity, having fallen quite soundly asleep at Freya's feet.

Freya clapped her hands together happily. "Oh," she gasped between guffaws. "If you could see your faces just now...it is too funny!"

"I've never seen a face turn so red," said Brynhild, referring to Barnabas' beet-like complexion.

Barnabas accidentally snorted as he chuckled. "And Wilfred looked as though he's swallowed a hive of bees!"

"I feel as if I've swallowed a hive of bees!" chortled Wilfred.

"You are the funniest creature. Brynhild, he is delightful!" said Freya, clapping her hands happily as the laughter subsided. "No one is ever honest with a goddess. It is very refreshing to hear someone speak plainly for a change."

"I am very glad that my comments did not offend," said Barnabas. He felt much more kindly disposed towards Freya of a sudden, and more inclined to believe in her innocence. "If you say that you know naught of the bowl, I shall take you at your word."

"Nonsense," said Freya. "You are kind to say so, but I feel that your honor would not let that sit easy with you. We shall have a proper trial!" She clapped her hands loudly. "Syn! Syn!" she looked around, as though expecting someone named Syn to magically appear. "Someone go fetch Syn immediately!"

They heard the sound of many scurrying footsteps outside

the chamber door, and servants' voices calling back and forth. "Have you seen Syn?" "Where has Syn gotten to?" And lastly, "Will someone *please* find Syn, for the love of gods!"

Freya waited patiently, her hands folded demurely upon her lap while a mischievous smile played upon her face. The pig Hildisvini let out a great hiccup, fluttered his eyelashes, then flopped about a few times before succumbing once more to sleep. Barnabas eyed the creature warily as it snorted and snored.

At last a woman burst through the door, walking briskly and with purpose. She wore what looked remarkably like the robes worn by the barristers at the Lincoln Inn in Holborn. She strode to the front of the chamber and stood there looking sternly at them all.

"This," said Freya, pointing to the woman, "is Syn. She is the defender of the accused in all of the realms. You may try your case with her, and she shall defend me."

"Oh my," said Barnabas. "I'm not entirely certain I'm quite prepared for a trial." He patted at his smelly cloak self-consciously.

Syn moved to stand beside Freya, carefully stepping over Freya's pet boar. "What charges do you bring against my client?" asked Syn peremptorily. "And hurry up about it, if you please. We don't have all day."

"Er…" said Barnabas.

"I would stop dilly dallying, if I were you," prompted Freya. "Syn is…efficient, you see. I'd hate for her to grow impatient with you."

Barnabas looked at Syn, who waggled her eyebrows impatiently at him. "Oh my," he repeated nervously.

"Your case?" demanded Syn. "Or, if you have no case, then I will close the matter once and for all."

"Which means you can never question me about it again," said Freya helpfully.

"If I could have a moment to confer with my colleagues?" asked Barnabas.

"No conferring!" said Syn. "Press your case, or end your case." She waited for half a second, then made as if to leave.

"Very well!" said Barnabas quickly. "I shall press my case." He took a deep breath (mostly to buy himself time to think; his thoughts were all jumbled up together and all of this *rushing* wasn't helping matters) but Syn was a relentless arbiter.

"Press it then!" she snapped. "At once!"

"I, well, that is, we thought, or perhaps thought is too strong of a word. Wondered, yes wondered is a better word, don't you think? Wilfred?" said Barnabas, somewhat nonsensically.

"Ah, yes," said Wilfred, no more certain of what to say than was his employer. "We wondered if perhaps, you know, the bowl?"

"We were talking to Sigyn, and she said that Freya was with her when her bowl was stolen. She also said that she had no knowledge as to *who* stole the bowl. Does she tell the truth?" said Brynhild, rolling her eyes at the two flustered detectives.

Syn bent down so that she and Freya might whisper back and forth for a few moments. At last Syn straightened and nodded to Freya, as though giving her approval to speak.

"Yes," said Freya simply. She folded her hands on her lap demurely, and affected an innocent expression on her face.

"Yes that you were with Sigyn?" asked Barnabas. "Or yes that Sigyn doesn't know who stole the bowl?"

Freya and Syn conferred. Finally they both turned back to face Barnabas.

"Yes," said Freya once more.

"Yes to both questions, then?" asked Barnabas, frowning in confusion.

"You've already asked that question," said Syn. "You are haranguing the witness."

"But I'm merely attempting to get a clear answer," pointed out Barnabas.

"Which was given," said Syn.

"I hardly think so!" protested Barnabas.

"'Yes' is what she said," said Syn.

"But to what?" said Barnabas.

"Perhaps, if I may?" interjected Wilfred, seeing his employer's annoyance mounting. Barnabas flapped his hands impotently, and motioned for Wilfred to proceed.

"I should like to ask another question," said Wilfred. "A *delicate* one, I believe."

"Ask, then," said Syn.

The boar snuffled and smacked his lips together wildly. Wilfred gave it a distracted glance, then continued on with his question.

"It has been suggested that Sigyn, and perhaps even Freya herself, may have some motivations for wishing for Loki's freedom. Namely, of course, that Loki is Sigyn's husband, and, further, that Sigyn's lover Balder shall be freed from death itself once Ragnarok is ended, which seems a desirable course of events for her. In addition, there is, of course, the matter of Freya's own father being held prisoner, and her husband being missing."

"Too much conjecture and speculation," said Syn to Freya. "Don't answer that."

"But I haven't even asked the question, exactly," argued Wilfred.

"Argumentative!" said Syn.

Barnabas, who had recovered himself somewhat, stepped in again, using a different approach. "Do you believe, Freya," he said, "that Sigyn may have colluded with anyone to effect the theft of the bowl?"

"Putting thoughts in the witness' head!" said Syn. "Freya shall most certainly *not* answer that."

"Oh!" cried Barnabas. He scrunched up his face in frustration and his hands clenched into tight little fists. His brows drew so close together and his agitation was so intense that Wilfred feared the poor man might suffer an apoplexy. "As trials go this is most absurd! How can one find out anything in this manner?"

"Freya," said Brynhild, "do you have any suspicions that Sigyn knows anything about the theft?"

Freya looked to Syn, who nodded her head. "No," said Freya.

"Did you yourself talk to anyone about taking the bowl?" continued Brynhild.

"No," said Freya.

"And can you think of anyone who might profit from the theft of the bowl?"

"Oh, yes," said Freya. "Lots of people." The boar at her feet kicked a foot spasmodically in the air before grunting and settling down to snore once more.

"Like who?" demanded Barnabas. He was thoroughly disgusted with the proceedings but was determined to have at least one of his questions answered, nonetheless. To his relief, Syn did not censure Freya this time.

"Well, besides Modi and Magni, there's Frigga."

"That's Balder's mother," supplied Brynhild.

"Hod himself might wish for Ragnarok. To undo what he did, so to speak."

"Hod is the one Loki tricked into killing Balder," said Brynhild.

"Then there's pretty much everyone in Niflheim and Helheim," mused Freya, pursing her lips and twisting them charmingly to the side as she thought.

"Where the dead go, if they don't die in battle. Very cold there," said Brynhild. "Not nice at all, really."

"I see," said Barnabas. "Perhaps I should have asked if there was anyone who *didn't* want the end of the world to happen."

"Well that's just silly," said Freya, even as Syn commented that the question was too open-ended and that Freya ought not to answer it. Barnabas threw his arms up in despair.

"If that does it, then?" said Syn. She looked at Barnabas, then Wilfred, then Brynhild. As all of them were too confused to think of anything to say, she nodded her head sharply. "The trial is over. My client is innocent of any wrongdoing. You are all excused." With that, she spun on her heels and left the room.

Barnabas shook his head in disbelief. "Is she both lawyer and judge at once?" he wondered.

"Yes," said Freya. The mischievous twinkle was back in

her eyes.

"Oh dear," sighed Barnabas defeatedly.

Freya softened and smiled kindly at Barnabas. "I really didn't have anything to do with the theft of the bowl, you know," she said. "Nor did Sigyn. Neither of us is eager for Loki to be free, no matter what motivations you think we might have."

Barnabas nodded. Freya's sincerity was evident. But that left them only with what information they could glean from the ridiculous trial (either too many suspects, or too few, depending on how one looked at it). "Thank you, my lady," he said. "You've been most helpful." He rose to take his leave. Wilfred and Brynhild followed suit.

"No, I have not been helpful at all," said Freya. "But that is only because I really don't know any more than you do."

"We have solved more obtuse cases than this," said Barnabas gamely. Wilfred nodded encouragingly. "I'm sure we shall discover something, in due time.

"Very well,' said Freya. "And good luck to you." She paused. "Might I suggest looking into Vidar first?" she said.

"Vidar?" asked Barnabas.

"Odin's son with Gird," said Freya. "I don't have any real reason to suspect him, other that he hates Loki."

"Meaning that he would be glad to see him suffer," said Barnabas.

"Yes," said Freya. "And, Vidar is destined to avenge Odin's death after Ragnarok."

"Wouldn't he wish to avoid the death of his own father?" asked Barnabas.

"I would think he'd be more eager for the glory of vengeance," said Freya. "And," she shrugged, "it's destined, so he might as well get on with it."

Barnabas sighed. He was beginning to find all this talk of destiny terribly tiresome. Still, he was thankful for the lead, and said so.

The three companions made their way to the door when a fresh bout of frenzied snuffling caused Barnabas to turn around. "Why is that pig twitching so?" he asked curiously.

Freya waved a hand dismissively. "Oh, it's just the Dark Elves from Svortalheim," she said, as though that explained everything.

"Dark Elves?" asked Barnabas. "Svortalheim?"

"The Dark Elves give nightmares," laughed Brynhild, ushering Barnabas and Wilfred through the door. "And they live in Svortalheim."

"We shan't have to go to Svortalheim, I should hope," said Barnabas, his eyes wide.

"Of course we will," said Brynhild. "It's one of the nine worlds, isn't it?" She walked on ahead of them, calling for a groom to bring Hynder. Barnabas and Wilfred followed behind, a bit reluctantly.

"Oh dear," said Barnabas. "Dark Elves. Nightmares." He shuddered.

"Oh dear, indeed," agreed Wilfred, shuddering as well.

Chapter Seven

"Do you know where we can find this Vidar fellow?" Barnabas asked Brynhild once they had left Freya's palace. A groom had brought Hynder to them, and they were all safely mounted (although safe was perhaps a strong word to apply to being seated three deep on a flying horse).

"Of course I do," replied Brynhild.

Barnabas waited a moment for her to expound on this statement to no avail. Brynhild, it seemed, felt that she had answered the question. Barnabas sighed resignedly. Even he had to admit that she had, in fact, answered precisely the question he had asked. No more, and no less. These Vikings, he thought, had no mind for hints and subtlety.

He blinked slowly to muster his patience, then tried again.

"*Where*, exactly, shall we find Vidar?" he asked.

"In Jutunheim," said Brynhild.

Wilfred, who was adept at reading his employer's moods, felt Barnabas' nerves begin to fray and stepped in smoothly.

"What, pray, can you tell us about Jutunheim? Will there be a palace like Freya's, or perhaps a great hall like Odin's?" he asked. Barnabas shot him a look of thanks.

"Not exactly,' said Brynhild. "Vidar has a home, yes, but it is not nearly as grand as a palace or a hall. Although it is rather big, which it would have to be, of course."

"Why would it have to be big?" asked Barnabas.

"How else would a giant live in it?" said Brynhild.

"A giant?" sputtered Barnabas. "A *giant* lives in it?"

"Of course he does!" said Brynhild. "I *told* you we were going to Jutunheim, didn't I? Where the Jutuns live."

"Presumably the Jutuns are giants," said Wilfred helpfully.

Barnabas tightened his lips and glared at Wilfred. "And I

suppose," he said wryly, "that Vidar must then, be a Jutun."

Brynhild nodded, and Barnabas closed his eyes as he breathed in deeply. "Lovely," he mumbled under his breath. "Splendid."

"Not really very splendid," said Brynhild, frowning. "It's actually pretty barren there. And very cold, since giants don't much like the heat." She pointed downwards as the grey stallion swooped sickeningly down from the sky. "See all that frost? And how all that grows are stunted brushwood and brown grasses?"

As she spoke Hynder alighted on a field of said grasses. They all climbed down (the process, though by no means easy, was at least getting easier with practice, so that they managed to alight with no villagers or grooms to assist them).

Brynhild removed Hynder's reins so that the stallion might graze more easily. Briskly, the skald began making ready a camp. "It is getting dark," she said. "We should rest, and talk to Vidar in the morning." She bent down and scooped up a handful of fallen brushwood.

"Is he nearby then? Or any other giants, for that matter?" asked Barnabas, looking about nervously for any signs of a giant walking about.

Brynhild handed the brushwood to Wilfred. "Pile it up," she said. "For a fire." Wilfred nodded and obliged. Then she turned to Barnabas. "There're plenty of giants," she said, "but if there was one in this field you'd know it."

"Comforting," said Barnabas sarcastically. He sat down heavily on the grass and waited for Brynhild and Wilfred to finish making the fire.

"You mentioned that giants don't like heat. What else don't they like?" asked Wilfred.

Barnabas barked a sarcastic laugh. "Detectives, probably," he remarked.

"I can't speak for *all* giants, of course," said Brynhild, "since they are all individuals and what they like or don't like is their own business. But Vidar doesn't like Loki at all. Besides, he is very loyal to his father…"

"Who is Odin," said Wilfred. "But Freya said that he might be the thief of the bowl, meaning that she thinks that he is not so loyal to Odin after all."

"I don't follow," said Brynhild.

"If Vidar stole the bowl in order to start Ragnarok, which Odin has hired us to prevent, then that puts Vidar and Odin at odds."

Brynhild's eyebrows knit together in consternation. "How so?" she asked.

"Because then one wants one thing whilst the other wants another," said Barnabas.

"So, if I want duck for dinner and you want boar, then does that make us enemies?" said Brynhild.

"That is preposterous," retorted Barnabas. "Of course not."

"So why, then, would Odin and Vidar be enemies if one tries to stop Ragnarok and the other does something to begin it?"

"Because," said Barnabas, "dinner choices and the end of the world are not comparable."

"But…"

"Odin will die in Ragnarok!" cried Barnabas. "So if Vidar were to try to start Ragnarok, then it follows that he is, essentially, effecting the murder of Odin. The logic is quite simple, really." He folded his arms obstinately.

"I don't know about logic," shrugged Brynhild, "but if it's destiny that made Vidar steal the bowl…"

"*If* he stole the bowl," interjected Wilfred.

"Yes," continued Brynhild, "*if* he stole the bowl it was preordained, so who can argue with that?"

"Bah!" exclaimed Barnabas, throwing up his hands in frustration. "A pox on preordination!"

Brynhild looked shocked. She made a strange hand gesture over her eyes and hissed. Barnabas quickly took a step back, alarmed. Wilfred, perceiving rapid deterioration of the conversation, deftly interceded to right the course.

"We seem to have gotten a bit off point," he said diplomatically. "Perhaps we should plan what we wish to ask

Vidar? We can't very well just go ask a giant straightaway if he stole something."

"A good point," acceded Barnabas. "One wouldn't wish to offend a giant, I suppose."

Brynhild lifted her brow sardonically. "Oh, so you can offend two goddesses by asking them straight out if they stole the bowl, but don't want to offend the giant?"

"I offend everyone in equal measure, thank you very much," retorted Barnabas. Brynhild stifled a laugh and raised her hands in a gesture for peace.

"All right, all right," she said. "So how do you suggest we find out if he took the bowl?"

"Well," said Wilfred, "we could tell him about the theft, and see how he reacts. That way, we can judge his feelings on the matter. See whether he is for or against it."

"We must try to outthink him," said Barnabas. "As we must all of our suspects. So, we ought to list our suspects, and the case for and against each of them."

"Wonderful idea!" said Wilfred.

"Let's begin with Sigyn," suggested Barnabas.

"Her motivation to begin Ragnarok would be to free Balder from Helheim," said Wilfred. "Or, perhaps it might go no further than merely wishing to cause Loki pain in allowing the snake's poison to drip, uncaught, onto his head."

"But she has an alibi in Freya, who is not known as a liar," said Brynhild. "And her motivation for keeping the bowl safe would be to keep Loki imprisoned, as revenge for causing Balder's death."

"Hold on," said Barnabas. "A motivation *for* stealing the bowl is to cause Loki pain. And yet a motivation for *not* stealing the bowl is to cause Loki pain."

"Yes," said Brynhild.

"Uh," said Barnabas. "Ought we not figure out which is the proper way to get revenge on Loki? Stealing the bowl or *not* stealing the bowl?"

"Either is a way of taking vengeance on Loki," said Brynhild.

"But that makes no sense!" protested Barnabas. "All of

our suspects will either wish to get vengeance on Loki, or else they might wish to save him. How are we to know who wants what if they both amount to the same thing?"

"Not all of the suspects," pointed out Brynhild. "It could simply be someone who profits from the end of the world, but has no feelings on Loki one way or the other."

"Which is how many people?" asked Barnabas.

"Let's see," said Brynhild, holding up her fingers so as to count off the list of suspects. "Thor's sons, who will inherit his hammer. Honir, one of the Vanir's Aesir hostages, although he is the god of indecisiveness so it's hard to imagine him plotting anything. Aegir, the sea god, who could conceivably become more important with the Aesir out of the way. Most of the goddesses are destined to survive, and gods know the goddesses hold more than a few grudges against all the various gods. Oh, and anyone who loves Balder and wishes to see him restored, which is pretty much everyone." She fluttered her fingers to indicate the uncountable-ness of the people who love Balder.

"But this is an unsolvable morass," groaned Barnabas miserably. "Isn't there a nice maid that we could suspect?" (One of Barnabas' few successful cases, conducted whilst he and Wilfred were still in the land of the living, of course, had ended with the indictment of the victim's maid. Since then he had developed the habit of viewing all serving folk with suspicion.)

"I don't think they have maids here," offered Wilfred, trying to steer his employer from this well-trod pathway to nowhere.

"Butlers, then?" asked Barnabas hopefully. Wilfred shook his head firmly. "No butlers, either."

"I don't know what you two are going on about," said Brynhild, "but I have a suggestion." She reached into her saddle bags and pulled out a small woven pouch. She opened the pouch, took its contents into her hand, and threw them onto the ground in front of her. She leaned over and studied them intently.

"Er," said Wilfred, peering at the small white shapes that

so interested Brynhild. "Are those *bones*?"

Indeed, the things looked like a collection of finger bones, on which markings had been made. "Of course," said Brynhild distractedly. "They're runes, what else would they be made of?"

Barnabas and Wilfred curled their lips in disgust. "That is horrid…" began Barnabas, but he was cut off by a peremptory wave of Brynhild's hand. "Shhh!" she hissed. "I'm trying to read."

Barnabas and Wilfred shared a glance, but obediently remained quiet whilst Brynhild stared at the little fingers in front of her. At last she began to speak, pointing at first to one bone, then another.

"There is pertho, the rune for mystery," she said. "It lies on top, so it is the most important one of all. It means that there is a great mystery to solve."

"I could have told you that without resorting to throwing fingers about," grumbled Barnabas. Brynhild ignored him and continued.

"This one is called rhaido," she said. "It means travel, but in combination with pertho it probably means that the travel we do is in search of our answer."

"Again, no need for finger throwing," mumbled Barnabas.

"Here we have nauthiz," said Brynhild. "The nauthiz rune says there will be delays, obstacles, difficulties. It also means that you must cultivate patience, and come to accept your fate."

Barnabas rolled his eyes, but Wilfred laid a calming hand on his arm to keep him from sharing his ideas about the concept of fate.

"Here we have eihwaz," said Brynhild. "It means that you are trustworthy and hardworking, and that you have a strong sense of purpose."

"Really?" said Barnabas, suddenly interested. "It says all of that?"

"And here's jera," continued Brynhild. "You shall harvest the fruits of your labor. A very promising sign."

"Well that is good news!" said Barnabas. He was smiling

approvingly now, warming up to the idea of the runes. "I never doubted our success, not once. Well, not really."

"This one, ah, this one," said Brynhild, pointing to one that lay a bit off to the side of the others. "This is the mannaz rune. It means intelligence, skill, and cooperation."

"Well, that sounds promising," said Barnabas happily.

"Except that it's in opposition," said Brynhild. "Meaning that we will be up against a clever foe, one who is cunning and tricky. Oh, and that there will be no help forthcoming."

"Oh," said Barnabas, disappointed. "Well. That's not so promising."

"Um, excuse me," said Wilfred, "but..."

"No need to look so glum," said Brynhild, ignoring Wilfred. "The runes only tell of what is fated to be."

"Well, I come from the age of reason," retorted Barnabas, "and therefore have no use for such an archaic thing as fate."

"I hate to interrupt," said Wilfred, "but it seems that..."

"But what will be, will be," said Brynhild. "There's nothing you can do about it so there's no use getting upset."

"Seriously, I really think you need to hear this," tried Wilfred.

"That is no comfort whatsoever," said Barnabas petulantly. In truth, he was heartily sick of all this talk of predestination and fate and so on.

Just then an enormous face leaned in over Barnabas' shoulder, so that its chin was hooked over Barnabas' collar bone. The face looked down at the runes and said, "Tough luck, there. That's too bad." A huge hand, presumably belonging to the same creature possessed of the enormous face, patted roughly Barnabas on the back.

"Ahhh!" screamed Barnabas shrilly.

"Ahhh!" squealed the enormous face, turning startled eyes to Barnabas' own terrified ones.

"Ahhh!" repeated Barnabas. He was unable to move, what with having a huge chin hooked in over his collar and a huge hand settled on his back, so he settled on the next best thing: a prolonged bout of screaming.

The owner of the enormous face simply stayed where he

was, yelling 'ahhh!' back at the little detective, so that they were nose to nose, locked in a dreadful, ear-splitting duet.

Brynhild, sitting across from Barnabas and the enormous face, laughed so hard at the spectacle that she snorted and nearly choked. Wilfred, meanwhile, stood off to the side, looking a bit exasperated. "I tried to tell you," said Wilfred. "There are giants here." Indeed, a second giant stood quietly next to Wilfred, calmly regarding the hysterical goings-on. This giant was so tall that Wilfred scarcely came up to his knees.

Barnabas, hearing Brynhild's laughter and the slightly annoyed calm of Wilfred's voice, stopped screaming. The enormous face followed suit. Without moving, Barnabas whispered loudly out of the side of his mouth. "*What*," he said, "is *this*?"

"As I've been trying to say for the last ten minutes, this is…" began Wilfred.

"Who," corrected the giant standing besides Wilfred.

"Who what?" whispered Barnabas.

"Eh?" asked the giant, confused. The enormous face merely blinked slowly at Barnabas, who blinked slowly back.

"He means that you should have said, 'who is this', not 'what is this'," said Wilfred.

"Who or what, I don't care," said Barnabas. "The question is, is it going to eat me?"

"Is *he* going to eat you," corrected the giant.

"That's what I'm asking you!" snipped Barnabas.

"I think perhaps you should stop calling that giant an 'it'," suggested Wilfred. "It might be taken as offensive."

"Oh dear," said Barnabas, "I'm terribly sorry. No insult intended, of course." Being properly British (and more than a little uptight, besides), his fear of being rude far outweighed his fear of being devoured by an enormous face.

The giant nodded his acceptance of Barnabas' apology. Barnabas looked from the giant to the enormous face, moving only his eyes. "So," he said nervously, "do we think *he* is going to eat me, or no?"

Brynhild, having got hold of herself, waved a dismissive

hand. "He would have already eaten you, if he was going to, don't you think?"

"Well, perhaps," said Barnabas, "but it always helps to make absolutely certain of these things."

"Right," said Brynhild. She took Barnabas hand and pulled him closer to her, so that he could see the owner of the enormous face, who in turn rose and went to stand beside his companion. "This," said Brynhild, gesturing to the giant who stood next to Wilfred, "is Vali. And this," she continued, pointing to the owner of the enormous face, "is his brother, Vidar."

Now that he looked at the two together. Barnabas could see that *both* were giants. Vidar's face had only seemed so large because it was so close to his own (although it was, to be sure, still an extraordinarily large head; still, that was only to be expected of a giant, Barnabas supposed).

"Well then!" said Barnabas. "Very nice to meet you!" He turned to Wilfred. "Why didn't you tell me there were *giants* here?" he asked accusingly.

Wilfred huffed and flung his hands in the air, but said nothing.

"I, for one, am glad to see the two of you," said Brynhild to Vidar and Vali. "We've come here to find you, and since you've found *us* instead we are spared the necessity of looking for *you*."

"Why are you looking for us?" asked Vali. He looked warily at all three humans. "You weren't sent by those infernal gods in Asgard, I hope?"

"I'll let Barnabas here tell you all about it," said Brynhild. "He's a detective you know." Vidar and Vali nodded, although from the looks and shrugs they gave each other it was clear they had no idea what a detective was.

Brynhild patted the ground beside her. "Come," she invited. "Sit with us. Share our fire."

Vidar and Vali moved closer to the fire, then lowered themselves to sit on the ground in cross-legged positions. They did so with a surprising degree of nimbleness, considering their size, a fact which did nothing to assuage

Barnabas' concerns about sitting in so close a proximity to two giants, one of whom was a suspect.

Once seated, both giants turned to stare expectantly at Barnabas. Flustered, he attempted to begin his interrogation.

"Yes, well, you see, we are here because...er, Freya said something, ah, well. Ahem. How do you do?" he concluded lamely.

Vidar looked quizzically at Barnabas. It was Vali who spoke.

"We've already gone through the greetings," he said. "Is this what a detective is? Some kind of interminable greeter, or something?"

"He'll get himself going in a minute," replied Brynhild. "Sometimes it takes him a bit to get started. Kind of a nervous sort, I think."

"I am not!" protested Barnabas nervously.

"He *should* be nervous," said Vali. "I saw those runes. I'm not a rune reader, but..." He whistled through his teeth and shuddered.

"What?" cried Barnabas. "What was wrong with the runes? Why should I be nervous?" he looked back and forth from Brynhild to Vali and back again so quickly that he looked quite a bit like a quizzical bird. Brynhild stifled a laugh.

"Nothing to fear," she said soothingly. (She had been watching how Wilfred handled Barnabas' nerves, and therefore was quickly learning how to do so herself.) "Everything's going to turn out great."

Barnabas heaved a sigh of relief, but then Vali spoke again. "Sure, it'll be great, if by great you mean torment, death, and destruction," he said blithely.

"What!" cried Barnabas. He looked to Brynhild. "You said the runes were good!"

"Well, I didn't exactly say *that*," said Brynhild. "But they're not as bad as Vali makes them sound, either."

"There's mannaz in opposition," pointed out Vali. "I'm not a professional rune reader, but even I know that's not good. I wouldn't want to come up against *that* foe, myself."

"But they also said I'm practical and resourceful and trustworthy," said Barnabas. "More than a match for any foe, no matter how cunning."

"And over there, isn't that the rune for obstacles? And there, the one for secrets?"

"Well, yes," admitted Brynhild.

"But you're just pointing out all the bad ones," complained Barnabas, "and ignoring all the good ones. Like the one about the fruits of my labors, and what-not."

"The fruits of your labors might be torment, death, and destruction," observed Vali.

"And there's also the one about travel," said Barnabas, drawing himself up primly. "A fellow cannot possibly travel if that fellow has suffered torment, death, or destruction, is what I always say."

Vali knit his eyebrows together, trying to make sense of that statement. "*Does* he always say that?" he asked.

"Yes," answered Wilfred and Brynhild at the same time.

"Huh," said Vali, scratching his chin, obviously trying (and failing) to figure out *if* a person really could travel after undergoing torment, death, and destruction, and *why* Barnabas would possibly say that all the time, besides.

"Anyway," said Brynhild, drawing out the word, "shall we get on with the questioning, then? I do believe our detective has shaken off his nerves now." She smiled encouragingly at Barnabas, who was looking off into the distance attempting to appear dignified. Indeed, he was trying very hard not to lose his temper entirely and say 'good day!' to Vali, an effort that made him purse his lips in a most severe fashion.

Seeing his employer struggling to compose himself, Wilfred stepped in to speak. "We are here," he began, "because Freya suggested that you might be of some assistance to us in our investigation."

"Oh?" asked Vali. "And what is this investigation about?"

"We are looking into the disappearance of the bowl that Sigyn uses to…"

"Yes, yes, to catch the poison before it drips on Loki," interrupted Vali, waving his hand impatiently. "What do I care what happens to Loki or his stupid bowl?"

Wilfred caught Barnabas' warning glare (actually, everyone present saw it, as it was far from subtle; indeed, with his waggling eyebrows, jerky tips of the head in Vali's direction, and wildly exaggerated facial expressions mimicking a madman one could hardly have missed it) and nodded his understanding: this giant seemed to have a short fuse and had best be handled delicately.

"Well," said Wilfred carefully, "it's not actually you Freya suggested we question, but Vidar. If I might just ask him a few questions?"

"You can ask me your questions," said Vali. "But make it quick."

"Of course we will be grateful for any answers you may give. But we should also greatly appreciate hearing what Vidar has to say."

Vali shrugged. "Go ahead, then. Ask." Something about the smug smirk on Vali's face made Wilfred nervous, but, seeing nothing for it, he proceeded nonetheless.

"Very well, then," he said, "and thank you." Then he turned to Vidar. "Freya mentioned that you, ah, well, that you had no liking for Loki. Further, she intimated that you may have cause to wish to see him, ah, come to harm."

Vidar remained silent. Wilfred glanced nervously at Barnabas, who nodded encouragingly, then tried again. "Please don't think that we are making any accusations, sir," he said. "Merely trying to ascertain the truth of the matter, if you will."

Vidar's silence continued. "*Do* you," tried Wilfred once more, "know anything whatsoever as to the whereabouts of the bowl? Or perhaps have any idea as to who else may have cause to remove it from Sigyn's possession?"

Still Vidar said nothing. He merely sat there, looking at everyone and blinking.

Barnabas leaned in closer to Vidar. He squinted his eyes and regarded the quiet giant thoughtfully. "Does he speak?" he asked at last. "I think that perhaps he might not speak."

"He screamed quite heartily just then," pointed out

Wilfred. "One would think he could speak, based on that fact alone."

"Vidar *can* speak, but he chooses not to most of the time," said Vali. "I *told* you to ask me the questions, didn't I?"

"Oh," said Wilfred.

"Hmmph," sniffed Barnabas. He walked off a few paces to sit by himself, making a show of rummaging through their packs. He picked out a large hunk of bread, then sat in the tall grass with his back to the others and began to eat.

"Looks like you've annoyed Barnabas, Vali," observed Brynhild.

"Oh no," said Vali sarcastically. "How terrible."

"Ahem," said Wilfred. "If I may try again?"

"Go on then," said Vali.

"Do you have any information pertaining to the questions that I asked Vidar?" said Wilfred. "Any reason that you can think of as to why, or why not, Vidar may have, or may have not, taken the bowl himself?"

"Speak plainly, little person!" snapped Vali.

Wilfred took a deep breath. "Very well," he said. "Did Vidar take the bowl?"

"No," said Vali. "He didn't. I know because he's my brother, and I know everything he does. And if he would have taken the bowl, I would have helped him. Probably."

"Oh, my," said Wilfred. "Barnabas? Did you hear that?" He looked about for his employer, who had been suspiciously quiet for quite a long time.

To Wilfred's surprise, Barnabas was still sitting in the tall grass a few yards away. But he was not alone. Instead, he was constructing makeshift bread and cheese sandwiches from the supplies in the pack and merrily sharing them with the three giants who sat beside him (who were happily devouring the sandwiches as fast as Barnabas could make them). The four of them whispered and giggled with their mouths full so that they looked like schoolgirls having a picnic.

"Barnabas!" gasped Wilfred. "Why didn't you tell us there were more giants here?" Barnabas startled guiltily and audibly swallowed a great bite of cheese sandwich.

"Actually," corrected Vali, "*those* are trolls. Vidar and myself are giants, although we much prefer the term *Jotun*."

"Barnabas?" demanded Wilfred. "I'm trying to interrogate our witness, and you sit over there having a snack with trolls? And don't think to say anything to anyone about it?"

"Well," said Barnabas primly, "now you know how it feels when someone doesn't alert you to things, don't you?" Wilfred threw his hands up in frustration.

"Might I trouble you for some assistance, please?" Wilfred said with exaggerated patience.

"But of course," replied Barnabas with a beleaguered sigh. He turned to his new troll friends. "Please excuse me for a moment," he said. "And please help yourself to more sandwiches. The trolls eagerly complied as Barnabas came over to stand beside Wilfred. "Well? What do you need me for?"

"Vali said that whilst neither he nor Vidar stole Loki's bowl, still he would have had Vidar asked him to," said Wilfred.

"Oh?? said Barnabas, turning to Vali. "Why did you say that?"

"Because Loki is a foul little twit," replied Vali. "I'd do just about anything to make him suffer."

"Why? What grudge do you hold against him?"

"He's caused the death of far too many Jotun," replied Vali. "And there was the time he humiliated Vidar. That was the last time I heard Vidar speak. Loki embarrassed my poor brother into silence! Not that he was ever much of a talker, mind you, but…"

"Yes, yes, I understand," interrupted Barnabas. "How, precisely, did Loki do this?"

"He flyted him," said Vali miserably.

"Oh," said Barnabas. He frowned, thinking. "Um, well, er, that is…what, pray, does being *flyted* entail?"

"It's when you insult someone using poems, of course," said Vali. "Everyone knows that."

"Ah, yes," replied Barnabas dryly, glancing sidewise towards Wilfred. "Of course. How could I forget. Insulting with poems is the worst type of insult."

"Right! The very worst! And for that, Loki deserves eternal torment," said Vali.

"For being a flyter most foul," observed Barnabas, trying (and failing) to hide a smile. Wilfred shot him a warning glance. Luckily, Vali was too immersed in his story to notice Barnabas' humor at his expense.

"*Most* foul," the giant agreed. "But still, as I said, Vidar didn't take the bowl and neither did I."

"You do seem to have cause, though," pointed out Barnabas. "And a very great capacity for vengeance, too, it seems."

"Yes, but I don't particularly want Ragnarok to happen," said Vali. "Vidar will make it through, but I won't. And I really hate all these earthquakes."

"Earthquakes?" said Barnabas. "Are you having earthquakes, then?"

"Oh yes," said Vali. "At least twice a day now. And they're getting worse with every day that goes by."

"If the earthquakes have begun," said Barnabas to Wilfred and Brynhild, "then our success in solving the case has become much more imperative."

"And it needs to happen faster," reiterated Brynhild needlessly. Barnabas pursed his lips again but said nothing.

"I don't like it when the earth shakes. Makes me queasy," said Vali.

"Right," said Barnabas. "We'd like to help you stop these earthquakes, but we shall require your help."

"I'd do anything to make the earth stay still," said Vali.

"Can you give us any idea of who the villain might be? We are sorely short on leads, thus far," said Barnabas.

"If I knew who took the bowl I'd merely squash them myself and take it back, wouldn't I?" pointed out Vali. Barnabas raised his eyebrows in alarm.

"Yes, I suppose you would, at that. And rightly so!" he added diplomatically. "Still, since the scoundrel, or scoundrels, remain un-squashed, then I suppose we must try to find another suspect." He sighed sadly at the enormity of his task.

"I'm not a detective," said Vali, "but it seems to me that if you can't find out who took the *old* bowl, you might want to make a *new* bowl."

Barnabas whirled to look at Brynhild. "Is that possible?" he asked.

"Well, yes, I guess so," she said.

Barnabas slapped himself on the forehead. "Why, oh why, didn't you mention this before?" he demanded dramatically.

"Because nobody asked me," replied Brynhild reasonably.

"Indeed, I am beset by unimaginable frustrations," he moaned. "Perhaps that is the insurmountable obstacles the runes foretold?" He rolled his eyes to the heavens, as though looking for divine aid.

"I don't know about all that," said Brynhild. "But I'd say the obstacle might be in getting the bowl made."

"Why?" said Barnabas. "We'll just find a silversmith, pay him, and there you have it!"

"You can't use just *any* bowl," said Vali. "It has to be made by the dwarves. And they are not always eager to help mortals."

"Of course not," said Barnabas. "And where, pray, shall we find these unhelpful dwarves?"

"In Nidavellir," answered Brynhild.

"Which is one of the nine worlds, I suppose?" asked Barnabas.

"Yes," answered Brynhild. "But it will be exciting! It's your first time in one of the worlds below the Earth."

"Nidavellir is an underworld?" said Barnabas. Brynhild nodded.

"Lovely," said Barnabas flatly.

"Lovely, indeed," agreed Wilfred.

Chapter Eight

After farewelling Vidar and Vali (and Barnabas' new troll friends, whom they left with a supply of their new favorite snack of cheese sandwiches, and who hugged Barnabas with effusive warmth, to Barnabas' great embarrassment and Wilfred and Brynhild's great amusement) the three travelers mounted Hynder and departed Jutunheim.

"What have you to say on the subject of Nidavellir and the dwarves?" asked Barnabas. His eyes were squinched tightly shut, as he had discovered that if he did so he could almost believe that he was sitting in his rocking chair in his sitting room in Marylebone rather than mounted aboard a flying horse in the midst of the Viking afterlife (insofar, of course, as he could ignore the fact that one did not sit astride a rocking chair as one did a flying horse. Also, of course, was the matter of the cold wind in his face, which he could ascribe to an open window, perhaps, though he would never in a million years have opened a window in such miserable weather; or the tremendous smell of horse emitted by Hynder; or the fact that Wilfred and Brynhild were sitting so terribly close to him, in a way that would most certainly not have occurred on a rocking chair in a sitting room in a proper English abode. Still, the pretense was all that kept Barnabas from succumbing to the absolute terror of being precariously perched atop a magical horse a thousand feet or more above ground, jumping from one world to the next, and so he clung to his purposeful delusion as tightly as he did to Wilfred's waist).

"Well," said Brynhild, "Nidavellir is underground, and is ruled by the dwarves."

"Yes, yes, yes," said Barnabas. He started to wave his

hand impatiently but immediately thought better of it. "We know *that*. What else?"

"There is a great hall of gold and gems, where the king Hredimar used to sit with his sons," said Brynhild.

"Gold and gems sound pleasant enough," said Barnabas.

"*Used* to sit?" said Wilfred.

"The king is dead," said Brynhild. "Killed by his sons."

"Oh dear," said Barnabas. "I *do* hope they have all been properly punished? Safely imprisoned?"

"They're all dead," replied Brynhild. Barnabas began to heave a sigh of relief, but Brynhild was not finished. "Except for one, Fafnir. He turned into a dragon and slew his brothers. Now it is he who sits in the hall of gold and gems."

"You don't mean…" began Barnabas.

"Fafnir is the one we must needs speak to, isn't he?" said Wilfred.

"Of course," said Brynhild matter-of-factly. "He's king now, isn't he?"

"I assume he's no longer, ah, entirely draconian, then?" asked Barnabas hopefully.

"Oh no, he's still a dragon," said Bryhild, as though this were not in the least bit alarming.

"You cannot mean that we are to beg a favor from a patricidal, fratricidal dragon?" exclaimed Barnabas. His eyes flew open, but a wave of vertigo overtook him as he beheld the view of the clouds scudding by below so he promptly closed them again.

"He's a reasonable enough fellow," said Brynhild, "so long as you don't annoy him."

"And how, pray tell," said Barnabas, "shall we avoid annoying a *homicidal* dragon?"

"Well," replied Brynhild, thinking. "Don't mention his father, of course. Or his brothers."

"Of course," replied Barnabas. "*That* would obviously be unwise."

"Although it will be hard not to, since he killed his father and brothers in order to get a ring that Odin gave to Hredimar in recompense for Loki killing Otr, who was one of Fafnir's

96

brothers."

"That is absurdly confusing," complained Barnabas.

"So Fafnir wanted this ring," said Wilfred, frowning with concentration as he tried to puzzle it out. "Why?"

"Because it makes gold and gems, and if there's anything a dwarf likes more than gold, it's gems," said Brynhild.

"And Odin gave the ring to the king because Loki killed one of his sons? Who was, therefore, one of Fafnir's brothers?"

"Exactly," said Brynhild. "The dwarves were furious at Loki for Otr's death. The ring was the only way to appease them."

"So Fafnir considers Loki an enemy?" queried Wilfred. "Because he killed Otr?"

"All of the dwarves are firmly set against Loki," said Brynhild.

"Let me get this straight," said Barnabas. "Fafnir hates Loki for killing his brother, and yet Fafnir killed the rest of his brothers himself."

"Yes," replied Brynhild. "That is so."

"And presumably, if Otr hadn't been killed by Loki, then Fafnir probably would have killed him himself."

"Probably," said Brynhild.

"So Fafnir is angry with Loki for doing something that Fafnir would have done anyway?" said Barnabas. "Doesn't that seem a bit, well, *convoluted*?"

"Excepting," interjected Wilfred, "that if Loki hadn't killed Otr, then there would be no ring, and therefore no reason for Fafnir to kill *any* of them."

"Again, I say," said Barnabas, "the politics of this place are impossibly impenetrable."

"It's simple," said Brynhild. "Don't mention Hreidmar, any of Fafnir's dead brothers, the ring, or Loki. That's all."

"Then there is no way to proceed!" exclaimed Barnabas.

"Why not?" asked Brynhild. "Just don't talk about anyone in Fafnir's family. Or Loki. Oh, and probably best not to mention Odin, either, since they're not on the best of terms."

"But Odin gave Hreidmar the ring that drove Fafnir to

murder, did he not?" pointed out Barnabas.

"Yes, but the ring was cursed, you see, so that whosoever should bear it is doomed to be killed during Ragnarok by the hero Sigurd."

"Then Fafnir should cast off the ring!" cried Barnabas. "If he doesn't want to be cursed, that is."

"But then he won't have all the gold, would he?" said Brynhild.

"Argh," moaned Barnabas, pressing his forehead between Wilfred's shoulder blades.

"The crux of the problem lies, I think," said Wilfred diplomatically, "in that we are here to ask Fafnir for a bowl."

"What's the problem?" said Brynhild. "I didn't say don't mention a *bowl*, did I?"

"No, but the bowl is for Loki. How are we to ask for the bowl if we are not to mention Loki?"

"Hmmm," said Brynhild, thinking.

"Wouldn't Fafnir be eager to stave off Ragnarok?" asked Barnabas. "Since he's going to die during it, one would think he'd be quite averse to the idea."

"Ah!" said Wilfred. "That's it! We present the idea of the bowl as a way to forestall Ragnarok, and therefore make Fafnir sympathetic to our cause."

"And we emphasize how, even though it may seem to be helping Loki to catch the poison from the snake, it is instead prolonging his suffering by preventing his thrashings from effecting his escape!" added Barnabas excitedly. "Fafnir is sure to be amenable to *that* idea, as he sounds like a bit of a *violent* fellow."

"A most violent fellow indeed," agreed Wilfred. "He should be most pleased to be integral in the continuation of Loki's punishment."

"And he will never suspect that we are using his very desire for vengeance against him," concluded Barnabas.

"Or," put in Brynhild, "we could simply ask him for the bowl, and pay him whatever he wants for it."

"Oh," said Barnabas and Wilfred in unison, their pride in their cleverness quickly deflating. Barnabas, disappointed, slumped as far as he might without falling off.

"Not that your plan wasn't very good," she added, feeling sorry for their dejection. "I just thought to save time…"

"No, no," sighed Barnabas. "You are quite right. Who needs a beautifully intricate plan when a blunt simple one will suffice." He sighed exaggeratedly.

"If you want to try your idea you can," said Brynhild, sorry that she had caused offense.

"Never mind," said Barnabas. "We'll do as you suggest." He turned his head and muttered under his breath, "As usual."

"Barnabas!" whispered Wilfred over his shoulder. "Please!"

"I can't help it if *someone* is a bit of a gobermouch," mumbled Barnabas primly.

"What?" said Brynhild, unable to hear Barnabas over the roar of the wind.

"Nothing!" said Wilfred hurriedly. "Just asking if we're nearly there, is all."

At that moment Hynder gave a sudden lurch, and they heard his hooves clatter on the cobblestones of a paved street. "We're here," announced Brynhild unnecessarily. She jumped down from Hynder's back, and held out a hand to help down first Wilfred and then Barnabas, who had carefully peeped open his eyes, one at a time.

Once he was certain that they were indeed safe on solid ground, he blinked both eyes fully open and looked around in great wonderment. "Ooh!" he exclaimed, as he dismounted most ungracefully despite Brynhild's assistance. He landed awkwardly on the cobbled street, and would have fallen flat on his face had he not face-planted into Hynder's flank instead.

"Mmmph," sputtered Barnabas, spitting horse hair from between his lips. Hynder nickered, and Barnabas patted him absentmindedly as he turned this way and that, getting a good look at the village in which they found themselves.

They had landed in the midst of what appeared to be the central square of a small dwarven town. The buildings that skirted the square were made all of the same dark color of stone, and, while not entirely the same were still similar enough in design so as to present an effect of careful planning and unity. Dark green shutters flanked each window, and planters bearing flowers of dark purple and deep red underlined each windowsill.

Four streets led outward from the square, centered precisely at the four cardinal points, their angles and positioning as accurate as if they had been surveyed with the most sophisticated of modern tools.

Scores of short, stocky dwarves, dressed sensibly in neat frocks and carefully tailored suits, bustled about their business in a way that appeared to Barnabas to be gratifyingly *busy*.

"Why, this is delightful!" he cried, all annoyance at Brynhild quite forgotten amidst the quaintness of the scene. "Are these little fellows…are these dwarves?" Brynhild nodded. "But they are nothing to be afraid of! Look at how, well, *small* they are! And so very orderly, as well." (Being a bit on the short side himself, Barnabas was very much relieved to find himself in the midst of an even smaller race of peoples, rather than the bulky Vikings, not to mention the extreme size of the giants and trolls, with whom he and Wilfred had been surrounded ever since Vinder had delivered them to Odin's hall.)

"Don't underestimate them," warned Brynhild. "Dwarves can be very dangerous. Especially Fafnir. He's a dragon, remember?"

"Bah! He's probably just a *little* dragon," said Barnabas. "Besides, how bad can he be, coming from such a wondrous place like this? And look at that, will you? Splendid! Just splendid." He pointed to the middle of the square, where a great golden statue stood. Cobblestones of uniform color, of a slightly darker color than those that comprised the cottages, were placed neatly in orderly rows around it, and pretty beds of flowers, all the same dark purple and deep red as those in the window boxes and all planted in straight little rows, accented its base.

"That is a statue of Fulla," said Brynhild. "This town is named after her."

"The town is called Fulla?" inquired Wilfred.

"Vollagarddal," replied Brynhild.

"Pardon?" asked Wilfred. "I don't think I heard you properly."

"Volla-gard-dal," repeated Brynhild slowly.

"Oh," said Wilfred. "I thought you said it was named after Fulla."

"It is," said Brynhild.

"I'm not entirely sure I follow," admitted Wilfred sheepishly.

"Volla is another form of the name 'Fulla'," explained Brynhild.

"And the 'gard-dal' part?" asked Wilfred.

"'Gard' means a farm, and 'dal' means a valley," said Brynhild.

"Ah!" said Wilfred. "I see! The town's name literally means 'Fulla's farm in a valley!'"

"Exactly," said Brynhild, nodding.

"Delightful!" said Wilfred, pleased at his small lesson in Viking semantics. "It's like piecing together a puzzle. Most satisfying. Isn't it fascinating, Barnabas?"

"Is that real gold?" asked Barnabas, who couldn't have cared less what they called the town and who had therefore kept his attention firmly fixated upon the beautiful statue. "Or merely painted?"

"It's real, through and through," said Brynhild.

"And the blue of her eyes, and the red accents on her gown? Surely they cannot all be sapphires and rubies," said Barnabas, marveling at the delicate beauty of the thing.

"All real," repeated Brynhild. "These are dwarves, after all."

"But it must be worth a fortune!" exclaimed Barnabas.

"I imagine it is," said Brynhild, bored.

"But where did they get such wealth to make such a fabulous thing?" pressed Barnabas. He gestured to the rest of the town, which, whilst charming, certainly did not seem to boast of great wealth. "The buildings look like homes for merchants and tradesmen," he said. Then he pointed to some of the people who hurried and scurried about the square. "And the people certainly appear to be of the most normal variety. So how did they come by such wealth?"

"How does anyone acquire wealth?" replied Brynhild. "Plunder and pillage, of course."

Barnabas frowned, displeased that his vision of amicable little dwarves in their charming little town was now tainted with the idea of those self-same dwarves on a murderous rampage, stealing and reaving for wealth.

"Surely not," he said. "Anyone who could build such an orderly place would surely not behave in such a way."

"You're probably right," said Brynhild. "People probably gave them their treasures of their own free will."

"Of course they did...oh," said Barnabas, catching Brynhild's sarcasm at last. He followed her as she led out of the square and down the northernmost of the four streets, casting suspicious glances at the little dwarves, who no longer appeared as innocuous as before. He stole one last look at the golden statue, which was still beautiful, despite its nefarious genesis. Then he frowned.

"Why," he asked, "is it holding cabbages?"

Wilfred turned to look and saw that in the statue's outstretched hands there were, indeed, quite a large number of cabbages balanced one upon the other. "That is most remarkable," he remarked. "What is that about?"

"Fulla is the goddess of agriculture and plenty," said Brynhild. "So the people give her offerings of whatever it is that they grow. Here, that happens to be cabbages."

Thinking on the idea of tiny dwarven marauders who also happened to be profilic growers of cabbages, Barnabas and Wilfred followed behind Brynhild in silence as they passed quickly out of the town and into a vast countryside (where, of course, many cabbages were growing). That cabbages could grow at all was quite surprising, really, since the sky never seemed to brighten to anything lighter than a deep azure color. "I don't suppose the sun will be up soon?" asked

Barnabas hopefully, whereupon Brynhild reminded him that Nidavellir was one of the underground worlds.

The whole place was really quite dark, and now that they were out in the open Barnabas and Wilfred found it quite oppressive. "I do hope that we are through with this *underground* business straightaway," whispered Barnabas to Wilfred. "It feels as if the sky itself is entirely too *close* down here, and I don't much like the idea of tiny dwarves who plunder and steal."

"Nor do I," said Wilfred. "Makes one feel quite claustrophobic, does it not?"

Barnabas nodded his agreement, and they plodded along, hoping that they'd come quickly to their destination.

They walked for a good many hours, however (so that Barnabas was complaining quite vociferously about his aching feet) before they came to a stop in front of the mouth of what looked to be an enormous cave.

"Lovely," said Barnabas. "Another cave." He rolled his eyes to what should have been the heavens, but was instead just a dark blue blur above them. "I suppose there are serpents in here as well?"

"Not really," replied Brynhild. She put her hand beneath her chin, thinking. "Unless you consider that dragons are actually a form of serpent, in a way. So I guess you *could* say there's at least one serpent in here, and a pretty large one at that…"

Barnabas shot her a withering look, and she quickly clamped her lips shut.

"Well," said Barnabas, stepping forward reluctantly into the mouth of the cave. "There's nothing for it, then. There's a dragon in there, and it's a dragon we must see. So in we go!" He lifted an arm as if to signal a cavalry charge, but his arm never came down and the charge never commenced (that is to say, Barnabas suddenly froze in place with his arm upraised so that he looked a bit like a triumphant statue).

"Ahem," prompted Wilfred after waiting some moments for Barnabas to move. "Shall we, then?"

"Shhh!" whispered Barnabas urgently. "No one speak, or

move, or do anything at all, really." He scarcely moved his lips as he spoke, causing Wilfred great consternation.

"Are you quite all right?" asked Wilfred, moving closer to inspect his immobile employer. "Is something the matter?"

Just then a terrible whooshing sound emanated from deeper within the cave. An awful smell wafted towards them, directly followed by three large winged shapes that soared along the cave's ceiling. The things swooped down and, with no further ado, picked up the three travelers by the scruffs of their cloaks and whisked them off into the depths of the cave.

"I told you," said Barnabas through clenched teeth as Wilfred's dragon (for that is what their abductors were) pulled up next to his own, "not to speak. Did I not?"

"Terribly sorry," said Wilfred. "I didn't realize…"

"Hmmph," snorted Barnabas. "And now we've been carried off by big smelly lizards."

"I wouldn't say things like that," warned Brynhild, whose own dragon had come up to join its fellows. "We don't want to anger them."

"Anger them?" said Barnabas sarcastically. "I truly fail to see what worse could happen than *this*." He gestured at the three of them, dangling from the wickedly sharp talons of the dragons, hurtling at great speed into a dark and dank cavern that seemingly went down into the very bowels of the earth, so far had they come already.

"They are probably just Fafnir's guards, come to escort us into his presence. It would be best if we arrived in as friendly a manner as possible," said Brynhild calmly.

"I do believe these stinky scallywags cast friendliness aside when they seized us in so abrupt a manner," said Barnabas.

"But they're not hurting us, are they?" pointed out Brynhild.

"They are being extraordinarily gentle with their claws," agreed Wilfred. He looked at the giant talon tipped with a claw the size of a hunting knife that clasped his cloak firmly in front of his shoulder, whilst somehow managing to avoid penetrating his skin, or even poking him in the slightest.

"They could be far more rough about the matter, I'm quite sure."

"Still," insisted Barnabas. "The whole 'plucking-people-off-the-ground-and-carrying-them-away-without-so-much-as-a-how-do-you-do' part is not to be borne. Really, it is most undignified."

And, while it was true that the dragons *were* being extraordinarily careful not to harm their passengers, it was also true that Barnabas was making out by far the worst of the three. Somehow, his cloak had managed to rise up (or, Barnabas himself had managed to slump down within it) so that its folds were uncomfortably high around his neck and his shoulders were hitched up entirely too far, which made his arms jut out at awkward angles. In truth, the entire effect was one of a grumpy kitten being forcibly hauled off by its mother under extreme protest.

"Perhaps if you'd stop kicking so," suggested Wilfred, "you might be more comfortable."

Barnabas grumbled unintelligibly in reply, but thankfully the impromptu dragon-ride had come to an end. The dragons (and their unwilling guests) swept into a great chamber, where a large number of dwarves dressed in splendid finery were gathered. The dwarves mingled and milled about amongst each other, but all clearly had at least part of their attention on the figure that lounged on an enormous chaise at the far end of the room.

"That," remarked Brynhild, "is Fafnir." The three dragons (who looked quite small, now that they could be compared to the tremendous bulk of the giant dragon whose body barely fit on the chaise, which was in itself nearly the size of a small carriage) flew over the heads of the assembled dwarves and dropped their passengers unceremoniously in front of Fafnir the dragon.

"Oomph!" said Barnabas as he landed heavily on the ground. He hastily jumped to his feet and patted himself down, sniffing indignantly as he did so. He cast a withering glance at the dragon that had carried him (at least, he *thought* he did; he hadn't really gotten a good look at the things before being picked up, and he certainly hadn't managed to do so whilst falling, either. Still, he thought, all three dragons were equally guilty, and so were also equally deserving of his reprobation. Therefore it followed that it didn't matter much, really, *which* dragon he silently chastised).

The dragon open its mouth and heaved in a great breath, but just before it was able to exhale straight into Barnabas' face (in what everyone assumed would be a fireball of dreadful proportions that would certainly turn Barnabas into a charred pot roast of sorts) the creature on the chaise spoke.

"Now, Cnub," said Fafnir, the dragon king of the dwarves. "That's enough. We've talked about how it's not polite to roast our guests, haven't we?"

Cnub the dragon quickly turned its head and gave a small, obviously fake cough, as though that was what it had been going to do all along, anyway, then flew over to join its fellows on a perch off to the side of the chaise.

"Hello, Fafnir," said Brynhild. "And thank you."

"Don't mention it," replied Fafnir. "Least I could do." He nodded his head graciously.

Fafnir's voice was not at all what one would expect from an enormous dragon. It was high-pitched and nasally, whilst bearing just a hint of the sibilant hissing sounds that put one in mind of snakes and other things that slithered about. Barnabas found it somehow adorable and terrifying at the same time.

"So," said Fafnir, "what brings Odin's favorite skald down to my humble abode?" The dragon-dwarf somehow imbued his words with so much loathing that Barnabas quickly amended his opinions on Fafnir's voice to tilt farther away from *adorable* and much closer to *terrifying*.

"We are here on business of the utmost importance," said Brynhild confidently, either unaware of the danger in Fafnir's voice or consciously choosing to ignore it. "We need your help in stopping Ragnarok."

"And why should I help you, a minion of Odin?" screeched Fafnir. All hint of *adorableness* was quite gone from his voice; indeed, now that he was yelling it sounded shrill and screechy and somehow *slimy* to Barnabas' ear. Barnabas and Wilfred shared a worried look, but Brynhild intrepidly pressed on.

"Because you, above all people, um, I mean, dragons, should want to keep Ragnarok from happening," she said.

"Do you have the nerve to refer to that stupid prophecy? The one about Sigurd and how he's going to kill me after Ragnarok?" hissed Fafnir, narrowing his eyes nastily.

"Well, it is something to think about," said Brynhild uncertainly. "Surely you'd like to avoid the situation?"

"Hah!" cried Fafnir. "Avoid a situation just because one of Odin's seers makes a silly proclamation? What does Odin and his ilk know of Fafnir, the Great Dragon of Nidavellir?" Fafnir spread his wings wide and looked expansively about the cavern. The gathered dwarves dutifully cheered in a rote sort of way, as though they went through this charade with some regularity and knew precisely what was expected of them.

"Runes don't lie, Fafnir," persisted Brynhild bravely.

"Don't they?" asked Fafnir, leaning in closer so that his nose was mere inches from Brynhild's. She shifted nervously from one foot to the other, but held her ground. Long moments passed as Fafnir stared down Brynhild. Barnabas and Wilfred watched, frozen in fear, afraid of what the clearly hostile dragon-dwarf might do.

Fafnir snarled menacingly as he continued. "Perhaps they don't. Perhaps it is not the runes that lie, but those who read them. And I wonder what happens to people who lie to Fafnir, be they Odin's pets or no?" He looked around the room again as though expecting an answer to come from one of his dwarven subjects.

"Charbroiled?" suggested one.

"Gobbled down whole?" said another.

"Yelled at severely?" called out yet another, somewhat less threateningly.

Barnabas saw Fafnir's snout begin to curl up in a nasty smile and knew that something dreadful was about to happen to Brynhild. She, too, saw it, and drew back, cringing a bit as she braced herself.

Without thinking, Barnabas leapt forward to stand between Fafnir and Brynhild (he had to wiggle a bit to insert himself, so close was Fafnir's nose to Brynhild, and in doing so he was forced to place his hands directly upon the dragon-dwarf's snout, which was extraordinarily rough to the touch and was covered with an unpleasantly slimy substance that transferred itself to Barnabas' fingertips. Still, it was what duty proclaimed he must do, and so he did it).

He drew himself up as best he could whilst every instinct in his body directed him to cower cravenly. He settled for a compromise between a heroic stance and a cowardly cringe, so that his head and neck were held high whilst his body was scrunched up protectively and his hands outstretched in a warding off gesture.

"Or," he cried, "you should give them a bowl!"

"Huh?" said Fafnir, cocking his head to the side quizzically.

"A bowl!" repeated Barnabas. "A magical bowl!"

"Why would I give a lying skald a magical bowl?" asked Fafnir.

"Because," said Barnabas, thinking quickly, "it would be a most, er, unexpected thing to do. People would think on how unpredictable you are, and quake with fear. 'Will he smite me in a fiery blaze,' they'll think, 'or will he give me a bowl?'" Barnabas shuddered dramatically for effect.

"Hah!" said Fafnir. "Hah! Hah!" His sides heaved and he waved his wings about haphazardly. It took Barnabas a moment to understand what was happening, but then he realized that the dragon was *laughing*. "A bowl!" howled Fafnir. "He says, he says, oh my, it's too much, who ever hear such a thing! A bowl!"

Barnabas feigned a polite chuckle, unsure of what the proper etiquette was when confronted with a hysterically laughing dragon. Wilfred and Brynhild took his cue and began to laugh as well. One by one the dwarves followed suit, until everyone in the chamber was laughing or chuckling or chortling.

Fafnir withdrew back onto his chaise, wiping a tear from his eye. "Well if that doesn't end it all," he said, still giggling a bit. "Who would have thought. A bowl! Where on earth did you get the idea of a bowl?"

"It's just that we saw such wealth, walking through your kingdom," began Barnabas, hoping to flatter Fafnir. Brynhild shot him a warning glance, but Barnabas was far too preoccupied with Fafnir the dragon to notice. "Your kingdom is so wealthy, and so impressive, that I thought it would be divine to possess a bowl made by such able craftsmen."

"Oh?" asked Fafnir casually. "And where, pray, did you see this impressive wealth?"

"It was in, ah, hmmm," began Barnabas. He turned to Brynhild and asked, "What did you say the town's name was?" She shook her head vehemently, but he misunderstood her message. "Oh come now, I'm certain you must remember. "Volla-something-or-other, I think it was."

"Vollagarddal?" asked Fafnir, leaning in.

"Yes! Yes, I'm sure that is it," replied Barnabas. "Such a lovely statue was there, all gold and rubies and sapphires. Why, I've never seen such workmanship!"

Brynhild slapped a hand to her forehead and groaned.

"I see," said Fafnir. "You know, I think I might be able to help you out with that bowl after all. If you'd just excuse me a moment?" The dragon-dwarf rose up from his chaise and took wing. With a great swoop of his wings he departed the chamber entirely, leaving his three visitors to stand alone.

"There," said Barnabas, proudly swiping his hands together. "That went swimmingly, don't you think?"

"Ummm…" said Brynhild.

Puzzled by her tone, Barnabas looked sharply at her but she refused to meet his gaze. He glanced around the room. The dwarves all seemed suddenly very tense and even Wilfred was shifting awkwardly from one foot to the other.

"What?" asked Barnabas. "What is it?"

"Oh, nothing, probably," replied Brynhild, suddenly taking a great interest of the workmanship of Fafnir's chaise. "Well, would you look at that!" she said to no one in particular. "Did they use a wire weave *and* a tablet weave, too? Incredible!" She edged closer to it and stuck her face nearly into the cushions, studying the weaving as though her life depended on it.

"Wilfred?" asked Barnabas. "What's the matter with her? What's the matter with them?" He nodded to the dwarves who were milling about and casting uncomfortable glances in the direction of the cave entrance. "What's the matter with *you*, for that matter?" he added. Indeed, Wilfred had turned a most alarming shade of red, and his eyebrows had migrated a good distance up his forehead. But Wilfred, feigning ignorance, merely shrugged his shoulders helplessly.

"Well," huffed Barnabas, "I certainly don't see what everyone is in such a bother about, of a sudden. Unless the two of you are envious that it was *I* who convinced Fafnir to help, which would be an exceedingly silly way to feel if you think about it, seeing as it's the end of the world we are talking about and a person should always cast aside his own egoism in cases like this and not get his feathers all ruffled simply because someone else, namely me, has done the part of the quest that will be sung about for ages to come, is what I always say."

During this speech Barnabas had gotten himself so worked up that his face had turned even redder than Wilfred's (although whether that was due to his budding self-righteous outrage or merely the fact that his sentence had gone on so long that he had nearly run entirely out of breath was unclear). He gulped down a few hasty breaths and had just opened his mouth to continue his diatribe (several salient points about selfless heroism and the importance of humility in the service of the greater good had popped into his mind and he was eager to drop this wisdom on his hapless assistant) when a rush of wind from the tunnel leading into the cave heralded the return of Fafnir.

A dreadful smell came with the wind; one of burnt charcoal and overly cooked produce.

"Ugh!" said Barnabas, his rant forgotten. "What is that smell?" He crinkled his nose. "It puts one in mind of cabbages left over-long on the...oh." With a sinking feeling Barnabas suddenly realized what the smell of roasted cabbages meant.

Moments later, Fafnir entered the cavern, and what he held in his giant claws confirmed Barnabas' fears. It was the beautiful golden statue of Fulla of which Barnabas had spoken so highly.

Fafnir dropped the thing in the center of the cavern (causing the dwarves who had been standing there to scramble to avoid being completely squished by the thing) and landed beside it. He shook his wings, sending a spray of soot and smoky ashes fluttering in a cloud about him. A few fire-blackened cabbages fell off his back and landed with a dusty plop on the cavern floor.

"Oh dear," said Barnabas miserably. "Oh, the village."

"And what a delightful little village it is!" proclaimed Fafnir. "Or, rather, *was*, I guess I should say." The dragon-dwarf cackled nastily, and Barnabas hung his head guiltily.

"No one would have guessed he would do *that*," said Wilfred diplomatically.

"*I* did," added Brynhild, rather *un*diplomatically. "*I* guessed it." Wilfred looked at her disapprovingly, and she returned to her feigned interest in weavework.

"You've done me a great service by reporting those gold-hoarders," said Fafnir to Barnabas. "To think that they thought *they* could hide this from *me*! Ha!" He caressed the golden statue lovingly.

"I don't suppose you limited your burning to only cabbages?" suggested Barnabas hopefully.

"Of course not, you ninny!" chortled Fafnir happily. "They'll have a Helheim of a time rebuilding Vollagarddal after all the glorious burning I've just done."

"Oh dear," said Barnabas sadly. "All those people, er, dwarves. All those beautiful buildings." He slumped, as though he were trying to sink into the very earth itself.

"Anyway," interrupted Brynhild, "now that you've got your statue and all, I guess we'll just be taking that bowl and heading on our way."

"Ah, yes!" said Fafnir. "The bowl." He reached out a forepaw as though waiting for a magical bowl to materialize on it. When it didn't, he shook his wings irritably. "The bowl, I said!" he demanded. A few puffs of smoke came out of his nostrils, and several dwarves jostled about, looking for the bowl in question. At last one of them found it and cautiously handed it to the king.

Brynhild reached out to take it, but Fafnir suddenly drew it back out of her reach. "But you have to pay for it first," he said with narrowed eyes.

"Pay for it?" said Brynhild. "Isn't the statue payment enough?"

Barnabas groaned and looked as though he were having trouble keeping his dinner down.

"It wasn't yours to give, though, was it?" pointed out Fafnir reasonably. "I had to fly all the way there, and burn all those houses, and get the smell of cabbages all over me..." Barnabas gasped at Fafnir's casual description of the horror he had brought upon the quaint little village, and Wilfred laid a calming hand on his shoulder, although he, too, was looking a little white about the gills.

"So what payment would you like?" asked Brynhild through gritted teeth.

"Gold, of course," replied Fafnir. Brynhild began to heave a sigh of relief (gold would be easily obtained, she thought) but then Fafnir continued. "From Freya."

"From Freya!" exclaimed Brynhild. "But she will never give us gold to give to you!"

"Precisely," said Fafnir. "You'll have to steal it."

"Steal gold from Freya? That's madness!" protested Brynhild.

"Do you want the bowl or not?" asked Fafnir implacably. "Steal me some gold from Freya, and I'll give you the bowl and the world won't end. Or *don't* steal the gold from Freya, and I *won't* give you the bowl and the world *will* end. Up to you." The dragon-dwarf studied his claws casually as he waited for their decision.

"You, sir, are...are...unconscionable!" cried Barnabas,

unable to contain his emotions any longer. "You destroyed that village, and now you seek to make thieves of upstanding, law-abiding citizens of the British Empire…"

"And me, too," added Brynhild. "Don't forget about me."

"And this nice, ah, Viking lady, too," finished Barnabas.

"Why, thank you," said Fafnir, confusingly. He nodded his head graciously, as though Barnabas had just paid him a great compliment. "I'll expect you back within a fortnight. After that I'll smelt down the bowl and make something else out of it. Like a bracelet, maybe, or a ring. Yes, I think a ring would be nice." Fafnir turned his back on the three companions and began to talk with the dwarf who had brought him the bowl. "Do you think a ring shaped like a snake would be good?" he said. "Oh! Or maybe a pretty necklace for the statue?"

"You scallywag!" cried Barnabas. "You…" He was interrupted by Brynhild, who clapped a hand over his mouth.

"It's time we go," she whispered. "*Quietly*."

"But…but…" protested Barnabas. He gestured towards the golden statue, marred with soot from the burned village of Vollagarddal. "It is too dreadful, too horrible, too appalling! He cannot just get away with it!"

"He's the king of Nidavellir," said Brynhild. "He'll get away with that and much more besides. Let's not give him any reasons to do something *appalling* to us."

"Oh, I cannot take it!" cried Barnabas, dramatically draping his forearm over his eyes. "It is too much! Too much, I say!"

"It is most dreadful," agreed Wilfred, sniffling sadly.

"Yes,' yes," said Brynhild, herding the two distraught detectives out of the cavern. "It is appalling, and dreadful, and we can think about it while we're on our way."

"On our way where?" asked Wilfred.

"To Freya's palace," answered Brynhild. "To steal her gold."

"Oh dear," said Barnabas.

"Oh dear, indeed," agreed Wilfred.

Chapter Nine

Together they hurried from the cave and back to Hynder. Such was their rush to get away from the capricious (and alarmingly violent) king of Nidavellir that they set an exceedingly fast pace and therefore had no breath left with which to speak of the atrocity that Fafnir had committed against the town of Vollagarddal.

Still, their distress was evident in their wide eyes and defeated postures (except, that is, for Brynhild; as a Viking she was all too accustomed to the sacking and pillaging of towns, and therefore didn't think too much of it aside from a slight regret that she hadn't prevented Barnabas from alerting Fafnir to the presence of the valuable gold statue).

Barnabas, in particular, was burdened by immense guilt over the thing. His eyes darted wildly from here to there, and he opened and closed his mouth like a fish passing water over its gills. Indeed, Barnabas was so markedly distraught, and his manner so distracted, that Wilfred feared he might slip entirely off of Hynder's back at a most unfortunate time. Wilfred, therefore, discretely made sure that his employer was in the middle, between himself and Brynhild, when they mounted, so that together they might hold him safely aboard.

Once all were settled and Hynder safely in the air, whisking them far away from Nidavellir, Wilfred encouraged the little detective to get some sleep, hoping that some rest might improve Barnabas' outlook on things.

"How can I sleep, after what has happened to all those dwarves in Vollagraddal?" said Barnabas. "*They* certainly shall not be sleeping, with their town all burned to a crisp, and, as the harbinger of their doom, I ought to also remain awake." He thought for a moment, then turned to look over his shoulder at Wilfred with his wild, stunned eyes. "Or, perhaps, they *are* sleeping, because they are, er, no longer entirely *alive*, and shall never do anything *other* than sleep. Oh, you don't think *that* is how it is, do you?" he cried.

"No, no, of course not," soothed Wilfred. "I'm certain that they must have heard the dragon coming, and been able to escape."

"Dragons fly rather quickly," said Brynhild. "I don't think...oof!" Somehow, Wilfred had managed to reach his leg all the way around Barnabas in order to deliver a sharp kick to her shin. "Then again," she said, taking the none-too-subtle hint, "they also make a lot of noise, so I'm sure everyone had *plenty* of time to get away."

"You really think so?" asked Barnabas hopefully.

"Sure," said Brynhild. "It's easy to run away, on foot, from a flying, fire-breathing dragon."

"Well, that doesn't sound..." began Barnabas, frowning. Wilfred hastily interrupted him, whilst giving Brynhild yet another kick.

"Oh yes, everyone knows it," Wilfred said. "Just think how much easier it would be to hide from a great, big thing that's in the air, rather than from a tiny, little, creeping thing that you'd never see coming."

"As in, you'd see a big hawk that was coming for you, but you'd never know a spider was there, until it bit you. So I'd much rather prefer the hawk I see, than the spider."

"Precisely," replied Wilfred.

"For the love of Odin," muttered Brynhild, rolling her eyes.

"But their homes," said Barnabas, unable to let go of his melancholia just yet. "All those lovely houses, burned to a crisp."

"Oh, but look," said Wilfred, pointing vaguely downwards. "I can see them. It looks as if they are already beginning to rebuild!" Of course, he had seen nothing of the kind, but was only making it up in order to calm his employer's fraught nerves.

"Really?" exclaimed Barnabas hopefully. He leaned over

to see for himself. Seeing nothing he leaned over even more, until he was dangling precariously off one side of the flying horse. Indeed, he would have tipped over entirely had Brynhild not reached back and taken a firm hold of the back of his cloak.

"I don't see anything," complained Barnabas.

"Really?" said Wilfred. "They're right there." He pointed in an altogether different direction than the one he had pointed to originally. "And they are carrying lumber, and stones, and what-not."

"That's not where you pointed before," said Barnabas suspiciously.

"Ah, well," stammered Wilfred, who was unaccustomed to lying and therefore wasn't very good at it. "I expect that's because there are so many of them, and because they are all so very busy," he said after a long pause.

"Hmmm," said Barnabas. "Yes, I suppose that makes sense. But really, I *would* like to see for myself. Why can't I see them?"

"Oh dear," said Wilfred. "Looks like we've gone above the clouds. I suppose *that's* why you can't see them."

"There aren't any clouds," pointed out Barnabas. He was still leaned over, trying in vain to see the busy little dwarves whom Wilfred had completely made up.

"We are too high to see the ground, anyway," said Brynhild, a bit snippily. "Now if you'd *please* sit up straight! My arm is killing me, holding you up like this."

"Oh my," said Barnabas. "I am *quite* sorry." He pulled himself upright, with no small effort, and sighed. "Still, even though they must be all right, if they are rebuilding their town already...they really are rebuilding, aren't they, Wilfred?" Wilfred nodded vehemently in the affirmative. "So they must be all right, at least *mostly* all right, although I can't help but think at least *some* of them must have met a gruesome end, and it is all my fault."

"No one could have foreseen what Fafnir did," said Wilfred. "It was most unexpected."

"It wasn't, really," pointed out Brynhild. "I *tried* to warn you. Ouch!"

"Really, Brynhild," said Wilfred, "I am getting *most* tired of having to kick you."

"What?" said Barnabas, looking confusedly back and forth between them (and developing quite a crick in his neck whilst so doing). "Why are you kicking Brynhild?"

"Did I say Brynhild?" said Wilfred with an innocent expression on his face. "I meant to say Hynder, of course."

"Oh," said Barnabas. "But why are you kicking Hynder?"

"Yes, Wilfred," said Brynhild snidely, "why *are* you kicking Hynder?"

"I would stop," said Wilfred, "if *he* would stop."

"Stop what?" said Barnabas. "What is he doing?"

"Nothing," said Brynhild, shaking her head. "I think *Hynder* will just be quiet now."

"Thank you very much. Hynder, I mean, of course. Thank *Hynder* very much," said Wilfred.

"Hynder says you're quite welcome," said Brynhild. "Now how about if everyone gets some rest? We've had a long day."

"Splendid idea," said Wilfred. "We can take turns. Barnabas, why don't you go first?"

"All right, I suppose," said Barnabas. "Although how I'll ever sleep…"

"Sometimes not talking anymore helps you fall asleep," pointed out Brynhild. Fortunately for her Wilfred was too tired to deliver any more kicks, and Barnabas was too tired to take offense. Instead he simply muttered, "Very well," and leaned his head against her back. In mere minutes he was snoring (and, truth be told, drooling just a little, as well).

He slept deeply for several hours (although his sleep was far from serene; several times he shouted things like, 'Ah! A dragon!' or 'Run, little fellows, run!', and several more times he muttered incoherent nonsense about overcooked cabbages).

It was Hynder's landing that jerked him awake, and he stretched sleepily, greatly refreshed by his rest. In contrast, Wilfred and Brynhild, who had not been able to sleep at all, seemed exhausted. They yawned repeatedly and blinked their reddened eyes in an attempt to keep them open.

"Where are we?" asked Barnabas.

"There's Freya's palace, over there," said Brynhild.

"Well, why didn't we just land in the courtyard, like we did before?" he said.

"Because we are here to steal things," said Brynhild. "Thieves don't come knocking at the front door, do they?"

"No need to be testy," said Barnabas, amiably enough. "I don't have the advantage of a life filled with nefarious doings, like you do, so of course I don't know about that sort of thing."

"What?" snapped Brynhild. She was certain that she'd been insulted in some way, but was too tired to figure out *how*, exactly.

"He only means that you should probably take the lead in this mission," said Wilfred smoothly.

"Right," said Brynhild. Moving to the edge of the ridge on which they had just landed, she surveyed the castle grounds that lay sprawled out in the valley below them. Men trained on the flowering fields that surrounded the place, whilst dozens of traders and workers scuttled to and fro on the lanes that led up to the front and back gates of the palace. High, windowless walls surrounded the palace complex.

Brynhild frowned, considering their options. "Well," she said, thinking aloud, "both of the gates look to be heavily guarded. We could try to fight our way through…" She glanced over at Barnabas' stocky, slightly pudgy form, and then at Wilfred's tall, slight body. "No, we'd best not try that," she concluded. "And besides, that would defeat the whole 'not alerting them to our presence' thing. I suppose we could wait till dark and try to climb over the walls somewhere near the gardens…"

"Those walls look awfully high," said Wilfred, who had joined her on the crest of the ridge.

"Only about twenty feet or so," said Brynhild.

"And I don't really see any handholds," said Wilfred. "Or *foot*holds, either, for that matter."

"Well, no, but you just have to sort of shimmy up," said Brynhild. "And then shimmy down on the other side."

"What if we accidentally shimmy *down* when we're supposed to be shimmying *up*?" said Wilfred. "Or if we shimmy down in too fast a manner?"

"I guess you'd probably break a leg or two," said Brynhild. "So it would be best not to do that."

"Oh dear," said Wilfred. "Perhaps we might come up with a slightly less dangerous plan?"

"We could try to fly Hynder in to the garden," said Brynhild. "Although a flying horse is far more likely to attract attention than three people scaling a wall."

"We might construct a ladder," suggested Wilfred. He looked around. "There are some sticks and twigs lying about. If we tied them together…"

"Ahem," said Barnabas.

"It would take forever," said Brynhild, ignoring him. "And would probably give way the second we got to the top."

"Surely we can think of something!" said Wilfred.

"Ahem!" said Barnabas again, more forcefully. "Ahem, I say!"

Brynhild turned to him. "Did you swallow a fly?" she asked.

"I most certainly did not!" huffed Barnabas. "I merely thought to alert you to the fact that your arguments on the matter are unnecessary, as I have solved the problem already."

"I thought you didn't know what to do in such 'nefarious' situations," pointed out Brynhhild.

"Ah, yes, well," said Barnabas. "I suppose I *did* say that. But it turns out that my deductive reasoning skills are up to any situation, be it nefarious or otherwise."

"Really?" asked Brynhild sardonically. "Do tell."

"It's quite simple, really," said Barnabas. He tilted his head so that his nose was pointing nearly up to the sky, trying to (and nearly succeeding at) affect a look of smug superiority. He tried to look down at Brynhild over the tip of his nose, but discovered that it was up so high that he could see only some distance above the top of her head. He adjusted himself, tilting and craning his head this way and that, until he found the proper angle. Wilfred nodded encouragingly, and he continued. "You see," he said, "all we must do is pretend to be merchants. Then we can go in the gates just as pretty as you please."

"Just as we did in Egypt!" said Wilfred. And indeed, the two detectives had tried just such a ploy to gain entrance into another castle, half a world away.

Brynhild frowned. "But we don't *look* at all like merchants," she said. "We don't have any wares to sell, for one."

"Oh," said Barnabas. "*That* is easy. We simply get some wares from one of those *real* merchants."

Brynhild put a hand beneath her chin and nodded. "And how do we get the wares?" she asked. Clearly she was warming to the idea.

"Why, we simply select one, lure him out of line, and, well, *you* know…"

"And *what*?" asked Brynhild.

"Oh, Barnabas, no," groaned Wilfred, knowing what was coming.

"Well, we just bonk him over the head, I suppose," said Barnabas.

"Barnabas!" chastised Wilfred. But Brynhild grinned and clapped her hands together, delighted.

"Perfect!" she cried. "It's a wonderful plan. That is what we will do, then."

"But, the bonking…" protested Wilfred.

"What about it?" asked Brynhild.

"Why, it's not right to take some poor, innocent merchant and just bonk him right over the head!" said Wilfred.

"Why not?" asked Brynhild, puzzled. Wilfred shook his head at the moral failings of the Vikings, and looked to Barnabas in appeal instead.

"It'll just be a little bonking," said Barnabas, reddening with embarrassment beneath the weight of Wilfred's disapprobation. "Hardly even a proper bonk at all, really."

"It is uncouth," said Wilfred, "and I am shocked that you would suggest such a thing."

"But it is a necessary uncouthness, is it not?" parried Barnabas. "If we don't bonk a merchant on the head, we don't get into the castle to steal Freya's gold, and the world will end."

"Well, yes, but…" said Wilfred.

"And which do you think the merchant would prefer? To be bonked on the head, or for the world to end?"

"I suppose he'd take the bonk, but certainly there must be something…"

"A bonk on the head today keeps the end of the world away, is what I always say," said Barnabas cheerfully. "Look, there's a fellow who looks promising." He pointed towards a man who was struggling to push a heavily laden apple cart. "A small fellow with a big cart, and off by himself besides. That's our man, right there!" So saying, he headed off towards the apple merchant.

Brynhild started to follow Barnabas, then turned and looked at Wilfred, who was still very unhappy with the plan. "We'll be very careful not to hurt him," she assured him over her shoulder. "It'll just be a tiny little bonk. I promise."

"Oh, very well," said Wilfred, knowing that he was beaten. Reluctantly he followed Brynhild towards the merchant.

"Although," said Brynhild, as Wilfred caught her up, "I suppose we could simply *buy* those apples from the man. Would that make you feel better about it?"

"Oh yes!" said Wilfred. "I would have no issue whatsoever with *that* plan."

"Good," said Brynhild. "It is settled then. I'll offer the merchant some silver, and he'll give us the cart…oh dear."

Unfortunately Barnabas had reached the merchant whilst Wilfred and Brynhild talked. Intent on carrying out his plan, and having mustered up the courage to do so besides, he had decided not to wait for his friends, but to simply commence the proceedings on his own. However, having never *actually* bonked someone on the head before, he wasn't entirely sure of precisely *how* to do so. Therefore, he had succeeded only in delivering an odd, open-palmed smack to the top of the man's head, which only managed to startle and annoy the fellow (and mess up his hair quite a good bit as well).

The merchant, of course, was confused and more than a little irate. "What was that for?" yelled the man, rubbing the top of his head and scowling. He snatched Barnabas by the front of the robe and shook him roughly. "Explain yourself, or I'll flatten you into the dirt." The merchant pulled back a meaty fist, and Barnabas yelped in terror.

"Oh dear, oh my!" he cried. "Please don't bonk *me*, good sir!"

"Oh dear, indeed," said Wilfred. "We'd best hurry." Brynhild nodded her agreement, and the two hurried towards Barnabas and the merchant.

"Tell me why you whacked me on the head, and maybe I will bonk you or maybe I won't," said the man, giving Barnabas another shake.

"I had to, you see, the end of the world, and the apples, and er, you know, the dragon," said Barnabas nonsensically.

"What?" said the man.

"Wait!" yelled Brynhild.

"Wait for what?" said the man.

"That's our friend there," said Wilfred. "If you'd just let us explain…"

"Explain why he came up out of the blue and smacked me on the head?" said the man. He was quite obviously still very irate at the situation.

"Uh, yes?" said Wilfred.

"It was a fly!" cried Barnabas.

"A *what*?" said the man.

"A fly," lied Barnabas. "A great big one."

"A great big fly?" asked the man, confused.

"One of those really bite-y ones," replied Barnabas. "It was on your head, and it was about to take a great big bite, so I smacked it away."

"Oh," said the man. He loosened his grip on Barnabas' cloak. "Really?" he asked suspiciously. "I think I would have felt that."

"I was too fast, I suppose," said Barnabas. "I must have smashed it before it could properly dig in."

"Huh," said the man. He let go of Barnabas entirely, but still looked a bit ruffled.

Barnabas patted at his cloak, straightening it. "You're *welcome*," he said pointedly.

"Eh?" said the man. "Oh, er, uh, thank you?"

"Hmmph," said Barnabas, sniffing.

"Anyway," interrupted Brynhild. "Now that we've got *that* straightened out, maybe we can get down to business?"

"Business?" asked the man, perking up a bit.

"We'd like to buy your apples," said Brynhild.

"I thought we were..." began Barnabas.

"...going to *buy* all of these apples," finished Brynhild firmly.

"Oh," said Barnabas. He sounded a trifle disappointed.

"All of the apples?" asked the merchant. He patted absentmindedly at his mussed up hair. "That's a lot of apples for just three people."

"And a horse," added Wilfred helpfully, pointing to where Hynder stood grazing on the slope behind them.

"Well, I guess that *is* a big horse," said the man doubtfully. "Still seems like an awful lot of apples, though."

"Will you sell them or not?" said Brynhild impatiently. She reached into her bag and grabbed a handful of silver coins, then shook them in her hand so that they jingled merrily. "If not, I'm sure we can find someone else a little less..."

"Inquisitive?" supplied Wilfred.

"In need of a good bonking on and about the head?" said Barnabas. "I think I see..." He flexed his fingers, eager to have another go at the apple merchant.

"*Difficult*," said Brynhild. "Someone a little less difficult." She made as if to put the coins back in her bag.

"All right, all right," said the man quickly. He reached his hand out, palm up. "The apples are yours."

"And the cart, too?" said Brynhild.

"Not the cart, just the apples," said the man.

"We'll just be on our way…" said Brynhild.

"No, no," said the man. "Hold on there! The cart too, then. Whatever you want."

Brynhild handed the merchant a fistful of silver, and he, in turn, left them with the cart full of apples. They watched the man walk off in the direction from which he had come (still scratching his head whilst trying to figure out what, exactly, the three strange travelers who had smacked him on the head and then bought his entire stock were about), then all three turned to face Freya's palace.

"Well," said Barnabas at last, "there's nothing for it now but to see if our plan works. To the palace to sell some apples!" He flourished a pointed finger in the air dramatically, then marched determinedly towards the palace gates, leaving Wilfred and Brynhild to manage the cart and the apples.

"Ugh," said Brynhild, rolling her eyes as she took hold of the cart handles and began to push. "Hynder!" she called over her shoulder. "You stay and graze out here. Wait for us to come back." Then she and Wilfred followed the intrepid Barnabas down the lane to the palace.

They caught up to the little detective just as he reached the guards at the gate.

"…turnip seller, I am!" he was saying to one of the guards. "On official turnip-selling business. My cart is, er, somewhere around here…" He turned to look for his companions. "Ah!" he said when he saw Brynhild and Wilfred approaching with the apple cart. "There are my turnips now. Do hurry with that cart, will you? Haven't got all day, you know." He turned to address the guard once more. "It's a busy thing, being a turnip merchant, you know," he explained. "And so difficult to find good help these days."

He jerked his head to indicate Brynhild, who was huffing and puffing behind the weight of the cart, and Wilfred, who was fluttering along beside her, trying to help but succeeding only in getting in her way.

Brynhild rolled her eyes and snorted.

"Uh," said the guard to Barnabas. "I thought you said you

were a turnips merchant."

"I did, at that," said Barnabas. "And only the finest turnips, too, if I do say so myself."

"Then why is that cart full of apples?" asked the guard.

"Well, why wouldn't it be?" asked Barnabas.

"Because a *turnip* merchant usually sells *turnips*, doesn't he?"

"Oh," said Barnabas, seeing his error. "Oh dear."

"What kind of merchant are you?" asked the guard suspiciously. He gestured to another guard, who was standing nearby, and waved for him to come over. "Borte, come here, will you? This fellow says he's a turnips merchant, but take a look inside his cart."

The guard named Borte came over and peered into the cart. "Those look like apples to me, Gunter," he said.

"That's what I thought," replied Gunter. "Makes you wonder why someone would say they sell turnips, but then try to pass through with a bunch of apples, doesn't it?"

"It sure does," replied Borte. He, too, looked over Barnabas suspiciously. "Where are you from?" he asked. "What is your business here? Why are you trying to pass off these apples as turnips?" Borte's eyebrows bristled and he put a hand to the hilt of his sword.

"Ahhh!" said Barnabas, alarmed. "I didn't mean, er, that is to say, I'm sure there's a mistake somewhere…Brynhild, *where* are my turnips?" he wailed at last.

Brynhild pursed her lips and shook her head, exasperated. But it was Wilfred who stepped forward and saved the situation.

"Don't you remember?" he said. "We traded our turnips for apples only just this morning." He smiled apologetically at the guards. "You must forgive us. It's been a long journey, and it's all too easy to misspeak when one is so very tired from the road."

"Ah yes!" said Barnabas, flapping his hands about in a flustered sort of way. "I remember now. The apples and the turnips and the trading and what-not. That's *exactly* what happened."

"Hmmm," said Borte. He and Gunter looked into the cart once more, then whispered to each other for a few moments. Barnabas gnawed nervously on his fingertips as they conferred, whilst Wilfred tried repeatedly (and failed just as many times) to pull his hands away inconspicuously.

At last Gunter and Borte finished their discussion. "Well," said Borte, "This has all been very strange, but since it really *is* just a cart of apples I suppose it's all right. You may go in." He stood aside and motioned for them to pass through the gates and into the palace. "The kitchens are across the courtyard and to the right."

"Thank you, thank you!" said Barnabas effusively. "Just a man and his turnips, passing through!"

"Apples, you mean," said Gunter tiredly.

"That's what I said," said Barnabas. Brynhild rolled her eyes again and shook her head. Then, together, the three phony turnips-merchants-turned-apple-sellers proceeded into the rear courtyard of Freya's palace.

"Well that went swimmingly," said Barnabas proudly.

"Well, it *went*, I guess," said Brynhild.

"There's the corridor that leads to the kitchens, I think," said Wilfred diplomatically. "I suggest we head in that direction, at least whilst Gunter and Borte are still watching. Then we can veer off and go in search of Freya's gold."

"Which would probably be in a locked treasury room. My guess is somewhere underground, perhaps near the dungeons," said Brynhild.

Following her lead, they fell in with all the rest of the merchants and servants who were heading towards the palace kitchens. Suddenly Brynhild stopped, forcing Wilfred (who had taken over control of the apple cart) to stop short behind her. The cart, of course, was quite heavy, and therefore difficult to stop, so that Wilfred had to veer off to the side to avoid running her over entirely. In doing so he barked the shins of a passerby.

The woman whom he clipped was a rather large and sturdy lady, wearing an extraordinarily dirty apron and an equally extraordinarily grumpy expression on her face.

"Oof!" exclaimed the grumpy-looking lady, as the apple cart came to an abrupt halt against her. "Watch where yer going, ye idiot!"

"Terribly sorry, madam," said Wilfred, appalled at his own clumsiness. He rushed over to her and began to pat her down as though looking for broken bones. "Are you quite all right? Can you stand? Can you walk? Do you have any bruises?"

The woman swatted at him irritably. "What'r ye doin?" she said. "Stop it. Are ye touched in the head or somethin'?"

Chastised, Wilfred backed away, his face red with embarrassment. The woman grabbed an apple from the cart, bit into it belligerently, and glared at him as if daring him to protest. "Ye'd best get them apples to the kitchen now, ye hear?" she said. "An' I'll be takin' this one for my troubles."

"Yes, ma'am," said Wilfred shamefacedly, as the woman gave him one last glare and stalked off.

"Well," said Barnabas, "*that* was a bit mortifying, wasn't it?"

"Anyway," said Brynhild quickly, "this stairway here looks promising. I think this is what we're looking for."

Barnabas peered into the dark, narrow staircase. It led downwards, but curved around on itself so that it was impossible to see where it went or how long it took to get there. A cold draft wafted up from it, and the air smelled dank and musty.

Barnabas sniffed. "It doesn't smell very nice down there," he said disapprovingly.

"Dungeons, as a rule, don't smell very nice," said Brynhild. "The storeroom has to be down here, I'm sure of it."

"*Or*," said Barnabas, "maybe…"

"It's down here," said Brynhild firmly. "Let's go."

"What shall we do with the cart?" asked Wilfred. "I don't think it will fit down the stairs."

"We'll just have to leave it," said Brynhild. "It's not like we need it anymore, anyway."

No one could think of a reason why they might need the apple cart again, nor could they think of anything else to do with it, so they left it abandoned in the corridor as they trouped, somewhat reluctantly, down the dark, smelly stairs.

The further they descended the worse the smell became, and after a few minutes they began to hear voices echoing in the stairwell. The voices sounded anything but happy, and grew louder and louder as they proceeded deeper and deeper underground.

"I say," said Barnabas, "those people sound quite *distressed*."

"People usually do when they're locked in a dungeon," said Brynhild drily. "It means we're going the right way."

At last they came to the bottom of the stairs. Two long hallways began at the landing and ran perpendicularly to each other. One hallway had smooth walls, unmarked by doorways or openings of any kind, whilst the other was perforated by openings barred by thick iron gates. It was this hallway from whence came the voices, and Barnabas peered down it fearfully.

"Ack!" he cried, jumping backwards in alarm as a dirty-face man with a knotted beard and sunken eye sockets pressed itself against the nearest of the iron bars. Wild eyes peeped out of the face and stared at Barnabas in mute appeal.

"Ugh," said Barnabas, trying not to make eye contact, "I think it's looking at me."

"*He* is looking at you," said Brynhild. "*That* is a *man* in there, not an *it*."

"Hardly, though," argued Barnabas. "*He* seems no more than an animal. And a rather unpleasant one, at that."

"That's not a very nice thing to say," chided Brynhild. "Who's to say what he's like, or who he was before he ended up here?"

"Well," sniffed Barnabas, "he must have done something quite dreadful to be locked up like this. They *all* must have." He gestured towards the cells, where more faces were beginning to appear, curious about the strange visitors.

"Something dreadful like stealing gold from a goddess?" asked Brynhild, raising an eyebrow.

"Precisely," said Barnabas, missing her point entirely. He

shook his head in dismissal. "Ne'er-do-wells, I say, the lot of them."

Brynhild opened her mouth to retort, but Wilfred hurriedly interrupted her before an argument could break out. "Let's take this other, less *populated*, corridor," he suggested, pointing to the hallway without cells. "Seems like a promising place for a storeroom."

Everyone agreed, and they all followed him down the hall and soon enough they were rewarded with the sight of a heavy, wooden door barred with a great oak beam.

"This must be it," said Brynhild. She took an axe from beneath the folds of her cloak ("Has she been hiding *that* all along?" whispered Barnabas to Wilfred, astounded) and made short work of the oak beam. She pushed open the door, and they all excitedly pushed to be the first to see what was within. After a certain amount of jostling (and no small amount of elbowing), they all managed to stick their heads into the door.

What they saw before them made all three of them gasp in awe. A small warren of rooms lay behind the door, and all, it seemed, were filled to the brim with gold and jewels and various other precious objects.

Brynhild was the first to recover herself. "We should hurry," she said. "Before anyone sees us." So saying, she maneuvered her way between heaps of gold and chests of silver to investigate the room to the left.

Wilfred followed suit. "I'll take the room to the right, then," he said. "We'll work faster if we split up." The two of them were soon hard at work collecting as much gold as they could stuff into their pouches and pockets and anywhere else they could think to put it.

Barnabas, however, was too taken aback by the wealth laid out before him, and merely stood where he was, ogling the sparkling riches.

"How much do you think we should take?" called out Wilfred.

"As much as we can carry," said Brynhild.

"Do you think Fafnir will be satisfied with that?" asked

Wilfred.

"I hope so," said Brynhild. "I would hate to have to come back and do this twice."

There was a great deal of tinkling as Wilfred rustled about. "Only gold, do you say? Or ought we to include some of these rubies and diamonds and such, as well?" he said.

"Ahem," whispered Barnabas suddenly. His two companions were too intent on their doings, however, to hear him.

"I think gold will suffice," said Brynhild.

"Ahem, ahem!" hissed Barnabas, a bit more urgently. Still, his companions ignored him as they sorted through the storerooms.

"It's only that there's a truly magnificent diamond here, and it might perhaps increase our odds of gaining Fafnir's satisfaction," said Wilfred.

"Turnips!" yelled Barnabas, somewhat hysterically.

"What?" said Brynhild and Wilfred in unison.

"This is not where the turnips go!" said Barnabas. "Oh dear, this is not at *all* where the turnips go."

"What are you going on about?" said Brynhild. She peered through the doorway of her storeroom to look curiously at Barnabas. Barnabas had turned white as the flesh of a turnip, and was gesticulating wildly down the hallway.

"Turnips! Oh turnips!" wailed Barnabas. "We should go to the kitchens at once, I say!"

"Nonsense," said Brynhild. "Wilfred, I think you are right. Grab that diamond and then we can be on our…"

"Be on your what?" said a silky, familiar voice, just as a heavily armed guard appeared in the doorway and grabbed Barnabas roughly by the arm. Several more guards crowded along beside the first, blocking the doorway and trapping Wilfred and Brynhild inside.

"Freya," said Brynhild flatly. "Oh no."

"Oh no, indeed," agreed Barnabas sadly.

Chapter Ten

Brynhild made an attempt to explain the suspicious circumstances, but Freya disgustedly waved her excuses away.

"You're standing in my storeroom, with your pockets full of my gold," pointed out Freya.

"But..." said Brynhild.

"But nothing," said Freya firmly, narrowing her eyes.

The grumpy woman from the upstairs corridor stood behind the guards, nodding with knowing satisfaction and talking to Freya and the guards.

"So I says to myself, '*Self*, them fellows in the hallway with that apple cart were sort of queer, ya know?' And so I thinks to myself that I ought go see what's takin' 'em so darn long gettin' to the kitchens with them apples, so I go back to see what's what and there's that cart, settin' all by itself just as pretty as ye please, with no queer fellows anywhere around. So then I thinks that they must be up to no good, bein' so queer and all and just leavin' them apples all alone like that, which nobody who's right in the head would ever do. Which is why I thought, well, I ought'n to go tell somebody, now shouldn't I? Which is just what I done, too. And just look! Here they are, stealin' and all, just like I says they would."

She looked around proudly, as though she had just performed a feat of remarkable heroism and was waiting for someone to pin an honorary medal to her dirty old apron. No one did so, of course, and so she was left disappointed.

The three companions were taken into custody and hustled off to the dungeons where they were all placed in separate cells, with no further ado (aside, of course, from Barnabas, who could be heard struggling and trying to convince the guards that they had merely been attempting to deliver turnips and nothing more, thereby explaining his earlier seemingly nonsensical outburst about turnips. Then, when it became clear that his captors were implacable and disinclined to believe the turnip subterfuge, Barnabas could be heard wailing for Wilfred. As the three of them were whisked farther and farther away from each other, however, and he could no longer hear Wilfred's answering cries, Barnabas desisted at last and merely hung limply in the guards' grasp).

To his complete horror, Barnabas was roughly shoved into the cell that contained the prisoner with the dirty face, knotted beard, and wild eyes.

"Oh dear me, no!" he cried. "You cannot lock me up with this ruffian!"

"I'm not really a ruffian, you know," said the dirty-faced man.

"Which ruffian would you prefer to be locked up with?" asked one of the guards, mockingly.

"I would prefer *no* ruffian, if you would be so kind," said Barnabas. "Really, I would prefer not to be locked up at all, if it's all the same to you."

"Sorry," said the guard, "but the whole 'not getting locked up with ruffians' thing is reserved for people who don't try to steal Freya's gold."

"But there are extenuating circumstances," said Barnabas. "I certainly don't deserve to be locked in with this scallywag."

"Really, all this name-calling is getting a bit insulting," said the prisoner.

"Tell it to the judge," said the guard, locking the metal door to the cell.

Barnabas grasped hold of the bars and pressed his face against the cold metal. "Please, oh please!" he cried. "You cannot leave me here! He'll tear me in two! He'll eat me alive! He'll...he'll...I can't even imagine the dreadful things he might do!"

"I'm actually quite nice, once one gets to know me," said

the prisoner.

"Should have thought of that before you became a thief," said the guard. Then the guards walked away, leaving Barnabas alone with his filthy cellmate.

"What are you going to do to me?" cried Barnabas, eying the man suspiciously.

"Uh, nothing?" said the man.

"Hmmph!" said Barnabas. "I'll be the judge of that." He looked the man up and down. "What *are* you, anyway? A murderer? A thief? A *debaucher*?" He shuddered.

"I'm a market manipulator," replied the man calmly.

"A what?" asked Barnabas. "I don't know what that is, but it must be *dreadful*."

"Oh, yes," said the man. "It's a terrifying crime. I worked for a group of grain farmers, and I attempted to convince Freya that the wheat supply was far less than what it really was, so as to drive up the price of wheat."

"You fibbed about how much *wheat* you had for sale?" asked Barnabas incredulously. The man nodded. "Well, that doesn't sound terribly dangerous," said Barnabas.

"Not at all," said the man. "Although *Freya* thought it was rather serious."

"How long have you been here?" asked Barnabas curiously. He edged over closer to the man, no longer afraid. He breathed in and got a nose-full of the prisoner's smell, however, so he scooched a bit farther back again.

"Five years, give or take," said the man.

"Five years!" gasped Barnabas. "For *wheat*?" The man nodded again. "But that's preposterous!" said Barnabas. "It's...it's...egregious!"

"I agree," said the man. "But Freya doesn't like to be swindled."

Barnabas sat down heavily. "I'm doomed," he said sadly. "I tried to steal gold from Freya, and now I'll be here forever."

The prisoner sat down beside Barnabas. "Well," he said, "since you're doomed, we may as well be friends. My name is Helg."

"How do you do, Helg?" replied Barnabas politely. "My name is Barnabas."

"So why were you stealing Freya's gold?" asked Helg.

"Because a dragon made me," said Barnabas.

"Huh?" said Helg. "I'm not certain *that* makes any sense to me at all."

"It's quite simple, really," said Barnabas, with a slight air of superiority. He turned to face Helg and began telling his tale with more than a little relish. "You see, Fafnir, who is the king of the dwarves, but somehow also a dragon, of course, demanded that we do so, in exchange for a bowl that could catch the poison from the snake that is dripping on Loki's forehead, which is causing him to thrash about and make earthquakes happen, which will eventually free Loki from his bonds and thereby bring about Ragnarok, although exactly *how* that will happen I'm not entirely clear on, but I *am* clear as to the fact that Odin hired us to stop Ragnarok, or at least slow it down; there's some nonsense about it being preordained and what-not but still, I take my responsibilities most seriously, which means that I had no choice but to steal Freya's gold, do you see?"

"Huh," said Helg again, scratching his beard. "I suppose so. Or, at least, I'll take your word for it."

"But the thing is," continued Barnabas. "The *thing* is that I seem to have botched things up quite a bit. And not just by being thrown into a dungeon. I, er, accidentally did something quite dreadful."

"Oh, come now!" said Helg. "I'm sure it couldn't have been *that* bad."

Barnabas heaved a heavy sigh and slumped his shoulders; indeed, he looked so dejected that he seemed about to sink into the very floor itself. "But it *is* that bad," he said after a long pause. "You see, I alerted Fafnir to the existence of a town wherein was kept a beautiful golden statue…"

"Why on earth would you do *that*?" exclaimed Helg. "Everyone knows a dragon is greedy for gold, and will stop at nothing to get more of it."

"Well," huffed Barnabas, "'*everyone*' didn't tell me about

that, did they? And I didn't *mean* any harm. How was I to know what would happen?"

"So what *did* happen?" asked Helg, more gently.

"Fafnir burned the village and took the statue," answered Barnabas miserably.

Helg shuddered sympathetically. "Well, if you didn't know about dragons, I suppose it could be called an honest mistake," he said.

Barnabas sighed again, and slumped down even further. "I suppose," he said sadly. "But it really does make one feel terribly guilty to see a town all burnt up because of something that one has said." He paused. "And, to tell the truth, it's not the first time I've inadvertently caused the destruction of a village. There was a thing in Egypt, with a flood and a great lot of crocodiles..." Distraught, Barnabas buried his face in his hands.

Helg patted him awkwardly on the shoulder. "There, there," he said. "Now, I hardly know you, but you seem like a nice enough fellow. I'm sure you didn't mean for any of those things to happen."

"It is terribly hard for me, all this misfortune," bemoaned Barnabas. "At least when I was still, well, *alive*, I suppose you could say, and working as an ordinary detective in Marylebone, my blunders were on a much smaller scale."

"Oh?" inquired Helg politely. "How so?"

"Well, back then, I only ever caused the untimely demise of one person at a time," said Barnabas. "Purely *accidentally*, of course."

"Of course," said Helg politely.

"But now I seem to have a penchant for setting certain events in motion, still purely accidentally, mind you, that result in quite a bit more, er, *carnage*," said Barnabas sadly.

"But if you didn't mean for those things to happen..." began Helg.

"Oh, I do so miss my old life," said Barnabas. "I had a cosy office in Marylebone, with a housekeeper, and my assistant Wilfred, of course."

"Sounds lovely," said Helg.

"And then we were whisked away on a most extraordinary case. It was in Egypt, you see. Or, at least, the afterlife of Egypt, because, of course, we were dead by then…"

"Aren't we all," commiserated Helg.

"And I had a special lady friend once, too," confessed Barnabas shyly. "Bindi was her name."

"Where is she now?" asked Helg.

"She's still in Egypt, I suppose," said Barnabas sadly. "Whilst I, of course, am here."

"What happened? Will you go to see her again, do you think?"

"I think I shall be lucky if I ever see the outside of this cell, don't you think?" said Barnabas.

"Well, perhaps Freya will be merciful," said Helg, but his tone made it clear that he did not believe that would be the case at all.

"Ah, well," said Barnabas. "Yes. Perhaps. But even so, Bindi is *there*, whilst my duties would have me *here*, in the nine worlds. And even were that not the case, it would *still* be unthinkable, impossible, even, for Bindi and I."

"Why so?" asked Helg.

"Because she is a *mouse,* of course," replied Barnabas. Seeing Helg's startled expression, he hurried to explain himself. "As was I, at the time."

"You're a *mouse*?" said Helg disbelievingly.

"I *was* a mouse," corrected Barnabas, with exaggerated patience. "Or, more precisely, I was temporarily possessed of a mouse head. Things are quite a bit strange in Egypt, you know."

"Sounds like it," said Helg.

"But now I shall never see Bindi again, I am sure," said Barnabas. "Nor my office in Marylebone, nor my housekeeper, nor any sort of proper civilization at all, it seems. And I seem to keep making people go dead, although if they're already dead, I suppose I'm making them go dead all over again, which could be worse, if you really think on it, to be dead not just *once* but *twice*." Tears welled up in his eyes as he contemplated the enormity of it all.

"But you didn't mean those people any harm?" said Helg.

"Of course not!" said Barnabas.

"And dragons are known for being rather tricky," said Helg. "There is no shame in being bamboozled by one, especially if you don't know what to expect."

"Exactly my point!" exclaimed Barnabas. "I've never spoken with a dragon before, so how was I to know what he'd do? Surely it isn't my fault. Is it?"

"I think not," said Helg supportively.

"Still, I would rather that it hadn't have happened at all," said Barnabas.

"I have an idea. Why don't you tell me about how you came to be talking to Fafnir in the first place?" suggested Helg. "Perhaps talking it out will make it all come clear, and mayhap soothe your conscience a bit as well."

"It's all so very complicated," said Barnabas.

"We have time," said Helg, raising an eyebrow. "I don't have any pressing plans, really. And neither, it would seem, do you."

"Right," said Barnabas. He sighed heavily. "Although I can't see how *talking* about it will help me figure out anything new."

"It'll pass the time," said Helg.

"It might at that," said Barnabas. "Very well. It all began, you see, when Wilfred, Brynhild, and I all went to Loki's cave to interrogate Sigyn…"

"Hold on," said Helg. "Why did you need to interrogate Sigyn?"

"Why, because she's Loki's wife, of course," said Barnabas. Seeing the confused look on Helg's face, he began again. "Someone has stolen the bowl that Sigyn uses to catch the poison that would otherwise drip on Loki's face. Odin hired Wilfred and me to find the bowl and catch the thief, and sent Brynhild with us as a guide, of sorts."

"Why is there poison dripping on Loki's face?" asked Helg, prompting a quizzical look from Barnabas.

"You don't know about Loki's punishment?" he exclaimed. "I thought *everyone* knew that story."

"I *have* been in here an awfully long time," said Helg.

"Ah," said Barnabas. "Well, then. I suppose I must recommence my story, and begin more at the, ah, well, *beginning*."

Helg sat there, waiting expectantly. Barnabas, taking on the role of orator, stood up tall, linked his arms behind his back, and puffed up his chest (as he imagined all great orators must do) and began again.

"Long ago," he said (a bit grandiosely, if truth be told), "Loki the Trickster did purposefully and willfully cause Hod to kill his beloved brother Balder. Since Loki was Odin's favorite son, and greatly loved by all, Odin was greatly wroth, and decreed that Loki be hunted down. Once caught, that foul villain was bound up most, well, *disgustingly*, by chains made of Jutun intestines..."

"Ew," interjected Helg.

"Yes, ew, indeed," agreed Barnabas. "Anyway, the chains are *nearly* unbreakable, but not entirely so. You see, there is a great serpent that hangs over Loki, and that drips its venom down upon the trickster's forehead. Should the venom touch his skin, he would thrash about most alarmingly. This would in turn cause earthquakes, which would eventually grow so great as to break apart Loki's bonds, thereby freeing him and bringing on the advent of Ragnarok."

"The end of the world!" gasped Helg.

"Precisely," said Barnabas. "However, Sigyn has sacrificed herself in order to hold a magical silver bowl over Loki's face, so that she might catch the venom within it and, so doing, prevent Ragnarok. Which is quite remarkable, really, considering that not only was Balder her illicit lover, which was most certainly why Loki wanted him dead, I'm sure, but also because the entrails that Odin used to make Loki's chains were that of her son, Narfi."

"Seems that she might not want to be so helpful, after all that," said Helg, scratching at his beard.

"She might not, at that," agreed Barnabas. "Which is why I knew that she must needs be our primary suspect, for three reasons. Firstly, that Loki caused the death of her lover, and so she must certainly want him to be punished, and not spend the rest of her life preventing the snake's poison from causing him pain. Secondly, that I would think she'd be loath to assist Odin, who used her son most cruelly. And thirdly, that she might indeed wish for Ragnarok to begin, since Balder is supposed to return from Niflheim after the world's end, which means that she may then be reunited with her lover."

"Hmmm," said Helg. "Seems to me that some of those motives might be a bit contradictory."

"Hmmph," said Barnabas. "Poppycock. You only think so because you are not a seasoned detective like myself, and therefore are not so practiced at thinking deductively about many clues at once."

"I *suppose* that could be it…" said Helg doubtfully. "Anyway, what happened when you interrogated Sigyn? Was she guilty in stealing her own bowl?"

Barnabas cast Helg a disparaging look, but continued on with his explanation. "No, it seems that she did not steal the bowl. The poor woman is quite mad, really, and furthermore has no wish for the end of the world, returned lover or no. Which leaves us, then, with so many suspects and a great deal fewer clues." He sighed dramatically at the enormity of his task.

"Who are the other suspects?" asked Helg.

"There's anyone who seeks to profit from Ragnarok," explained Barnabas. "There're those who seek merely to thwart Odin, or to uproot the status quo. And then, of course, there's anyone who loves Balder, and either wishes to avenge him or wants him to be freed from Niflheim."

"Sounds like it could be just about anyone," observed Helg.

"Indeed it does," said Barnabas, "and therein lies our conundrum."

Helg thought it over for a moment. "You know," he said at last, "I'm just a simple prisoner, but it seems to me that Balder's name came up quite a few times in your story. Perhaps you should go pay him a visit."

"Visit Balder?" said Barnabas. "In…in…Niflheim?" He

uncrossed his arms, moved them forward to re-cross them again in front of his chest, and slouched his shoulders nervously.

"If he's as kind as he's rumored to be, and connected to so many of your suspects, then he might have something to offer," said Helg, oblivious to his cellmate's discomfort at the idea of Niflheim.

"Oh dear," said Barnabas. "The idea *does* have merit. Still, I have little wish to go to Niflheim. Isn't that some sort of, um, *pit* in the middle of Helheim, which sounds, in itself, dreadful enough?" He swallowed audibly.

"That's the place," said Helg cheerfully. "All you need to do is go to Helheim and then get past the dragon that guards the entrance to Niflheim." He brushed his hands together, as though that settled *that*.

"Oh, that's all," said Barnabas sarcastically. "But I suppose you are right. Balder is the key to all of this, and we cannot possibly solve the case without speaking to him." He paused, then visibly gathered his courage. He straightened up once more, and lifted his chin as high as it would go. "So, there's nothing for it, then. To Niflheim I go!"

He turned and would have gone to Niflheim that very instant, had he not come up against a very real reminder that he was imprisoned in Freya's dungeons by slamming his upturned nose directly into the bars of the cell.

"Oof!" he cried, rubbing his injured nose. He turned to Helg. "You could have warned me that was there!" he remonstrated.

"How was I to know you'd walk straight into it?" pointed out Helg reasonably. Just then, footsteps and voices sounded in the corridor outside, and soon several figures appeared on the other side of the bars.

"Wilfred! Brynhild!" cried Barnabas, jumping up hastily and running over to grasp the bars of his cell. "No one has ever been more pleased to see someone in all the history of everyone!"

"Are you quite all right?" asked Wilfred. He eyed Helg suspiciously. "Are you unharmed?"

"Unharmed?" asked Barnabas, confused. He followed Wilfred's gaze, and laughed. "Oh, Helg, you mean? He's quite a fine fellow, quite brilliant really, once you get past the smell and what-not."

"I *can* hear you, you know," said Helg.

"But I am beyond famished, and quite thirsty, as well," continued Barnabas. "My kingdom for a proper tea!"

"It's been an hour," pointed out Brynhild. "We've been in the dungeon for an *hour*."

"Still, it's been a *busy* hour," said Barnabas, "and busyness makes a fellow hungry."

"Busy?" asked Wilfred. "How so?"

"Well, I've solved our problem, for one," said Barnabas. "I've figured out how to save the world."

"With my help," added Helg. "Don't forget I helped."

"Yes, yes," said Barnabas. "Helg was a great help, I'm sure. The important thing is that we must be released, so as to put my plan…"

"Our plan," interrupted Helg.

"…into action," finished Barnabas.

"We *are* released, as you can see," said Brynhild. "Whilst you and…" she waved her hand distractedly towards Helg.

"Helg," supplied Helg.

"….were sitting in here talking, *I* was busy working out a deal to get us a hearing with Freya. Syn has generously agreed to represent us, so if you'd just come along, we can get started. Syn is waiting, and we really oughtn't delay."

"Yes, of course, at once," said Barnabas as one of the guards unlocked the bars and allowed him to pass. "May I get some refreshments, please?" he said to the fellow.

"You never did tell me how you came to tell Fafnir about the golden statue!" called out Helg.

"Well thank you very much for reminding me that!" snapped Barnabas. He shook his head and leaned in to Wilfred. "Honestly, do people in dungeons lose all sense of the social niceties?" he whispered loudly.

"I can still hear you," said Helg.

"Oh," said Barnabas. "Quite sorry." He paused for a

moment, thinking on what the proper protocol might be in a case like this. "Very nice to meet you, Mr. Helg. I *do* hope you enjoy your day," he said at last.

"I'm sure my day will be just as fabulous as the last two thousand or so have been," said Helg sarcastically.

"Smashing," said Barnabas. "Now, about that tea…."

They were hustled along the corridor and back up the stairs from whence they had originally come (no one bothered to answer Barnabas' inquiry into tea, which he found exceedingly rude) and then down another corridor, up another flight of steps, and along yet another corridor.

At last they were ushered into a large chamber that was obviously a courtroom of sorts. Long wooden benches had been placed in a series of rows, flanking a wide central aisle. At the head of each of the rows was a shorter bench, each with a high podium just in front of it. And at the very front of the room, perched upon a high dais, was a very imposing wooden desk that clearly served as the judges' bench.

Along the walls at the sides and to the front of the courtroom were pictures and statues depicting varying degrees of justice. Barnabas looked at each of them in turn, his mild interest (and annoyance at having his hunger ignored) quickly turning to nervousness and finally to extreme trepidation.

To his left was a statue of a man in shackles being dragged behind a guard. To his right was yet another man in shackles kneeling with his head bowed, as though pleading for mercy. But the worst was the painting that hung directly behind and above the judges' bench. It depicted a man (shackled, of course), his hands extended in a pleading gesture, whilst a stony faced judge in black robes (who looked suspiciously like Freya; indeed, a bit of feather like the ones Freya had been wearing at their last meeting appeared to peak out from the neckline of her robe) swung an enormous sword above her head. It didn't take much imagination to see that the arc of the sword, once completed, would remove the poor man's head entirely.

Barnabas shuddered. "Horrible!" he said. "Is *that* intended to frighten us? Or is it *really* how prisoners are treated here?"

"I certainly hope not," said Wilfred. He, too, was looking at the painting, and wringing his hands together nervously. "I very much desire to keep my head precisely where it is, thank you very much."

"*Should* we be frightened?" demanded Barnabas of Brynhild. "Oughtn't we to send round for Odin? A telegram, perhaps, or a messenger?" Before she could answer he turned to one of the guards and plucked at his sleeve. "Who do I speak to about sending a message, please?" he asked.

"Hush!" hissed Brynhild. "*Both* of you! Do you *want* to be shackled?" She gestured towards the foot of the nearest bench, and Barnabas and Wilfred saw that there was a metal ring wrapped around it, with a short metal chain and a thing that looked like a handcuff affixed to it.

"I merely wanted to get Odin to…" began Barnabas.

Brynhild cut him off. "To override Freya, and undermine her authority in her own palace?" she suggested. "I'm sure *that* will go over wonderfully." She rolled her eyes.

Barnabas looked to the guard whom he had asked to send a message, and saw that the man was indeed pursing his lips in a most irate sort of way. "Oh," he said. "Er, yes, well. Ahem. Never mind," he finished lamely. The guard merely shook his head in exasperation, but made no move to report Barnabas' faux pas to anyone else.

Barnabas heaved a sigh of relief that was stopped mid-exhale by the arrival of Syn. Dressed, as she had been before, in her severe robes (and with a stern expression on her face), she entered the room through a small side door and marched over to one of the podiums at the front of the room even as the three prisoners were pushed none-too-gently onto the short bench just behind her.

The side door opened once more and Freya appeared (although she was scarcely recognizable, thought Barnabas, with her sober judge's robes and that serious look on her face; still it was clear from the portrait that this was indeed Freya in her role as judge.). A slightly mischievous glint was in her eyes, belying her efforts to appear stately, but the look was a trifle more predatory than the playful one she had worn in her chambers.

Her pet pig, Hildisvini, followed at her heels.

"What, pray, is happ—" began Barnabas.

"Shhh!" whispered Brynhild.

"Shush!" hissed Syn at the same time. Intimidated, Barnabas dutifully shushed.

Freya, meanwhile, had seated herself behind the judges' bench and picked up a ridiculously large gavel. Hoisting it high above her head, she brought it back down sharply upon the hard wood of the desk, making everyone jump with the noise of it. Hildisvini let out a great snort, and looked as though he might jump clear off the ground, if only he wasn't quite so fat. Only Syn was unaffected; she offered not so much as a twitch at the banging of Freya's gavel, and merely stood there staring serenely at the goddess.

"All rise!" called a guard stentoriously. Barnabas, Wilfred, and Brynhild hesitantly started to stand, but the guards directly beside them kept pushing them back down on their benches. Unsure of whether they ought to obey the command of the guard at the door, bidding them to stand, or to comply with the guards at their sides, who were firmly pushing them back down again, they all three ended up moving up and down repeatedly like a family of alarmed hedgehogs popping their heads out of their hidey-holes.

Freya rolled her eyes in exasperation. "Oh, do sit, will you!" she cried. She looked at the guard who had told everyone to stand. "You're meant to say that when I walk in, *not* after I'm seated. We've *talked* about this!"

The guard mumbled incoherently and shuffled his feet. "Well, haven't we?" demanded Freya.

The guard mumbled again, then turned to address the prisoners once more. "You may sit," he said. Gratefully they lowered themselves out of their uncomfortable squatting positions and settled back down on the bench.

Hildisvini likewise laid down beside Freya's bench, and immediately fell asleep. The boar's snores echoed around the chamber. Barnabas looked at Wilfred, and they both raised their eyebrows at the oddity.

Freya rolled her eyes again and shook her head. "Ridiculous," she muttered. Then she brightened. "All right, then, shall we get on with the trial? Is the defense ready?"

"We are," agreed Syn.

"We are?" asked Barnabas.

"Hush!" snapped Syn.

"Is there a problem?" asked Freya archly.

"No problem," said Syn, with a warning glance at Barnabas. "You may state your case."

"Very well," said Freya. "The case against the accused is as follows. They did enter my palace unlawfully, with the intent to steal my gold. They were caught red-handed, or should I say *gold*-handed. As prosecutor, I will present such evidence to myself, as judge, so as to be assured of only one possible verdict: guilty."

"Now just one moment!" protested Barnabas. "You cannot be both prosecutor and judge at once!"

"Objection!" yelled Freya. "The defendant is out of order!"

"Upheld," agreed Freya the judge. "The defendant shall be silent…"

"This is unconscionable!" sputtered Barnabas. "No court of law could possible work this way…"

"…or he shall be thrown back in the dungeon with no further ado," finished Freya.

Barnabas' eyes widened, and he sat back with his lips firmly pressed together to prevent another outbutst.

"Thank you, Judge Freya," said Freya. Barnabas' lips pushed together even more firmly, until they went quite white with the pressure, but he managed to hold his tongue.

Freya, acting as prosecutor, now began to present her case. Mercilessly did she present the details of their wrongdoings, from their subterfuge at the castle gates, to their entering restricted areas of the castle without permission, to their being found in the storeroom with her gold in their hands and pockets.

Gone was the playful, friendly goddess they had met in her

chambers not that long ago. In her place was the most aggressive prosecutor Barnabas or Wilfred had ever seen.

At last, having laid out the last of the damning details, she nodded to Syn. "The prosecution is finished," she said. "The defense may now speak. Syn, you may proceed."

"My defense is simple," said Syn. "They were fated to do all of those things, and so they had no choice but to do them."

Everyone in the courtroom gasped. Guards began to whisper amongst themselves, people seated in the benches behind the accused (who had somehow snuck in during the prosecution, it seemed) held excited conversations behind their hands. Even Hildisvini chirped a few times in his sleep before kicking out a leg spasmodically and settling back down.

Aghast at this unforeseen turn in the trial, Barnabas unpursed his lips and exclaimed in protest. "This is most unfair," he cried. "If I had known that my lawyer would offer a defense of such, such, *poppycock*, I would never have agreed to it!"

"Order, I say!" cried Freya. The command in her voice was undeniable, and the courtroom immediately fell silent.

"Syn," the goddess said at last. "Your client doesn't seem to like his defense."

"He doesn't *have* to like it," said Syn calmly. "It was his fate to steal your gold, and it is his fate to have fate as his only defense."

"Well, of all the most inane things!" exclaimed Barnabas. "I refuse to be a party to this. Je refuse!"

"Oh, do be quiet," whispered Brynhild.

"Are you saying," said Freya to Barnabas, "that it was not your fate that made you steal my gold?"

"The accused will *not* answer that," ordered Syn, with a stern glance at Barnabas.

"Of course I am saying that!" said Barnabas. "The very idea of fate is so unreasonable, so preposterous, that I cannot even fathom how it is possible that we are even discussing it!"

"Perhaps it's best if we allow Syn to handle this," suggested Wilfred carefully, looking from Freya to Barnabas with alarmed eyes.

"So you mock our beliefs?" asked Freya. "And you take full responsibility for stealing my gold? It is your assertion that you took my gold of your own free will?"

Freya looked intently at Barnabas. Her eyes narrowed considerably and one eyebrow twitched upwards, putting Barnabas even more in mind of a feline on the hunt. Indeed, beneath her gaze he began to feel quite a bit like a bug about to have its legs plucked off by a mean-spirited cat.

He shifted uncomfortably in his seat, and began to realize that perhaps he oughtn't to have said anything, after all. He looked desperately to Syn for help.

Syn shook her head in annoyance. "Clearly, he was fated to say such things," said Syn. "In order to fulfill his final destiny."

"Which is?" asked Freya.

"Why, to find Od, of course," replied Syn.

"My husband?" exclaimed Freya. "He is fated to find my husband?"

"Obviously," said Syn. "Together with his companions, of course."

"Of course,' agreed Freya. "Why didn't you just say that before we began?"

"Things must proceed as they will," said Syn.

Barnabas and Wilfred shared a confused glance, unable to fathom the strange twist of logic that somehow connected their theft to this new development of being slated to discover the whereabouts of Freya's prodigal husband Od. They turned to Brynhild, but she appeared as bemused as they were.

"Very well,' said Freya. "The prisoners are freed, providing that they find Od and bring him hence." She brought her gavel down with a great bang, startling everyone once more (excepting for Hildisvini, who simply twitched a bit more in his sleep. Barnabas stared at him curiously, an idea beginning to take hold in his mind).

Freya rose and left the courtroom through the side door, followed by the guards. The onlookers also filed out quickly out of the back doors (looking a bit disappointed; many of them had hoped to see an execution). Syn nodded to Barnabas, Wilfred, and Brynhild before exiting through the side door as well, leaving the confused companions to themselves with only Hildisvini the sleeping pig as company.

"Well, what do we do now?" asked Wilfred.

"I suppose we should go find Od," said Brynhild.

"But what of Balder?" asked Barnabas. "We simply must find him for our case to proceed."

"He *could* prove useful in finding Od, as well," said Brynhild thoughtfully. "But I don't see how we can get to him. Even Hynder can't fly into Niflheim, and there is the matter of the dragon guarding the entrance."

"We might tempt him with food?" suggested Wilfred.

"There is nothing the dragon would like to eat more than two detectives and a Viking lady," said Brynhild.

"A distraction, of sorts, perhaps?" tried Wilfred.

"I fear that whosoever provides the distraction would also then provide dinner for the dragon, if you know what I mean," said Brynhild.

"Surely the creature sleeps?" asked Wilfred.

"Never," said Brynhild. "No one has ever managed to get past him. Ever."

Barnabas, feeling a bit defeated, sat with his chin cradled in his hands and sadly watched Hildisvini jerk and groan in his sleep.

"It is no use," concluded Wilfred sadly. "We must come up with another plan. One that doesn't involve Balder."

Suddenly, Barnabas lifted his head. "The Dark Elves!" he cried.

"Huh?" said Brynhild. She looked to Wilfred, but he simply shook his head, as perplexed as she was.

"The Dark Elves, and the pig, and the dragon!" said Barnabas, nearly yelping in his excitement. He stamped his foot impatiently and pointed at Hildisvini the twitching pig. "Nightmares!"

Chapter Eleven

"Um," said Brynhild. "Do you think you could be a bit more specific?"

"I'm sure I don't know how much more clear I could possibly be," stated Barnabas, still pointing at Hildisvini excitedly. He began to count off the points he had made on his fingers, one by one. "The pig. The Dark Elves. The nightmares. The dragon. See? It's perfectly simple."

"Perfectly obtuse, is more like it," muttered Brynhild.

"What say you?" said Barnabas, affronted. "It's hardly *my* fault that you're too…"

"Perhaps if you slowed down just a bit," interrupted Wilfred diplomatically. "So that we might follow along more easily. Not being privy to the inner workings of your mind, and whatnot, and so on and so forth, you see."

"Well, of course, Wilfred, since you put it so *politely*," said Barnabas, with a snarky glance towards Brynhild. "I'd be happy to help you to understand my deductions."

"How very *kind* of you," retorted Brynhild.

"Yes, indeed," said Wilfred quickly. "I, for one, am most eager to hear the explanation." He gestured for Barnabas to begin with a slightly overdone bow and florid hand gesture. Brynhild rolled her eyes at Wilfred's obsequiousness, but Barnabas beamed.

He straightened his robes and lifted his chin high, like an orator about to deliver a speech (which, in a way, is *exactly* what he was, just now). He looked dramatically down his nose, lips primly pursed, first at Brynhild, then to Wilfred, and then back again, before speaking.

"Ahem," he said at last, once he was certain that he had everyone's attention. "It is all quite simple, really, if one has the mind of a detective, which, of course, I do, or else I wouldn't be here, because I would instead be somewhere *else*, and most definitely *not* being a detective, I suppose…"

"Quite right, quite right," interrupted Wilfred, to hurry him along. "And so, the pig?"

"Of course, I was *getting* to that," said Barnabas. "You see, I noticed right away that the pig was still having nightmares, which put me in mind of something Freya said when first we were in her sitting room. The pig, of course, was sleeping then, as well, and yet was twitching and snorting and behaving exceedingly *oddly* for a sleeping pig. When I inquired about it, she told us that the Dark Elves were giving him nightmares. Do you remember?"

"I do!" said Wilfred. "I do remember her saying *something* about Dark Elves, at least."

"The Dark Elves are nasty creatures, who delight in giving nightmares to animals. What possible use could that be to us?" said Brynhild.

"Why, think on it!" said Barnabas, ready to drive home his point. "*What*, pray, is a dragon?"

"A big scaly lizard?" supplied Wilfred, trying to be helpful.

"A thing that could fry us into charcoal if we so much as annoy it?" said Brynhild, less helpfully.

"Yes, yes," said Barnabas impatiently. "I suppose both are correct. But the point is that a *dragon* is an *animal*. Do you see? Do you *see*?"

Brynhild looked confused, but comprehension began to dawn upon Wilfred's face. He furrowed his brow as he concentrated, trying to work it out, and Barnabas smiled proudly at him.

"So," said Wilfred slowly, "Nidhug is a dragon, which is of course an animal. And the Dark Elves give animals nightmares. So…"

"So we get the Dark Elves to give Nidhug nightmares!" exclaimed Barnabas.

"And then," said Wilfred excitedly, "whilst the dragon is dreaming…"

"We sneak right by him!" finished Barnabas. He stopped to regard his rapt audience of two, his face flushed a bit with pride at his own deductive skills.

"But, that is brilliant!" cried Wilfred. "Genius!"

"Well," said Barnabas, shuffling his feet with (mostly) faux modesty, "you are too kind."

"Our problem of how to get to Balder is solved," said Wilfred happily. "Oh, but this is most exciting. Is it not, Brynhild?" He turned to Brynhild, who was chewing thoughtfully on her lower lip.

"It *could* work..." she said at last.

"It *will* work," interrupted Barnabas confidently.

"...but we *do* have to find Od first, for Freya," continued Brynhild.

"But..." protested Barnabas.

"We *must*," insisted Brynhild. "Or would you prefer to try to sneak past a dreaming dragon with an angry goddess on our tail?"

"Oh. Well. Humph," said Barnabas. "I suppose, then, that we can find Od first. And then the dragon, straightaway!"

"Well, yes, although we still need a way to get the Dark Elves to do this for us," warned Brynhild. "And they're not the *easiest* creatures in the worlds to deal with."

"We'll just have to convince them, then," said Barnabas. "I'm sure it won't be so difficult as all that."

"Hmmm," said Brynhild.

"Our problems are solved, then, and our way is set," said Barnabas. "First we find Od, then we go to the Dark Elves."

"I'm not sure it will be so easy as that," said Brynhild carefully. But Barnabas, full of bubbling excitement at what he thought a terrifically clever solution to their problems, was unperturbed by her pessimism.

"When one sees a pig having nightmares, one takes notice, is what I always say," said Barnabas jauntily, despite never having said such a ridiculous thing. "So, with no further ado...to Od!" And with that he spun on his heels and, taking extraordinarily long and determined strides, stalked out of the room.

"Well," admitted Brynhild grudgingly, "I suppose that it is a good plan, after all."

"You see?" replied Wilfred. "I know that you and Barnabas don't always get on quite so well as I might hope, but you must understand that I know him better than anyone, and I know that he is capable of the most remarkable feats. And furthermore, I know that when he becomes all overwrought and overexcited like that, well, it means that something of great genius is about to simply burst right out of him. You oughtn't doubt him so."

"I doubt everyone so," teased Brynhild with a wicked smile. She grabbed Wilfred's hand and squeezed it for a moment before letting it go and hurrying out of the courtroom to follow Barnabas. Wilfred followed behind her, his face as red as an overripe beet.

They had to hurry quite a bit to catch up to the little detective (filled with exuberance, he was still taking those great long strides and had managed to cover a surprising amount of distance with them) but at last Wilfred and Brynhild came up alongside him just as he was preparing to mount Hynder (whom the palace grooms had brought out) all by himself.

"Would you like some help?" asked Brynhild, stifling a laugh at the sight of Barnabas jumping up and down beside Hynder. His robes flapped about rather comically as he tried in vain to gain enough height that he might grab hold of the horse's flanks and thereby heave himself aboard.

"Do I *look* like I need help?" snipped Barnabas. He squatted down in a deep plie, then frog-kicked his legs as powerfully as he could. His feet kicked out to the sides as his arms stretched out as far as they could go above his head. It was a most impressive jump (being rather unused to exercise, it was really quite remarkable that Barnabas was able to jump at all), and Brynhild and Wilfred shared a bemused glance.

Still, it was not enough; even though his head cleared Hynder's back he was unable to gain purchase with his flailing arms and therefore fell heavily back to the ground with a thump.

"Perhaps just a leg up would be of use?" suggested Wilfred.

"Poppycock!" said Barnabas. "I almost had it, just there, didn't you see?" Without waiting for a reply, Barnabas began to bounce up and down in the strangest manner.

"*What* is he doing?" whispered Brynhild, her eyebrows raised so far up her forehead that they threatened to disappear entirely into her hair.

"I'm not certain that I know," replied Wilfred dubiously. "Perhaps a mounting block?" he called out to Barnabas.

"Hah!" cried Barnabas, ignoring Wilfred as he completed one last small bounce and then leapt with surprising grace straight up into the air. At the top of the leap he arced his body into a crescent shape, so that his chest landed squarely on Hynder's back.

He squirmed and wriggled to work himself farther onto the poor, beleaguered horse's back (it was no small thing to have a man of Barnabas' not-inconsequential weight repeatedly flinging himself upon one's spine, after all) but unfortunately could make it only so far before becoming quite stuck, with his head and chest dangling down one side of the horse and his legs down the other, with his bottom end sticking high up towards the sky.

Triumphantly, he lifted his head to call out to his companions. "See?" he said. "It's all about persistence, and building the momentum. I refused to give up, and look where I am now!" His face beamed with pride even as his legs kicked uselessly in the air.

"Dangling like a carcass with your arse in the air?" said Brynhild, laughing. Wilfred delivered her a pointed glance, and she covered her smile with her hand.

"I am most certainly *not* dangling," said Barnabas huffily. "I am instead very nearly *aboard* this horse, as you would see if you had any sense whatsoever." His legs kicked valiantly to and fro as he tried to work one of them up and over whilst leaving the other behind. Wilfred quietly snuck up behind his employer and gave him a gentle push on the behind, helping to slide him into place, then stepped back hurriedly before

Barnabas could turn all the way about.

"There!" exclaimed Barnabas, once he had maneuvered himself into place. "I did it, and without any help whatsoever."

"Well, Wilfred..." she began, then yelped as Wilfred aimed a surreptitious kick at her ankle.

"Yes, Wilfred will need some help in getting up," said Wilfred smoothly.

"Of course, no shame in that. We all learn at our own pace," said Barnabas (somewhat pedantically, thought Brynhild, for someone who had just mounted a horse in such a ridiculous sort of way; Wilfred, of course, was accustomed to his employer's foibles and found Barnabas' prickly and somewhat fragile pride entirely tolerable, if not endearing). "The key, of course," continued Barnabas blithely, "is to never give up. If one is clever and has a will to do something, well, then, one will do it eventually, is what I always say!"

"He certainly does have a certain tenacity about him," admitted Brynhild as she stooped to give Wilfred a leg up.

"Which is very admirable," added Wilfred pointedly.

"It is at that," said Brynhild. She hoisted Wilfred onto Hynder's back and then swung herself up (with a good deal less effort than Barnabas, which made the little detective press his lips tightly together in annoyance).

"What a fustylugs," whispered Barnabas in Wilfred's ear, "showing off like that!" Wilfred, seated between the two, merely sighed and shook his head tiredly. Then, after a few moments of slightly awkward silence, he said more loudly, "Shall we go fetch Od, then?" He thought for a moment. "*Where*, precisely, is Od?"

"Huh," replied Brynhild. "That's a good question."

"To which the answer is...," prompted Barnabas.

"I have no idea, really," said Brynhild.

"Well *I* certainly don't know where he is," stated Barnabas.

"Nor do I," added Wilfred. "And I would be unable to even venture a guess as to his whereabouts, I'm quite sure."

"He could be just about anywhere, in all the nine worlds,"

said Brynhild, rather unhelpfully.

"Well," said Barnabas, "*how*, may I ask, are we to find this person, who might be anywhere at all, doing any manner of thing, with any manner of persons?" He thought, then, of the giants they had met, and, the dwarvish folk, and of the dragons. "Or," he amended, "with any manner of, er, well, not-quite-persons?"

"I suppose," said Brynhild blithely, "that finding Od is a quest that we are fated to embark upon."

"Hmmph!" said Barnabas (who found the Viking preoccupation with the idea of fate and predestination particularly maddening). He closed his eyes and breathed in deeply, collecting his thoughts. "I suppose," he said at last, "that as we have no real information upon which to base our search, we must instead use logic and reason to discover the location of our quarry."

"We might begin by interviewing his friends, to see if they know ought of where he went," suggested Wilfred.

"A fine idea," said Barnabas, "but I suspect that Freya would have already done so, and discovered nothing of any help, else she would not require our assistance in the matter. No, we must be more wily than that." He scrunched up his face, so that he looked as though he had just eaten the world's largest, sourest lemon whole, as he thought through their conundrum.

"I simply can't wait to hear your wily idea," said Brynhild dryly, earning herself another kick in the shin from Wilfred.

"Well, then, you shall be delighted straightaway," said Barnabas (who was so wrapped up in his thinking that he had entirely missed Brynhild's sarcasm and Wilfred's subsequent censure of it). "What, pray, do you know of Od's habits?"

"His habits?" asked Brynhild doubtfully.

"Yes, yes," said Barnabas, waving his hands impatiently. "What sort of place does he frequent? What type of activities does he prefer? And with what sort of person does he enjoy these things?"

"Oh," said Brynhild. "Well, I have heard that he enjoys hunting and drinking quite a bit. But then, so do most

Vikings, really."

"Does he associate with anyone in particular, whilst he hunts and drinks?" asked Barnabas.

"I have seen him in the company of Honir once or twice," said Brynhild.

"Honir, Honir," said Barnabas, tapping his fingers on his chin and thinking. "Why does that name sound familiar?"

"Wasn't that one of the fellows someone mentioned as a possible suspect in the theft of the bowl?" ventured Wilfred. "I cannot remember for the life of me who said it, but I feel certain that is the context in which I heard the name."

"It could be," said Brynhild. "He *is* fated to survive Ragnorok." Her voice, however, sounded doubtful.

"But?" prodded Barnabas.

"But he's ridiculously indecisive," said Brynhild. "He has one opinion one moment, and then another the very next. I cannot imagine him being able to come up with a plot to end the world. Or, I suppose, I can't imagine him *sticking* with the plot."

"But," asserted Barnabas, "if someone else were to think of the plan, and then propose it to him, and lay it out in the most attractive of terms…well, an indecisive fellow may very well go along with whatsoever he is told, might he not?"

"He might," conceded Brynhild. "I hadn't really thought of it like that."

"Which is why *I* am the detective, my dear girl," said Barnabas (a bit smugly, if truth be told). "It is a skill that not everyone possesses; indeed, it must be cultivated over many years of hard work, assuming, of course, one has the proper natural aptitude."

"You can take your natural aptitude and stick it—" began Brynhild.

"So," interjected Wilfred quickly, before a fracas could ensue, "what else do you know about Honir, Brynhild?"

"He's one of the Aesir," said Brynhild. "He was sent here as a hostage after the Aesir and Vanir had their war."

"So he may have a grudge against, well, either side really?" said Wilfred. "Against Odin for *sending* him as a hostage, or against Freya for *taking* him as one?"

"I suppose," said Brynhild doubtfully. "But, as I said, he's so very indecisive…"

"Which makes him a perfect pawn for a nefarious ne'er-do-well's shenanigans," said Barnabas. "And besides, when one hears a man's name come up repeatedly during an investigation, it behooves one to look more closely at that man."

"Maybe," replied Brynhild, "but I have no more idea of where to find Honir than I do of where to find Od."

Barnabas sighed beleaguredly. "I don't suppose Honir enjoys hunting, as well?" he asked.

"Of course, as I said, you'd be hard-pressed to find a Viking who does not," said Brynhild.

"So," continued Barnabas, "perhaps we ought to look in the places where one might go hunting."

"Where we might find either Od, or Honir, or both!" surmised Wilfred excitedly.

"Precisely, my boy," said Barnabas.

"All right," said Brynhild. "It's a plan, at least."

"Where, then, does the hunting occur?" asked Barnabas.

"Pretty much everywhere," said Brynhild.

"Oh dear," said Barnabas.

"Oh dear, indeed," agreed Wilfred.

"But," continued Brynhild, "we *could* visit Skadi."

"Skadi?" asked Barnabas. "Who is…?"

"The goddess of the hunt," said Brynhild. "She'll know where the best hunting is to be had this time of year."

"Then we must needs see her," said Barnabas. "To Skadi!" He paused for a moment. "*Where*, precisely, is Skadi?"

"She's in Midgard," said Brynhild.

"Not anywhere near that terrible cave, with the snake and the crazy lady, I hope?" cried Barnabas in consternation.

"Doubtful," said Brynhild. "My guess is that we'd find her in a tavern. Skadi *does* enjoy her drink."

"Good, then," said Barnabas. "Not that I was afraid to go back to Loki's cave, mind you…"

"Of course not," said Brynhild, with a knowing glance

over her shoulder at Wilfred.

"I'd readily go back in, if need be, and do battle with that snake as many times as is necessary," insisted Barnabas. "Only, if there's no *need* to do so, then there is no *point* in doing it, now, is there?"

"No point whatsoever," said Wilfred. "I, for my part, will much prefer a tavern over a snake-infested cave."

Brynhild shook her head at the silliness of the two detectives, gave Hynder a gentle kick to the flank, and they were off to Midgard once more.

Conversation slowed as they traveled (what with the noise of the wind whistling in their ears along with the need to stay mounted upon Hynder and not lean off in either direction it was quite difficult to hear one another). Within short order, however, they had arrived in Midgard and alighted in front of a tavern.

Though it was daylight still, the tavern was doing a brisk business. Boisterous, rowdy sounds emanated from the open door, putting Barnabas in mind of the rambunctiousness of the crowd in Odin's hall.

"Oh my," he said, with no small degree of trepidation. Nothing made Barnabas so nervous as unruliness (not even snakes, flying horses, or being locked in a dungeon). "It sounds as though the place were filled to the brim with hooligans!"

"And there's the hooligan we're looking for!" said Brynhild cheerfully. "Skadi!" she called out, waving into the darkness within the tavern. "Skadi! Out here!"

To Barnabas' great relief, a woman came to the front door of the tavern. She saw Brynhild, and came outside to meet them where they stood beside Hynder. "Brynhild!" said the woman. "It is good to see you!"

"And you! It's been too long," said Brynhild, giving the woman a warm hug.

The woman looked much the same as the rest of the Viking women they had seen thus far; that is to say, not much different from the men, save for the lack of a beard. She wore long thick robes, and her hair was wild and stuck out in every which direction. Her skin was tanned and lined, and her eyes were sharp and keen, like a predator's.

Indeed, thought Barnabas, *most* of the people (or people-like creatures) they had met in the nine worlds thus far put him a bit in mind of predators, so forthright were their stares and so *appraising* their demeanor. Even the way people walked here seemed more assertive, more aggressive, even, than the polite, quiet way in which a proper English person moved about.

He suppressed a shudder and fervently hoped that none of them ever thought of himself or Wilfred as prey.

Luckily, Skadi proved friendly. When Brynhild pointed out the two detectives and told Skadi their names, the goddess lumbered over and gave Barnabas a hearty (and altogether rather stifling) bear hug. Barnabas thought that he would have much preferred to simply bow and say "how do you do", but he was glad, at least, that no one was throwing him in jail or burning down quaint little village, so he merely smiled mildly and watched in sympathy as Wilfred suffered the same treatment.

"So, Brynhild," said Skadi, once she had completed her friendly suffocation of Wilfred, "what brings you to Midgard?"

"We are looking for Freya's husband," replied Brynhild.

"Od?" said Skadi. "Bad luck, then! You've just missed him."

"He was here?" said Barnabas, leaning forward eagerly. "Do you know where he went? Do you know the identities of his companions, if any?"

"I do know the answer to both of those things," replied Skadi, with a hard glance at Barnabas. "But first you must answer *my* question: *what* is all that to you, and *why* are you so eager to know?"

"We are detectives, on official—" began Barnabas indignantly.

"It's for Freya," interrupted Brynhild. She smiled conspiratorially at Skadi. "You know how she hates when Od takes off like this." Barnabas huffed, but Wilfred shook his head to dissuade him from speaking any further so he merely pressed his lips together in disapproval.

Skadi laughed, Brynhild's words and manner having put her at ease once more. She whistled through her teeth and said, "Don't I know it. She really ought to keep a tighter leash on her husband."

"A tighter leash!" exclaimed Barnabas, outraged. "How dare...ow!" he cried, as Wilfred stepped heavily on his toe. "What*ever* are you about, Wilfred?" said Barnabas plaintively, hopping about wildly as though he might hop entirely away from the pain of his stubbed toe.

Wilfred said nothing, but pulled a dramatic face and nodded jerkily in the direction of Skadi whilst shaking his head even more emphatically.

Skadi watched them, her head tilted and her eyes narrowed. At last she turned to Brynhild. "Odd little fellows, aren't they?" she said.

Brynhild sighed and shook her own head. "Don't I know it," she replied, making Skadi laugh once more.

The two women talked, then, of Od and his whereabouts, whilst Barnabas and Wilfred argued over the injured toe. Skadi finally went back inside, and Brynhild began walking towards the back of the tavern.

"Wait, where are you going?" called Barnabas, seeing her leave. "We mustn't leave! We haven't found out about Od's whereabouts, yet!"

"He's in Midgard Forest," said Brynhild calmly.

"What?" sputtered Barnabas. "*How* did you come by *this* information?"

"Skadi told me," said Brynhild. "While you two were arguing and stomping on each other's feet."

"Oh," said Barnabas, sharing a chastened look with Wilfred. "Well, then. Good work, I suppose."

"You're welcome," said Brynhild.

"Thank you?" said Barnabas. "Er, I mean, yes, thank you very much."

Brynhild sighed again. "Shall we?" she said. "Midgard Forest is just behind the tavern. We can take that trail over there."

Barnabas looked to where she gestured, and eyed the dark shadows beneath the enormous trees warily. "Mightn't we ride Hynder?" he suggested. "Because, er, well…"

"Because we can ride faster than we can walk?" supplied Wilfred helpfully.

"Precisely!" agreed Barnabas, even as the howl of a wolf echoed out from the depths of the forest.

"And because Hynder can run faster than a wolf, whereas we cannot?" added Wilfred.

"Yes, yes," said Barnabas, nodding his head vigorously. Another wolf added its voice to the first's, and Barnabas suppressed a nervous twitch. Seeing Brynhild's skeptical (and somewhat judgemental, he thought) expression, he tried to put a brave face on things and appeal to her sense of logic. "Good point, that," he said. "Not that we'd necessarily be *running*, precisely, indeed it may very well be the *wolves* who are running from *us*, as we are certainly nearly as fearsome as they, although it is always prudent to have several plans in place at once, just in case of, say, a *particularly* aggressive wolf, who may or may not recognize quite *how* fearsome we really are, and might, as such, seek to make a morsel of one or all of us…" Yet another howl sounded from within the trees (and not too terribly far away, either, thought Barnabas, with no small amount of trepidation). He hastened to add, "It is, perhaps, prudent to be mounted on a flying horse when one encounters a particularly aggressive *pack* of wolves, is what I always say."

Brynhild shrugged. "That's a wonderful idea," she said. "But Hynder can't fly through all those trees, and the undergrowth is too thick to risk his legs with. So Hynder will stay here, and we'll just have to walk. I don't think it's terribly far to the nearest hunting lodge, anyway, which is probably where we'll find Od, or at least some news of him."

"Splendid," muttered Barnabas, dropping his pretense. "It will be quite comforting to know that we're *not too terribly far* from the hunting lodge whilst we are being devoured by wolves."

"Well," said Brynhild doubtfully, "I can't see how it would make much difference *where* we're devoured. Seems like it would be equally unpleasant in one location as much as another."

"I'm sure I would prefer not to be devoured at all, whatsoever," sniffed Barnabas.

"As would I," agreed Brynhhild. "But if we're fated to be eaten by wolves, then eaten by wolves we shall be." She paused, then brightened. "If you're eaten, then you might very well end up in Helheim with Balder. Problem solved!" She slapped her hands together as though brushing crumbs off of them, and strode off down the trail.

She was quickly swallowed by the gloomy shadows as Barnabas and Wilfred prevaricated at the wood's edge.

"Well," said Barnabas. "I suppose there's nothing for it but to follow her." To his credit, his voice trembled only the slightest bit, although his knees were in danger of knocking together, so shaky were they.

Wilfred took a deep breath, then exhaled, marshalling his own courage. "I suppose so," he said. "Besides, it's probably best if we stay close to Brynhild. Safer, I mean to say."

"Safer, perhaps, but also more grating to the nerves," said Barnabas. "I know that she has been of immense help, but all her talk of fate puts me quite out of temper, I must confess."

"Well," said Wilfred, "I for one find the idea of fate and predestination quite fascinating. And you cannot deny that she is unflappably brave."

Barnabas looked quizzically at his friend, for the younger man's face had taken on a funny sort of bemused expression that Barnabas found impossible to read. Seeing Barnabas' scrutiny, Wilfred flushed and turned away. "We ought to hurry," he said quickly. "We don't want to fall behind."

Then he, too, disappeared beneath the trees, leaving Barnabas to scurry after him.

The two detectives hurried down the trail after Brynhild, with the near-constant howling of the wolves giving speed to their feet. Indeed, each time the wolves cried out, so, too, did both Barnabas and Wilfred. They scurried faster and faster as the wolves seemed to draw closer and closer, each trying to put the other between himself and the wolf pack (without meaning to, of course, since neither would have willingly put the other in danger; however, the reflexes of fear are powerful and nearly uncontrollable under such circumstances). They bumped into one another and clutched at each other's robes and tripped each other's feet with their wild, erratic steps, so that they advanced down the path, not in a straight line, as would have been more efficient, but in a sort of zig-zagging, lurching pattern punctuated by the occasional full circle when the howls sounded particularly threatening and so sent them into near panic.

When they emerged at last into a clearing, where Brynhild stood waiting for them, they nearly fell, so tangled up were their feet and arms. She looked at them, wondering what they were about, then shook her head. "What are you...oh, never mind," she said. "We've reached the hunting lodge, and it looks like there are people within."

"Oh, thank heavens," cried Barnabas, too relieved to pretend at bravery.

"Best hurry inside before those wolves eat you," teased Brynhild. But Barnabas was already scrambling across the clearing as fast as his little legs would take him, towards the lodge and away from the wolves.

Wilfred, feeling a good deal less frightened now that Brynhild was next to him (he suspected she would know how to comport herself effectively in case of a wolf attack), followed at a more relaxed pace. Indeed, as they approached the steps that led up to the long porch that fronted the lodge, he paused.

"Perhaps we ought to have a plan, of sorts," he suggested. "Rather than simply bursting into the place, all a-panicked, you know."

"I figured we'd just ask around, see if anyone has seen Od," said Brynhild.

"I wonder, though," mused Wilfred, "if a bit of subterfuge might prove more effective?"

"Why so?" asked Brynhild. "They've either seen him or

they haven't, and if they have, they'll either tell us or they won't. I can't see how subterfuge would change that."

"Well," said Wilfred, "if Od were to be, say, hiding, from his wife, you know, then perhaps his hunting friends might not tell agents of his wife his whereabouts. However, if we were to be, instead, friends of Od, and looking for him to propose, for example, a hunting trip…" he trailed off, allowing Brynhild to reach the logical conclusion.

"Ohhh," said Brynhild admiringly. "That is very clever." She nodded with approval. "I think you are right. From this moment forth we are simply friends of Od, hoping to whisk him off for some fun." A burst of rowdy laughter emanated from the lodge, interrupting her for a moment. "Perhaps," she continued, "we'd best go in, before Barnabas gets himself into a pickle. I have a feeling that a room full of drunk hunters might make him just a little bit *nervous*."

Wilfred agreed, and together they stepped onto the lodge's porch. However, by the time he and Brynhild opened the door to the lodge, Barnabas was already inside and seated at a table with two very rough-looking women, Thor's son Modi, and a remarkably long-legged fellow, who was apparently having an impossible time at deciding between two horns of ale.

The lodge, filled as it was with Viking hunters in various stages of drunkenness, was quite noisy. The people at the table at which Barnabas was seated were, however, easily the loudest of the bunch. They laughed uproariously as they shouted and waved their arms, signaling for more ale as they apparently reenacted some hunting adventure or another with great animation.

Incredibly, Barnabas himself had already somehow procured for himself a horn of ale, and was in the process of drinking the entire thing down in one gulp when he saw Wilfred and Brynhild at the door.

"Hullo!" he called. "What took you so long? Over here, over here!" He put the empty horn down on the table, where it was promptly filled by a serving boy who carried a large flask about for just that purpose.

Wilfred and Brynhild came up to the table, quizzical looks on their faces. "What are you doing?" whispered Wilfred in Barnabas' ear. "Have you forgotten we're here to look for Od?"

"Of course not, my boy," replied Barnabas, wiping ale froth from the tips of his mustache. He was whispering far too loudly (Wilfred suspected that his employer was beginning to be a bit *drunk*, if truth be told), but no one seemed to pay him any mind, so engrossed were they in their ale horns and their raucous conversation. He leaned in to Wilfred and stage-whispered, "Saga and Fulla and Modi just returned from a fishing trip with Od. Can you believe the luck? And they were just about to tell me the story, about the fish they caught…"

"It was as big as Barnabas!" yelled one of the women.

"As big as me, can you believe it?" said Barnabas.

"Not really," muttered Brynhild.

"I'm sure that's splendid," said Wilfred, "but do they know where Od is?"

"Patience, Wilfred!" said Barnabas. "They'll tell us, I'm sure. In due time, in due time." He leaned even closer, and said, with a conspiratorially wink at Wilfred, "And *that* fellow right there is none other than Honir. And we were just looking for him, too, which I told him, to which he replied, 'well, you've found me, then, haven't you!' What luck, I say!"

"Yes, yes," said Wilfred quickly, "but I think we were, perhaps, hoping to play our cards a bit closer to the vest. To be, perhaps, a bit more *subtle* in our questioning?"

"Subtle, schmubtle," said Barnabas, waving his now empty horn in the air for another refill. "No need for subtlety here! They're all friends of ours, and our mission, they've assured me of such. You've met Modi, of course, at Odin's hall. And this, you see," he said, pointing to one of the women," is Saga, who is the best of friends with Odin. And *this,"* he continued, pointing at another of the women, "is… er, ah, let's see…"

"Fulla," said the woman in question. "I'm Frigga's maidservant."

"A maid!! Do you see?" exclaimed Barnabas happily. "Maids always know more than they let on, you know."

"Yes, we do," agreed Fulla. "Loads more."

For some reason the group found this exchange hilarious, and everyone (excepting for Wilfred and Brynhild, who were still terribly confused and more than a little alarmed) laughed uproariously.

"Come, sit," said Barnabas scooting his stool over to make room for his friends. "Modi was just telling us how he nearly caught a moose…"

"I would have had him, too," said Modi.

"We know," said Saga sarcastically. "If only you'd had your father's hammer, right?"

"Well, it's not fair," said Modi petulantly. "He could let me *borrow* it sometimes, you know."

"Not till Ragnarok," teased Honir, looking up from the table, where he was still apparently debating between one horn of ale and the other. "Then you can get all the mooses you can eat."

"Bah!" said Modi. "I wanted *that* one."

"Modi and Honir have been talking quite a bit about what could be done with that hammer," said Barnabas. "It's very impressive. You've got to hear it." He turned to face Modi, and asked cheerfully, "What is it you were saying, Modi, about the hammer?" He waggled his eyebrows suggestively at Wilfred, who wondered if his employer was not nearly as intoxicated as he made himself out to be.

"Well," said Modi, "for starters I'd be a much better hunter."

"Very important in the Viking world, I think," said Barnabas.

"Yes!" said Modi. "And I would be nearly invincible!"

"A better fighter than you are now?" asked Barnabas, his eyes widened as though in innocent admiration.

"So much better!" said Modi.

"And don't forget," added Honir, trying to take a swig out

of both horns at the same time. "what you could do in Jutunheim…"

"Ooooh," said Barnabas. "The place with the giants?"

"I could rule it!" boasted Modi. "As I was meant to!"

Saga and Fulla rolled their eyes. "Prideful idiot," said Saga, shaking her head. "Can't even get his own moose for dinner and he wants to rule the giants."

"Well," muttered Modi, "I *could* if I only had that hammer."

"Which you don't," said Saga "So can we please change the subject? I'm tired of all this male boasting."

Triumpantly, Barnabas reached for his newly filled ale horn. Brynhild, however, deftly intercepted it, earning herself a glowering glance from the little detective. "Yes, let's change the subject," said Brynhild. "Back to Od, perhaps. You say you last saw him on a fishing boat?"

"Well, sort of," said Fulla, looking down guiltily.

"What do you mean 'sort of'?" demanded Brynhild.

Fulla sighed. "He was there, on the boat, you see," she said. "And then he wasn't."

"Meaning?" prodded Brynhild.

"Might as well just be out with it," said Saga pragmatically. She turned to Brynhild. "He must have fallen overboard. I was busy with my Barnabas-sized fish, and the next thing I knew Od was in the water."

"And then Ran got him," added Fulla.

"Ran?" asked Barnabas and Wilfred in unison.

"The goddess of the sea," said Brynhild grimly. "Od is at the bottom of the sea."

"Oh dear," said Barnabas.

"Oh dear, indeed," agreed Wilfred.

Chapter Twelve

Saga, Fulla, and Modi began to argue amongst themselves over whose fault it was that Od had fallen overboard. Meanwhile, Barnabas, Brynhild, and Wilfred hastily crept away once the others' attention was fixed firmly upon each other.

"Well, Barnabas," said Brynhild, once they were safely ensconced in a relatively quiet corner, alone. "You certainly know how to get yourself into trouble, don't you?"

"I most certainly do not know anything of the kind!" huffed Barnabas. "Any *trouble* I was in was quite purposeful, I assure you."

Brynhild frowned. "That's sort of exactly what I just said," she said.

"'Tis not," muttered Barnabas petulantly. "'Tis entirely the *opposite*."

"No, you see, it's the *same*. I said…" began Brynhild.

"I think the point is," interrupted Wilfred smoothly, "that we have now found out a good deal of information." He turned to Barnabas. "Good acting job, that. You had me convinced that you were three sheets to the wind, for a moment."

Barnabas lifted his nose into the air so that he might gaze down at Brynhild with an air of triumph. Then he hiccupped, blushed with embarrassment, and tried to appear as sober as Wilfred apparently thought him. (Unfortunately he did so by sitting as bolt-upright as was humanly possible whilst holding his eyes as widely open as they could go, blinking slowly all the while. In the end, the effect was more one of a groundhog that had just been startled awake, more than one of a clever, confident, and entirely sober detective.)

"Yes, well," said Wilfred diplomatically, seeing Barnabas' efforts. "Perhaps a nice drink of cold water?" He signaled for the serving boy, and once a glass of water had been brought to all he continued. "So," he said, "we now know, for one thing, that Modi cannot possibly be involved in the theft of Loki's bowl, as he has a strong alibi."

"Hmmm," said Barnabas.

"Hmmmm?" asked Wilfred.

"It's just that, well, something didn't sit right with me. Something with the way Modi and Honir spoke was a bit, er, *off*, I suppose you could say."

"I agree that Modi clearly harbors a great deal of resentment towards Thor," said Wilfred, "especially in regards to that hammer. And Honir did seem to instigate those feelings quite a bit. But one cannot discount the fact that both of them were fishing with Od, Saga, and Fulla at the time of the crime."

"Yes, well, you know what I always say," said Barnabas. Wilfred and Brynhild merely looked at him, obviously not knowing what, in particular, he always said that applied to this moment. "It's always the maid," said Barnabas impatiently. "'It's always the maid', is what I always say. And Fulla is a maid, is she not?"

"But she's Frigga's maid," interjected Brynhild. "And Frigga is Odin's wife. Why in nine earths would Odin's wife's maid get involved with a plot to end the world?"

"Why wouldn't she?" demanded Barnabas, somewhat nonsensically. As there was no way to answer that question, Brynhild remained silent, shaking her head in perplexity. Barnabas sniffed. "See?" he said. "You cannot say. And I'm sure that Wilfred sees my point as well."

"Ahhh," said Wilfred.

"Wilfred?" said Barnabas. "You *do* agree, do you not?"

"I'm sure that what you say is *possible*," said Wilfred carefully. "But I also think it would be, um, *prudent* to keep our minds open to other possibilities as well."

"Et tu, Wilfred, et tu?" cried Barnabas. "I expect *Brynhild* to disagree with me, since disagreement is what she does best, but you?"

"Hey!" protested Brynhild.

"I'm merely suggesting that we investigate all angles," said Wilfred. "Just as you taught me."

"Huh," said Barnabas grumpily. "I suppose I *did* teach you that."

"And I was remembering how well it worked for us in Egypt, when you abandoned your initial suspect and followed a new line of inquiry."

"Well, it did at that," said Barnabas, still not quite mollified.

An awkward silence descended upon the trio, until Brynhild piped up. "It's all well and good," she said, "to argue about suspects, but we do have a more *immediate* problem."

"Which is?" prompted Barnabas dourly.

"That Od is at the bottom of the sea," she replied. "And if we don't return him to Freya, she'll throw us back in the dungeon for a very long time."

"Then we shall simply have to go fetch him," said Barnabas, simply.

"Oh?" said Brynhild sarcastically. "Is that all? Shall we turn into fish and swim down to him? Or shall we ask the Sun to dry up all the water?"

Barnabas thought for a moment. Indeed, his brow was furrowed so deeply, and his expression was so intense, that Wilfred and Brynhild began to fear that he might be in the midst of an apoplexy.

"Is he all right?" whispered Brynhild to Wilfred, after several minutes had passed thusly.

"I think so," said Wilfred doubtfully. "He's either thinking very hard, or is quite ill."

"Should we do something?" asked Brynhild.

"I'd hate to interrupt him if he's thinking," said Wilfred, "and irritate him further. But on the other hand he *did* drink far more ale that what he is accustomed to, so perhaps we *ought* to do something."

"What should we…" began Brynhild. She was unable to

finish, however, because at that very moment Barnabas let out a triumphant cry.

"Aha!" yelled Barnabas quite loudly (indeed, if they had been in any other place, any *civilized* place, that is, he would have drawn quite a bit of attention to himself with that yell; they were, however, in a hunting lodge full of drunken Vikings, so that his cry merely blended in with the general din).

"Aha, what?" inquired Brynhild.

"We shall indeed ask the Sun for help!" exclaimed Barnabas. "And the Moon as well!"

"I'm not certain I follow," said Wilfred uncertainly. Brynhild merely shook her head, as confused as Wilfred.

"Don't you people have a god or goddess of the sun and moon?" asked Barnabas.

"Well, yes," said Brynhild. "Sol is the goddess of the sun, and Mani is the god of the moon. They both have chariots that fly through the sky, pulling the sun and moon behind them. In fact, the horses that pull those chariots are Hynder's cousins."

"Splendid!" cried Barnabas, clapping his hands together, his earlier annoyance with Wilfred quite forgotten in his excitement.

"I'm sure I still don't understand," said Wilfred.

"Nor do I," added Brynhild.

"Think on it!" said Barnabas. "Think of the tides of the Thames, or of the sea at Cornwall in the summer."

"I've never seen those places," pointed out Brynhild.

"I *have* seen those places," said Wilfred, "but I must be hopelessly slow, because I don't see how the tides of the Thames will help us retrieve Od."

"Bah!" said Barnabas. "Think!" (He said this impatiently, but was, in truth, greatly enjoying the feeling of having made a very clever deduction, one that no one else could quite understand as of yet, and he wanted to draw out the moment a bit.)

"You're going to have to explain it," said Brynhild at last.

"It's quite simple, really," said Barnabas, a bit pedantically (earning himself an eye roll from Brynhild). "When are the tides the highest?"

"After a storm?" said Wilfred.

"When it's windy?" tried Brynhild.

"Well, yes," said Barnabas. "But also when the sun and the moon are in alignment directly above the waters. So the tides are the lowest…"

"When the sun and the moon are in alignment directly opposite the waters!" interrupted Wilfred excitedly.

"Hmmph," said Barnabas, displeased at having his dramatic moment robbed of him so easily. "Precisely. So we ask Sol and Mani to simply move to the other side of the earth, temporarily…"

"And the tide will go so low that we can simply walk in and retrieve Od!" said Wilfred.

"*Will* you stop interrupting, for heaven's sake!" said Barnabas.

"Oh, yes," said Wilfred, abashed. "Quite sorry."

"Hmmph," said Barnabas again. "So, yes, the tide will become very low, and then we can, well, as you said, walk in a retrieve Od."

"What do *you* think, Brynhild?" asked Wilfred.

"It's actually quite a good plan," she said. "And Sol and Mani are likely to want to help us, since they are fated to be run down by wolves during Ragnarok."

Barnabas and Wilfred shuddered at that, and thought of the pack of wolves that might, even now, be waiting for them outside of the lodge.

"Well," said Barnabas at last, "We must to Sol and Mani go, and our way is through the wolf-infested woods, so I guess there's nothing for it but to go, and hope for the best."

Their course decided, they left the lodge together. They hesitated on the porch for a moment, straining their ears for a sound that might betray the location of the wolves.

"I think they've moved on," said Brynhild at last, stepping confidently off the porch and down onto the grassy clearing below.

"Are you quite certain?" hissed Barnabas doubtfully. He

was trying to extend his foot down upon the first step, so that he might follow her, but it kept pulling itself back up, seemingly of its own volition. "Best to be sure of such things, I say."

"Of course I'm certain," retorted Brynhild over her shoulder. "I know these woods better than anyone."

Wilfred looked at Barnabas and shrugged. "We'd best be after her, then," he said, stepping down from the porch to follow Brynhild.

"But…" protested Barnabas nervously. He looked after his companions, heading off into the cold, dark, and possibly wolf-infested forest. Then he cast a longing glance back at the warm, well-lit, and completely wolf-free lodge behind him.

Finally he sighed, squared his shoulders (as best he could; they were trembling mightily, so highly wrought were his nerves at the thought of entering the forest) and forced his feet to carry him after Brynhild and Wilfred.

He had not gone more than a hundred paces or so when a cacophony of wolf cries broke through the silent night air. Brynhild had just reached the edge of the woods, where the trail opened up onto the clearing in front of the lodge. Wilfred was just behind her, and Barnabas (who had been walking with great haste, not wanting to be left behind) was mere steps behind Wilfred.

"Wolves!" exclaimed Barnabas, quite needlessly.

"Where are they?" cried Wilfred. "They seem to be everywhere at once!" Indeed, the wolves' howling echoed through the open meadow and off the trees, so that the origin of the sound could not be determined.

"We must make haste back to the lodge!" said Barnabas.

Brynhild, however, was accustomed to wolves, and hunting (or, more precisely, *being* hunted) and the trickiness of sounds in the woods at night. Also, she had looked back towards the lodge, and saw through the darkness of the night, what Barnabas and Wilfred had not yet seen: dark lupine shapes crouched low in the clearing, creeping stealthily towards the three companions.

"They are between us and the lodge," said Brynhild, as calmly as she could manage. "We must run to Hynder."

"We'll never make it!" protested Barnabas. "You cannot think that we can outrun *wolves*!"

"It is either *try*, and have a chance at escaping," replied Brynhild, "or stand here, and have no chance whatsoever. So run!" So saying, she grasped hold of Barnabas' hand with one of her own, and Wilfred's with the other, and forcefully pushed them in front of her down the path.

"Run!" she yelled, walloping them both on the rumps, as one would a reluctant horse. Panicked, they obeyed blindly, running wildly down the path, screaming and flailing their arms. The moon began to come up behind them, but its light was still quite meager and was unable to filter down through the dense canopy. Because of this, Wilfred, who was in the lead, could not see the path very well. He ran off it entirely, so that they were soon crashing through the undergrowth, with no clear trail before them.

"I think we have fallen off the trail," pointed out Barnabas. Indeed, even as he spoke the words, the moon's light grew stronger and illuminated the terrain before them, proving his point. Nothing but dense shrubbery and thorny bushes lay before them. The trail was nowhere in sight.

"We cannot go back to find it," said Brynhild. "The wolves are right behind us. Push on!"

They pushed and stumbled and tore their robes (and skin) on the prickly thorns and branches, but still the sounds of the pursuing wolves drew ever closer even as the light of the moon grew stronger and stronger.

After a short time of this Brynhild noticed that some of the wolves had run up on either side of them, and were beginning to pull ahead. "They are flanking us," called Brynhild from behind.

"What does that mean?" yelped Barnabas, gasping for breath.

"It means that they mean to encircle us, to cut off our escape," replied Brynhild.

"What shall we do?" wailed Barnabas.

"Can you climb trees?" asked Brynhild.

"I'm sure we can, if we must," said Wilfred.

"Ack!" cried Barnabas, who was afraid of heights and most emphatically could not climb trees.

"Very well," said Brynhild, taking this as an affirmative answer. "So we climb. That oak over there looks like it might hold the three of us."

Unfortunately, Wilfred did not know an oak from a poplar from a beech tree, so he simply took hold of the nearest trunk and flung himself up as high as he could jump. Then he began to inchworm his way up, with an astonishing amount of haste. Barnabas hesitated at the bottom, but Brynhild took hold of his bottom and hoisted him up so that he had no choice but to cling to the trunk with his arms and legs.

"Up!" she commanded, poking at his rump. He obeyed, moving as swiftly as he could whilst trying to ignore the sensation of being up far too high, and the feeling of the tree trunk swinging precariously this way and that as they climbed.

At last Wilfred, thirty feet or more above the ground, came to a place where the trunk was too thin, and the branches too flimsy, to support any further upward movement. "I cannot go any higher, I fear," he called down. "Is everyone out of reach of the wolves?"

"I think so," said Brynhild. She looked up to where Wilfred clung precariously to the terribly narrow trunk. The moonlight was quite strong now, especially as high as they were, and she could see that their position in the tree was tenuous at best. "Don't go any higher. The boughs won't bear your weight."

"Should the tree be moving so much?" asked Barnabas, as the tree swayed alarmingly from one side to another.

"It's kind of a small tree," said Brynhild. "Too small to hold the weight of all three of us, I think."

"You *said* to climb it!" said Barnabas.

"I said to climb the *oak*," replied Brynhild. "Which is the *big* tree. Over there. *This* is an *ash*."

"Oh dear," said Wilfred. "Terribly sorry about that."

"It should be fine," said Brynhild. "So long as we all stop wriggling so much," she added, with a pointed look at Barnabas, who was shifting his feet this way and that trying to gain better purchase on the slender trunk.

"Oh, of course, blame me…" began Barnabas in exasperation. He was interrupted, however, when the tree lurched violently to one side. "Ohhhh!" he cried. "I don't like that, I don't like that at all! What is happening?"

Brynhild looked down, then pressed her lips grimly together. "The wolves," she said. "The wolves are jumping on the trunk. I think they're trying to knock the tree down."

"They can't do that!" yelped Barnabas. "Wolves can't knock down a tree! Can they? Arghh!" He groaned as the tree swung abruptly to the other side, nearly dislodging him entirely. "Can they?" he repeated, once the tree (and his stomach, which was becoming quite queasy from all the motion) had steadied.

"I fear they can," said Brynhild. "We shall have to fight."

"Fight?" repeated Barnabas. "Fight wolves? Surely you jest!"

"What else would you suggest?" said Brynhild. "We are surrounded, and about to be knocked out of this tree."

"Oh, they will eat us for certain!" wailed Barnabas. "Why, oh why, must there always be something trying to devour me whole?"

"Well, I don't think they'll devour you whole," said Brynhild with maddening calmness. "I think they'd probably eat you bite by bite."

"That is decidedly *un*helpful," said Barnabas dourly.

"Mightn't we try to make a leap for that other tree, over there?" suggested Wilfred. "It's not too far. I think we might make it."

Just then the trunk of the ash tree cracked, and began leaning drunkenly to one side. Brynhild quickly assessed the situation, looking towards the nearest tree (which, even now, Wilfred was leaning over to grasp hold of one of the branches in an attempt to pull it closer), then down to the trunk of their own tree (which would surely break at any moment).

"You two try," she said. "I will jump down and keep the wolves occupied. That should give you enough time to make it, I think."

"Surely you cannot mean to do that!" protested Barnabas. "There must be twenty wolves down there!"

"I'm sure we can all make it to the other tree," said Wilfred. "If only we hurry." Frantically, he tugged at the boughs in his hands, trying, with little success, to get the other tree close enough to jump onto.

"It is our only chance," said Brynhild. "If I don't go down there and fight them, they will keep pushing on this tree until it breaks. Then they will eat us all."

"But if you jump down by yourself, then they shall surely eat *you*," said Barnabas.

"Perhaps. Or perhaps not," said Brynhild. "I'm quite tough, you know. I may make it to the other tree just fine."

"But you probably will not," said Barnabas. "I cannot allow you to do this."

"You cannot stop me," said Brynhild.

"You are a lady," insisted Barnabas. "And no gentlemen would let a lady do what is *his* job to do. And if it is anyone's task to jump down there, and, er, *distract* the wolves, then it is mine, as the lead detective of this case."

"This *lady*," huffed Brynhild, "is more capable of fighting those wolves than you are, I can assure you."

"For once," said Barnabas with resignation in his voice, "we are in agreement about something. But…still." So saying, he took a deep breath and leapt from the trunk.

Gasping with shock, Brynhild and Wilfred could hear tree branches breaking as Barnabas fell to the earth. They heard him yell out, in a voice that quavered only a little, "For Queen and for Country!" then, more defiantly, "Here I come, you lupine gibfaces!" even as the wolves barked excitedly at the prospect of an easy dinner.

Suddenly, a bright light flashed through the forest, blinding everyone momentarily. Wilfred and Brynhild heard Barnabas say, "What? Eh? Oh my!" Then a loud crashing sound erupted, as though something large were crashing through the trees, and the wolves, yipping in fear, scampered away.

Wilfred and Brynhild peered down towards the ground, blinking against the intense light, to see what was happening. "Barnabas? Barnabas!" they called. "Oh dear, what has happened?"

"I don't know," said Brynhild. "But something has scared all the wolves away."

"It must be dreadful indeed to have done so," bemoaned Wilfred. "I am certain that Barnabas is perished!"

"Maybe not, but we don't know if whatever it is be friend or foe, so it's best to be quiet, just now," warned Brynhild.

"It is all my fault!" cried Wilfred, ignoring her. "If only I had chosen the right tree! Or if only I had held on to his cloak, to prevent him from jumping! But I did not, and now he is surely lost. Oh, the cruelty of it all!"

"Lost?" said Barnabas' voice cheerfully, from above. "On the contrary, I am quite found. Or, more precisely, saved, I suppose you could say. We all are!"

Startled, Wilfred and Brynhild looked up to see Barnabas leaning down from above the trees, smiling. He was standing in a great chariot, which was led by a magnificently black flying horse. And beside him was a very handsome youth, dressed all in silver and black.

"Wilfred, Brynhild," said Barnabas, with a formal flourish of his hand towards his new companion. "Meet Mani, god of the Moon. Our deliverer."

Chapter Thirteen

With the wolves dispersed (they had run in fear of the glowing orb of the moon that was drawn behind Mani's chariot, and which had, indeed, rescued Barnabas from the wolves in catching him up before he landed), Wilfred and Brynhild were able to easily make the climb from the boughs of the tree into the chariot to join Barnabas and his godly rescuer.

Once all were safely aboard, Barnabas immediately commenced explaining precisely what had happened after his bold leap from the tree.

"I was descending from our tree to the ground..." he began, but he was interrupted by Mani.

"It sounded a good deal more like *falling*, really, than *descending*, per se," said the god, amicably enough. "Lots of branches breaking, and such."

Barnabas flicked his eyes sideways towards Mani, and his lips pursed nearly imperceptibly, but he gamely continued on.

"...as I said, I was *descending* with great haste, and rather heroically, I might add, if I were to say so myself..."

"I heard a great lot of screaming," said Mani.

Barnabas inhaled sharply in exasperation. "...calling out a *challenge* to those dreadful wolves..."

"A terribly high-pitched challenge, if you ask me," added Mani.

"...*loudly* calling out a challenge to the wolves, in a pitch they were certain to hear, much like a dog whistle, you know. And it was working, as the wolves were yelping with nervousness as I drew closer..."

"Barking with glee at the imminent arrival of their dinner, I should say," said Mani.

"Oh!" cried Barnabas, unable to contain his annoyance at having his moment of glory undermined any longer. He stamped his foot on the chariot's floor. "*Must* you?"

"I'm simply adding on to your story," said Mani. "Do go on."

"But you have made me sound like a helpless baby bird, fallen from its nest and sure to be devoured, whilst quite ignoring the fact that I leapt from that tree in a moment of nearly unimaginable bravery…"

"He really did," interjected Brynhild, earning herself a rare grateful look from Barnabas. "He sacrificed himself, so that we might escape."

"Well," conceded Mani, "that *does* sound brave, indeed. But really, there's no shame in screaming just a bit when one is about to be eaten alive by a pack of ravenous wolves."

"*Thank* you," said Barnabas, responding to Mani's admission of his bravery. Then he belatedly understood the rest of Mani's statement. "Huh," he said, unwilling to admit the fact that he had, in fact, been screaming in terror the entire way down. "Yes, well, quite so, it *would* have been understandable for someone in that situation to scream, of course, though it is in no way an entirely *accurate* representation of the particular situation in which I, personally, found myself. I think."

Wilfred quickly stepped in before Mani could reply to this. "It isn't the first time I've been saved by an action of Barnabas', and I daresay it shan't be the last!" he proclaimed (a bit *too* heartily, if truth be told; indeed, Brynhild found his intense loyalty so amusing that she had to duck her head and feign a cough in order to hide a giggle). "Still," continued Wilfred, "it is a great thing to be plucked out of a tree by none other than the moon. The moon!" he gestured expansively at the bright orb floating behind the chariot.

"Er, yes, about *that*," said Mani, "you're very welcome, of course, but since you're quite completely rescued, I really should get back to the task of hoisting this thing across the sky."

"Certainly," said Barnabas. "Of course you must. Only, we

must ask for yet another boon, if it's not too much trouble."

"Of course," said Mani graciously (although he looked with some impatience to his horse, which was restlessly pawing at the air, then back to his moon). "Easy, Sentvaken," he soothed. Sentvaken the horse snorted grumpily in reply.

"It's just that we have a terribly important message for Sol. She is your sister, I believe?"

"Yes, she is," agreed Mani. "She pulls the sun with *her* chariot."

"Quite so," said Barnabas. "And it is truly critical that we get a message to her, which means that it is great luck that we happened to come upon you, here…"

"'Be *rescued* by', I think you mean," corrected Mani.

"Hmmph," said Barnabas. "Yes, well. Certainly. I suppose."

"So," said Wilfred, "can you take us to her?"

"Hmmm," said Mani, prevaricating. "We're really not supposed to be in the same place at the same time, really. It wreaks havoc with the tides, and what-not."

"You don't say?" remarked Barnabas, putting on a face that was so extraordinarily innocent-looking that it in actuality had quite the opposite effect, and looked quite a bit suspicious, instead. Luckily Mani didn't notice (or, at least, said nothing), and Barnabas pressed on. "I'm quite sure it will be fine, just for the once. It really is quite important."

"Still, I think it best that I don't," said Mani. "I can take you out of the woods, and leave you at the edge, but as for anything further…"

Barnabas leaned forward conspiratorially. "The thing is," he said, "is that we simply *must* deliver the message. And we must be helped in doing so by none other than you. It is…" he broke off and swallowed heavily, as though choking on the words he must now utter. "It is," he said at last, "*fated* that you do so."

"Fated, you say?" said Mani.

Barnabas nodded as encouragingly as he could, with a phony smile plastered on his face.

"Well, then," said Mani. "I suppose I must, then. Off we

go!"

So saying, he clucked to Sentvaken, and they were off, flying up over the tops of the trees and away from the forest towards the west. As they passed over the place where Hynder waited, Brynhild called down to the gray horse. Immediately Hynder jumped into the air and happily flew alongside her cousin Sentvaken. The two horses nickered together, apparently discussing things of great equine importance that went altogether unheeded by the human passengers behind them.

Soon enough they saw the sea looming on the horizon. Hovering above the waters was the sun, Sol.

Barnabas stared at the sight for a moment, chewing on his lip in perturbation. At last, he leaned in to Brynhild. "*That*," he whispered, "is the sun, no?"

"Obviously," replied Brynhild sardonically.

"And is *that*," he continued, gesturing towards the sea, "the same sea in which we hope to find Ran and Od?"

"It is," said Brynhild.

"Oh dear," said Barnabas. He stared down at the water, towards which they were drawing ever closer, along with the now less-distant sun. The waves were high and choppy. "Oh dear indeed!" cried Barnabas, a bit hysterically. "This will not do!"

"Whatever is the matter?" asked Wilfred.

"Sol is right there, over the water, where Od is," said Barnabas. "Which means that *we* shall soon be over the water, as well, together with Mani."

"Oh!" exclaimed Wilfred, understanding. "The sun and the moon together!"

"And exactly opposite of where they must needs be," agreed Barnabas. "This is just terrible."

"Dreadful, indeed," said Wilfred.

"What are you two blathering on about?" asked Brynhild. "I thought we wanted the sun and the moon together."

"Yes," answered Barnabas, "but over there…" (he waved his hand distractedly behind them to the east) "…rather than here. If they converge here it will simply make the tides higher."

"Meaning that we won't be able to access the sea floor," explained Wilfred (rather needlessly, as Brynhild had already understood the implications).

"We've got to stop this chariot!" she hissed urgently. "But how?"

"I have an idea!" said Barnabas. Immediately he doubled over, as though in great pain, and began coughing and retching dramatically. Wilfred and Brynhild shared a bemused look, and Mani turned back to look at his passengers in some consternation.

"Is everything quite all right back there?" he asked.

"It is not!" said Barnabas between coughs. "I have a dreadful pain. We must stop the chariot immediately!"

"But, we are almost to my sister," protested Mani. "Can you hang on for just a few more moments, please?"

"Ack!" cried Barnabas piteously. "I fear I cannot wait even one moment. We must put down straightaway!"

"But what is the matter with you?" asked Mani. "Perhaps..."

"No, no," interrupted Barnabas. "I need to be off this chariot immediately. Put down on the beach, please."

"If you're sure you can't make it," said Mani doubtfully, unwilling to stop. Still, he pulled back slightly on Sentvaken's reins, which was encouraging.

Barnabas redoubled his efforts at once, sensing that his ploy was close to succeeding. Attempting to appear as ill as possible, he pressed the back of his hand to his forehead. "Oh!" he cried. "Oh, but I am so terribly ill, I am certain to be sick immediately!" To increase his affect of severe distress, he scrunched up his face whilst lifting his eyebrows up as high as they could go, so that they nearly disappeared into his hairline.

"Oh, *do* set us upon the ground at once," added Wilfred helpfully. "This is just like the last time he became ill in a flying chariot..." (Although, of course, such a thing had never happened, still Wilfred managed a very convincing shudder at the false memory. Barnabas beamed in admiration at his assistant's acting skill, whilst Brynhild merely shook her head and sighed.) "Well, let's just say that I don't think you'd wish for such a thing to happen in *your* chariot. The smell alone…"

Mani cast one more doubtful look at Barnabas (who was now pretending to gag just a bit, to increase the feeling of urgency) and immediately steered the chariot down towards the beach. Indeed, he did so with such haste that the passengers within the chariot, which lurched most alarmingly with the precipitous descent, were jostled about so violently that Barnabas feared he might actually become sick, and no longer need to pretend. He emitted a genuine groan then, and clutched his stomach.

Wilfred saw Barnabas pale, and leaned in to whisper in his ear. "Good job, there," he said, patting Barnabas' shoulder approvingly. "And how on earth are you managing to turn yourself so, well, *green*?"

Barnabas, who could not have managed to utter anything further than a few guttural moans, was spared the need to attempt to do so by the chariot's abrupt landing upon the beach. Sand flew in all directions from the impact, covering everyone is a light dusting of the briny smelling granules.

Barnabas climbed as quickly as he could from the chariot. He plunked himself down most ungracefully upon the strand and sat there, miserably wiping sand from his eyes and mouth. Wilfred soon followed and did the same, but Brynhild lingered in the chariot.

"Will he be all right now?" asked Mani of Brynhild.

"I'm sure he will," she said. "He's not really one for flying, you know."

"I see," said Mani. "Well, I suppose fate will be satisfied just as well if I deliver the message to my sister without you. So I'll just be on my way…"

"Ack!" yelped Barnabas incoherently. He was still a bit queasy, if truth be told, and he had swallowed a great lot of sand. Still, he was able to gesture feebly to the sun which, though it had moved further away, was still far too close for their plan to work. Luckily, Brynhild took his meaning immediately.

"Of course," she said smoothly. "But first we must make sure you know precisely what to tell her."

"Can't you just give me the gist of it?" said Mani, clearly anxious to be off (and away from these strange and somewhat annoying travelers).

"Oh no," said Brynhild. "That won't do. Won't do at all. The wording must be absolutely perfect. Because, you know…fate."

Mani sighed. "Very well," he said, with no small degree of resignation in his voice. "Go on then. What am I to say to my sister?"

Brynhild began, then, to make up an exceedingly long (and rather nonsensical) message for Mani to deliver to his sister Sol, making the beleaguered moon god repeat each sentence as she said them. While she spoke she glanced surreptitiously at Barnabas, who jerked his head towards the slowly disappearing sun and shook his head.

Finally, the sun disappeared over the horizon and Barnabas nodded subtly, indicating that it was time. Brynhild stopped mid-sentence and slapped her hands together. "And that's that!" she proclaimed to Mani.

"That's that?" he asked, confused. "But, *that* doesn't make any sense!"

"Ah, yes, well, you know the gods!" Brynhild said cheerfully.

"Perhaps it is Sol's fate to decipher the riddle?" added Wilfred astutely.

"Oh," said Mani, thinking this over. "Yes, well, you are probably right. I'll be off, and will deliver the message to Sol just as you gave it to me."

"Splendid!" said Wilfred. Brynhild climbed out of the chariot to join her companions on the beach, and Mani and his chariot hurried away, before they could ask any more of him.

Brynhild thumped Barnabas heartily on the back. "Good acting!" she congratulated. "Even *I* almost believed you were truly sick."

"Errr," said Barnabas, still battling waves of nausea. "Acting."

"So," continued Brynhild, oblivious to Barnabas' struggles, "I suppose we simply wait here until Mani catches up to Sol and the tides go down?"

Barnabas nodded. "Rest a bit, perhaps?" he muttered, and lay down to sleep, curled up in the sand.

Wilfred and Brynhild spoke quietly together, so as not to wake the sleeping detective, for several hours. With the sun and the moon both headed to the opposite side of the world, it soon became incredibly dark. Still, after a couple of hours of waiting they were able to sense the tide receding at a rapid pace, and Wilfred leaned over to gently shake Barnabas awake.

"It is time," he whispered gently, causing Barnabas to mutter in his sleep and turn over grumpily.

Brynhild sighed. "Hullo!" she yelled, giving Barnabas a great shove as she did so. "Wake up!"

"Ahhh!" cried Barnabas, jumping to his feet. "Dragons!"

"What?" exclaimed Wilfred and Brynhild in unison.

"Argh," said Barnabas, shaking the sleep from his head. "Ah, what?"

"You yelled 'dragons', just now," said Brynhild.

"No I didn't," said Barnabas, clearly embarrassed.

"But, you *did*," insisted Brynhild.

"Don't be silly," retorted Barnabas. "Why are you wasting time talking about dragons? Can't you see how low the water is? We'd best see about rescuing Od straightaway. If you are quite done making nonsensical accusations, that is?"

Brynhild opened her mouth to retort as Barnabas turned on his heel and began to stride after the receding seawater, but Wilfred kicked her ankle.

"Ow!" she yelped. "Why do you…"

"It's just easier," sighed Wilfred. "Come. Let us stay together. I can scarcely see Barnabas anymore, and it wouldn't do to be split up in this darkness."

Indeed, Barnabas had all but disappeared into the blackness of the night sea, and Wilfred and Brynhild had to scurry over the wet sand to catch him up.

Surprisingly, the ocean was receding faster than any of them had expected, so that although Barnabas had walked a good way out by the time Wilfred and Brynhild caught up to him, the water barely rose above their ankles.

"Just as I had planned!" crowed Barnabas (although, in truth, expecting to get a good deal more wet than he had thus far he had spent the past moments gritting his teeth against the expected dousing of cold, northern seawater, and in truth had more than half expected to be thoroughly drowned by now. Still, he believed that it was always better to put a brave face on things and to pretend at confidence even when one's knees were knocking together with nervousness). "The sea is following Mani and Sol, and getting out of our way entirely." He paused and frowned, squinting his eyes as he tried to peer through the utter blackness of the moonless night. "But I'm quite sure I have no idea of where, precisely, to find Ran. I thought you said her palace was at the bottom of the sea?"

"It *is*," said Brynhild. "But the sea is a big place."

"Well, shouldn't you know *where* it might be, or at least in which *direction* it might lie?" asked Barnabas, a bit testily.

"How in nine earths would I know that?" replied Bynhild, equally testily. "No one has ever mapped out the bottom of the ocean, as far as I know. Being as the only people who've ever gone to the bottom of the ocean tend to not make it back up, being drowned and such."

"I only meant that you might have an idea of which way we ought to *go*, now that we are standing here in the middle of the ocean, and what-not," retorted Barnabas.

"What *should* be the bottom of the ocean," corrected a new voice. Barnabas and Brynhild, however, ignored it, immersed as they were in their disagreement.

"I'm a *skald*," said Brynhild, "not an omnipotent knower-of-everything."

"Errr, did you hear that?" interjected Wilfred, looking around for the source of the voice.

"Well you certainly could have fooled me," said Barnabas, ignoring Wilfred and pursing his lips and affecting an obviously feigned expression of benign innocence.

"Oh!" cried Brynhild, stamping her foot and sending a spray of cold water everywhere. "What is *that* supposed to mean?"

"Do you *mind*?" said the voice irritably. "You just smashed my garden gazebo."

"Oh, *nothing*," sniped Barnabas. "Only that you seem to know *exactly* what we should do at all times, excepting for *now*, when we are standing all alone in the middle of the ocean and it would be quite welcome if *someone* knew what to do!"

"I'm not certain that we *are* all alone," tried Wilfred, to no avail.

"Well, it's a good thing that *someone* knows what they're about!" cried Brynhild.

"Really, you're lucky that you didn't stamp on any of my guppies. Thank Odin they fled from your big, clumsy land-feet," said the voice.

"And that someone is *me*," said Barnabas prissily.

"Do you land-dwellers really need to speak so loudly?" asked the voice. The tone of it was beginning to sound quite testy, and Wilfred feared that ignoring it might result in serious repercussions.

"I believe that someone is here with us…," began Wilfred, only to be cut off by Brynhild's angry response.

"You seem to forget who got you out of Freya's dungeon," she yelled.

"I'm seriously thinking of calling up a tidal wave just to get rid of your infernal noise," said the voice. "Don't think I won't!"

"And you seem to forget who saved us from the wolves!" cried Barnabas at Brynhild.

"Ahhhhhh!" shouted Wilfred at the top of his lungs. "Ahhh! Ahhhh! Ahhhh!"

Barnabas and Brynhild stopped their argument to give Wilfred a bemused look.

"Why in the worlds are you screaming like that?" asked Brynhild.

"Really," said Barnabas, "are you *quite* all right, Wilfred?"

"I believe he's trying to get your attention," said the voice, from a place just next to Barnabas. Barnabas jumped in startlement, then stuck his head out as far as it would go so that he might clearly see the speaker.

A very grumpy-looking woman sat cross-legged in the wet sand, slumped down with her hands at her feet and staring balefully back at Barnabas. Algae and seaweed stuck to her hair, and mud stained her face and arms.

"Oh my," said Barnabas. "Are you...are you Ran, perchance?"

"I am, and you are wrecking my palace," said the voice (which did, indeed, belong to the sea goddess Ran).

"Look, everyone!" cried Barnabas happily, his rancor at Brynhild immediately forgotten. "It's Ran! Just the person for whom we've been searching." He clapped a sympathetic hand on Wilfred's shoulder. "See? There's no reason to shout so. We've found her."

Wilfred exhaled noisily through his nostrils, and Ran and Brynhild both cast him a sympathetic look.

"So, Ms. Ran?" said Barnabas, oblivious to the sensibilities of his companions. "We've come to ask you a few questions, if you don't mind?"

Ran sighed. "Will you go away, then, and send the water back?" she asked tiredly.

"But of course," said Barnabas. "We have no wish to trouble you."

"Then perhaps you oughtn't have drained my palace," said Ran dryly.

"Oh," said Barnabas, looking a bit chagrined. "Quite so. I do hope that it hasn't been too much of an inconvenience."

"Oh, no," said Ran. "It's been lovely, having all my fish dragged off to the other side of the world and my sea gardens dried out."

"I'm terribly sorry," said Barnabas. "I didn't think of those things, in truth I did not."

"Just as I'm sure you're not thinking about how you are standing on my tail," said Ran.

"Oh, dear," said Barnabas. "Oh, dear." Flustered, he jumped back, so as to stop treading on the goddess's tail, and immediately lost his balance and fell over. He landed with a heavy *plop*, and everyone heard a loud cracking sound. Barnabas cried out in pain.

"Ow!" he yelped. "I've been stabbed!" He kicked and flailed so violently in his efforts to get up that a small maelstrom began to form in the water around him.

Ran shook her head dejectedly. "You've sat upon my coral arboretum," she said sadly. "I'm sure you've destroyed it."

"Quite sorry, truly I am," said Barnabas, intensifying his efforts to stand. More cracking sounds ensued, and Barnabas unsuccessfully stifled further gasps of pain as the broken coral poked mercilessly at his bottom.

"Do stop," said Ran. "You're making it worse."

"If I could just…" began Barnabas, but was cut off when he fell backwards and his head went under water. He kicked out in a panic, and Wilfred hurried over to assist him, accidentally kicking at further areas of Ran's palace as he ran.

"Excuse me, begging your pardon," he apologized as he went.

Ran looked helplessly at Brynhild. "What do they want? I'll give them anything, if only they'd leave!" she cried.

Brynhild smiled to herself. Ran was known for being a merciless denizen of the northern waters; a woman who dragged hapless sailors to the bottom of the ocean with her net, heedless of their pleas for mercy. Yet somehow, it seemed that Barnabas' combination of obliviousness and determination had managed to defeat the ruthless goddess of the sea.

"We'll go if only you deliver Od into our keeping," said Brynhild.

"Yes, yes," agreed Ran. "Take him. Take him and go. Now please!" She waved a hand under the ankle-deep water (which, amazingly, had now somehow engulfed both Wilfred and Barnabas so that they were completely unaware of the exchange between Brynhild and Ran). Wilfred had fallen on top of Barnabas, and the two detectives rolled and fumbled in sputtering confusion as they struggled to get up. "Do hurry!" admonished Ran, even as a very cautious seahorse approached, leading a man whose hands and ankles were tied with shackles of sea grass.

Brynhild took hold of the grassy chain tied to Od's restraints, and with her other hand lifted first Wilfred, then Barnabas from the water. "Come," she said. "We've got what we came for. Let's go."

"But, the palace!" protested Wilfred. "We've quite wrecked it."

"Yes, you have," whispered Brynhild, "and a good thing too. Now we must go!"

Wilfred caught the impetus in her voice, and hastened to follow her back towards the shore. Barnabas followed a bit behind, stepping gingerly and rubbing his sore bottom.

The sound of the waters moving noisily behind them hurried his steps, however (Mani must have concluded his meeting with Sol, as the sea was rising quite rapidly by the time they neared the edge of the land). Still, they were wet to the waist when they at last set foot on the sandy beach.

"We'd best mount Hynder and get Od back to Freya straightaway," said Brynhild.

"But I don't want to go home yet," complained Od.

"And I am far too sore to sit upon a horse!" added Barnabas.

Brynhild gave them both a withering look, and, chastened, the two men sheepishly clamped their mouths shut and protested no more, but climbed dutifully aboard Hynder (though Barnabas winced and moaned rather dramatically as he settled his injured buttocks upon the horse's flank).

They were all cold from being wet, and rather miserable, but thankfully Freya's palace was not far (at least, not for Hynder) and soon enough they had landed in the cobbled courtyard of the palace.

Chapter Fourteen

"Od!" came Freya's voice, almost immediately, once they had landed. Od immediately moved to hide behind Barnabas, whilst trying to make himself appear as small as possible. His efforts were a bit ridiculous, however, as Barnabas was rather on the short side of things, and Od was quite tall, even by Viking standards. Therefore, Od's bearded face and broad shoulders peeked out over the top of Barnabas' head, even though he was hunched down as low as he could go.

Freya, of course, was not fooled, and marched directly up to Od. She thrust Barnabas abruptly out of the way and took hold of her husband by the ear.

"I say!" huffed Barnabas. Freya ignored him entirely and proceeded to drag Od across the courtyard towards the palace, ear first.

"How dare you run off like that?" she chided. "Without so much as a word! And you smell like seaweed." Her nose wrinkled in disgust.

Od began to mumble (ostensibly he was making an excuse of some sort, although his muttering was so low as to be unintelligible so that no one could understand a word of what he said; this was, however, of no matter, as Freya cut him off immediately with a vicious twist of his ear lobe. Od uttered an extraordinarily profane curse of pain, which everyone understood quite well).

"Oh, my!" exclaimed Barnabas. "I have a general idea of what he meant, of course, but what, precisely, is a…"

"Never mind that," said Brynhild quickly. "We should leave."

"But," argued Barnabas, "oughtn't we speak to Freya first? Perhaps she can give us some advice on what to expect in

Svortalheim. And I, for one, would feel much better if she were to officially pardon us. I have no desire to end up in her dungeon again!" He leaned forward to address Freya, who had by now neared the palace entrance with her husband in tow. "Ms. Freya?" he called. "Pardon me?" He paused, then chuckled a bit at his unintentional pun. "I beg your *pardon*," he repeated, "but are we *pardoned*?"

Wilfred laughed appreciatively, whilst Brynhild rolled her eyes and shook her head.

"Well, I know someone who *isn't* pardoned," said Freya, letting go of Od's ear to slap playfully at his chest. "I know *someone* who is going to be punished terribly." She batted her eyes and disappeared into the palace.

Od's face broke out in a silly smile, and he happily trotted after his wife as she passed through the palace doors.

Barnabas turned to his companions, his confusion written comically upon his face. "Why is he smiling about being punished?" he asked. "Those dungeons are *dreadful!*"

Brynhild let out a guffaw, to Barnabas' further consternation. His eyebrows furrowed as he thought over the dilemma. "I fail to see what's so funny about Freya's punishments," he said. "And as for Od…why, he didn't even *try* to plead his case! Nor did he even so much as offer a 'thank you very much for saving me from the bottom of the sea'." He leaned forward and yelled out loudly after Od's retreating figure, "You're *welcome*! It was no trouble whatsoever to align the *sun* and the *moon* and nearly drown! I'm certain *anyone* would have done the same!"

There was no answer other than the sound of the door closing behind Od.

"Well," huffed Barnabas, "if he'd rather go be punished by his wife than properly thank his rescuers, I suppose he deserves what he gets, the ungrateful scallywag!"

"I think that Od may not mind his punishment at all," suggested Brynhild. "Indeed, he seems quite eager to take it."

"Why would anyone be eager to take a punishment?" snapped Barnabas. "That is absurd." He crossed his arms and furrowed his brows even more, until they had lowered so much that they threatened to block out his eyesight entirely.

"Freya hasn't seen her husband for a long time," said Brynhild, by way of explanation. "I think you can see where I'm going with this…"

"I cannot," said Barnabas. "I'm sure I am wholly confused by the matter, and by the abominable manners that we have seen displayed here today."

"Well," said Brynhild carefully, "I think that perhaps this 'punishment' will be taking place somewhere other than the dungeons."

"Is there a torture chamber, then?" gasped Barnabas, appalled. Brynhild let out another guffaw, and Wilfred shuffled his feet in embarrassment.

"I think, perhaps, that they might be going to talk in private," said Wilfred carefully. "About personal husband-and-wife sorts of things."

"Yes, I'm sure they're going to *talk*. I'm sure they have quite a lot to *say* to each other," replied Brynhild, gales of laughter erupting from her.

Barnabas looked from the laughing Viking skald to his suddenly bashful assistant, and slowly the truth of the matter dawned upon him. "Oh," he said, his eyes widening. "Oh!"

"There, you see?" said Brynhild, still chuckling. "Od will be quite all right. And we should be on our way now."

She walked over to where Hynder waited, with Wilfred just behind her. Barnabas followed, his feet moving slowly as his mind worked over the shocking developments. "But, it's *daytime!*" he said, as Brynhild hoisted him up onto the horse's back. Brynhild squealed with laughter at that, and continued to chuckle quietly to herself as she mounted Hynder herself. Indeed, she laughed almost all of the way to Svortalfheim, where the Dark Elves dwelt.

Her mood sobered considerably as they entered that place, as did the moods of Barnabas and Wilfred. Indeed, Barnabas forgot all about his offense at not being thanked by Freya and Od, and his outrage at their shockingly indecent behavior, as he looked out at the bleak views below them.

Svoralfheim was a dark and dinghy place: the sky was a

muddy grey, the ground was a slightly darker version of the same color, and there were no trees or growing things of any kind to break up the dismal dreariness. The two detectives looked about them at the dreary scenery, and felt their spirits sink.

"Well I don't care much for this at all," said Barnabas at last. "Why is it so dark here? Where's the sun?" His eyes widened as he considered a dreadful possibility. "It hasn't anything to do with what *we* did, sending Sol and Mani off their courses, does it?"

Brynhild shook her head. "No, Barnabas," she said gently. "It's not our fault. Svoralfheim is one of the underground worlds, and so there is never sun here."

"Why would these Dark Elves want to live here then, if there's no sun, ever?" asked Barnabas.

"Not all creatures crave the sun," explained Brynhhild. "In fact, there are many who much prefer the shadows."

Barnabas shuddered. "I'm certain I don't want to meet any creatures like *that,*" he stated.

"Errr," said Wilfred.

"What is it?" asked Barnabas.

"It's only that I rather suspect that the Dark Elves may very well be creatures 'like that'," replied Wilfred.

"Well, how do *you* know?" asked Barnabas, somewhat snippily. "Have you some experience with Dark Elves? In *Marylebone*, perhaps?"

"I'm merely drawing an assumption based on the fact that they've chosen to live *here*, and also that they are called the *Dark* Elves, rather than the Happy Friendly *Rainbow* Elves," said Wilfred.

"Oh," said Barnabas. "Quite right, I suppose." He pursed his lips. "Still, no reason to act quite so *superior* about it, really."

"Anyway," interrupted Brynhild hastily, "it's no matter who is acting snippy or superior or whether or not we still wish to meet the Dark Elves, because we are here and we are meeting them regardless."

As if to punctuate her words, several Dark Elves had

appeared on the ground below them, and were even now calling up to them.

"Put that horse down at once, and present yourselves," the Elves yelled. One of them proffered a bow, took an arrow from a quiver upon his back, and dipped it into a darkly molten reddish liquid that flowed like a viscous river upon the ground. The tip of the arrow caught fire as the elf lifted it up.

"What is he doing?" asked Barnabas, peering down. "Oh dear, oh dear, I think he might…ahhhh! Duck!" he yelped, as the elf nocked the arrow and sent it whizzing up into the sky towards them. It passed within a yard of Hynder's flanks, and Wilfred and Barnabas clutched each other in terror as they saw the elf reach back to his quiver for yet another arrow.

"Land the horse immediately!" yelled the elf with the bow and the flaming arrows. "*That* one was a warning. The next one won't be."

"Lava arrows?" shouted Brynhild to the elves contemptuously. "I wasn't expecting a *warm* welcome from the Dark Elves, but don't you think the arrows are a *bit* much, even for *Svortalfheim* dwellers?" She infused the word 'Svortalfheim' with so much derision that Barnabas cringed.

"Must you antagonize them?" he hissed. "Seems that a *friendlier* approach might behoove us here."

"Aggression is the only thing these creatures understand," answered Brynhild. "We must show no fear."

"This is just dreadful," bemoaned Barnabas as Brynhild angled Hynder down towards the elves on the ground. Thankfully, the elf with the arrow held back, and shot no further flaming missiles their way, although he held one in a threatening manner in his hand, clearly ready to nock it at any moment. "I would never have agreed to come here, had I known it would be like this."

"It was *your* idea," pointed out Brynhild reasonably.

"And a *terrible* one it was, at that," snapped Barnabas. "And, really, whose fault is it for agreeing to it?" He glared at Brynhild and Wilfred in turn.

"Mine, I suppose," sighed Brynhild. She looked up as a

new Dark Elf approached. "Hail, Maledokkalfar!" she called out to a new figure that was approaching. Dressed all in black, with voluminous robes that swirled as he walked, this new elf strode with sinuous steps closer to the travelers. The other elves bowed their heads and stepped aside to make way for him.

Barnabas considered the new elf, whom Brynhild had called Maledokkalfar. An air of evil seeped from him (although, *how*, exactly, Barnabas could not say, nor could he quite pinpoint the e*xact* source of his aversion to the fellow; he only knew that menace radiated from Malefokkalfar like sweet smells radiated from lavender fields). The elf had a hood that covered his face, but removed it dramatically as he neared Hynder.

Maledokkalfar was quite black in color (which was not entirely unexpected, given the name of his kind and would not have, in itself, been cause for alarm). However, his face was not merely *dark*, but entirely black, and more than a little shiny, so that it didn't look as though it were covered in *skin* so much as some terrible sort of pliable obsidian. Even worse were his eyes, which glowed with the same reddish color as did the fiery molten river that had set the arrows afire. The eyes bored into each of the companions in turn, so intently that it felt as though Maledokkalfar's gaze might burn one's soul up entirely.

Barnabas and Wilfred couldn't suppress gasps of horror. Brynhild skillfully sent an elbow into the ribs of both of them in warning. "Shhh!" she hissed. "Show no fear!"

"As if we *would*," scoffed Barnabas (although, in truth, his bulging eyes that cast about wildly from elf to elf gave him more an appearance of a nervous rabbit that had suddenly found itself somehow plunked down into the middle of a busy eagle eyrie than of a fearless detective whose very presence struck fear into the hearts of the guilty). "*I*, for one, am most definitely *not* afraid in the slightest." He glanced towards Wilfred. "Are *you* afraid, Wilfred?"

"Not in the least," replied Wilfred, his voice wavering and his eyes bulging nearly as badly as Barnabas'.

"Then *why*," asked Brynhild, "are you clinging to one another so?"

Barnabas and Wilfred looked at each other and saw that they were, in fact, huddled very closely together and gripping tightly to one another's cloaks. Abashed, they pulled away and shuffled their feet sheepishly.

"That's better," whispered Brynhild. "Maledokkalfar doesn't like it when…"

They never did get to find out what Maledokkalfar didn't like, as the fellow himself came into earshot and addressed them directly.

"Welcome, my fine guests," he said, his voice as oily as his rippling skin. "I trust that you have been made to feel welcome?"

"As welcome as anyone would feel with a barrage of arrows to escort them in," retorted Brynhild defiantly.

Maledokkalfar laughed, a sound that was utterly devoid of actual mirth or friendliness. "But that is part of the fun of visiting Svortalfheim," he said. "One *knows* that there will be arrows, but one is never quite sure *where* they'll land." He put a finger to his lips and pretended to ponder the issue of the location of the arrows' strike. "Will they fly *past* me? Will they hit my precious *horse*? Will they strike *me*?"

The Dark Elf king laughed again as he looked at Barnabas and Wilfred, who had both begun to cringe again at his nasty words. He leaned forward suddenly and poked a narrow finger into Barnabas' face. "Bah!" he yelled, causing Barnabas to jerk backwards in startlement, which only added to Maledokkalfar's evil mirth.

"I *say*!" said Barnabas, affronted.

"You *say* what?" asked Maledokkalfar, his lava eyes glittering with malice.

"Barnabas…" warned Wilfred and Brynhild in unison.

"Let the man speak," said Maledokkalfar, his voice a sinister mockery of a conscientious host concerned with his guests' wellbeing. "I'd like to know what is making him so jumpy. If my *hospitality* is lacking, I'm sure I should like to know about it."

Wilfred, seeing Barnabas' face begin to redden and his features set with temper, tried to intercede. "Our welcome has been quite lovely, I'm sure. We are all unharmed, at least, as you can see…"

"I mean, we've been nearly shot out of the sky by a group of *exceedingly* grumpy elves, and now here's yet *another* exceedingly grumpy elf made of melted rocks with eyes made of magma, so no, I cannot say what might *possibly* be making us nervous," sniped Barnabas.

Maledokkalfar's eyebrows shot up onto his forehead with surprise. The other elves surrounding him muttered angrily, and the one with the bow casually pulled another arrow out of his quiver, set it afire in the lava river, and placed it in his bow, ready to shoot.

"We're dead," said Brynhild matter-of-factly to Wilfred, shaking her head. "He just *can't* hold his tongue, and now we're, you know, *dead*."

"Oh dear," said Wilfred. "Oh dear, indeed."

"Exceedingly *grumpy*?" exclaimed Maledokkalfar. "*Exceedingly* grumpy?"

The elf with the flaming arrow nocked it, drew his arm back, and took aim at the three companions. Wilfred pranced in place nervously, trying to decide if he could take arrows for both Brynhild and Barnabas at the same time or, if not, whom to prioritize: ought he dive in front of the employer to whom he owed his loyalty, and with whom he'd been through so much, or ought he instead to dive first between the only lady present and the arrow meant for her, as chivalry (and, if truth be told, a certain tenderness of feeling) dictated?

Brynhild, meanwhile, stood stock still, stoically resigned to their fate.

Barnabas, however, had been greatly peeved at being made fun of, and his annoyance outweighed his fears of the Dark Elves and their flaming arrows. He took a step closer to Maledokkalfar and, without blinking, poked his own finger into the Dark Elvish king's face.

"*Ex*ceedingly!" he said pointedly.

To everyone's surprise, Maledokkalfar burst into laughter,

and this time it was not feigned, nor even particularly evil-sounding. Indeed, the king seemed to be taken by a fit of genuine mirth, so that he guffawed and chortled and snorted with glee.

"Oh!" cried Maledokkalfar. "We shoot flaming arrows at him and he calls us 'exceedingly grumpy'! Oh, but it is too funny!"

The other elves took their leaders cue and began to laugh as well. Wilfred and Brynhild looked at each other with surprise, then began to laugh as well (although their laughter was borne more of relief than of amusement). Barnabas smiled but held his ground, pleased and proud that he had stood up to the Dark Elf king and had somehow come out on top (or, at least, not dead).

At last Maledokkalfar's laughter faded, and everyone stood there, uncertain of what might come next. Maledokkalfar emitted a few more last giggles, wiped his eyes, and looked back at Barnabas. "Well, I suppose I should ask what it is that brings you here, so that I am not accused of further 'exceedingly grumpiness'?" He chuckled again at his own joke, and the others laughed politely.

"We've come here," began Brynhild, "on a quest from Odin himself, that is of the utmost importance, and that…"

"We wish for you to give the dragon Nidhug nightmares," interrupted Barnabas.

"Give Nidhug nightmares?" asked Maledokkalfar. "But why would you want that?"

"Our reasons are our own," said Barnabas primly. His eyes flashed with a touch of mischievousness as he added, "And I'm certain that you'd enjoy doing so, what with your being so exceedingly grumpy and what-not."

"Oh dear," said Wilfred once more.

"And now we're dead again," replied Brynhild, aghast.

But Maledokkalfar merely laughed and clapped Barnabas cheerily on the shoulder. Barnabas winced a bit, as the blow was in actuality quite rough (not to mention the fact that the king was, truly, made of rock, albeit molten rock, and therefore more than a little hard to the touch) and a small cloud of what looked to be volcanic dust erupted from the king's hand and settled onto Barnabas' cloak.

"You've got me there, good fellow," said Maledokkalfar amiably. "I do *so* enjoy giving creatures nightmares."

"Splendid!" said Barnabas. "It's settled, you'll send the nightmares to Nidhug and we'll be on our way…"

"Welllll," said Maledokkalfar, spreading his hands out and shrugging in an apologetic gesture.

"Well *what*?" asked Barnabas.

"I said I'd enjoy giving the dragon nightmares, but I certainly didn't say I'd do it for free, did I?"

"Well, no, I suppose not, but…"

"But nothing. Will you pay my price?" asked Maledokkalfar.

"Not until you tell us what it is!" said Brynhild.

"And then we must discuss it," added Wilfred. "To compare the difficulty of your price, with the benefit of the nightmares, and decide rationally on what is the best course…"

"We'll do it!" said Barnabas, ignoring his two companions and sticking out his hand to shake on the deal.

"Wonderful!" said Maledokkalfar, shaking Barnabas' hand heartily. "And a deal well done."

Barnabas beamed happily whilst Wilfred blinked unhappily and Brynhild buried her face in her hands. She opened her fingers a bit so she could peer out from between them.

"And *what*," she asked through gritted teeth, "is the price?"

"Nothing much," said Maledokkalfar, with a rather terrifying air of feigned innocence. "I only need you to get the fire sword from the giant Surt. You know, the one who guards Muspelheim?"

"A fire sword. From a giant. In Muspelheim," repeated Brynhild flatly.

"Precisely!" crowed Maledokkalfar. "See, that's not so bad, now, is it?"

"And if we cannot?" asked Brynhild.

"Well, then I kill you," said Maledokkalfar simply. "Best be off now. I really *do* want that sword, you know. And soon." With that, he smiled and turned, allowing his cloak to sweep dramatically about his ankles as he strode away, followed by his minions.

"Well then," said Brynhild through gritted teeth. "I suppose we're off to Muspelheim. To steal a sword from a giant."

"Will that be *terribly* difficult, do you think?" asked Barnabas.

"On, no, I'm certain we'll have no problem whatsoever *stealing a sword from a giant*," said Brynhild.

"Splendid, then!" said Barnabas, oblivious to the sarcasm in Brynhild's voice. "What are we waiting for? Off we go! To Muspelheim!" He began to scramble back atop Hynder (Wilfred came up behind him and gave his rump a push to help him aboard). So occupied, he didn't see the apologetic shrug that Wilfred gave to Brynhild, nor did he see the set of the skald's jaw as she shook her head and sighed.

"To Muspelheim," she repeated (albeit with a great deal less enthusiasm), once she and Wilfred had likewise mounted Hynder. "To steal a fire sword."

Chapter Fifteen

"So," ventured Wilfred, once they were underway. "What might we expect in Muspelheim? Is it a terrible sort of place?" (He said this more to break the awkward silence that had developed between Barnabas and Brynhild than out of any real desire to know what Muspelheim was really like; indeed, he had surmised enough from Brynhild's attitude that it was not the sort of place that one might wish to visit. Further, any place that was inhabited by things called Fire Giants was most definitely not going to be terribly pleasant.)

"Yes," said Brynhild. "It is *very* terrible."

"Oh," said Wilfred. "That is, well, er, terrible," he concluded, rather lamely.

"Very *astute* observation, Wilfred," observed Barnabas wryly. "I'm certain the *terrible* place is *terribly* terrible." He chuckled a bit at his joke (which he had thought was quite clever and very amusing indeed), but was more than a little surprised when Brynhild reacted vehemently.

"At least *Wilfred* didn't antagonize the king of the Dark Elves and then promise him we'd go to this *terrible* place, to get a *terrible* sword from an unimaginably *terrible* giant!" she snapped.

"Well," huffed Barnabas, taken aback, "*someone* had to talk us out of our predicament with the lava-elves…"

"Dark Elves," corrected Wilfred helpfully.

"Yes, yes, I *know*," said Barnabas. "But the name 'Dark Elves' really doesn't reflect how dreadfully *creepy* they were, does it? 'Lava elves' seems much more apropos."

"I suppose not," said Wilfred. He frowned doubtfully. "Although I'm not certain they were made of lava, necessarily. They appeared to me to be made of some type of rock."

"Quite so," said Barnabas, "but the rock they were made of was most definitely lava."

"Or obsidian, perhaps?" said Wilfred. "Isn't that what lava is called once it cools off and hardens?"

"I thought it was pumice," said Brynhild. "Doesn't lava solidify into pumice?"

"Hmmm," said Wilfred thoughtfully. "That could be, but I believe that pumice is quite porous and covered in pockmarks, whilst the Dark Elves seemed more, well, smooth and shiny."

"Granite?" tried Brynhild.

"Or basalt?" added Wilfred.

"Oh, yes," said Brynhild, "I do believe you're right. Basalt is dark, and smooth, and shiny, and I think it *does* come from volcanoes…"

Barnabas, who had been watching this exchange with ever-increasing irritiation, suddenly erupted. "Lava is a pseudoplastic mixture of molten minerals that is fluid when it is hot and solidifies when it has cooled," he cried, flapping his arms in a temper.

Brynhild and Wilfred turned to look at him, eyes wide and mouths agape with surprise.

"It matters nought which state it is in; be it fluid or solid it is lava," continued Barnabas, in a huff. "Therefore, they *are*, in fact, the Lava Elves, and that is that." He crossed his arms over his chest (which is no mean feat when one is balancing upon a flying horse) and stared haughtily off into the distance.

"Oh," said Wilfred, trying to smooth things over. "Quite so."

Brynhild, however, was not to be cowed so easily. "Wonderful," she said. "So, as I was saying, it wasn't *Wilfred* who promised the, ahem, '*Lava* Elves' that we'd steal a sword from a Fire Giant. Unless, that is, you think the Fire Giants ought to be called something else?"

She narrowed her eyes at Barnabas, who looked further away so as to pretend not to see her. Brynhild leaned in closer, until she was bent over nearly backwards over Hynder, to bring her face closer to Barnabas'. Barnabas merely turned his head further away, and upon his face affected an expression of someone who was peacefully enjoying the scenery on a train ride, rather than that of a man who is currently having an argument with a Viking skald about nasty elves and dangerous giants aboard a flying horse.

Wilfred, squinched between the two, shifted uncomfortably. "Oh my," he said. "It seems we've all got a bit heated…"

"You mean like some pseudo…some pseudo, ah…." said Brynhild, fumbling for the word.

"Pseudoplastic," muttered Barnabas under his breath. "Pseudoplastic nincompoops."

"What did you say?" said Brynhild.

"I called you a…" began Barnabas, but Wilfred, inexplicably, began to loudly hum a polka, so that Barnabas' words were lost in the music.

"What?" yelled Brynhild.

"I said, that…" called back Barnabas to no avail, as Wilfred merely increased his volume.

"What is he doing?" cried Brynhild.

"I have no idea," responded Barnabas. He poked Wilfred in the ribs. "I say, dear boy, what on God's green earth are you about?"

"I am singing," said Wilfred simply.

"Yes, yes, we can see that. Or, rather, *hear* that. But why?" asked Barnabas.

"I've decided I'm going to sing every time the two of you begin to argue," said Wilfred.

"But then you'll be singing most of the time," pointed out Brynhild.

"And your singing is far, far worse than any argument Brynhild and I might have," added Barnabas.

"I don't like it any better than you do," said Wilfred, in between stanzas. "But I will do what I must." He took up the tune with renewed gusto, and Barnabas and Brynhild cringed.

"Oh, do stop!" said Barnabas. "We'll promise never to

argue again, won't we, Brynhild?"

"Actually," said Brynhild, "this has all given me an idea."

"An idea?" asked Barnabas. "An idea for what?"

"Fire Giants like music," she replied. Wilfred, seeing that the conversation was heading into more productive territory, stopped singing at just that moment so that Brynhild's voice, still pitched high to be heard over Wilfred's polka, echoed loudly through the air. Everyone shook their heads to clear the ringing in their ears, and Brynhild continued at a more normal volume. "They like music," she repeated. "It lulls them to sleep."

"Aha!" said Barnabas. "So we have Wilfred sing to Surt, which makes him fall asleep, and we steal his sword!"

"Not exactly," said Brynhild, with an apologetic look at Wilfred. "I think the music ought to be a bit more, well, *pleasant.*" She put a conciliatory hand on Wilfred's arm, and Wilfred colored and ducked his head in embarrassment. Barnabas, watching, noted Wilfred's sudden bashfulness. He cocked his head thoughtfully as he regarded his assistant, but said nothing. *Later, he thought. I'll bring it up later, when we are alone. No sense embarrassing the lad further.*

"So," Barnabas said instead, "who shall sing for the giant? *My* voice is no better than Wilfred's, I'm afraid, so unless *you* have some hidden talent…"

"Not I," said Brynhild. "But I know who does."

"Who?" asked Barnabas.

"The Light Elves," replied Brynhild. "They are known for the beauty of their musical instruments. We can go to them and ask them for one."

"Will they be as, errr, *helpful* as the Lava Elves?" asked Barnabas doubtfully. "Will they shoot arrows of, oh I don't know, *light*, at us?"

"Not at all," said Brynhild. "In fact, they are very kind. I think that you'll find Alfheimer to your liking."

"Alfheimer?" said Barnabas.

"The home of the Light Elves," said Brynhild. "It is a place of great beauty, and peace."

"Well, that sounds all right," admitted Barnabas. He

brightened. "Do you think they'll have some proper tea there?"

"I don't know about tea," replied Brynhild. "But they *do* have ambrosia."

"I'm sure that's well and good for *you*, but I'm sure it won't do for *me*, unless it's Earl Grey ambrosia, and served with a proper watercress sandwich," mumbled Barnabas.

Brynhild sighed as she steered Hynder towards Alfheimer and the Light Elves, whilst settling in for the ride. At first Barnabas thought only of ambrosia, and if perhaps Brynhild might be wrong and the elves might put on a proper spread, complete with tea and sandwiches and biscuits, but after a while he tired of thinking of that and instead began to contemplate Wilfred's strange, shy silence.

Indeed, Wilfred hadn't spoken since the odd exchange with Brynhild, when she had touched his arm and the young man had flushed and fallen quiet immediately. Having recently experienced a time in his life when he, too, had suffered from a sudden affliction of feeling that had left him awkward and miserable (caused by a mouse-headed waitress named Bindi in the deserts of the Egyptian underworld) he had a suspicion of what might be going on with Wilfred. It wouldn't do to speak outright of such a thing, of course, as he might be wrong in his assumption and to say something in such a case would cause no small degree of embarrassment for both detectives. Still, he resolved to keep watch over his assistant in case any more clues were forthcoming as to his emotions.

His musings on the matter of Wilfred's feelings were cut short, as Hynder had begun to descend and was even now breaking through the cloud cover above Alfheimer, the world of the Light Elves. Barnabas gasped in astonishment as the landscape came into view below them. Brynhild smiled knowingly, and Wilfred ceased his uncharacteristic brooding to cry out in wonder.

"Oh!" said Wilfred. "Oh, but look at that. *Do* look!"

"Yes, *do*," teased Brynhild, causing Wilfred to blush all over again.

"Well," said Barnabas, finding himself in the position of making things *un*awkward (which was usually Wilfred's duty and, if truth be told, that poor fellow was far more suited to such a role than was Barnabas). "Well," he repeated again.

"Yes, right?" said Wilfred, somehow catching his meaning. Brynhild looked, bemused, from one to the other, shaking her head.

"Entirely," agreed Barnabas.

"Quite so," added Wilfred.

"I assume you find Alfheimer to your liking?" asked Brynhild, her left eyebrow lifted in amusement.

"Yes, well," said Barnabas. "It is, well, it is, ah, *just so*."

This was, of course, a rather nonsensical statement, but both Wilfred and Brynhild knew precisely what he meant by it, because they knew the sorts of things that Barnabas would like, and because things in Alfheimer were, indeed, *just so*.

The trees were uniform in size and shape, having been trimmed into smooth, neat trunks with perfectly rounded poofs at the top for greenery, and had all been planted in nice, straight rows. The lawns were obviously carefully tended, so that not a weed nor a dandelion showed amongst the short green stems of the grass. Snow-white flowers had been carefully placed in tidy little beds that were carefully delineated by delicately filigreed garden fences of bronze, that were perfectly positioned to highlight the marvelously carved marbled fountains that dotted the lawns at regular intervals.

The lanes that ran between the trees were of a soft tan color that almost magically offset the emerald green of the lawns, and were arranged in concentric circles, forming an enormous spoked wheel pattern that converged at the center at a gloriously symmetrical limestone castle.

Everything here, it seemed, had been put where it was thoughtfully and considerately, so that it looked as though each and every thing was precisely where it was meant to be, and no other placement would be nearly so good as the place that the thing currently occupied.

"Just so," repeated Barnabas, nodding approvingly.

"It *is* magnificent, is it not?" said Brynhild.

"It is, why, it is even nicer than an English garden," said Barnabas in a whisper, as though he were speaking some sort of blasphemous thing (and, in a way, he was; to him, all things British were the gold standard, and to believe something to be superior to the English way of doing things had been, for him, unthinkable. At least it *had* been, until this very moment).

"And the castle," said Wilfred, still a bit stunned by the magnificence of the place. "How *ever* did they get the turrets so round?"

"And the arch of the windows is in perfect harmony with the curve of the walls, do you see?" said Barnabas.

"And do you see how the shutters are made of the same filigree that rings the flower beds?" pointed out Wilfred.

"Oh, my, do you see?" said Barnabas, pointing excitedly down to the wide lane that led to what was, presumably, the front doors of the castle. A group of elves, tiny in the distance, were mounted on snow-white horses, and were riding out in perfect formation, with tiny green and tan flags snapping smartly in the breeze.

"Their livery matches the gardens," said Wilfred. "It is as though they are part of the very landscape!"

A soft musical sound drifted up from the elvish party. It was a bit difficult to hear, as they were still rather high up, so that Barnabas had to cock his head in order to catch the melody more clearly.

"Is that a harp I hear?" he asked, amazed. "Are they truly playing the harp whilst riding horses?"

"Welcome to Alfheimer," said Brynhild, gesturing expansively with both hands.

"But it is marvelous!" exclaimed Barnabas, clapping his hands. "Although," he said, glancing at Brynhild's arms, which were still opened wide as though she might be trying to embrace the whole of Alfheimer, "perhaps you ought to put your hands back on the reins, don't you think?"

Brynhild laughed. "You should know by now that Hynder doesn't need reins," she said. Still, she obligingly took both reins in one hand as she guided Hynder down to the ground, where the stallioncame to a rest a few yards away from the elvish riders.

One of the riders cantered forward to greet them. His white-blond hair streamed out from beneath his tan and green plumed helmet (which, in truth, was more like a fancy headdress than any sort of protective device). His tunic and leggings (which were astonishingly tight, to Barnabas' thinking) were similarly colored, but were woven of some sort of sparkly thread, so that they shimmered and glimmered as the elf moved.

It was the elf's skin, though, which was the most remarkable. As pale white as freshly fallen snow, it seemed to glow as if the fellow were lit from within by the brightest lamp imaginable. Indeed, looking directly at this elf was akin to staring directly into the most intense gaslight possible.

"Well," whispered Barnabas, squinting as he tried to keep his eyes on the approaching figure. "He certainly is *bright*, is he not?"

"Extraordinarily so," agreed Wilfred, who was blinking his own eyes with some discomfort. "And it does no good to look at the others instead," he added, by way of warning. "They are *all* quite bright."

"It gives one a bit of a headache, does it not?" said Barnabas.

"Most definitely," said Wilfred, putting a hand above his brow in a futile attempt to shade his eyes. "It's like looking into the sun!"

"Hush!" said Brynhild. "You don't want them to hear you, do you?"

"Perhaps if they did they might, ah, *dim* themselves a bit?" suggested Barnabas.

"Oh yes," said Wilfred, "just a little bit would suffice. Like turning down a lantern, I should think."

"They are *Light* Elves," said Brynhild, rolling her eyes in exasperation. "They cannot 'dim themselves just a bit'. This is how they *are*. It's in their *name*."

"Hmmph," said Barnabas. "One can be *light* without

burning out people's eyeballs, is what I always say."

Wilfred nodded his head sagely, as though he had indeed heard his employer say just that many times (although, of course, he hadn't, as Barnabas had never said such a thing in his life). Brynhild merely shook her head in resignation. She was spared from any further discussion on the topic of the excessive brightness of the Light Elves by the arrival of the leading elf in front of them.

"Hail to the travelers," he said, bowing gallantly. "And welcome to Alfheimer! My name is Bjaarte, and on behalf of our queen I can assure you that we will be most pleased to have you as our esteemed guests."

"Thank you very…" began Brynhild, before Barnabas cut her off abruptly.

"How does your queen know that we are *esteemed* guests, rather than *unsavory* ones?" he demanded. His time in the Nine Worlds had made him a bit suspicious, to say the least, and the discomfort of his eyes had put him into a bit of a temper. "And if we are so esteemed, perhaps we might be given a tonic of sorts, to help with…"

"Headaches from our travels," interrupted Brynhild.

"Eyestrain!" corrected Barnabas indignantly. He had his eyes so squinched up against the brightness of the elf that it was a wonder he could see at all, and he had placed one hand dramatically over his face so that he might peep through his spread fingers.

"Please excuse him," said Brynhild hastily. "He's from very far away, and I fear our recent adventures may have soured his mood. She shot a glance of reprimand towards Barnabas, but it was Wilfred who spoke next.

"Not to be of any trouble, of course, but I too would appreciate a tonic for my head, if one were to be on hand, that is," he said shyly, with an apologetic look at both Bjarte and Brynhild.

Luckily, Bjarte simply laughed good-naturedly. "Of course you may both have a tonic," he said. "And whatever else you might require for your comfort. Please, if you'll follow me?" He turned his horse and began to walk the creature back in the direction of the beautiful palace. He turned briefly to look over his shoulder, smiling kindly. "I know we can be a bit hard on the eyes at first," he assured them. "But you will grow accustomed to it soon enough."

"Oh," said Barnabas bashfully, as there was nothing else to say, really. Bjarte's good manners had put his own rather shabby ones to shame, and he was terribly embarrassed.

Bjarte merely nodded courteously, and clucked his horse forward. The three companions obediently followed Bjarte, and they, in turn, were followed by the other elves in the company, who had resumed their harp-playing so that they all entered the palace in a soothing fanfare of melodious music.

They were led through a series of magnificent rooms and corridors, each one more splendiferous than the last. Everything (walls, floor tiles, carpets, even the ceilings) was of the same pleasing color scheme as the outside areas; all of the artwork upon the walls was beautifully painted and perfectly complementary. The entire place was the epitome of orderliness and understated luxury, and had a most soothing effect.

At last they entered a large room.

"The throne room," whispered Wilfred (rather unnecessarily, as at the front of the room were two very large and very ornate chairs that could only be thrones, and upon those chairs sat two very marvelously dressed elves).

"Splendid detective work," said Barnabas, a trifle sarcastically. "I had thought those two, sitting on those fancy chairs, to whom everyone is bowing and genuflecting and otherwise showing great deference, must of course be the *butler* and the *housekeeper*."

Wilfred reddened and cast an abashed look in Brynhild's direction. Barnabas observed his assistant's strange reaction, and again resolved to speak with him about it later. He also felt a bit ashamed of himself, for speaking so snippily to poor Wilfred and causing him embarrassment.

"Although," he said quickly, in order to make amends, "I suppose you must have thought that I was still quite blinded by the extreme, er, *lightness* of these Light Elves, and was unable, therefore, to see anything whatsoever. And indeed, you are quite right to think so. I am having the most abominable time with my eyes, I must say." And indeed, Barnabas did seem to be struggling quite a bit. His eyes were still terribly squinted, and he was blinking at a most alarming rate.

"Are you quite all right?" asked Wilfred with concern.

"Yes, yes, I'm fine," said Barnabas. "Aside from the fact that everywhere I look I see bright ghost images of whichever elf I happened to look at last. Sort of like when you look at a bright lamp, and then look away and see flashes of that lamp, except for with elves instead of overly bright lamps." He looked around, still blinking, as though to clear away the flashes of light from his vision.

Wilfred patted his arm consolingly, but was unable to offer any words of advice as the two figures seated upon the thrones beckoned them forwards.

"Greetings, Barnabas, Wilfred, and Brynhild," said the woman (who was, presumably, the queen). "I am Asta, and this is my husband Asmund, Queen and King of the Light Elves. We trust you have found our home pleasing? And that you have been made to feel most welcome?"

"Why, yes, we have found it most pleasing…wait a moment, how did you know our names?" replied Barnabas, frowning. The effect on his face was most unfortunate, since he was still squinting against the light and therefore ended up looking quite a bit like a grumpy mole that had been unexpectedly brought up out of its nice, dark den.

"Bjarte told us," replied the queen. Seeing Barnabas open his mouth to argue, she continued. "With his mind," she said. "Which is why you didn't hear him announce you."

"Light Elves are clairvoyant," whispered Brynhild.

"And you didn't think to tell us that beforehand?" hissed Barnabas. He looked towards the king and queen, saw them watching him expectantly and bowed nervously. He was suddenly aware that, if they could speak to each others' minds, then they could most assuredly look into his as well. Of course, as soon as he had that realization, the most embarrassing, arbitrary, and inappropriate thoughts flooded into his brain. The harder he tried to shove those thoughts aside, the faster they came along, until he was nearly paralyzed with mortification.

The queen laughed gently. "Do not worry," she said. "You cannot shock us, no matter what." She turned to look at Brynhild, and her eyes creased with merriment. "Now Brynhild, on the other hand..."

"I say!" said Wilfred, stepping forward in front of Brynhild, as though to shield her from the queen's prying.

"No offense meant," assured the queen, laughing. "I only meant that Brynhild is an *interesting* person, and we elves do so enjoy interesting persons."

"It's fine," said Brynhild, who looked completely unperturbed by the queen's intrusive attentions. "She's not wrong, you know."

Wilfred looked confused, and flushed with upset. The queen merely smiled kindly at him, with something that looked like pity in her eyes.

"*Anyway*," said the king, rolling his eyes good-naturedly at his meddlesome wife. "You are here to ask us for the gift of music, are you not?"

"How did..." began Barnabas, then stopped himself. Of course they knew everything about the companions, including the reason for their visit.

"And, of course, we shall be pleased to assist you." The king gestured for a page to bring him an item wrapped in a thickly emrodiered green and tan brocade. Asmund unwrapped the brocade to reveal a beautiful silver flute. "This is an enchanted flute," he explained, proferring it to the three supplicants. "It will surely put the giant Surt straight to sleep."

"Too bad it doesn't work on dwarf-dragons," said Asta, shuddering. "Oh, that poor town!" She winked at Barnabas. "It's really not your fault, you know," she said. "At least, not entirely. What I mean to say is that you didn't *mean* for that to happen."

Barnabas colored, knowing that she was referring to the

dwarf king Fafnir, who was also a dragon, and his destruction of the charming town of Vollagardal. At that moment, another elf offered him a large cup of a sweet-smelling amber liquid, and, without thinking, he quaffed it down in its entirety.

Immediately Barnabas' guilt lifted off of his shoulders, and floated away like an errant balloon (indeed, he imagined that he could *see* the guilt as it drifted up towards the ceiling and then, remarkably, disappeared).

His eyes, too, felt better. He could still see how very bright were the elves, but their light did not bother him so much, anymore. As he opened his eyes and looked more directly at the elves, he fancied that they were actually made of rainbows, rather than of flesh and bone, and said as much.

"Oh dear," said Asta, although her voice seemed to be coming from very far away. "You're only supposed to take sips of it, really."

Wilfred and Brynhild, who had each taken only one small draught of the stuff, looked from one to another with concern.

"It won't harm him," said Asmund. "He'll merely be, well, extraordinarily *happy* for a time."

And, in truth, Barnabas was exceedingly happy. His headache was quite gone, and his worries had dissipated as well. Alfheimer was the perfect place, to his mind; everything was orderly and peaceful and how it ought to be. Indeed, he could think of no other place better than this one. And how amiable were the elves themselves! So unlike their brethren in Svortalheim.

Incredibly, there was also a most beautiful marble statue of a mouse in the throne room. In Egypt, Barnabas had become quite enamored with a waitress named Bindi who was, unfortunately, also a mouse. (Of course, Barnabas had also been a mouse at the time, or at least *partly* so, which had removed any strangeness or impropriety from the matter).

He walked over to the statue to admire it, and then, to Wilfred's mortification (and everyone else's great amusement) embraced it. Wilfred fruitlessly attempted to pull his employer away from the statue, whilst Brynhild and all of the elves present laughed appreciatively.

"It's the perfect statue, in a perfect place, and surrounded by all these perfect elves!" proclaimed Barnabas. Wilfred took hold of his fingers and tried to pry them from the statue, but to no avail. Barnabas merely dug in all the deeper.

"I apologize for this behavior," said Wilfred. "I assure you it is most unlike him. It must needs be the drink that has caused this."

"Oh yes, thank you, my boy!" said Barnabas. "I had nearly forgotten all about the perfect drink, in the perfect place that has the perfect statue and is full of all the perfect elves. Might I have some more of that, please?"

"No!" said everyone in unison.

"At least, not right now," added the queen. "But you are welcome to stay here and abide with us, for as long as you like."

"Splendid!" agreed Barnabas. "Did you hear that, Wilfred? We can stay with the Light Elves, and drink wonderful drinks, and spend time with this wonderful statue!"

"I'm certain that would be most *wonderful*," said Wilfred drily. "But we have a job to do, remember?"

"A case which isn't going very well at all," said Barnabas cheerfully. "This place is much better than that case, I am sure."

"But we are to prevent the end of the world," protested Wilfred.

"The world cannot possibly end in Alfheimer," said Barnabas. "It's too pretty here."

"I don't think Ragnorok cares whether things are pretty or not," said Wilfred.

"Why, then Ragnorok is a scoundrel, and a scallywag!" proclaimed Barnabas nonsensically.

Just then the entire palace began to shake. Cracks formed on the floor and in the ceiling, so that plaster rained down upon all those in the throne room. Paintings fell askew, or were knocked off the walls entirely. A stained glass window (of tan, white, and green, of course), shattered and fell to the floor with a pretty tinkling sound. Elves gasped in shock as the moving floor jostled them about, causing them to fall as well.

"Earthquake!" yelped Brynhild. She grabbed Wilfred and pulled him down to crouch upon the floor with her, whilst Barnabas stayed clinging to the mouse statue. At last, the tail of the statue broke off and Barnabas fell heavily to the floor, tail in hand.

At last the tremors stopped. Barnabas, still sitting on the floor, regarded the broken marble tail in his hands sadly, then glanced around to see the damage done to the beautiful palace of the Light Elves. Nothing was in order anymore, and fear was apparent on the faces of the shining elves.

"Oh dear," he said.

"Oh dear, indeed," replied Wilfred.

"I suppose we must go," said Barnabas. "And at least *try* to stop Ragnorok, before it ruins everything of beauty." He sighed. "Even though I fear we shall fail."

"We shan't," said Wilfred, placing his hand on his employer's shoulder by way of comfort.

"Well, we either shall or shan't, but if we shan't it shall not be for want of trying!" said Barnabas with as much bravado as he could muster.

"Hear, hear," said Brynhild approvingly.

"Hear what?" asked Barnabas.

"No," corrected Brynhild, "hear, hear. It's a *saying*."

"Yes, of course," said Barnabas irritably (in truth, the lovely drink seemed to be wearing off rather rapidly). "We are *here*, and now we are going (he thought that a clever joke). Wait, where's the flute?"

Wilfred rose and headed up to the thrones. Asmund handed him the flute with a nod. "Good luck," said the king. Wilfred rejoined his friends, and together they walked out of the throne room to the cheers of the elves (which was a splendid feeling, to be farewelled as heroes, thought Barnabas). They found their way out easily enough through the logically arranged corridors and were soon back on Hynder, flying away from the pleasant world of Alfheimer towards the far less pleasant world of Muspelheim.

"You know," observed Wilfred once they were aloft, "we never did get that gold to the dwarves."

"Gold to the dwarves?" asked Barnabas, perplexed.

"Remember, we were supposed to steal Freya's gold for Fafnir, so that he might make a replacement bowl to catch the poison from Loki's snake?" said Wilfred.

"Heavens," said Barnabas. "I had quite forgotten all about that." He frowned, considering. "Oh well, I suppose it can't be helped. To Muspelheim!" He stuck out his arm like a charging soldier, and it was off to Muspelheim for the two detectives, their Viking guide, and their magical horse.

Chapter Sixteen

Barnabas dozed off as they flew, and had the most dreadful dream, in which he had somehow managed to get himself placed inside of an oven, and was currently being roasted. At last, the heat inside the oven became too much to bear, and he awoke with a start to find that reality had, in fact, intruded upon his dreams, as he was indeed in a situation of the most extreme and uncomfortable warmness.

In his sleep he had fallen into a leaning position upon Wilfred's back (although, somehow, Wilfred had managed to wriggle out of his heavy fur cloak without waking Barnabas, so that he was clad only in the thin cotton robes they had got in Egypt. Barnabas sat upright on Hynder, grumbling grumpily.

"You might have warned me that it would be this hot here," he said accusingly to Brynhild, who had also removed her warm cloak and was now wearing only a lightweight short tunic of cotton or somesuch material. Barnabas was, of course, far too cross with his own discomfort to be properly shocked at her lack of attire.

"Well, it is a fire realm," said Brynhild reasonably.

"And with fire giants, as well," added Wilfred helpfully. "I would imagine they add to the heat quite a bit, being rather large, I would assume, and on fire."

"Huh," replied Barnabas, fumbling to wriggle out of his cloak without upsetting his seat upon Hynder. "At least you could have warned me to take my cloak off. I'm sweating like a mudlark in August."

"We didn't wish to wake you," explained Wilfred. "You were sleeping quite soundly."

"I'm sure I was, as I was being roasted..." He trailed off

as he happened to glance at Wilfred's back. There, on the thin fabric of Wilfred's robe, was the sweaty imprint of a man that could only have been made by Barnabas himself. He narrowed his eyes in order to better see, and was slightly appalled to notice that one could clearly see the shape of his shoulders, the slight swell of his somewhat rounded waistline (which, he had to admit, looking at the image critically, had narrowed considerably since he had left his cosy parlour in Marylebone), and even the point of his nose sticking out from where his face had turned to the side.

"Um. Er. Eh. Wilfred?" he began. He grimaced and reached out a tentative hand, as though to perhaps pat away the embarrassing stain, then thought better of it and lowered his hand once more.

"Yes?" asked Wilfred.

"What?" said Barnabas.

"You were going to tell me something?" said Wilfred.

"I was not," said Barnabas.

"You said my name," said Wilfred.

"I most certainly did not," said Barnabas, looking away guiltily. He was hoping that the stain might dry, or be obscured in time by Wilfred's own sweat. It was too embarrassing a prospect to have to admit to having sweated an image of oneself onto someone else, much less to be subjected to an inquisition about it.

"You did so," said Brynhild. "I heard you too."

"It seems we are at an impasse, then," replied Barnabas, "as the two of you are intent on insisting I said 'Wilfred' whilst I shall continue to insist that I most assuredly did not."

"I only thought perhaps you had something you wished to say," sniffed Wilfred, somewhat offended by Barnabas' inexplicably prickly mood.

"Oh, do stop haranguing me!" cried Barnabas. "It is far too hot for such torture!"

Wilfred and Brynhild exchanged a bemused look, then both shrugged and let the matter drop.

There was silence for several minutes after that, as Brynhild carefully steered Hynder around several mountains that were, somehow, entirely on fire (which emitted a fearsome heat that made Barnabas feel certain that he might utterly melt, like a pat of butter on a frying pan). Nor was the rest of the landscape any more inviting, really, dotted as it was with fire-burned rocks that gave off a dusty ash that clogged the lungs whenever a breeze blew, as well as other places that were more actively afire, which threw up great clouds of grey smoke that similarly choked the travelers.

Looking down, Barnabas at last saw a moving, living figure on the bleak landscape. As large as an oversized boulder, albeit in a relatively man-shaped form, the creature lumbered slowly across the dark rocks. The thing was quite dark yet also possessed of a reddish glow, like the blackened charcoal at the bottom of a cooking pit that still harbored a bit of the fire that had initially ignited it.

"Wilfred?" said Barnabas.

Wilfred said nothing in reply, but continued to look about.

"Wilfred," said Barnabas again. To his intense annoyance, Wilfred not only didn't reply, but (quite maddeningly) began to softly hum, "When the Swallows Homeward Fly".

"Wilfred, I say!" exclaimed Barnabas. "'Tis no time for parlour music! Have you taken leave of your hearing, man!"

"Pardon?" said Wilfred blandly, affecting a look of surprised innocence. "I'm quite sure I must not have heard you."

"I called your name twice!" sputtered Barnabas. "And, as I am sitting directly behind you, I am certain that it is quite impossible that you did not hear."

"I had thought I had, but did not wish to be in error once more and cause offense again," said Wilfred implacably. Brynhild stifled a chuckle, rather unsuccessfully.

"I'm sure it's all terribly amusing," retorted Barnabas, sticking his nose up into the air as high as it would go, in order to appear as haughty as possible, "I'm sure that you are truly enjoying yourself, having your fun at my expense. In the meanwhile, of course, I shall be keeping my eye upon that very large person who appears to be made of fire directly below us."

"You mean, the Fire Giant?" asked Brynhild. "The thing we were coming here to see? And in particular the one in front of which we are about to land?"

Barnabas, intent upon his outrage, had not noticed that Hynder was, indeed, descending, and was, in fact, doing so directly in front of the fiery creature.

"Oh," he said. "Yes. Hmmph."

"I'm surprised that you didn't see how close we were getting to Surt, since you were going to such great trouble to point him out in the first place," said Brynhild.

""Yes, well, perhaps I *would* have, had everyone not been behaving in quite so difficult a fashion," said Barnabas.

"I mean, we *are* within ten feet of him, you know," added Brynhild.

"We are within ten feet of a lot of things," said Barnabas implacably (which was not particularly true, unless one counted rocks when one was speaking of 'lots of things').

"And did you not notice how the temperature went up?" persisted Brynhild.

"Why, certainly," replied Barnabas sarcastically, wiping the copious sweat from his brow with a dramatic flourish. "I'm quite sure I noticed that it went from forty degrees to forty-one degrees. Really, it was altogether balmy before we landed at the feet of a Fire Giant, and now it's just a wee bit on the warm side."

Brynhild muttered unintelligibly under her breath as she dropped down from Hynder, and Barnabas sniffed victoriously. His pleasure was short lived, however, as he turned to look at Surt, who was rather more dreadful looking now that they were closer and could see him in more detail.

Surt's skin was, indeed, made of some sort of brittle rock. Having already seen the Dark Elves, with their skin of molten obsidian, this was not as shocking to the two detectives as it might have been. What was shocking, however, was the red glow that emanated from between the many cracks in Surt's skin. It looked as though the poor fellow was completely on fire within, and that fire was, even now, charring the blackened skin from the inside out.

Also quite terrible was the *smell*. Surt smelled quite a bit like a very intense cookout; or, rather, a cookout that had been done some time ago and the remnants left out overly long, so that they had all gone a bit *off*.

Still, it didn't do to judge a fellow by his appearance (or his smell, for that matter) so Barnabas put a brave face on and smiled politely at the giant as he approached Brynhild.

"Maybe he'll be friendly?" he whispered to Wilfred (both were still atop Hynder, whilst Brynhild stood just off to the side). "Like the delightful giants in Jutunheim?"

"Hail, Surt!" called out Brynhild to the giant, bowing formally as she did so. "We are…"

She was prevented from finishing her greeting, however, when Surt reached out a crumbly hand and snatched her up in his enormous fist. She kicked her feet helplessly as he hoisted her up towards his face.

"Mmmm," said Surt. "Dinner came to Surt!"

"Ahhhhh!" yelped Brynhild, punching and pulling at the giant's fingers in vain.

"Ahhhhh!" echoed Barnabas and Wilfred in unison.

"Mmmmm," said Surt again, smacking his lips and opening his mouth. His tongue (gruesome in its hot wetness, and preceded by a wall of breath that was overpowering with its stinky humidity) emerged from his open maw and delivered a great sticky lick to Brynhild's face. "Dinner is tasty," said Surt, nodding approvingly. "Surt is going to like dinner."

Barnabas, shocked into action, leapt down from the horse, picked up a rock and flung it as hard as he could towards Surt. "Take that, you foul-smelling ne'er-do-well!" he yelled. He bent down, picked up another rock, and heaved that one at Surt as well. The rocks bounced (rather harmlessly, if truth be told, as Barnabas was not a terribly strong fellow, nor was he athletically inclined) from Surt's things. Little pieces of dust drifted off from where the rocks had sloughed off a bit of charcoal-skin, but that appeared to be the extent of the damage.

"Ow," said Surt. "Dinner is annoying Surt." Surt bent

down and, with no further ado, lifted a screaming and kicking Barnabas off the ground and held him level with Brynhild.

"Thanks," said Brynhild. "Very brave of you to try."

Despite his abject terror at the prospect of being momentarily eaten up by a giant who was not only on fire but who was also possessed of the most dreadful breath Barnabas had ever smelled, he beamed a bit at the praise. He made a gesture as though he were gallantly tipping an imaginary hat, and inclined his head towards Brynhild. "It was no less than my duty," he said. "I wonder which one of us he shall devour first?" He sighed. "I do rather wish that we were not here, about to be eaten up by a Fire Giant."

"As do I," said Brynhild sadly.

"This sort of thing doesn't happen in Marylebone," observed Barnabas. "Indeed, the worst that might happen there is a pickpocket, or perhaps a splashing by a careless carriage driver."

"Then, how did you end up in the land of the dead, rather than in this Marylebone place?" asked Brynhild.

"Wilfred and I were dispatched, quite dreadfully and as a terrible surprise, by a mummy that we had gone to see in a museum," said Barnabas, as if this sort of thing were quite commonplace, and not at all strange.

"Huh," said Brynhild, flinching a little as Surt's fist brought them closer and closer to his open mouth. "That sounds a bit worse than a pickpocket, I think."

"Yes, well," said Barnabas, "such things hardly ever happen, really. I fear I'm not explaining it properly…"

Their conversation was cut short by two things: a wave of hot, smelly breath as Surt's fists (and the two terrified people therein, passed between his lips and hovered there with the giant's crooked teeth both above and below them, and the sound of Wilfred clumsily singing "When the Swallows Homeward Fly."

"Really, Wilfred!" snapped Barnabas. "Is *now* really the time for your infernal singing? Can't a fellow be devoured alive in peace?"

"Louder, Wilfred!" called Brynhild, rather inexplicably.

"*Louder?*" asked Barnabas. "You wish to be eaten whilst listening to Wilfred's caterwauling?"

"No," said Brynhild, "look! We're moving backwards!"

Barnabas looked and, indeed, the fists in which they were contained had left the interior of Surt's mouth and now hovered somewhere just in front of the giant's lips. Confused, he turned puzzled eyes towards Brynhild. "It's the music!" she whispered. "Remember? Fire Giants are charmed by music!"

"You mean, if Wilfred sings we won't be devoured entirely?" asked Barnabas hopefully.

"We won't be devoured at all if he does it properly," replied Brynhild.

"Oh dear," said Barnabas, listening to the off-key sound of Wilfred's singing and shaking his head sadly. "We are doomed."

"The flute, Wilfred!" yelled Brynhild. "Use the flute!"

"Oh, yes, the flute!" agreed Barnabas. "Precisely what I was about to say."

Brynhild narrowed her eyes at him and shook her head, but said nothing. Her eyes brightened with hope, however, as the sounds of Wilfred's flute playing reached their ears and Surt's hands began to lower.

Barnabas looked up and saw that a look of sleepiness had come over the giant's eyes. "It's working!" he whispered loudly to Brynhild. "Oh, sweet heavens, we shall not be devoured today!"

Wilfred continued to play, and Surt's fists continued to lower, until at last Barnabas and Brynhild were safely on the ground once more. Carefully, they extricated themselves from the now-sleeping giant's grasp. Brynhild darted forwards and slipped Surt's fire sword from the scabbard (which, luckily, was not nearly so large as one might have expected a giant's sword to be, and, further, lay upon the ground, having fallen whilst the giant was preoccupied with thoughts of his dinner). She wrapped the sword in her cloak and quickly began to ready Hynder for their flight out of Muspelheim.

"We should..." she began, then broke off when she saw the look on Barnabas' face. His skin had gone pasty white, excepting for two little blotches on his cheeks the size and color of crabapples. His eyes were as wide and round as twin moons at the height of their waxing, whilst his mouth was screwed up in some sort of odd upside-down grin. His eyelids lowered and then opened again in great slow blinks. "Are you..." she said, "are you, well, is everything all right?"

"Fine," squeaked Barnabas in a strange, high voice. Then, remarkably, he sat down with a heavy thud, emitted a loud sob, and began to cry.

Brynhild, surprised, looked helplessly at Wilfred. Wilfred lowered the flute and rushed to his employer's side. "I say!" he said. "Is there something the matter?"

"Huh?" came the sleepy voice of the giant Surt from behind them.

"Don't stop playing!" cried Brynhild. "Surt will wake up."

Wilfred hurriedly placed the flute back up to his lips and began to play once more.

"Why are you crying?" asked Brynhild, once the giant was safely lulled back to sleep. Wilfred, unable to speak properly, arched his eyebrows questioningly and nodded sympathetically at Barnabas.

"Oh, why is everyone staring at me?" wailed Barnabas. "Haven't you ever seen a grown man from London wearing an Egyptian toga covered in charcoal from a ridiculously burnt-up Viking fire world whilst standing in front of a hypnotized giant and having a bit of a cry?" he flapped his robes in frustration and, indeed, quite a bit of charcoal dust, presumably from where Surt's hands had rubbed off a bit, floated away in a dark cloud.

Wilfred and Brynhild looked at each other quizzically, both shaking their heads. "Nope," said Brynhild at last. "I don't believe either one of us has ever seen such a thing."

"Well, now you have," snapped Barnabas. "And you're welcome!" he added emphatically (and somewhat nonsensically).

"Uh," said Brynhild. "Sure." She looked at Wilfred, who

was staring with great concern at Barnabas and attempting to give him a comforting pat on the shoulder whilst still maintaining the playing of the flute. "Hynder and I are going to walk over there," she said, pointing to a large rocky outcropping some distance away. "Join us when you're ready."

So saying, she walked away, with Hynder following at her heels. She glanced back over her shoulder as she walked. "And don't stop playing, whatever you do. Surt waking up is the last thing we need right now."

Wilfred nodded his aggreance, and the two detectives were left alone.

"Can you at least stop playing that song?" said Barnabas miserably. "It is so sad, I cannot bear it!"

Wilfred nodded, and immediately launched into a rendition of "Come into the Garden, Maude".

"Oh, but that is hardly better," said Barnabas. "Really, your taste in music is quite morose."

Wilfred shrugged apologetically, but continued to play.

"I suppose," said Barnabas, sniffling a bit, "that nearly *any* song might put me into a state right now. It *does* wreak havoc with one's emotions, being nearly eaten by a Fire Giant, you know."

Wilfred nodded sympathetically.

Barnabas sighed. "And it is becoming most tiresome, really, all these episodes of nearly dying. Snakes, wolves, angry giants…why, it is unconscionable!" He paused, and looked off into the distance. "Still, I must admit that is not the true cause of my distress, if you must continue to press me so," he said (although Wilfred, who was still playing the flute, had by no means pressed him on the topic in any way). "Indeed, I fear to tell you what grieves me so."

Barnabas looked shyly at Wilfred, who nodded encouragingly.

"Very well," said Barnabas, "if you insist I suppose I must tell you. My but you are a relentless inquisitor!" Wilfred shrugged and attempted a smile, which was no mean feat considering that his lips were pursed to blow into the mouthpiece of the flute.

"So," continued Barnabas, "as you well know, I had developed some feelings of the tender variety towards Bindi. Ah, Bindi, the lovely mouse-headed waitress in the Egyptian desert! And I'm certain that you recollect that is was quite impossible for me to pursue a relationship with her, for the obvious reason that she lives in Egypt, whilst my duty has taken me to this forsaken place."

"And she's a mouse," added Wilfred quickly before launching into the next verse of the song.

"Well, possessed of a mouse head, I should say, rather," said Barnabas. "What may surprise you is that, whilst at the home of the Light Elves in Alfheimer, I had allowed myself to fancy that I might stay there and abide."

Wilfred opened his eyes wide in feigned shock, as though Barnabas' desire to stay with with Light Elves hadn't been readily apparent to everyone present.

"And, similarly, I allowed my fancies to stray even farther afield. You see, the beauty and the wonder of Alfheimer planted a seed of hope within my heart, that perhaps Asta and Asmund might be possessed of some magic that might make it possible to bring Bindi hence, and so we might dwell there, in Alfheimer, ever after. And further, the thought germinated in my mind that the elves might either change Bindi into a fully human sort of person, or perhaps cause me to revert to my former mouse-headed self. You do remember how, in Egypt, our heads were turned into mouse heads for a time?"

Wilfred inclined his head in remembrance, and attempted to pat Barnabas' shoulder with his elbow by way of comfort.

"So you see, when you began to play that song, and my emotions were already heightened by the experience of being on the inside of a Fire Giant's mouth, rather than on the outside, where one belongs…well, I'm certain that you can understand how one's emotions might get the best of him." Barnabas pursed his lips and exhaled heavily, as though he, too, were playing a flute. "But now we come to the crux of things," he said. "You see, all these thoughts of my own emotional state have been exacerbated by my perceptions of *your* emotions."

Barnabas paused to see the effect these words had on his assistant. Wilfred raised his eyebrows warily but said nothing, so Barnabas, thusly encouraged, continued. "As your employer, nay, as your friend, and as one who has experienced quite the same range of feelings that I believe that you yourself are currently in the midst of, well, I would simply like to say that I, well…"

Wilfred waved a pinky finger to hurry Barnabas along. "I suppose it's better to just get on with it," said Barnabas. He exhaled noisily once more. "I know that you've developed some tenderness of feeling of your own," he said. "For Brynhild."

Wilfred's playing faltered a bit, but he quickly got hold of himself and continued with the song (which was now on the third repetition, so long had Barnabas talked). The reddening of his cheeks, however, confirmed that Barnabas' suspicions were correct.

"Let me assure you," said Barnabas, "that, despite my own inability to find a satisfactory resolution to my situation with Bindi, I am very happy for you." Wilfred's eyebrows shot up in surprise. "I know, I know," said Barnabas, "you think that I do not like Brynhild. But you are completely incorrect in that matter. In point of fact, I like her very much indeed."

Wilfred stared quizzically at Barnabas. "Really?" he said, then placed the flute back to his lips and recommensed with his song.

"Why, of course I do!" said Barnabas. "She is brave, and intelligent, and, beneath that *absurdly* gruff exterior, quite kind at heart, I do believe. Truly, she is an extraordinary woman!"

Wilfred flushed happily, then glanced to where Brynhild waited in the distance with Hynder.

"Quite right," said Barnabas, wiping the last of the tears from his cheeks. "We ought to be going." He stood up and together they began to walk towards Brynhild, away from the still-mesmerized Surt. "Although," he added, "I *do* think she is a bit of a know-it-all. Really, she does *insist* on being right all of the time, which is quite patently silly, because most of the time I know that it is *myself* that is correct."

Wilfred shook his head and sighed, so that the last note came out in a long, warbling trill.

Chapter Seventeen

The ride back to Svortalfheim was made quickly and in somewhat of an awkward silence. Barnabas was mortified by his outburst in Muspelheim (or, rather, the fact that people, Brynhild in particular, had witnessed it). Wilfred was embarrassed because of his employer's discovery of his feelings towards Brynhild. And Brynhild, for her part, had no idea of what to say or do after one has witnessed a grown man weeping hysterically, was made uncomfortable by Barnabas' red-rimmed eyes and tear-stained cheeks, which served as a reminder of the incident.

Therefore, no one spoke beyond the barest necessity, and even felt a bit of relief at the sight of the rather malevolent-looking party of Dark Elves who converged upon them the moment they landed in order to escort them to Maledokkalfar's lair, as the presence of the Dark Elves prevented the possibility of the event being spoken of any further.

"Well," said Barnabas, with a bit of forced gaiety, "at least they didn't shoot flaming arrows at us this time."

"Quite so," agreed Wilfred politely.

"Everything is better when nothing is on fire!" proclaimed Barnabas. As no one could really disagree with that, everyone merely smiled and nodded.

The party of Dark Elves came to within hailing distance of the travelers and stopped. "Come," said one, a glowering, swarthy fellow who looked as though his face might crack in two if a smile were to cross it. Indeed, a myriad of small cracks already emanated out from around his eyes and lips (although Barnabas suspected that these were made not by smiling, but from scowling instead, so mirthless was the elf's expression). "You're going to see Maledokkalfar. "You'd better hope you have the sword he wants. If you don't, you won't be coming back.

With that cheery welcome, the elf turned on his heels and strode back the way he had come, clearly expecting to be followed. The other elves, however, remained behind and arrayed themselves in a triangular formation so that they formed something of a funnel around the three companions. Obviously the intention was to flank them and then come around behind so that they would have no choice but to follow."

"There's nothing for it but to follow him, I suppose!" said Barnabas. He was still trying to assert a sense of bravado that he did not feel in the slightest, in order to lighten the mood. He slid down from Hynder's back and busied himself with rummaging through their packs as the others likewise dismounted. Soon enough Barnabas found the sword, and lifted it, still wrapped up in Brynhild's cloak, out of the bag in which Brynhild had stashed it.

"Be careful with that," warned Brynhild. "It is more dangerous than you know."

"I am more than capable of handling things of any sort of danger, whether I know it or not, thank you very much," retorted Barnabas.

"Perhaps Brynhild ought carry the sword?" suggested Wilfred tactfully. "Since she recoverd it from Surt, that is." He gave Brynhild a shy glance, and then looked away, blushing. She, seeing Wilfred's manner, stared quizzically at him and looked as though she might say something.

The moment was interrupted by Barnabas.

"Nonsense," he said. "It makes no difference whatsoever *who* carries the sword, just so long as it *is* carried. And as I am the one who is currently carrying it, well, then, I shall continue to do so."

So saying he lifted his nose into the air and walked off briskly in pursuit of the Dark Elf. Wilfred and Brynhild hurried to catch up, and the other elves fell in behind.

At last they came to the place where Maledokkalfar dwelt,

and paused at the entrance as the leading elf (Barnabas had dubbed him "Crackly Face" in his mind) shouted to the guards at the door to let them in.

Maledokkalfar's abode was, of course, not in a proper sort of palace (or really a proper sort of *house* whatsoever). It was, instead, located inside of a dark, deep cave. Barnabas and Wilfred shared a nervous glance as they entered, but as Brynhild stepped bravely inside, following the glowering elf who led the way, and as there were several rather glowering elves walking impatiently behind the two detectives, they had no choice but to enter the cave as well.

They were led down a series of dark corridors that put them much in mind of the dwarven tunnels in Nidavellir.

"I do so dislike these underground places," whispered Barnabas to Wilfred. "They do not suit me at all, I say."

"It makes one wish for just one Light Elf, to light the way," agreed Wilfred, squinting his eyes in order to see in the dim light.

"Or some of that delightful tea they served," said Barnabas wistfully.

"I think perhaps not," replied Wilfred. "Indeed, I would suggest that you stay away from that tea entirely."

"On the contrary," said Barnabas. "In point of fact, I should like to have it for breakfast, afternoon tea, and supper each and every day!"

"Truly," said Wilfred, frowning. "I do not think *that* is a good idea at all. Perhaps a nice chamomile concoction, instead?"

"Chamomile?" said Barnabas. "Don't be silly. Why, you didn't even try the tea. It really gave one the most astounding feeling of relaxation." He clapped Wilfred sympathetically on the shoulder. "You really must try it yourself. You seem a bit uptight lately."

Wilfred began to sputter an indignant reply, but they had at last come into Maledokkalfar's throne room and so Wilfred was forced to swallow his retort.

It was difficult to see in the darkness, but Barnabas could make out the figure of Maledokkalfar seated on a high chair flanked by sconces across the wide expanse of the room. Dark Elves clustered around either side of a long aisle that led up to the chair. They were pressed closely together, and this, combined with the dim light of the place, made it impossible to accurately judge their numbers, but Barnabas thought that there were perhaps several hundred of the creatures present.

Barnabas, Wilfred, and Brynhild were herded down the aisle to stand at the foot of Maledokkalfar's throne. The flames of the sconces on either side cast a flickering light across the king's face, making him appear even more malevolent than he had seemed outside, threatening a fiery death if they failed to bring him the sword.

"So," said Maledokkalfar, with absolutely no pretense at the normal pleasantries, "do you have Surt's sword?"

"Indeed we do!" said Barnabas, stepping forward. He hefted the sword high up into the air. As he did so, Brynhild's cloak came unwound from around the sword and slipped down to the ground. The flames of the exposed sword flared brightly in the darkness, and cast a harsh, unwavering light upon the cave walls and the appalled faces of the Dark Elves who were congregated in the throne room.

Feeling the eyes of everyone on him, hearing the utter lack of sound uttered by anyone, and thinking, therefore, that the elves were overawed by the presence of the sword, Barnabas found that he felt terribly important. He straightened his spine as though he were a general addressing his troops, gave the sword a dramatic flourish, and waved it about. Reaching the sword up as high as his arms could stretch (and even standing on his tip-toes just a bit so as to appear just a bit taller) he pivoted on his toes and turned from one side to the other, so that all might have a better view.

The eyes of the elves were turned, as one, to him, and they were all as round as a poupette's. Similarly, their mouths were formed into perfect circles, which neatly echoed the widened shape of their eyes.

Feeling proud of himself for being the bearer of such a mighty object, Barnabas looked to his friends to see if they, too, were enjoying his triumphant moment. Wilfred, however, merely looked confused, whilst Brynhild had turned entirely white and was pressing her fingertips harshly into her temples as though she were mightily displeased. Barnabas raised a questioning eyebrow at her, but then shook his head, dismissing the distraction of her disapproval. Brynhild was often, after all, quite critical, and so Barnabas decided to pay her no more heed. Instead, he turned back to bask in what he perceived as the admiration of the elves.

However, Barnabas had gravely misinterpreted the reaction of the Dark Elves to the sword. Their silence was not one of impressment, but rather one of shock and more than a little fear. Indeed, the utter silence in the chamber had merely been a momentary lull before the true sounds of appalled horror commenced.

Suddenly, the chamber erupted into a cacophony of shrieking terror. The open mouths of the elves, which Barnabas had thought to be preparing to utter things like, 'ooooh' and 'ahhhhh', were now emitting screams of an ear-crippling pitch. The eyes, only moments ago wide with shock, were now squeezed shut as though to block out the sight of Barnabas and his sword, and arms were flung up to cover the faces of the cringing, shrieking elves.

Confused, Barnabas turned this way and that, swinging the sword with him. "What?" he cried. "What is it? Why is everyone carrying on so?" However, each time he turned, he set off a new chorus of screams in whichever direction he was facing.

Whilst most of the Dark Elves were flailing and screaming and cringing about the room, a few of them were completely silent and immobile, and simply stared blankly at him with the widened eyes that he had, moments before, mistook for approbation. Others appeared to be stuck in varying aspects of a fleeing motion, or a cringing one, or, in the case of one particularly disturbing elf, one of complete rage (this one's lips were curled up tight over his teeth, his brows lowered dangerously over his eyes, and his arm raised in a most menacing fashion. Even more disturbingly, he had come up quite close behind Barnabas, so that when Barnabas turned in that direction he was given quite a startle, so close was the angry elf. However, the fellow seemed to have frozen there, just before delivering what promised to be a mighty blow to the back of Barnabas' head).

"Ack!" yelped Barnabas, taking a step away from the nasty-looking elf. Mystified, he looked about with wild eyes. "Truly, whatever is the matter with everyone? Why are you all screaming and running about? And why is this fellow playing at being a statue? And in such a strange and unsettling pose, I might add."

"He's not playing," said Brynhild (rather incomprehensibly, thought Barnabas).

Annoyed with her cryptic answer, Barnabas looked for Maledokkalfar, to see if he might shed some light, so to speak, on the situation. Incredibly, the king himself was cowering behind one of the immobilized elves, and was peeking around with his fingers spread out over his eyes.

"Cover it, you idiot!" yelled the king.

"Cover it?" asked Barnabas, blinking slowly. "Cover what?"

"The sword!" said Maledokkalfar. "Can't you see you've won? Must you continue to torment us so?"

"The sword?" said Barnabas, confused. "I've won? Torment? I must say, you really do need to be more clear about things, if you expect anyone to understand you at all."

Brynhild sighed heavily behind him, and he heard her mutter under her breath.

"The sword," she said, in an exhausted voice. "An uncovered sword from a Fire Giant turns Dark Elves to stone."

"Stone?" asked Barnabas, still not comprehending. Then, looking at all of the elves 'playing statue', and the others running amok in abject terror, understanding slowly dawned upon him. "Oh," he said, chagrined. "Oh, dear."

"Oh dear, indeed," agreed Wilfred.

"Cover it!" cried Maledokkalfar.

Sheepishly, Barnabas bent to retrieve Brynhild's cloak,

and quickly placed it back over the sword. "I'm terribly sorry," he said. "Truly, it was not my intention..." He held out the sword to Maledokkalfar, by way of offering peace, but the cloak began to slip off once more, revealing the tip of the sword.

"Ahhhh!" yelled Maledokkalfar, ducking more fully behind the statue of his stony erstwhile courtier.

"Oh my," said Barnabas, fumbling with the cloak. "Frightfully sorry, didn't mean to do that, the cloak slipped is all, won't happen again..."

"Leave it!" yelled Maledokkalfar from behind the statue. "Just put it on the floor and leave!"

"Quite right, quite right," said Barnabas. He bent down and gingerly placed the wrapped sword on the floor, then rose up and began to back away from the dreadful scene of carnage that he had, quite accidentally, wrought. Everywhere one looked were elves who had either been turned entirely to stone, whilst those who had not been were cringing and wailing from their hiding places.

Barnabas looked regretfully at the nearest statue and felt a wave of remorse. "*Terribly* sorry," he repeated. He took a fold of his robe in one hand and began to dust the thing off in a clumsy attempt to make amends.

"That won't help," said Maledokkalfar, who had ventured to peer around the stony shoulders of the courtier's statue once more. "He's a *statue*. He doesn't care if he's *dusty*."

"Certainly," said Barnabas. "I'm sure you must be right. It's just that I feel quite dreadfully about this whole thing, you see."

"Good!" snapped Maledokkalfar. "As well you should."

"And, it comes to mind that I wouldn't want anyone else to be punished for my mistake. Meaning, of course, that it would only compound the tragedy were our quest to fail and Ragnorok to occur, simply because I didn't know how Dark Elves might react to a fire sword."

"What are you prattling on about?" demanded the king.

"I believe he's asking if you still intend to give the dragon Nidhug nightmares, as per our original agreement," supplied

Wilfred helpfully.

"You want me to *help* you?" replied Maledokkalfar, astounded.

"You'll honor the agreement," interjected Brynhild, "unless you'd like us to wave that sword around again."

"Oh my!" cried Barnabas and Wilfred in unison, shocked at Brynhild's ruthlessness.

"Fine!" spat Maledokkalfar. "I'll give your stupid dragon nightmares. Just please go now and never come back."

"Of course," said Barnabas, trying to smooth things over. "As you wish. We are most grateful, and pleased to be of service, and…"

"Gooooo!" yelled Maledokkalfar. Wilfred grabbed him by his arm, urging him away and, with a final apology, the three companions hurried out of the chamber and down the corridors. Fearful of reprisal, their footsteps quickened until they were nearly running down the hallways and out of the door, and no one spoke until they were safely aboard Hynder and away from the place.

As Hynder rose higher and higher, and Svortalfheim sunk farther and farther beneath them, everyone began, at last, to relax.

"You know," ventured Barnabas, "I really *didn't* do that on purpose."

"It was a misunderstanding that anyone could make," soothed Wilfred.

"Anyone at all!" agreed Barnabas heartily. "Who would have guessed that would happen?" He shuddered at the thought of the screaming elves, with the terrified looks on their faces, some of whom would be stuck with such a visage until the end of days (which, he thought, might come sooner rather than later, if they didn't make progress on this dreadful case).

"Except," said Brynhild, "that I *did* warn you to keep it covered."

"You did no so thing," contradicted Barnabas.

"Indeed I did," insisted Brynhild. "I said, 'keep it covered'. Just like that."

"You most assuredly did not," huffed Barnabas. "If you had done so, I would most certainly have done so."

"Well, I did say it, and then you most certainly did flash it about uncovered anyway," retorted Brynhild.

"Your memory is most faulty, I must say," said Barnabas. He looked to Wilfred for support. "Is her memory not mistaken, Wilfred?" Wilfred coughed, reddened, and looked away, affecting not to hear.

Barnabas, in a temper, stamped his foot several times before remembering that he was aboard a flying horse and could therefore succeed only in stamping the air. Frustrated, he attempted to flap his arms about with indignation, but as he needed to hold onto Brynhild in front of him in order to avoid falling from Hynder and plummeting back down to Svortalfheim he was only able to flap one at a time, which was not terribly satisfying.

"When you first picked the sword up and my cloak started to slip," continued Brynhild implacably, ignoring Barnabas' flailings behind her. "I called out to you, and you put the cloak back around it."

"That never…" began Barnabas, before the memory of that very thing occurring began to assert itself in his mind. He blushed and froze mid-flap, his left arm extended awkwardly out to the side, fingers balled into a tight fist. One by one he loosened his fingers, then lowered his arm slowly. "Oh," he said. "Oh, dear."

"Oh dear, indeed," said Brynhild, copying Wilfred's manner of replying to his employer.

"Oh, but those poor elves!" cried Barnabas, as the full import of his failing struck him. "I've turned them to stone!"

"That you did," agreed Brynhild.

"I am a horrible person!" cried Barnabas, disconsolate. "If only it were I that turned to stone, rather than those innocent elves!" He flung his arm up so that the back of his hand rested dramatically upon his forehead. "Even Crackly Face," he wailed. "Now he is stuck forever that way, with no hope of ever achieving a better complexion." (In truth, Barnabas did not know if Crackly Face had been turned into a statue, but he fancied that he *may* have been, which, to Barnabas' mind, was much the same, in the end.)

"Dark Elves are nasty creatures," said Brynhild. "I would guess that any one of them deserved to be turned to stone."

"No, no," disagreed Barnabas, determined to berate himself. "It was a grievous thing, and I am the one who caused it. I am a reprobate beyond repair."

"Remember that they shot flaming arrows at us," said Wilfred.

"*Now* you speak," muttered Barnabas beneath his breath.

"Pardon?" said Wilfred, who had not heard what Barnabas said.

"And they have shot *many* people with flaming arrows," said Brynhild (who had heard what Barnabas said) quickly.

"Really?" asked Barnabas hopefully.

"Yes, really," said Brynhild.

"So," said Barnabas, "essentially you are saying that, by statue-ifying those Dark Elves, I have prevented them from shooting people with fiery arrows?"

"I suppose you could look at it that way," said Brynhild, furrowing her brow.

"Which, in essence, means that I have done well to brandish the sword so, in that I have removed an evil from the land," said Barnabas.

"Yes, splendid, well done," said Brynhild sarcastically. She rolled her eyes and shook her head in exasperation.

Barnabas, of course, did not see any of that, as he was sitting behind her, and therefore took her words to heart. He pulled his hand from his brow and sat up as tall as he might, attempting to portray a sense of noble heroism. "It is a hard thing, sometimes," he said gravely, "to serve the greater good."

"Indeed," said Brynhild, a small smirk playing across her face. "The worlds are better off with a few less Dark Elves running about. Not at all like the incident at Vollagarddal, really."

Barnabas immediately deflated at the reminder of how he had inadvertenly caused the destruction of Vollagarddal, and fell quiet for a moment, in memory of the quaint little dwarven town. It was not long, however, before present concerns asserted themselves in his mind, and he shifted a bit on Hynder's back.

"I say," he said, "is there a reason why it is so dark here? And cold, too!" He shivered and clutched his robe around his arms as best he could, wishing that his heavy cloak was not safely tucked away in his bag, quite out of reach. Brynhild's cloak was, of course, presumably still wrapped around the fire sword in Maledokkalfar's throne room, but she didn't seem to be terribly affected by the creeping onset of the cold that had so subtly crept up upon them that Barnabas couldn't tell when the atmosphere had changed from the sweltering miasma of the Svortalfheim air to this rather brisk and breezy place in which they found themselves now.

"We have entered Niflheim," explained Brynhild. "The Mist World, they call it, where it is always dark, frozen, and cold. Where the dragon Nidhug lives, and guards the Well of Hvergelmin."

"Must all of the worlds be so terribly unpleasant?" sniped Barnabas, shivering in earnest now. Indeed, the temperature was rapidly dropping, and it was all he could do to keep his teeth from clacking together.

"You seemed to like Alfheimer just fine," pointed out Brynhild.

"And Vannaheim was quite nice, as well," added Wilfred.

"Yes, yes, but those were ages ago," complained Barnabas. He looked around, squinting into the dark mist as though looking for something. "I don't suppose that there's an inn, or a tavern, or what-not?" he said. "Where we might obtain a spot of tea, and perhaps a biscuit or two?"

"And a cosy fireplace," added Wilfred. "And a room with a nice, fluffy bed."

"Oh, yes, a bed!" agreed Barnabas. "I cannot for the life of me remember the last time we slept in a bed."

"And one does tire of sleeping out of doors, wrapped up in our smelly cloaks," said Wilfred.

"My kingdom for a laundress!" said Barnabas. "And a

proper tea service, too," he added.

"At least you both still *have* cloaks," grumbled Brynhild.

"You may have mine," said Barnabas and Wilfred in unison.

Brynhild shook her head, bemused, at their habitual gallantry, which they offered without question despite the fact that they were clearly suffering far more than she from the cold. "No need," she said, deftly landing Hynder on the ground. "I don't intend to be here for long. See?" she said, pointing towards a dim shape only vaguely visible through the hazy mists of the place. "There's the well."

"Which means Nidhug must be nearby," said Barnabas unnecessarily, as everyone knew that Nidhug would of course be there, guarding the well. "And what, pray, is that disgusting noise?"

He was referring to a moist, smacking, crunching sort of sound that was coming from the area of the well. "That," said Brynhild, as she jumped down from Hynder and helped first Barnabas and then Wilfred down as well, "is probably Nidhug, chewing on the corpses of the dead. Or, perhaps, he might be eating away at the roots of Yggdrasil, which, as you remember I'm sure, is the Tree of Life from which all of the worlds hang."

"Of course I remember," snapped Barnabas (who remembered no such thing). "But, which is it?"

"Which is what?" asked Brynhild.

"Which is he eating? Corpses, or tree roots?"

"The smacking noises sound rather corpse-like to me," observed Wilfred, wrinkling his nose.

"But the cracking ones sound like tree roots being gnawed through," argued Barnabas.

"Or bones," suggested Wilfred.

"Or both," said Brynhild. "I can't see how it matters *what* the dragon is currently eating, since we have to go by him either way."

"Well, it matters quite a lot. Better to deal with a tree-eating dragon than a dead person-eating one, is what I always say," said Barnabas (although he had never, of course, had occasion to say that, or anything like it, really).

"But," said Wilfred, "I believe the true question is this: why is the dragon eating when he's supposed to be sleeping and having nightmares?"

"*That*," said Brynhild, "is a good question. I suppose he might be eating in his sleep?"

"Perhaps," said Wilfred doubtfully.

"Maledokkalfar *promised* to give the dragon nightmares," said Barnabas, earning himself a skeptical look from both Wilfred and Brynhild.

"I'm sure you can see how Maledokkalfar's promises may not be something to hang your hat on," pointed out Brynhild. "Particularly considering the situation with the sword…"

"Quite so, quite so," interrupted Barnabas quickly. "But we *must* see Balder, and to do so we *must* get into the well, which *means* we must needs pass by the dragon, nightmares or no."

They all saw the sense of this, and slowly, carefully, crept closer to where Nidhug the dragon lay, curled around a well made of blackened, rotten-looking wood. In one mighty paw was held a corpse in a most distressing state of decomposition, and in the other was snatched up a root from the base of the mighty tree Yggdrassill.

Barnabas and Wilfred, who had not had occasion to see the tree whilst in Asgard (where the upper limits of the branches were located and where, presumably, the tree was much *prettier*) were caught between marveling at the sheer enormity of the roots as they spread out to enclose both the well, and the dragon (and a plethora of corpses, as well) in a bizarre and rather unsettling sort of bower.

"It is," observed Barnabas, "awe-inspiring and yet also revolting, all at once, is it not?"

Wilfred nodded his wholehearted agreement.

Nidhug stirred at the sound of Barnabas' voice, and fixed one half-open eye upon the travelers. A cranky snort emanated from the dragon's nostrils, which steamed the air and smelled rather like the corpses upon which the dragon fed.

"Quick!" hissed Barnabas. "Act nightmarish!" So saying, he stepped forward and began waving his arms oddly. "Ooooooh," he cried, in an affectation of a ghostly sort of voice. He twirled about, like a whirling dervish, calling, 'Oooooh, I'm a ghost!' whilst he did so.

Wilfred, following Barnabas' lead, leaped forward as well. He extended his arms out to either side and began running around in a wide circle, so that he looked quite a bit like a bird riding the winds. "Eeeeee!" he squealed. "I'm a ghost too! A *bird*-ghost!"

"What a terrible nightmare you are having, Corpse Breath!" cried Barnabas, still speaking in that queer, wavering voice. "You are surrounded by ghosts, it is terrible indeed!" He twirled and flapped whilst Wilfred arced and screeched.

Brynhild, shaking her head in wonder at the oddness of the two detectives, stepped forward and, with no further ado, jumped straight into the well. She emerged a moment later with Balder in tow.

Barnabas and Wilfred froze in the middle of their performance.

"Well," said Barnabas, stuck in mid-twirl, "that's *one* way to go about it, I suppose."

Chapter Eighteen

Together with Balder, the three companions walked some distance away from the well (until they couldn't hear the sounds of Nidhug's munching anymore), then sat down to talk. Barnabas meant to offer Brynhild his cloak, and would have done so, but when he turned around he saw that Wilfred and she were already sharing Wilfred's cloak, and he smiled a bit to himself at the sight.

A loud snuffling sound came from behind them, interrupting Barnabas' pleasure at the thought of Wilfred and Brynhild together. He jumped in alarm.

"I say!" he said. "Are we quite far enough? Can the dragon not see us? Or hear us?" He paused and sniffed doubtfully at his own cloak. "Or, ahhh, smell us?" he added. The cloak had smelled none too fresh when they had purchased it, a problem which had only been compounded by their adventures in the frightfully hot worlds in which they had found themselves of late. Not to mention the fact that he (along with his cloak) had come into terrifically close proximity to the giant Surt's mouth. He sighed ruefully. Every so often, if he moved just so, he fancied that a whiff of the giant's breath emanated from the cloak. It was a smell of rot, and decay, and stale meat (and, oddly enough, coconut, which perplexed Barnabas a great deal but did little to mask the subtle stench).

Balder put a comforting hand on his shoulder. "It is far enough," he said. "Nidhug only concerns herself with things that are going *in* the well, not those that are coming *out* of it."

"Well, then," said Barnabas slowly, "if I may be so bold?"

Balder, who was a short, rounded man (indeed, he looked somewhat alike to Barnabas, albeit a great deal more hirsute, as was the northern way, and his smile was a bit more ready than was Barnabas'. Balder's eyes, too, sparkled with a great deal of mischievousness, whilst Barnabas' own were filled with earnestness.

"You may speak freely, friend," Balder replied kindly, his hand still on Barnabas' shoulder.

"I was wondering, I mean, the question had occurred to me, you see, when you mentioned just now that the dragon doesn't pay notice to those coming out of the well, and, of course, I do not mean to question you or to cause offense in any way, as we came all this way simply to speak with you, so of course your counsel is…"

"He wants to know why you stay in the Helheim if the way out isn't guarded," interrupted Brynhild.

"I beg your pardon!" snapped Barnabas.

"Well, that *is* what you were going to ask, isn't it?" asked Brynhild.

"Well, yes," said Barnabas reddening, "but I would have phrased it far less bluntly."

"And you would have taken all day to do so," pointed out Brynhild reasonably. "I was helping."

"It is a question that had occurred to me, as well," interjected Wilfred, seeing that Barnabas was getting a bit out of temper. "If you can get out, why not do so?"

"Because I am supposed to be in Helheim," said Balder calmly. His hand slid from Barnabas' shoulder, and he sat down with a heavy plop on the hard, cold ground. The others followed suit.

"Well, you are out now," said Barnabas once he was seated. "I suppose that must be a great relief to you?"

"I am glad to be here," said Balder, "and I am pleased to be speaking with you. And, when we are finished with our conversation, I shall be content to jump back into the well."

"Back into the well!" exclaimed Barnabas loudly, earning himself a snort of attention from the not-distant-enough Nidhug and a round of 'shush'es from his companions. "Back into the well?" he repeated, more quietly. "Is Helheim so pleasant, then, that you would return?"

"Oh, no," said Balder cheerfully. "It is quite dreadful. And boring. It's filled with loads of old, dead people."

"Wait a moment," said Wilfred. "Aren't we all dead, here?"

"Well, yes," said Balder, "but *these* people are dead in a different, *Helheim* sort of way."

"I'm not dead," chimed in Brynhild.

"You're not dead?" said Wilfred. "But, how, then, are you *here*?"

"I'm from Midgard," said Brynhild. "Odin sometimes brings mortals to Valhalla to do work for him. That's how I came to be here."

Barnabas, watching the exchange, saw that Wilfred had gone quite white, nearly as white as the ice that surrounded them, and that his eyes were wide and blinking far too quickly. Suddenly the full import of the exchange struck him. If Brynhild was of the land of the mortals, whilst himself and Wilfred were now, irrevocably it seemed, of the afterlife… well, it was as impossible an impasse as the gulf between himself and his beloved mouse-headed Bindi. "Oh, dear," he said.

"Oh dear, indeed," whispered Wilfred.

"Oh dear, *what*?" asked Brynhild, confused.

"It is nothing," said Wilfred, trying (and failing rather spectacularly) to put on a reassuring smile. The attempt, however, ended up looking more like a comical grimace, with just his lips pulled up high over his clenched teeth, whilst the rest of his face remained the very picture of misery.

"It is *something*," insisted Brynhild, regarding Wilfred's strange expression with no small degree of consternation. "No one just looks like that for no reason."

"It is something that shall remain nothing," observed Balder with cryptic wisdom.

"It is *something* that you didn't mention the fact that you were *alive*," said Barnabas. He was angered by the misery that was apparent on his assistant's face, and, in truth, he felt a bit betrayed in his own right. "It seems as though you might have disclosed such a thing."

"Well," retorted Brynhild, "I can't see why. Did you say, 'oh, hello, nice to meet you, I'm dead, how do you do'?"

"Of course not," said Barnabas, "because, considering where we met, being *dead* would be the logical assumption. One does not expect to meet anything *other* than dead people in Asgard, does one?"

"As though you are suddenly an expert on Asgard!" snapped Brynhild. "And, anyway, I fail to see how it matters, whether I am dead or not."

"It matters because…because…" sputtered Barnabas, but he was unable to think of anything to say that would not give away Wilfred's secret. "Oh!" he cried in frustration. "It just does." He turned his nose up towards the air and pointedly looked away from Brynhild. "So *good day*, I say to you, and nothing further."

"Whatever do you…" tried Brynhild, thoroughly confused.

Barnabas held up a hand towards her. "I said good day!" he repeated firmly.

"But…" said Brynhild, but Wilfred stopped her.

"Once he's said 'good day' it means the conversation is over," said Wilfred. "No use trying, just now."

Brynhild sighed and shook her head.

Balder, on the other hand, was unperturbed. "Good," he said. "Now that we've got *that* out of the way, perhaps we can get to the crux of the matter. Namely, why have you fetched me from Helheim?"

"We wanted to ask your advice on the theft of Loki's silver bowl," said Brynhild.

"We came to ask you if you had any insights into who may have stolen Loki's silver bowl," said Barnabas loudly, as though Brynhild hadn't spoken.

"Is he going to just pretend I'm not even here?" whispered Brynhild to Wilfred.

"Probably," said Wilfred apologetically. He had gained some control over his facial expression, but he still kept his eyes averted from her. Brynhild flung up her hands in exasperation and leaned back, clamping her lips firmly shut as she shook her head.

"Well," said Balder, as calmly as if a trio of squabbling detectives snatching him out of Helheim were of no particular note, "what do *you* think?"

"Why, I think that, as we have no real clues in this case, then we must needs follow the motive," said Barnabas.

"And who do you think has motive?" said Balder.

"Pretty much everyone," admitted Barnabas sadly.

"But who has the strongest motive?" pressed Balder.

"That there are very many people who will prosper from Ragnorak," said Barnabas. "Yourself included."

"Barnabas!" chided Wilfred, shocked at his employer's audacity.

"That is so, I suppose," said Balder, unperterbed by the offensive observation.

"Although you have been in Helheim all of this time, meaning that you wouldn't have the opportunity. And I cannot think, from what I have heard of you, that you would countenance such a thing being done in your name," said Barnabas.

"That is so, as well," agreed Balder.

"Which leaves us with, well, almost *everyone* else," continued Barnabas, musing aloud. "Vidar, who will be able to take vengeance on Loki after Ragnorak, although I cannot see him being possessed of the guile required to orchestrate such a plot. Honir, who would benefit from the world's end but who is, by all accounts, far too indecisive to do much of anything. Sigyn, who, although she seemed quite innocent, would still yet be quite glad to be freed from sitting over Loki holding that silver bowl for all eternity. Your own mother, acting on her own accord, in order to have you back with her." He paused and heaved a heavy breath. "You see? The list of suspects goes on and on, and there is not a shred of evidence to favor one over the other."

"But what does your instinct tell you?" asked Balder.

"That Modi, who shall inherit Thor's sword after Ragnorak, has something to hide," replied Barnabas.

"But he has an alibi," said Wilfred. "He was with Od and Fulla, fishing, remember?"

"Yes, yes," said Barnabas, "but still...there is something *fishy* about it all."

Balder laughed and slapped his knee. "A delightful pun," he said merrily. "With wit like that, you are sure to solve the case."

"Hmm, well, yes," said Barnabas (who had not meant to deliver a pun, in any way, and who was, indeed, unsure of what the pun he had made *was*, precisely).

"But what shall we *do*, now?" persisted Wilfred.

"Investigate your suspects," said Balder simply. "As you have been doing."

"Yes, but what else?" said Wilfred. "We simply don't seem to be getting anywhere. That is to say, we are *going* to lots of places, but we are not making much progress, at the same time."

"And you should carry on doing so," said Balder (rather unhelpfully, thought Barnabas, and he said as much).

"Well," replied Balder, "you've said you're suspicious of Modi, so perhaps you might follow him a bit?"

"I suppose that is something, although it is not anything we hadn't thought of ourselves," grumbled Barnabas.

"Splendid!" said Balder, jumping to his feet. "Pleased to be of service." He dusted off his robe, which had gotten a layer of ice stuck to the back of it where his weight had pressed it into the cold ground. "And now it is time for me to go back to Helheim."

"But, why would you go back, when you might stay out here with us, and help prevent Ragnorak?" asked Barnabas, his brow furrowed in confusion. "Indeed, why would *anyone* go back to Helheim? It sounds a dreadful place!"

"Because it is where I am *fated* to go," said Balder. "It is where I *belong*, just now."

"Argh!" exclaimed Barnabas. "Fate!" He sniffed derisively at the idea.

"Barnabas doesn't hold to the idea of fate," explained Brynhild.

"Nor should I," said Barnabas, forgetting that he had intended to ignore her. "The very thought of it is preposterous. A man makes his own fate, is what I always say."

"Well, then," said Balder amicably, "then perhaps I am creating my own fate by following the one woven to me by the Norns. Either way, it is off to Helheim with me." So saying, he turned and strode off in the direction of Nidhug, and the well, and Helheim which lay beyond the well. As he walked, he turned his head to call over his shoulder. "Perhaps you might pay the Norns a visit, on your way to Modi's abode," he said, and was gone.

"The Norns?" asked Barnabas. "Who are the Norns?"

"They are the Fates," said Brynhild. "They live in Asgard and they see the past, present, and future."

"Well, *that* would be helpful," said Barnabas snidely. "Why haven't you mentioned the existence of these all-seeing beings before?"

"You didn't ask," answered Brynhild.

"One would have thought that one would impart such pertinent knowledge unprompted," snorted Barnabas (a bit haughtily).

"One would have thought that a detective would have asked in particular if there were any such creatures," retorted Brynhild.

"One would never have guessed that a detective would be required if there were beings who already knew everything!" yelped Barnabas, outraged.

"Well, they might know everything," said Brynhild, "but that doesn't mean that it's any help."

"Whatever do you mean by that?" asked Barnabas, looking at her side-eyed.

"The Norns are notorious for being extremely cryptic," replied Brynhild. "It is impossible to get a straight answer out of them."

"Bah!" exclaimed Barnabas. "Nothing is impossible. Not whilst Barnabas Tew is on the case! To the Norns!" He raised a finger, and aimed it pointedly in first one direction, then the next. He turned about in confusion, obviously not entirely certain in which direction the Norns might be, until Brynhild sighed, took his hand, and pointed it towards Asgard.

"I suppose we may as well go see them now, since Balder said we should." She looked over to where Barnabas was standing next to Hynder. The little detective was jumping up and down, trying in vain to mount the tall steed. "And Barnabas seems quite intent on the plan as well." Brynhild shook her head and began making preparations to depart, ending the conversation and leaving Wilfred no choice but to follow suit. Wilfred followed her with an air of sadness about him, whilst Barnabas intrepidly repeated his valiant efforts at climbing aboard Hynder on his own. In the end Brynhild surreptitiously gave Barnabas a well-timed push from behind, just as he reached the apogee of a leap, then gave Wilfred a helping hand as well. At last she too mounted Hynder and they were off, to Asgard and the Norns.

Their second trip over the rainbow bridge went much better than the first, as both Barnabas and Wilfred were by now thoroughly accustomed to, if not completely comfortable with, the experience of flying over great heights. Indeed, this time they were better able to appreciate the beauty of the thing, and to marvel at the multi-colored lights that glinted off of the icy surface of the bridge. Even Wilfred's mood seemed to lift at the sight, so that he no longer wore an expression of glum moroseness by the time they landed on solid ground in Asgard.

As they dismounted, they soon saw that they were near to the base of an enormous tree, and that the tree was itself near to a massive stone well. A great crowd of gods and various other personages had gathered round the tree, including Odin himself. When the king of the gods saw Barnabas, Wilfred, and Brynhild, he hallooed out a bellicose greeting and beckoned for them to join him at the foot of the tree.

With some difficulty the three companions pushed their way through the crowd until they came to stand next to Odin.

"Yggdrasil!" said he proudly, as though that in itself were some sort of understandably impressive comment.

"Errr," said Barnabas uncertainly, unwilling to admit that he had no idea what the god was talking about. "Ah, ahem. Yes, the great yrrg, erm, the amazing yrrrg…ah, well, it is something, I see," he concluded lamely.

"That it is!" proclaimed Odin, nodding with approval. "Nothing like it in all the worlds." He pointed up at the branches of the tree. "Do you see there? That's the door to Midgard, and there's the one to Alfheimer."

"Doors? To Midgard? To Alfheimer?" repeated Barnabas, slow to understand the implications.

"Of course! And on the other side you'd see the doors to Vanaheim and Jutunheim, and up just a little higher the ones to Muspelheim and Asgard…"

"Wait a moment," interrupted Wilfred. "Aren't we *in* Asgard?"

"Well, yes," said Odin, frowning. "So?"

"So why would there be a door to Asgard, *within* Asgard?" said Wilfred.

Odin's frown deepened as he tried to puzzle this out, then his expression cleared and he waved Wilfred away with a great swipe of his meaty hand through the air. "Because there has to be a door to *all* the worlds, of course. How else would a person *get* to Asgard, if there wasn't one?"

"I'd say that if one is already *in* Asgard, that would be a moot point," pointed out Barnabas.

"And we came in twice through the rainbow bridge," added Wilfred helpfully.

"That we did," agreed Barnabas. He thought for a moment, chewing on his lower lip. "So, you're saying that there are doors to all of the worlds, right here, in this, ah, this yrrg…"

"Yggdrasil," corrected Odin.

"Yes, that's what I said," said Barnabas impatiently. "There are doors that lead to the worlds in, ah, this tree?"

"Of course there are," said Odin, getting a bit annoyed at the repetiveness of Barnabas' questions. "That's what the tree is there for."

"So why in heaven's name did we spend the better part of

a month flying about on a horse, when we could have simply used those doors?" cried Barnabas. "A horse, I say!"

"I don't know," said Odin. "Why *did* you? Seems like it would have been a *lot* easier to just use the doors."

"Because you never told us about the doors!" said Barnabas, his color rising.

"I just did tell you," pointed out Odin.

"Yes, but after we've already run all about the place, riding atop a flying horse!" said Barnabas. His eyes were beginning to bulge out like an angry bullfrog's, and Wilfred placed a hand on his shoulder and gave him a soothing pat.

"Why would you do that, when you've got all these doors right here?" asked Odin.

"Aaaah!" cried Barnabas, flapping his arms about in annoyance. He shook off Wilfred's hand, and stomped off. Soon enough he realized that he had no particular place to stomp off *to*. The place was utterly crowded with gods and deceased warriors, and even if he were to push a path through the throng he still had nowhere else to go. It was not as if he could merely hail a cab and be off to Marylebone.

With his dramatic exit foiled, his frustration overcame him. His forward motion ceased (although his feet continued to stomp angrily at the ground as he turned from one direction to the next). His hands balled into fists and he began to punch the air, cursing profusely as he did so. "Insufferable ratbag! Hare-copped mumble-cove!" he grumbled as he stamped and flailed and lurched.

Odin looked quizzically at Barnabas (whose machinations, in truth, looked quite a bit like some odd sort of dance). "He's a strange little fellow, isn't he?" he observed.

Wilfred quickly stepped in to change the subject. "We returned to Asgard to see the Norns," he said. "Might you direct us to them?"

Barnabas, who had not gone so far as to be out of earshot, called back, "And you could have mentioned the Norns, too, you…you…*nincompoop*!"

"Nincompoop?" asked Odin, frowning. "What is a nincompoop?" His eyebrows bristled menacingly. "Is he *insulting* me?"

"Oh no," said Wilfred in alarm, whilst Brynhild stifled a giggle. "Not at all, I assure you!"

"Then what does nincompoop mean?" persisted Odin.

The god's glowering expression intimidated Wilfred to the extent that he turned quite pale, and found it difficult to speak, much less to think of a convincing lie as to expound the meaning of the word 'nincompoop'. "It means, well, that is to say, it is a compliment of the highest order, you know, a term of respect, really…"

"What does it mean?" bellowed Odin, his patience worn thin.

"A smart person?" suggested Brynhild slyly.

"Maybe it means 'a king'?" suggested one of the dead warriors who happened to be standing nearby, rather helpfully. Soon all of the warriors and gods within hearing were offering their own guesses as to what the word meant, until it became quite a game.

"It's a great warrior," called out one. "A clever person!" yelled another. "A type of spotted pigeon," tried another, rather nonsensically. Everyone ignored this, however, and continued to venture guesses of their own, all complimentary and designed, it seemed, to flatter Odin's pride.

"Well," demanded Odin at last. "Which of those guesses were correct?"

"Ummm," said Wilfred uncertainly.

"Which one?" persisted Odin.

"Yes," said Wilfred, too flustered to formulate a proper answer.

Remarkably, Odin was satisfied with this answer, and nodded his head with approval. "Good," he said. Then he clapped his hands together loudly, making Wilfred jump. "Now let's introduce you to the Norns." The great god turned and began to lead the way out of the throng, then looked back to where Barnabas was in the final throes of his fit of temper. "If your friend is finished with dancing, that is…" He raised a questioning eyebrow, and Wilfred hurried off to collect Barnabas so that they might follow Odin to meet the Norns.

Chapter Nineteen

Once Wilfred had cajoled Barnabas into returning to the group (which took a great deal of coaxing and pleading and, in the end, more than a little forcible man-handling) they followed Odin around the great trunk of Yggdrasil. There, in the lee of the tree, sat three ladies.

One was very young, one was of middle age, and the last appeared to be extraordinarily old. "These are the Norns," said Odin by way of introduction. "Good luck." And with no further ado, the greatest of all the Norse gods, turned on his heel and left them alone with the three Fates.

"Hello," said the youngest.

"Welcome," said the middle-aged Norn.

"We are the Norns," said the eldest, rather redundantly.

Barnabas, though his temper was still piqued, remembered himself enough to greet the women courteously. "Hello," he said. He bent into a gently bow and made as though to tip his hat before remembering that he no longer had a hat to tip, causing the gesture to appear instead like an odd sort of salute. "Ahem," he coughed to hide his embarrassment. He turned to the eldest Norn. "You must be the Norn of the past," he said. "You," he continued, gesturing towards the middle-aged lady, "must be of the present. And the younger would of course be of the future."

"Wrong," said the youngest and the oldest in unison.

"Correct," said the middle Norn.

"Pardon?" said Barnabas, confused. He looked quizzically at Brynhild and Wilfred, but they appeared to be as mystified as he was.

"I am Verdandi, the Norn of the present," replied the middle-aged Norn.

"And I," said the youngest, "am Urd. I am the Fate of the past."

"Whilst I am Skuld," said the oldest, "and my province is the future."

"But, that doesn't quite make sense," protested Barnabas. "Clearly age should represent the past, whilst youth must needs represent the future?"

"Sometimes," said Skuld, as though that explained everything.

"Huh," said Barnabas, perplexed.

"Huh, indeed," whispered Wilfred into his ear.

"It is what it is," said Verdandi.

"And will become what it shall become," said Skuld.

"But formed, as always, by the past," added Urd.

They all three nodded, as if they had just made a statement of profound wisdom.

"Yes," said Barnabas, raising his eyebrows. He was beginning to suspect that this conversation might prove to be more than a little trying. "Well." He cleared his throat. "Anyway. We have come to seek your guidance…" he began, but Urd cut him off.

"Because Loki's bowl has been stolen and Loki has been freed," she said.

"Loki is free?" gasped Barnabas, aghast. "Oh dear, then we are too late! Too late, I say!"

"It is not too late," said Verdandi. "It is the time that it is supposed to be."

"I'm sorry…what?" asked Barnabas, frowning.

"There is the possibility of Ragnarok occurring, now that Loki is freed. If it does, many will die in a terrible battle, and the black void will swallow us all," said Skuld cheerfully.

"But that is dreadful!" exclaimed Barnabas.

"Truly dreadful," agreed Wilfred.

"Just as dreadful as what happened to all those dwarves in Vollagarddal," replied Urd. Barnabas colored with shame, and shifted from one foot to the other.

"So of course those dwarves have no future anymore," added Skuld, compounding Barnabas' discomfort.

"I did apologize, you know," he mumbled. "I never meant for them to be burnt up like that."

"Barnabas rarely causes people to die, you know," said Wilfred helpfully.

"And when he does," said Brynhild, "it's always an accident."

"And, besides," said Barnabas, "we must now look to the future." He looked at Skuld. "What do we *do*, is the question? To prevent Ragnarok?"

"Perhaps you'd best ask Verdandi," replied Skuld, "since it is something that is in the process of happening."

"I would think Urd would be the one to ask," said Verdandi. "Since it has all happened before. Numerous times, even."

"I am terribly confused," said Barnabas. "If the world ended already…"

"The world ended and began again. Now the bowl was stolen and Loki has been freed, the cycle begins anew," said Urd.

"All right," said Barnabas slowly. "Assuming that we accept, err, well…*that*…" (the inflection he put on the word made it quite clear that he considered *that* to be a rather unbelievable statement of pure poppycock). "Assuming that all of *that* is true, what shall we *do*?"

"Well," said Verdandi, "right now you are questioning us and we are telling you things."

"Things we already know!" protested Barnabas. "But we need your assistance, not a summary of what has brought us here in the first place!"

"So you came to us," stated Urd. "Because balder suggested that you should. You wanted our help."

"Which we are currently giving you," added Verdandi, nodding sagely.

"Yes, we know all this," said Barnabas, stamping his foot impatiently. "And I am not certain that I would call *this* helping," he added under his breath to Wilfred. Wilfred nodded his head sympathetically.

"But we will only continue helping you until Ragnarok

commences," said Urd. "Then we won't help you anymore."

"Excepting, of course, for the help we already gave you," added Urd.

"And that we are giving you now," said Verdandi.

"And will give again later, *after* Ragnarok," said Skuld.

"But not while Ragnarok is occurring, of course," said Verdandi.

"Or during Ragnarok's *past*, either," said Urd.

The Norns continued to talk in circles thusly, with no end in sight. Barnabas (with a tug on the sleeve and a subtle tilt of his head) indicated to Wilfred that they ought to leave, and Wilfred in turn did the same to Brynhild. Slowly, the three companions backed away.

"Well," they overheard Verdandi say, just before they passed out of earshot, "they are leaving."

"As I knew they would," said Skuld.

"But we really helped them while they were here," said Urd.

Barnabas shook his head, bemused. "Well *that* was most unhelpful," he said.

"Indeed, I have never been quite so confused in all my life," said Wilfred.

"The Norns can be a bit, well, frustrating," said Brynhild.

"Which means that we are once more left to our own devices," said Barnabas. "And we have no more idea of what to do than when we did before."

"Psst!" said a soft voice. It was coming from the large holly bushes that were just a few feet behind them.

"Well, you had some suspicions about Modi," said Brynhild. "We could investigate him a bit further."

"Psst!" came the voice again, a bit louder.

"I suppose," sighed Barnabas, ignoring the voice. "Still, it is a just a *feeling*, really, that makes me suspect Modi. We still have no real evidence whatsoever."

"We have solved a case with less to go on than this," said Wilfred encouragingly. "Remember that case for Anubis… why, we had *dozens* of suspects at first!"

"Pssst! Pssst! Pssst!" said the voice insistently.

"Yes, but we seemed to make more progess on things, then," said Barnabas morosely. "Now I feel as though we are getting nowhere."

"I SAID PSST!" cried the voice at last, as the man to whom it belonged extricated himself from the prickly holly bush. Everyone jumped at his sudden appearance, and watched as he brushed the thorns from his arms and stumbled in their general direction. The newcomer, however, missed them by about three feet to the left, and continued walking as though he would leave them entirely.

"I say," said Barnabas, "it is quite strange to pop out at people, and interrupt them so rudely, only to walk away from them with no explanation whatsoever."

At the sound of Barnabas' voice the fellow stopped and readjusted his course so that he was once more heading towards the group. "Can you *please*," he said, "keep talking? How else am I to find you?"

"Why, we are right here…oh!" said Barnabas, as he got a better look at the fellow's face and saw that he was, in fact, completely blind. "Oh my heavens, but I am terribly sorry. Here, let me help you." Barnabas hurried over and took the man's arm and guided him gently.

"This is Hod, Balder's brother," said Brynhild.

"I figured that much," said Barnabas, "once I saw that he was blind. Oh dear, I ought not to have said that."

"It is fine," said Hod. "I *am* aware that I am blind, you know."

"Of course you are," said Barnabas.

"I mean, it is quite apparent to one when one cannot *see* anything at *all*," said Hod (a bit huffily, thought Barnabas).

"Is that why you were hiding in the holly bush?" asked Wilfred helpfully. "Because you couldn't see where you were?"

"Oh!" cried Hod. "Of course not! I was in the bush because I was *hiding*, obviously."

"Wilfred, *do* hush," admonished Barnabas in a noisy whisper. "It is terribly impolite to draw attention to someone's…er, *incapacities*."

"My incapacities don't require your notice," snipped Hod, greatly offended now. "Not that I consider myself incapacitated in any way, thank you very much."

"Oh dear," said Barnabas. "I do believe you've offended him, Wilfred."

"Oh dear, indeed," replied Wilfred, looking abashed. He turned to Hod and bowed apologetically (and, of course, superfluously, as Hod, naturally, could not see it). "I meant no offense. I was merely curious, is all."

"And of course if you were in the holly bush that is precisely where you meant to be," added Barnabas. "I can think of lots of reasons for a fellow to be in a holly bush, rather than somewhere less prickly."

"I'm sure that if someone were hiding, then a prickly place is just the thing, as no one would ever think to look there," said Wilfred.

"Unless, perhaps, they were attempting to hide, as well," said Barnabas, his finger under his chin as he considered all of the possible reasons one might have to either peer into or climb inside of a holly bush.

"And there are all sorts of reasons for wishing to hide," said Wilfred.

"If one were attempting to, say, *spy* on someone else," said Barnabas. "That would be a good reason for hiding."

"Or to avoid someone who isn't entirely amiable," said Wilfred.

"Or to sneak in a quick nap," said Barnabas, warming to the game.

"Or if one were hunting, of course," added Wilfred. "One could remain unseen, and then pop out and shoot—"

"Wilfred!" gasped Barnabas and Brynhild in unison. Then Barnabas hissed sharply, "Don't mention hunting! Remember he's the one who shot Balder with an arrow!"

"Oh dear!" cried Wilfred, aghast. "Terribly sorry!"

"I simply cannot believe you said that," said Barnabas primly, earning himself a look of bemused disbelief from everyone there, as both Wilfred and Brynhild had heard Barnabas say far more imprudent things many times over, and even Hod had experienced such in the few minutes of their acquaintance.

Hod looked sadly at Brynhild and sighed. "Well, I'm not entirely certain that I wish to help them anymore," he said.

"You mustn't mind them," said Brynhild. "They don't mean any harm. They are just…well…"

"Simple?" asked Hod.

"Beg pardon!" cried Barnabas. "If anyone is to call me simple, it shall be myself and none other!" Brynhild stifled a smile, and Hod guffawed outright.

"Yes, well, then," said Hod. "Would you like my help or no?"

There was a long pause whilst everyone waited for Barnabas to respond. He had pressed his lips firmly together and affected an air of aggrieved offense, but quickly realized that this had no effect whatsoever on the blind Hod. He sighed loudly to get his point across audibly rather than visually.

"Help of any sort would be most, well *helpful*," prodded Wilfred gently.

"Hmmph," said Barnabas, crossing his arms.

"He means yes, we would be very grateful for your help," said Brynhild to Hod. "What have you to tell us?"

Hod leaned forward to whisper conspiratorially to Brynhild. "Only that Loki's silver bowl has turned up in the Well of Wisdom," he said, turning his head from side to side dramatically.

"The Well of Wisdom?" said Barnabas, reluctantly interested. "And where is this Well?"

"It is in Jutenheim," replied Hod. "Near Jarnsaxa's house."

"Oh, *Jutenheim*!" cried Barnabas, delighted. "The place where we met Vidar and all of those delightful trolls, you mean? I *did* so enjoy myself there."

"Er, yes, I'm sure," said Hod doubtfully. "But I fear that you may be missing the point…"

"Of course I'm not," said Barnabas. "I get the point precisely."

"So what is the point?" asked Brynhild in a teasing tone,

earning herself a none-to-subtle kick in the ankles from Wilfred.

"It is...it is...well, but a good detective never explains his deductions," said Barnabas. "Better that Hod explain what *he* thinks the point is, and then we shall see if the point I have taken aligns with what Hod has said."

"I do believe that Jarnsaxa is Magni and Modi's mother, is she not?" said Wilfred.

"That she is," replied Brynhild grimly. "Meaning that it looks as if Magni and Modi might be involved after all."

"Which is precisely what I've been saying all along!" cried Barnabas triumphantly. "If it's not the son, it's the mother, is what I always say."

Hod frowned quizzically. "*Does* he always say that?" he asked. "Why on earths would he *ever* say that?"

Wilfred merely sighed beleaguredly in response, whilst Brynhild rounded on Barnabas.

"You never once said anything about Jarnsaxa," she pointed out.

"I'm certain that I did," insisted Barnabas. "You must not have been paying attention."

"I'm sure I would remember if you had," said Brynhild.

"Actually..." began Wilfred sheepishly.

"Yes?" said Barnabas and Brynhild at once.

"Barnabas did say that he had a bad feeling about Modi," said Wilfred.

"You see?" said Barnabas, pointing victoriously at Wilfred. "Oh," he said, thinking of a sudden of Hod. "Terribly sorry."

"All right," acquiesced Brynhild. "I suppose he did mention Modi, but certainly not Jarnasaxa or Magni."

"It was *implied*," said Barnabas imperturbedly.

"That you suspected Magni? Or Jarnsaxa?" asked Brynhild.

"Yes," said Barnabas, rather unhelpfully.

Brynhild slapped the back of her hand against her forehead and exhaled noisily. Hod put a sympathetic hand on her shoulder as she shook her head in exasperation.

"So it's all settled then," said Barnabas, in a snooty, self-satisfied sort of way. "My suspicions of Modi have been proven correct…"

"Except that Modi still has an alibi," corrected Wilfred. "He was with Od the whole time, remember?"

"Yes, but isn't that alibi terribly *convenient*?" asked Barnabas.

"I think that *all* alibis are convenient," interjected Hod. "In fact, I believe that is the very definition of an alibi."

"In that it serves to throw suspicion off of Modi, whilst all the while he was conspiring with his entire family in order to commence Ragnarok," continued Barnabas, ignoring Hod's interruption.

"It *does* make sense," conceded Wilfred.

"So there you have it," said Barnabas. "Our culprits are Modi and Magni and their mother."

"Who just happens to be a giantess," said Brynhild.

"Which is why we are exceedingly happy to have you with us, Brynhild," said Barnabas, giving her a hearty pat on the back. "So…to Jutenheim, to apprehend a giantess!" And with that, he was off, leaving Wilfred and Brynhild to take leave of Hod and follow him with no further ado.

"Thank you for the information," said Wilfred to Hod, bowing once more awkwardly before scurrying off.

Hod shook his head and snorted. "Good luck with those two," he said to Brynhild. "They seem quite a, well, *handful*."

Brynhild laughed. "You don't know the half of it," she said wryly. "But they *do* grow on you, you know." She looked to where Barnabas was quickly striding away (in the completely wrong direction, as if he were attempting to find Hynder, which, of course, he was), with Wilfred not far behind. "And so I'm off to Jutenheim. To capture a giantess," she proclaimed.

And with that she too, was off, to collect the two wayward detectives and take them to the Land of the Giants.

Chapter Twenty

It took no time at all for the three travelers to make the trip back to Jutenheim, once Barnabas and Wilfred had been turned round and pointed in the right direction. Soon enough they were mounted on Hynder and off to the Land of the Giants aboard the magical flying horse (Barnabas, always a creature of habit, had grown quite accustomed to riding Hynder by now and, loath to try the heretofore unheard of doors, had not protested when Brynhild had led them to the horse rather than the Tree where the doors were housed).

Barnabas chattered excitedly throughout the entire trip, cheerily delineating the proceedings of Magni and Modi's maleficent plan (or, at least, the details of how he now deducted it must have gone).

"Clearly," he said, "Modi and Magni must needs have a great desire to be possessed of their father's hammer, which we know they shall receive during Ragnarok and which we ourselves witnessed them arguing over the moment we first stepped foot out of Odin's hall. I remember I felt that there was something amiss about the two of them right there and then! I'm sure you remember me saying as much."

"I don't remember you saying anything about Modi and Magni," said Brynhild. "But I *do* remember that you got a bit carried away with that hammer, yourself." She and Wilfred exchanged an amused look as Barnabas flushed deeply.

"Oh!" he said, embarrassed as he remembered how he had taken hold of the hammer that had lain momentarily forgotten on Odin's lawns and had immediately become overwhelmed with such an intense feeling of uncharacteristic aggression that he had run around swinging the hammer above his head like a maniac. "Oh dear," he sighed at last. "I suppose I did, at that."

There was a bit of a silence whilst Barnabas steeped in his humiliation. "You were speaking of Modi and Magni's motivations," prompted Wilfred helpfully in order to smooth things over. "And I, for one, would hear more of your deductions, if you please."

"Certainly!" said Barnabas, his embarrassment immediately cast aside as he remembered that he had been in the process of describing his own cleverness. "So, Modi and Magni wish for the hammer, but must needs begin the commencement of Ragnarok to get it. They steal the bowl and carry it hence to their mother's abode, for a mother of course must needs do whatsoever she can to help her children. How the bowl came to be lost from Jarnsaxa's house and fallen into the well instead, of course, remains to be seen, as does the minor detail as to whether Jarnsaxa was implicit in the planning of the misdeed, or if she was merely acting to protect her sons."

"How do you account for the fact that Modi was with Freya's husband, fishing?" asked Brynhild.

"Why, that is a subterfuge of the most obvious kind, of course," replied Barnabas proudly. "The moment I met him in that tavern...you remember, just before we were accosted by those vile wolves in the forest?"

"You mean the tavern where you got drunk with Modi and his friends?" said Brynhild.

"Precisely," said Barnabas. "Er, well, except that you must remember I wasn't truly intoxicated at all, but was merely *pretending* to be."

"I suppose," said Brynhild. "But I think you were at least a *little* drunk."

"But not nearly as drunk as he made out to be," said Wilfred, rather defensively. Barnabas shot him a grateful look.

"Indeed," he said. "And that is all beside the point, anyway." He waved a dismissive hand. "The point is that I had an ill feeling about Modi straightaway, as though he were keeping a secret of some kind, and trying far too hard to emphasize the idea that he had been with Od the entire while. At the time I wasn't quite certain what to make of it, but now it is most obvious."

"Obvious?" asked Brynhild, frowning. "Obvious, how?"

"That Modi wanted most desperately for us to know about his alibi, so that we wouldn't investigate himself or his family any further. Because whilst he was out ostentatiously fishing with Od, either his brother or his mother, or both, were busily stealing Loki's bowl and thereby precipitating the end of the world and the delivery of Thor's hammer to Modi and Magni."

"And Od's kidnapping?" asked Brynhild. "How does *that* fit in to your theory?"

"Of that I cannot be certain, but I strongly suspect that Modi orchestrated that as well, so that we would remain occupied elsewhere. It would be a simple matter for him to tell Ran where they would be, and to 'accidentally' knock Od overboard so that she might capture him," replied Barnabas. "It is so simple, and yet also so ingenius, really. We truly did spend a great deal of time following his false trails." He shook his head ruefully at the thought of a rapscallion such as Modi manipulating their actions.

"Huh," said Brynhild at last. "I must admit, it all makes sense. I can see no flaws in your logic whatsoever."

"Of course you cannot," sniffed Barnabas proudly. "My deductive skills are impeccable, you know."

"As is your modesty," sniped Brynhild.

"My modesty is better than…oh, heavens, *what* is *that*?" said Barnabas.

They had arrived in Jutenheim whilst they spoke, and Barnabas had been too intent on their conversation to notice that they were fast approaching a very large mountain that had, incredibly, an enormous face. The face was not carved into the mountain, but was instead apparently part of the mountain. Disturbingly, the face was rather alive, it seemed, as it was, even now, calling out to them, which is what had suddenly drawn Barnabas' attention to it.

"That," replied Brynhild, "is Mimir. He was killed by the

Vanir in the last uprising and became part of the mountain afterwards."

"*How*," said Barnabas, "does one become part of a mountain whilst one is dead?"

"That is a story for another day," said Brynhild as she waved back at beckoning Mimir-mountain. "He really doesn't like to think of it, as I'm sure you can understand, so it's best we stop talking about it now."

Barnabas, looking up at the massive face, and deeming that it wouldn't do to offend a mountain, agreed.

"Hallo!" said the mountain (in a tone that was, thought Barnabas, far too loud. Indeed, it rather rattled the ear drums quite uncomfortably, so that his ears began to ring with an echo of Mimir's voice). "How goes it with you? How come you to Jutenheim?"

"Eh?" asked Barnabas, shaking his head in an attempt to clear it of the ringing.

Brynhild, however, seemed imperturbed by the noisiness of Mimir. "We've come in search of Loki's bowl," she said. "We've heard that it may have been seen in the Well of Wisdom."

"You've heard right," boomed Mimir. "Modgud threw it into the Gjoll, and from there it washed down into the well. Not two days ago, it was."

"The jowl?" asked Barnabas, squinching up his face. "Mud God?"

"The Gjoll," whispered Brynhild. "It's a river, and Modgud is a goddess who guards the bridge over it."

"Well, we must go to this bridge then," said Barnabas. "At once!"

"We will," said Brynhild grimly. "Because it is the only way to Jarnsaxa's castle."

Barnabas clapped his hands delightedly. "Which can only support my theory," he crowed. "Oh, but this is delightful news indeed!"

"Yes," said Brynhild with a sarcastic smirk, "it is delightful that we are going to accuse a giantess and her two half-giant, half-god sons. What could go wrong?"

"Oh," said Barnabas, momentarily deflated. Then he perked up again. "'Tis a good thing we have you, my dear!" he said, merrily clapping Brynhild on the back. Then he set off down the little road that led down towards the river (which he had found quite easily since the road ran directly by the foot of the mountain, and the river was clearly visible from there). "Thank you, Mister, eh, Mister Mountain!" he called back over his shoulder.

Brynhild and Wilfred nodded their thanks as well, and ran to catch up with Barnabas. Barnabas, excited at the prospect of catching a ne'er-do-well at last, set a brisk pace, and they soon came to the bridge over the river Gjoll where Modgud made her home.

The river was a large one, and had carved out a great gorge in the landscape so that the road must needs descend rather precipitously down in order to meet the bridge that spanned it. An enormous house, clearly built for a person of great stature, arose from the side of one of the bridge's abutments.

"Modgud's house?" asked Barnabas (rather redundantly, as this had been their destination all along, and there was no one else who might have their house on a bridge over this particular river).

"Mmmm. Perhaps I ought to speak to her first," suggested Brynhild. "Alone."

Barnabas made to protest, but then noticed the look on Wilfred's face as he regarded Brynild. Wilfred's eyes shone with an amalgamation of admiration of the Viking skald's bravery, combined with an obvious profound, wistful sadness, that Barnabas was reminded that his assistant had only recently discovered that his tender feelings towards the woman were, apparently, unreturned. Having recently suffered from his own impossible romantic situation (from his ill-fated hopes towards a particular waitress whilst afflicted with the curse that had made both himself and Wilfred rather more rodent-like than was usual), Barnabas was struck with a poignant empathy for his young assistant.

Surprising everyone, he immediately acquiesced, and

allowed Brynhild to pick her way down the rocky incline that led to the bridge and Modgud's abode without a word of protest. As soon as she was out of earshot, he patted Wilfred consolingly on the shoulder.

"Bad luck that, eh?" he ventured.

"What, that our villains our giants?" asked Wilfred.

"No," said Barnabas. "Er, well, yes, I suppose one could view that as a spot of bad luck. But it is the bad luck with Brynhild of which I speak."

"With Brynhild?" asked Wilfred.

"Meaning that it is a hard thing, her being, well, *alive* and such," explained Barnabas.

"And I am glad for her that she *is*," said Wilfred firmly.

"But of course you are," said Barnabas. "I do not mean to imply…I mean only that it is a hard thing that *she* is alive whilst *you* are, well…"

"Dead," supplied Wilfred sadly.

"No need to put it so harshly," said Barnabas. "I prefer to think that we are currently absorbed in our *second* lives, if you please."

Wilfred sighed. "And I suppose that is a perfectly correct way of looking at it," he said.

"Because," added Barnabas, "we are still running about and *doing* things, instead of just lying there as one would imagine a *dead* person might do."

"Still, whether we be dead or merely somehow alive for the second time, it still makes little difference, does it?" said Wilfred.

"No, I suppose it does not," said Barnabas. He looked down at the ground and shuffled his feet. "I am sorry that our being not-precisely-dead is an obstacle between you and your heart's desire. I do understand the pain of an impossible situation all too well, you know."

Wilfred looked at Barnabas in much surprise, for it was quite uncharacteristic for the little detective to display such depth of emotion. "Thank you," said Wilfred simply.

"Yes, well, there you have it. We are a couple of silly, romantic fools," said Barnabas. He gave an embarrassed snort then, and made a show of standing up with perfect posture, chin raised, like a proper Englishman. "Chin up, then, I say, and let us ignore our heartaches like the gentlemen we are." He glanced down towards Modgud's house. "Brynhild has been there for a time," he said. "Shall we see what is afoot?"

"Certainly," said Wilfred, with as much dignity as he could manage. His eyes blinked just a bit too rapidly, however, and his jaw was set rather tensely. Barnabas politely averted his eyes so as not to embarrass the poor fellow by witnessing his obvious distress. Still, the moment was an uncomfortable one for both, and Barnabas was relieved to see Brynhild emerging from beneath the bridge and heading back up the slope towards them before they'd taken so much as a dozen steps in awkward silence.

"Hullo, there!" called Barnabas (a bit too heartily, if truth be told, and far too loudly as well). "What news from the troll 'neath the bridge?"

"Ssshhh!" hissed Brynhild, with an anxious glance over her shoulder. She scrambled up the last few feet of the embankment and gave Barnabas a reproving look. "Don't say such things!"

"Whyever not?" asked Barnabas. "Is Modgud not a troll? I thought that there was naught in Jutenheim *but* giants and trolls."

"Well, yes, she *is*," replied Brynhild, "but…"

"And does she not dwell beneath a bridge?" interrupted Barnabas. By now he had fully affected an impression of a barrister trying a case in a courtroom, and swirled his cloak dramatically about his legs as he pivoted from Brynhild to Wilfred as though from witness to jury.

"Well, yes, she *does*," said Brynhild, "but…"

"So as she is, in fact, a troll, and she does, indeed, live under that bridge, then one might safely conclude that referring to Modgud as 'the troll 'neath the bridge' is not only accurate, but also…"

"Yes, yes," interrupted Brynhild impatiently. "But you don't need to *say* so, do you? It is terribly impolite. No one likes to be called a troll."

"Merely establishing the facts of the case, madame," said Barnabas. Thoroughly enjoying his barrister act now, he wrinkled his nose and peered down at Brynhild in what he believed was an expression of triumph, but that looked in actuality as though he had smelt something rather unpleasant. "Which *are*," he continued imperiously, "that Modgud is a troll, and she…"

"Oh, hush before she hears you!" cried Brynhild. "Do you *want* to be stomped into mush? And us with you?"

"Stomped into mush?" repeated Barnabas anxiously. "Is *that* an option?"

"It is if you persist in—" began Brynhild, but Wilfred cut her off.

"I don't think Modgud will be stomping anyone, at least not just now," he said.

"I'm sorry to disagree," said Brynhild, "but really, I know Modgud, and I'm sure that she would think no more of stomping on Barnabas than she would a bug."

"I am much more difficult to stomp than a bug," sniffed Barnabas, affronted. "And I'm certain that she would think quite a bit about it, after she had done so."

"Only in that it would be more of a mess on the bottom of her boot," sniped Brynhild.

"Well, of all the rotten things to say!" cried Barnabas. He would have pursued the argument further, but Wilfred flapped his hands impatiently in Barnabas' face. "I say, Wilfred," said Barnabas, confused. "What are you about, with all that flapping and whatnot?"

"I'm trying to tell you," replied Wilfred, "if the two of you would cease your incessant bickering and listen, for once!" Barnabas and Brynhild gave each other guilty glances, and shuffled their feet. "There," said Wilfred. "That's better. Now, if you please, look over there." He pointed towards the far side of the bridge, where the road continued on towards Jarnsaxa's castle, the top of which was just visible over the horizon.

Immediately they saw what had stirred Wilfred up so.

There, scurrying down the road, was Modgud. The guardian of the bridge was running as fast as her thick legs could take her, with her skirts hiked up to her knees. She ran hunched over, as though trying to make herself as small as possible (which was rather absurd, considering that, being a troll, she was of rather large stature, a fact which no amount of hunching could possibly ameliorate). She also kept looking back at the three travelers surreptitiously, as though checking to be sure they hadn't yet spied her. Clearly, she was trying to sneak off without being seen.

"Why, what is she about?" cried Barnabas. "Why is our witness running away?"

"And towards Jarnsaxa's castle, no less," grumbled Brynhild. "Methinks that Modgud lied to me."

"What did she say to you?" asked Barnabas.

"I asked her if she had thrown the bowl into the river, as Mimir said she had done. She admitted to it, but when I asked her why she said that she had stumbled upon the bowl out on the road one day. She thought it was ugly, so she carelessly tossed it into the river."

"She threw Loki's bowl into the river, without so much as a 'how-do-you-do', nor even a 'perhaps-I-ought-not-start-Ragnarok'?" asked Barnabas with an air of shocked incredulity.

"She said she didn't know it was Loki's bowl," replied Brynhild.

"And you *believed* her?" demanded Barnabas.

"Why shouldn't I have?" said Brynhild. "Can *you* tell one silver bowl from another?"

"I'm certain I would find it highly suspicious if a silver bowl simply showed up, sitting on the road," retorted Barnabas. "And I would be even *more* suspicious of anyone who claimed that they blithely stumble upon such things as a matter of every day occurrence!"

"Well then, why didn't *you* question her, if you're so much better at it than everyone else?" yelled Brynhild.

"I most definitely would have done, if you'd not have hurried off to do so yourself!" cried Barnabas, in a fine temper.

"And whilst we sit here arguing over whether or not to call Modgud a troll, and who should have said what and when, our material witness if getting away!" cried Wilfred, thoroughly annoyed now. "Well, I for one am going after her!"

And with that, he stomped off after the fleeing Modgud, taking care to stay out of her sight by ducking behind first this bush and then that so that he ran in a strange zig-zagging pattern.

"Huh," said Barnabas, staring after his oddly-running assistant. "He can be so very *dramatic* about things, sometimes," he said, shaking his head in bemusement, completely unaware of the irony of himself making such a statement.

Brynhild barked out a loud guffaw at that, startling Barnabas even further. "Indeed," she said, still laughing, and set out to follow Wilfred's crooked path after Modgud.

Barnabas, terribly confused, watched the three figures hurrying down the road: Modgud, then Wilfred, and lastly Brynhild. "I suppose there's nothing for it," he said to himself after a long moment. "Though it will take *forever* to get down the road running like that." Then he shrugged, gathered up his robes in his fists, hunched over, and followed after everyone, darting and zig-zagging just as they had.

Chapter Twenty-One

It did, in fact, take quite a long time for Modgud and her three unseen followers to travel the relatively short distance to Jarnsaxa's castle in this way (and, to make matters worse, the entire exercise left Barnabas feeling terribly ridiculous, as though he were an unwilling participant in an impromptu and rather absurd parade). Still, they all arrived at their destination at last, with Modgud none the wiser that she had been pursued at all.

Modgud entered the castle by the front gates as Barnabas, Brynhild, and Wilfred congregated together on the grassy lawn, partially hidden from view by a gnarled and stunted fir tree.

"Well," said Barnabas primly, "*that* was an interesting tactic."

"We were *sneaking*," said Brynhild. "That is how one *sneaks*."

"Hmmm," said Barnabas, pointedly considering his fingernails as he lifted his eyebrows disdainfully.

"Would you rather have had her see us?" snapped Brynhild defensively.

"I'm relatively certain that the difference between her seeing us and not seeing us had little to nothing to do with our running after her like three scrunched up chickens," retorted Barnabas.

"You only think that because you know nothing about subtlety and subterfuge," said Brynhild.

"Oh!" cried Barnabas. "I'm quite sure that I know more than you!"

"About how to get caught following people!" shot back Brynhild.

Barnabas opened his mouth to retort, but was cut short by Wilfred, who was jumping up and down whilst flapping his arms about in frustration. His face had gone beet-red, so that he looked like an extraordinarily distraught tomato.

"Will you please!" shouted the young fellow. "Is there no *end* to your arguing?"

"See?" said Barnabas to Brynhild. "You've gone and upset Wilfred again."

"Again?" asked Brynhild, perplexed. "When did I upset him before?"

"Oh dear," said Barnabas, realizing that he had been on the verge of spilling Wilfred's secret admiration for Brynhild, and the romantic disappointment that had come from it. "Oh dear," repeated Barnabas, now nearly as flustered as Wilfred.

"Oh dear, indeed!" yelled Wilfred. "It is not *Brynhild* who is upsetting me. Or, rather, I should say it is not *only* Brynhild. It is the both of you, together."

"Why, I'm sure I have no idea what you are talking about," said Barnabas. He looked to Brynhild. "Do you?" She shook her head, just as mystified as Barnabas.

"The two of you bicker incessantly," said Wilfred. "Really, it is unbearable."

"Well," said Barnabas, "in that case you are upset for nothing, as I, for one, do not *bicker* at all."

"You were just doing so, just now," insisted Wilfred.

"We were *discussing*," said Barnabas. "Not bickering."

"Perhaps disagreeing, a bit," added Brynhild.

"But of course it is important that I, as the leader, point out when she is in error," said Barnabas. "Most respectfully, of course."

"Just as it is important that I, as the only one who has even a chance of apprehending our suspect, point out when our leader is being a goose," said Brynhild. "Most respectfully, of course," she added with an obviously insincere sweet smile upon her face.

"A very clever goose, you mean," said Barnabas, "as I have spied, even whilst we speak, that Modgud is now standing in the window over there, with a giantess whom I must assume is Jarnsaxa, as well as Modi and Magni."

He pointed to a window on the third floor of the nearest turret where, indeed, the quartet of giants were standing, having an animated conversation of their own. A wooden trellis covered completely in some sort of creeping ivy reached all the way up to the top of the turret. The ivy-covered trellis passed directly underneath and around the window in which the suspects were now framed, and Barnabas nodded with satisfaction.

"See?" he said jovially, patting Wilfred heartily on the back. "It is all settled. Brynhild and I do not argue, and our suspects are ripe for the picking." He turned to Brynhild and gave a gentlemanly bow. "And now, madame, I am going to climb up that trellis so that I might spy on the villains. And we shall see if there is only one of us who has a chance of apprehending them, as you say!"

With that, he flounced off, leaving Brynhild and Wilfred to stare after him, dumbfounded. Both of their mouths hung agape for several moments. Brynhild was the first to recover.

"You don't think he'll really try to confront them, do you?" she asked, still staring at the little detective as he hoisted himself (with no small amount of effort and a great deal of grunting and slipping) onto the lowest rung of the trellis.

"I rather do think he might," said Wilfred.

"Oh, dear," said Brynhild.

"Oh dear, indeed," agreed Wilfred. "I suppose we ought to follow him up there, to prevent, well...you know."

"Yes, I do," said Brynhild. "I wouldn't like to see him get smushed by Jarnsaxa. I've become rather fond of the little menace."

"You have?" asked Wilfed, astonished.

"But of course," said Brynhild. She reached out and gave Wilfred's hand a squeeze. "And I've become quite fond of you, too." She turned, then, and headed off to follow Barnabas up the trellis, so that she didn't see the renewed flush on Wilfred's cheeks, nor the glint of happy hopefulness that sparkled in his eyes.

Brynhild and Wilfred quickly caught up to Barnabas, who had made rather slow (and terribly noisy) work of climbing the trellis. As soon as they came level with his feet, he looked down with a gleeful expression on his face.

"They have the bowl!" he cried excitedly. "They must have retrieved it from the well!"

"Shhh!" hissed Brynhild in warning.

"And Magni and Modi have Thor's hammer already! They are fighting over it!" yelled Barnabas, heedless of Brynhild's admonition.

Luckily the four giants within had very loud voices, which they were using to their fullest extents, so that they didn't hear the relatively small sound of Barnabas' voice as he yelped and crowed with the delight of a case solved just outside their window.

"I stole the bowl," they heard Magni say. "So I should get the hammer first!"

"But I was the one who threw those annoying detectives off of our trail," protested Modi. "You'd never have gotten away with it, if I hadn't!"

"But I disposed of the bowl for you," said Modgud. "What is *my* reward?"

"Bah!" scoffed Jarnsaxa. "You disposed of it, all right... right into the Well of Wisdom! You could have foiled all of our plans, with *that* particular bit of stupidity!"

"Very good," whispered Brynhild. "We have clear proof of their guilt. We should descend now, and go tell Odin..."

"Tell Odin!" cried Barnabas. "Tell Odin! Nay, I shall return to Odin with the ne'er-do-wells in custody, or I shall return not at all!"

So saying, he pushed himself upwards so that his face was neatly framed in the window. He hoisted one arm, finger pointed, high above his head (causing himself to wobble quite a bit on his precarious perch; such was his excitement, however, that he scarcely seemed to notice the dangerous way in which he lurched and swayed on the flimsy trellis). At last he managed to swing his arm down, so that his finger was pointing directly into the room where Jarnsaxa, Modgud,

Magni, and Modi were arguing over who would get which spoils during Ragnarok.

"J'accuse!" yelled Barnabas, before Wilfred took hold of his foot and delivered a mighty pull. There was a brief moment of struggle, and then they were falling, together, to land in a heap between the castle wall and the trellis.

"Oof! I say! What are you ab-mmmph!" yelped Barnabas, but was immediately shushed by Wilfred's hand as it clamped down tightly over his mouth.

"Shhh!" hissed Wilfred urgently, his eyes a bit wild as he panted from the exertion of leaping up and man-handling Barnabas down off the trellis. "Giants!" he added (rather unnecessarily, thought Barnabas).

"Did you hear that?" boomed a voice from high above them. Barnabas, who had spent enough time in the window to link each voice to a particular giant, recognized it as belonging to Jarnsaxa.

"Hear what?" came another overly loud voice from the window (whether it be Modi or Magni, Barnabas could not tell; the brothers not only looked alike but sounded alike as well).

"I thought I heard voices," said Jarnsaxa. A loud rustling from the ivy above indicated that the giantess was leaning out of the window, and, for all they knew, peering down directly at the place where they lay, scarcely hidden between the trellis and the castle wall.

"Brynhild!" gasped Wilfred, his eyes widening even more so that they looked as though they might bulge out of their sockets entirely. "She'll be discovered!" He began to rise up, and reached up for the trellis as if to begin climbing, straight into the view of the giants who were still arguing in the open window.

Now it was Barnabas' turn to restrain Wilfred, which was no mean feat as the little detective was flat on his back and still quite winded from the hard fall they had taken. Still, he managed to loop his legs around his assistant's waist and lock his ankles, so that, struggle though he might, Wilfred was powerless to extricate himself from his clutch.

"I must help Brynhild!" protested Wilfred. "Surely they will hurt her if they find her lurking outside their window!"

"If anyone can handle themself, it is Brynhild," insisted Barnabas. "And I do not believe they have seen her."

"How can you know?" asked Wilfred, still struggling (valiantly but in vain) against the vise grip of Barnbas' legs.

"Because the giants are arguing over whether or not anyone heard anything at all," said Barnabas. "Listen."

Wilfred paused in his struggles and listened for a moment. Sure enough, Jarnsaxa and whichever brother happened to be in the window with her were still carrying on an animated and exceedingly noisy conversation.

"I didn't hear anything," said the male voice doubtfully.

"But *I* did, Modi," said Jarnsaxa.

"Well, what did you hear?" asked Modi.

"I don't *know*," said Jarnsaxa. "Which is why I'm asking if anyone else heard anything, obviously."

"If you don't know what you heard, then you didn't hear anything worth talking about," said Modi. Remarkably, his convoluted logic seemed to appease Jarnsaxa.

"That's true," she said, as a second rustling of the ivy above indicated that the giants had withdrawn their heads back inside. Suddenly, another loud sound made both detectives jump. They jumped again as a heavy object landed on the ground beside them, and then stared at each other with amazement as they saw what it was that had fallen. Without a word, Barnabas reached out and picked up the object: an intricately engraved bowl of solid silver.

Soundlessly, Brynhild appeared feet-first, gracefully climbing down the trellis like a mountain goat. "That was close!" she proclaimed. "If Jarnsaxa had turned her head just a bit to the left...what?" she broke off, looking at the raised eyebrows and rapidly blinking eyes of her companions.

Still too stunned by this stroke of good luck to speak, Barnabas merely held out the bowl to Brynhild and watched as her eyes, too, opened wide with surprise. "Loki's bowl!" she cried. "But how...?"

The answer came from a loud screech above. "You fool!"

yelled Jarnsaxa. "You dropped the bowl!"

"Well, if you hadn't had me leaning out the window for no reason, I wouldn't have!" defended Modi.

"Ugh," said Jarnsaxa, disgust dripping from her voice. "Just...just go down and get it, would you." It was a command, not a question.

Some grumbling followed, and then the sound of heavy footsteps receding into the interior of the castle.

"We should go," said Barnabas, and this time Brynhild didn't argue. She helped Barnabas and Wilfred scramble to their feet, and the three companions scurried quickly back up the road from whence they had come.

Though they feared pursuit, none was forthcoming and they made it back to the Well of Wisdom, where Hynder waited patiently, without incident.

Chapter Twenty-Two

The three companions arrived back in Asgard weary from their efforts but with a great sense of satisfaction at the successful completion of their quest. True, Barnabas was a bit disappointed that they had been unable to take the four nefarious giants from Jutenheim into custody (and thereby make a splendidly triumphant procession into Odin's hall, impressing and silencing all of the warriors who had looked upon them so disdainfully on the occasion of their first visit), yet still he was on the whole pleased with the outcome of their work and its satisfactory resolution.

They all dismounted and Barnabas and Wilfred gave Hynder a few farewell pats upon his neck before Brynhild led the mighty horse away to be reunited with his equine friends. Barnabas watched the retreating figures with a genuinely wistful look in his eye.

"I shall miss that horse," he said, astonishing Wilfred.

"I thought you found riding a flying horse, well, *disconcerting*, to say the least," said Wilfred.

"I *did*," agreed Barnabas. "Until, all at once, I *didn't* anymore. Indeed, I have become rather fond of that particular mode of transportation, I must say. Most useful, it is."

"Indeed it is," agreed Wilfred. The two detectives stood in silence for a few moments, watching Brynhild lead the magnificent steed away towards the stables and the horse pastures.

"Perhaps," ventured Barnabas after a time, "perhaps Odin will restore us to our lives in Marylebone."

"Do you think that he can?" asked Wilfred. "Anubis wasn't able to…"

"Or didn't *wish* to, which is a different sort of thing

entirely," pointed out Barnabas.

"Mayhap that is true," said Wilfred. "I suppose it doesn't much matter, as the end effect is the same."

"Still, I hold on to the hope that someone will be both able and willing," said Barnabas.

"To return us to London?" asked Wilfred.

"Just so," said Barnabas. "And, of course...Well, *you* know." What he had meant to say, but could not bring himself to, was his dearly held wish to be returned to life itself, not just to London. He was heartily sick of the afterlife, and the extraordinarily provoking characters to be found there.

"Indeed," nodded Wilfred. He coughed into his hand, and reddened a bit in the cheeks as he heaved a heavy sigh. "And, errr, I wonder if, well, that is to say, I was thinking that, perhaps..."

"That what?" queried Barnabas. "Spit it out, my good fellow."

"Well, I was wondering, I mean...do you think it possible, that Brynhild might enjoy London as well?"

"Brynhild! In London!" cried Barnabas. Now it was his turn to be astonished.

"It is not so far-fetched an idea," said Wilfred, blushing furiously now. "Indeed, if we can make it *here*, then surely she could find a way to be *there*."

"I don't doubt that she would do splendidly, wherever she went," said Barnabas. "I only meant that you had quite *stifled* those feelings of yours towards her."

"I *had* done so," said Wilfred. "That is, I *tried* to do so. Still, hope *will* spring eternal, and when you brought up the thought of us returning to our lives, which was, indeed, the main impediment towards my future with Brynhild...You can see how the idea might rekindle, yes?"

"I do," agreed Barnabas, nodding sagely. "I do understand it all too well, I'm afraid." He shook his head sadly. "Still, I must tell you that I think the odds are against such a happy outcome. Indeed, I feel that the odds are against Odin sending us back to London. I should never have brought it up, and stirred up your hopes so."

"It was a hope that would have stirred no matter what you had said or not said," said Wilfred kindly. "In fact, it is a hope so strong that I must pursue it."

"What if Odin denies our request, and we are doomed to wander through afterlife after afterlife?" asked Barnabas.

"Why, then, I shall ask Brynhild if she should like to join us," said Wilfred.

Barnabas pursed his lips. "Perhaps I should have done the same," he said. "Perhaps Bindi would have enjoyed a bit of travel." He thought of the mouse-headed hostess from the restaurant in the Egyptian desert, and shook his head sadly, knowing that his own hopes in that matter were far more unlikely than Wilfred's were in the matter of Brynhild. "I wish you luck, my friend," he said simply. Wilfred, delighted with his employer's approval, didn't notice the glint of sadness in his eyes, nor the somewhat dejected slump of his shoulders.

Just at that moment, Odin himself came walking out of his hall, flanked by a contingent of large, hirsute, and raucously laughing warriors. The mighty god spied the two detectives conversing on his front lawn, and boomed a greeting.

"Hallo, detectives!" he called. "What news on Ragnarok?"

Shaking off his thoughts of Bindi and unrequited love, Barnabas waved back and affected a triumphant smile that, whilst tinged with an underlying melancholy, was genuine enough.

"It is prevented!" he called back as Odin drew nearer. "That is, it will be once you have taken the criminals into custody. Whom, of course, we have identified," he added hastily.

"Who were the culprits?" asked Odin.

"'Twere Modi, Magni, and Jarnsaxa, with help from Modgud," replied Barnabas.

"Splendid! I am glad to hear it. Good work, good work!" With that, Odin beckoned to his warriors and began to walk off.

"But...wait!" called Barnabas, confused. "Are you going

now to apprehend them? Shall we accompany you?"

"Why would I apprehend them?" asked Odin.

"Because they are criminals," said Barnabas. "And we have found them out. If it is a matter of proof, I can certainly present a most compelling case."

"Oh, pshaw," said Odin. "That sounds rather boring, don't you think? No, I'm just on my way to go hunting. Would you like to come along?"

"Hunting!" cried Barnabas. "But, we must arrest the giants and place Loki back into Sigyn's keeping, straightaway." Flustered, he flapped and flailed his arms about, like a disturbed fur-clad bird.

"What is that you have in your hand?" asked Odin. Barnabas, in his upset, had very nearly forgotten about Loki's bowl, which was still in his hand.

Barnabas paused and looked at his hand, and the bowl held within. "Oh, yes, this. Why, it is the bowl that Sigyn uses, or, I should say, used, to catch the poison from the serpent above Loki's head. It is part of our proof, you see, and it is ready to be restored to its rightful place. Of course, we shall need you to come with us, as we cannot possibly apprehend giants on our own, let alone Loki…"

Odin, scarcely listening to Barnabas, reached out and took the bowl. He turned it about in his hands, considering it, then handed it to the nearest of the warriors. "Here, Eskil," he said. "Take this back into the hall and tell someone to fill it with fruit."

"Fruit!" sputtered Barnabas. "Fruit! How can Sigyn use it if it's filled with *fruit*?"

"Why would Sigyn need to use it?" asked Odin.

"To catch the poison before it drips on Loki's forehead," said Barnabas. "Just as she did before."

"But Loki isn't there," pointed out Odin, as though this explained everything.

"But aren't you going to put him back there?" demanded Barnabas.

"Why would I do that?" asked Odin, looking quizzically at the little detective.

"To prevent Ragnarok, of course!" exclaimed Barnabas.

"But, it's fated to happen," said Odin. "It's no use fighting fate, you know."

"So why bring us here at all?" asked Barnabas, growing visibly frustrated.

"Why, to solve the mystery of course," said Odin. "Which you did. Well done!" He reached over and awkwardly patted Barnabas on the head.

Barnabas shook his head to dislodge the god's mighty paw. "Hmmph!" he cried. "That does no good to anyone if you don't put Loki back into his cave."

"Truly," added Wilfred, "our activities do seem a bit, well, unnecessary, if nothing is to be done because of them."

"Ah well," said Odin, seemingly imperturbed. "I suppose that's one way to look at it. I, for one, am pleased that you have done all that I asked you to do."

"Yes, but to what end?" asked Barnabas.

"The end that was meant to be, of course," said Odin. "Which is just the beginning, really, if you think of it."

"I have no idea what that means," said Barnabas. "But I do know that Ragnarok is imminent if you don't do something."

"Yes, well, Vor said that it would all turn out this way," said Odin. "So that is how it should be, then, isn't it?"

"Who is Vor?" asked Barnabas.

"The goddess who knows everything," answered Odin.

"So," said Barnabas, mulling over this new bit of information, "if this Vor knew everything already, why bring us here in the first place?"

"To do everything that you have done," said Odin.

"But why? Why not just listen to Vor? Or tell us about her, for that matter?" said Barnabas. "It would have spared us a world of trouble, had we had an omniscient goddess to help us, you know."

"*Worlds* of trouble, no doubt," quipped Wilfred.

Odin shrugged. "Fate is strange, I suppose," he said.

"Oh!" cried Barnabas. "That is the most absurd…"

Seeing Odin's pleasant smile begin to turn into a rather frightening glare at Barnabas' words, Wilfred hurriedly cut him off.

"...Absurdly wonderful ending to a case, is what he's trying to say. More wonderful than we could have expected!" he said brightly.

Odin looked doubtfully from the apoplectic face of Barnabas to the overly amiable one of Wilfred, then shrugged again. "Very well," he said. "Congratulations, and thank you." With that, he left, trailed by his entourage of warriors, leaving the two detectives to stare in confounded bemusement after him.

"Of all the uncanny, absolutely stupid things!" said Barnabas, stamping his feet. "That could not have gone any worse, I am certain of it."

"Quite right," said Wilfred. "It is all too strange to be believed."

"And incredibly frustrating!" added Barnabas. "I am sure that I have no idea what to do now."

"We could capture Loki and the brothers ourselves," said a new, feminine voice from behind them. Barnabas and Wilfred turned to see Brynhild coming back towards them, accompanied by none other than Freya. It was the goddess who had spoken.

"You would help us in this?" asked Barnabas, feeling the beginnings of hope spark anew in his chest.

"After what they did to Od?" said Freya, laughing musically. "Dragging him off to be kidnapped by Ran? Of *course* I will help."

"Oh dear," said Barnabas, suddenly deflated. "But Odin has taken Loki's bowl and turned it into a fruit container."

"That is no matter," said Freya, airily waving a hand.

"Freya has already commissioned Fafnir to produce a new bowl," explained Brynhild. "You remember...the dragon king of the dwarves? She told me so when I ran into her at the stables. In fact, the bowl was set to be delivered to Sigyn today."

"And it cost me a good deal more than it might have," added Freya. "In order to recompense the dwarves for the destruction of Vollagardal."

"But, but..." stammered Barnabas, torn between chagrine and outrage. "I did not mean for the town to be destroyed, and it was Fafnir himself who destroyed it!"

"Yes, well," said Freya. "None of that matters much. In case you haven't noticed, things are not always entirely *rational* here, are they?"

"No, I suppose not," agreed Barnabas.

"So," said the goddess, clapping her hands together as though to hurry them along. "We must go if we wish to catch our victims, ah, I mean, our *villains*, in the cave."

"How shall we lure them there?" asked Barnabas, flummoxed.

"Freya has already done so," said Brynhild happily.

"How on earth did you manage such a thing?" exclaimed Barnabas.

"Why, it was easy," said Freya. "I sent Modi and Magni an invitation from Od, to go fishing in the pool below the cave. As for Loki, well, I merely told him that I would be visiting Sigyn, and that I'd be bringing Hildisvini with me..."

"The pig?" asked Barnabas, confused.

"The one that snores, if I'm not misremembering," added Wilfred. "I believe the Dark Elves gave him nightmares."

"Ah, yes, the Dark Elves," said Barnabas, shuddering. "Awful creatures, really. Just awful. Not at all like the Light Elves. I wonder if the Light Elves would still have us, do you think?"

"Perhaps!" said Wilfred. "Brynhild, did you not find the home of the Light Elves amenable as well?" It was as bold a statement as anyone had ever heard Wilfred make, and Barnabas and Brynhild stared at him, openmouthed. Brynhild was spared from responding, however, by Freya's interruption of the conversation.

"Enough!" snapped the goddess irritably. "You may discuss the elves of whatever variety you please after we've tied Loki back up. Now if you'd all just hold hands, please..."

Sheepishly, everyone obeyed, clasping hands as they formed a small semicircle. Freya stepped forward to fill in the gap between Barnabas and Brynhild, and suddenly, the entire world began to spin in a sickening fashion, and then all went black.

Chapter Twenty-Three

Moments later they landed, disoriented and dizzy, upon a rocky floor.

"Oh," said Barnabas, clutching either side of his head. "Of all the most abominable things, I do believe that *spinning* is the worst."

"Really?" said Freya, who was still spinning about though she no longer had a real reason to do so. "I find spinning divine." Her head was thrown back and arms spread wide, and Barnabas looked at her askew.

"I'm certain," he said primly, lips pursed together, "that you do. Now, *where* are we?"

The three companions looked about them as best they might, considering that it was quite dark currently, and the only source of light was a dim glow that seemed to come from everywhere and nowhere at once. A loud, rhythmic rumbling sound echoed rather alarmingly around them, making Barnabas jolt and twitch each time he heard it.

"Don't you recognize it?" asked Freya. "You've been here before, after all."

"Hmmm," said Barnabas, chewing his lip as he considered the environs. "Well, the floor is quite hard, as is evidenced by the myriad of lumps and bruises upon my person after our ungainly landing." He cast a disparaging look towards Freya, but she was too caught up in her happy spinning to pay it any mind.

"Yes, yes," she said. "A hard floor. Very good! Now what else?"

"It is dark, that is for certain," said Barnabas.

"Most dark, indeed," agreed Wilfred.

"And what little light there *is* is somewhat odd," said

Barnabas.

"Most odd," said Wilfred. "And it flickers, as though from a torch of some sort."

"Yes, yes," said Barnabas snippily, not happy at having Wilfred reach a conclusion before he himself had got there. "As I was about to say, of course."

"Of course," said Wilfred graciously.

"And there is a great racket being made," added Barnabas, referring to the rumbling sound. "Like giant machinery, or whatnot."

"Errr," said Freya, gracefully bringing her swinging to a stop and regarding the detectives with no indication whatsoever that she was at all dizzy.

"So, a hard floor, flickering torchlight, and a great mechanical rumble can only mean one thing," said Barnabas, lifting up a finger as though about to disclose a deduction of monumental proportions.

"Yes?" prompted Freya, as Barnabas paused for dramatic effect.

"A subterranean train station!" he announced proudly. "We are in London, of course, and a train will be along any moment now. See how the sound grows louder?"

Brynhild shook her head in exasperation. "We are in Loki's cave," she corrected. "Or, to be more precise, we are in the cave directly *behind* Loki's cave. The flickering light is from the fire Sigyn keeps lit within."

"Ha!" scoffed Barnabas. "Preposterous! To get to Loki's cave the first time we had to climb up a great lot of stairs, if I do recall."

"Which we didn't have to do this time, since Freya transported us directly into the cave," said Brynhild.

"Brynhild is correct," said Freya. "We are, of course, in Loki's cave. I rather thought that would be an easy question, since I announced that we were *going* there before we even *went*, if you remember."

"Of course I remember that we were going to go to Loki's cave," snapped Barnabas. "But that doesn't mean that we weren't to make a stop somewhere else, first."

"I suppose not," said Brynhild. "But since we are in Loki's cave, as Freya has confirmed, perhaps we might…"

"And you are not even accounting for the mechanical sounds," continued Barnabas, ignoring her. "I am certain that there is no possibility of there being a train in Loki's cave." He slapped his hands together as if to brush Brynhild's theory away as poppycock.

"Unless it is not a train at all," said Brynhild. "But is instead Hildisvini, breathing in his sleep."

"The snoring pig?" asked Barnabas, cocking his head to the side quizzically.

"He's a boar, but yes, that is him," answered Freya.

"Well, one must admit that he does sound quite a bit like a train," said Barnabas. "And when one *hears* a train, one always assumes that there *is* a train, is what I always say."

"Or a snoring pig," added Wilfred, less than helpfully.

"Well," said Freya tactfully. "I'm sure that this cave is something like a…a…what did you call it?"

"A train station," said Barnabas. "An underground one, for which you can be forgiven for knowing nothing of, since they are quite new, of course."

"Of course," said Freya, rolling her eyes. "Now, shush, if you please. I believe I hear our guests coming up the stairs even now.

Everyone dutifully shushed, and followed Freya as she crept to the other end of the cave. There, they discovered an opening that gave way into the main cave, where Barnabas and Wilfred had first met Sigyn (and, of course, where Barnabas had entered into a fruitless and rather terrifying battle with the giant snake that still lurked about in the high ceiling. Barnabas cast a suspicious look in its direction but, as it was bothering no one else, he looked down to where Loki and company were entering the cave).

"Freya?" he whispered. She pretended not to hear him for a moment, but as he persisted she acknowledged him with a sigh.

"Yes, Barnabas?" she said.

"Why did you bring your pig?" he asked.

Brynhild stifled a snort of laughter as Freya bit back a smile.

"Why, because Loki loves Hildisvini," answered the goddess.

"He does?" asked Barnabas. "But why?"

Freya shook her head. "I have no idea," she said. "But he's never turned down a chance to visit with Hildisvini."

"Which is why you used the pig as bait?" pressed Barnabas.

"Not as bait," said Freya. "As a lure, I would say."

"Huh," said Barnabas to Wilfred. "Who'd have thought the end of the world would be prevented by a *pig*?"

"A *boar*," corrected Brynhild. "But look! Here comes Loki!"

And there, framed in the opening to the cave, was the great trickster god himself. Barnabas, seeing how short and slender Loki was, thought immediately that it would be no difficult task in securing him to his table beneath the nasty snake once more. However, his hopes of an easy resolution were dashed as first Modi and then Magni walked in behind Loki, with Modi swinging Thor's hammer carelessly in one hand.

Immediately Loki saw (or heard) the snoring Hildisvini, and cried out with glee. "Hildisvini!" he exclaimed, rushing over to pet the sleeping boar. "How's my favorite pig?" He fawned over the creature for a time before noticing his wife, Sigyn, sitting in a chair along the cave's wall. "Oh, hallo, dearest wife," added Loki in a far less enthused tone, causing Sigyn to shake her head sadly. (In truth, Barnabas had not seen her either, and immediately felt bad for overlooking the poor, beleaguered woman.)

Modi and Magni bade Sigyn perfunctory greetings as well before joining Loki. They too wished to pet Hildisvini, and paid no more mind to Loki's patient wife. Remarkably, Modi was so intent on petting the pig that he dropped his father's hammer to lay, momentarily forgotten, on the cave floor.

"Here's the plan," began Freya, but Barnabas paid her no mind. His eyes were fixated on the hammer on the floor; the self-same hammer that he had picked up there on the lawns of Valhalla so long ago and which had nearly overcome him with violent impulses.

"Barnabas, no," said Wilfred, seeing the overly excited glint in his employer's eye, but to no avail. Barnabas, with no further ado, leapt forward and streaked across the cave towards the god, the two giants, and the hammer.

"Stop!" commanded Freya. "You cannot do this!"

"Can so!" called back Barnabas as he bent down and scooped up the hammer and began to swing it about (rather clumsily, if truth be told). "As is evidenced by the fact that I am, in fact, doing it!"

Brynhild slapped her hand across her forehead and shook her head, exhaling heavily.

"You cannot!" boomed Freya. "It is preordained that it is I who must..."

"Preordain *this*!" yelped Barnabas. He had managed by now to gain some control over the swing of the hammer, and it whirled about in crazy circles through the air. Immediately, he set upon Loki and the two giant brothers with a whoop, and began to whack them on and about their heads with the hammer (which were within his reach, as they were all kneeling beside the still-sleeping Hildisvini). "J'accuse!" cried the little detective, as the culprits tried unsuccessfully to fend off his ferocious attack.

Remarkably, Loki fell to the ground, insensible, after being clocked only once upon the jaw with the hammer, and Magni and Modi took only three and four strikes before likewise falling beside him. Everyone stared in wonder at the three unconscious scallywags and the crazed little detective who had brought them down.

Barnabas, still in the throes of battle-rage and consumed in no small part by the effects of the hammer, stood triumphantly over his fallen foes. "Rise, you lily-livered cowards!" he yelped. "So that I might deliver you another great blow, and then another, and another..." Each word was punctuated by a swift swing of Thor's hammer, and there was a maniacal glint in his eyes that no one particularly cared for.

"Barnabas," said Freya. "That is enough. You may set the

hammer down now."

"Nonsense!" cried Barnabas. "There must be someone else that needs a good whacking!"

"Really, no, I think you have done all the whacking that is required, just now," said Freya.

"But, I'm sure there must be *someone*," protested Barnabas, unwilling to let go of the powerful hammer. His eyes fixed upon the snake that still hung from the ceiling, regarding the goings-on with a baleful eye. "How about that snake? I could smite the snake, surely?"

"No!" cried everyone at once.

"Just a little smiting?" said Barnabas. "Really, that snake deserves it."

"Barnabas, do not smite that snake," warned Freya, slowly advancing on the crazed detective. "I am ordering you to drop the hammer and leave the snake alone."

"Ordering me?" said Barnabas, backing away from the goddess. "*Ordering* me? But I have Thor's hammer, don't I? Perhaps I will order you to…to…well, I can't think of just *what*, right now, but I'm sure that I *will*, given time!"

"Give me that hammer!" yelled Freya angrily. She reached forward as though to take it, but Barnabas leapt back nimbly.

"Maybe it is *fate* that *I* keep the hammer!" cried Barnabas. Freya gave chase to him, but Barnabas leapt about the cave as fast as a billy goat, always staying out of her reach. "Maybe it is fate that I run about the Nine Worlds, smiting ne'er-do-wells! Why, I'll be the god of…of…smoting! Smiting? Smiteness?"

"You will drop that hammer this minute!" shouted Freya, truly alarmed now. Wilfred and Brynhild looked at each other helplessly, knowing that the hammer had completely possessed their friend but unsure of how to stop the terrible situation that was unfolding before their eyes.

"I will drop it when I want to," taunted Barnabas. "Which will be never, so there…ack!" This last was uttered as Barnabas, in his unhinged glee, failed to pay heed to where he was stepping, and therefore tripped and fell over the bulky body of the sleeping pig.

The hammer flew from his hands as he landed with a heavy thud, directly in front of the two giants and the god (who were all, thankfully, still completely unconscious).

The crazy light went out of Barnabas' eyes and he blinked several times in confusion as his senses returned to him. Seeing himself face-to-face with the criminals, he gave a startled little cry and skittered back.

"Oh dear!" he cried. "They've got me! Oh, *do* help!"

"No one has got you," said Freya. She removed a large piece of fabric from a fold of her robe and carefully wrapped it around the fallen hammer. Then, with noticeable effort, she pushed it away, out of reach. "And you most assuredly do not need help," she added sardonically.

"If they haven't got me, then why am I on the floor next to them?" A safe distance away now, he looked at the three sleeping figures curiously. "And why are *they* on the floor, pray?"

"Probably because you knocked them out," said Freya, scowling. "Even though I told you not to."

"I, er, that is, I did...*what*?" asked Barnabas, thoroughly perplexed.

Freya looked sharply at him. "You don't remember?" she asked.

"It was like this before," said Brynhild. "The first time he picked up the hammer. He just scooped it up and went all berserk, almost exactly like what just happened."

"Excepting that no one was knocked unconscious that time," supplied Wilfred.

"Only because Hynder kicked him in the hand before he could get around to it," said Brynhild.

"I assure you," said Barnabas, "that I most certainly do *not* go *berserk*. Not under any circumstance, I am sure of it." The extraordinary redness of his cheeks and his refusal to meet anyone's eye whilst he said this gave the lie to his words, however.

"Except that you *do*," insisted Brynhild. "Go berserk, that is."

"But only when he handles that accursed hammer," added

Wilfred, trying to ameliorate the statement.

"He picked up the hammer before?" demanded Freya. "And no one thought to tell me this?"

"And then he remembers nothing of what happened, afterwards," added Brynhild, not quite answering Freya's question.

"It's as if it takes control of him," added Wilfred. "It is rather frightening, if you ask me."

"Frightening, indeed," said Brynhild, rolling her eyes.

"I say," said Barnabas, who, although he truly did not have any memory of what, precisely, had happened whilst he wielded Thor's hammer, *did* have enough presence of mind to put together the things the others were saying with the obviously unconscious state of Loki and the two brothers, and decide that he had, in all likelihood, behaved in a most untoward manner. "I say," he repeated, eager to change the subject, "it is enough, I believe, that the criminals are captured. No need for any further discussion on how they were captured, I'm sure."

"Quite so," said Freya. "Only, please, in the future, don't allow him near any more magical hammers. *Please.*"

Everyone nodded their agreeance to this, and, satisfied, Freya patted down her robes. "Very well, then," she said. "I just need to tie up Loki once more, and we can be on our way. Now where is that rope?"

"Is this the rope you're looking for?" asked Wilfred, picking up a thick length of rope from the ground.

"Ah, yes!" said Freya. "I must have dropped it whilst chasing Barnabas about." Barnabas looked down and shuffled his feet in embarrassment, but was quickly saved from further mortification by Freya's next words, which she uttered as she accepted the rope from Wilfred. "Ah, yes, this is it. Only rope made from the strongest of troll intestines will do, you know," she said with a wink.

"What?" yelped the three companions in unison. Wilfred, horrified, wiped his hands on his robes and grimaced.

"Um," said Freya, seeing their complete discomfiture. "Uhhhh, nothing. No troll intestines here!" she said, then lodged her tongue firmly into her cheek and looked shiftily about.

The goddess proceeded to tie Loki back up where he had been, and handed Sigyn the new silver bowl with which to catch the snake's venom as it dripped onto Loki's forehead, so that all would be as it had been before. (Sigyn thanked her for the bowl, but it seemed that only Barnabas could see the look of dull resignation on her face and hear the note of resigned insincerity in her voice. Sigyn, he thought, was far from pleased with her fate.)

Whilst Freya worked, Magni and Modi began to stir. One at a time they opened their eyes to behold each other lying there, side by side, on the cavern floor. They looked over to see Freya busily tying up Loki and their eyes hardened. For a moment Barnabas was sure that the two rascals would cause some further trouble, but then their eyes alighted on Barnabas. They both let out a terrified cry and, jumping to their feet, fled the cave.

Their feet could be heard stamping rapidly down the stairs outside as they beat a hasty retreat, still screaming. Barnabas gave an embarrassed shrug as Brynhild shot him an amused glance and raised an eyebrow.

"There," said Freya, as the cries of the escaping giants drew further away. "All done. Loki won't escape so easily next time," she declared, stepping back to admire her handiwork.

"Shan't we recollect Modi and Magni?" asked Barnabas after a pause, when it became clear that Freya was not going to pursue the brothers without a prompting.

"Why would we do that?" asked Freya.

"Because they are scallywags who nearly ended the world?" suggested Barnabas.

"And because they dropped Od into the ocean, to be kidnapped by the underwater goddess Ran?" added Wilfred helpfully.

"Bah," said Freya, waving a hand in dismissal. "They were fated to do that, I am sure. And all's well that ends well! Besides, I do believe that it is time for lunch."

"Oh, bother," said Barnabas, too weary to argue with such convoluted logic.

"Bother, indeed," agreed Wilfred.

"So, Brynhild," continued Freya. "Are you coming with me? I can drop you off at Ran's on my way home."

"Ran's?" cried Wilfred, surprised. "Why are we going to that dreadful place?"

"Not *you*," said Freya. "Just Brynhild."

Wilfred looked as though someone had just delivered him a terrible blow to his manparts. He blinked rapidly as his face turned first red, then purple, then white, then back to purple again before deciding upon a complexion comprised of an alarming mottling of the three.

"I'm sorry," said Brynhild gently. "When I was taking Hynder to the pastures in Asgard Freya told me that Ran has need of my services and wishes me to come to her the moment we finished up here. I meant to tell you, but then we came here straight away and then Barnabas took hold of the hammer and things, well…you know."

"I thought, well, I thought that perhaps, maybe, only, oh, I don't know!" said Wilfred, his obvious disappointment of feeling tying his tongue.

"That perhaps we might have a bit of time to sojourn with the Light Elves," supplied Barnabas, rescuing Wilfred from embarrassment. "The three of us together. To discuss the case, of course, and to tie up loose ends."

Wilfred, who had not entirely regained control of his faculties yet, merely nodded miserably.

"Oh no," said Freya. "We mustn't keep Ran waiting. Come, Brynhild." So saying, the goddess beckoned for Brynhild. The skald reached out to take first Barnabas' hand in farewell and then Wilfred's, giving the poor young fellow's hand an apologetic squeeze before moving to stand next to Freya.

Freya took hold of Brynhild as they prepared to leave. "And as for the two of you," said the goddess, "there'll be scant time for visiting Light Elves, or Dark Elves, or really elves of any kind, because I have a friend across the sea who has need of you. As soon as I deliver Brynhild to Ran I'll be back to take you to her. Ixchel is her name. I'm sure you'll handle yourselves well."

"Oh dear," said Barnabas sadly. "Another case? No Light Elves?"

"No Light Elves," said Freya firmly.

"Oh dear, indeed," said Wilfred sadly.

"Very well then," said Freya. "Shall we?" Without waiting for an answer, the goddess wrapped her arms fully around Brynhild and began to spin.

"Goodbye to you both," called Brynhild. "I'll miss you!"

"Farewell, dearest Brynhild!" said Barnabas, in an unprecedented display of affection for the young woman who had not only helped them solve their case but who had come to occupy the heart of his dearest friend.

"Fare thee well, dear Brynhild," whispered Wilfred at last, but whether she heard him or not was unclear as Freya's spinning had rapidly accelerated, thereby commencing the transportation process, and the two women had disappeared before Wilfred could finish.

"I am truly sorry, my dear boy," said Barnabas, seeing the look of stricken chagrin on Wilfred's face. He awkwardly patted him atop the head. "There, there," he added lamely.

Wilfred sighed, then composed his features into a stoic expression. "It is a disappointment to be sure," he said, "but life *will* go on."

Barnabas thought that this was not an entirely accurate statement, as the two detectives were not precisely entirely *alive* anymore, but decided against pointing out that particular detail just now. "Quite right," he said heartily. "A stiff upper lip cures all ills, is what I always say. And we have a new case to keep us occupied." He pursed his lips and rested his chin on his hand. "I wonder who this *Ixchel* person is?" he mused. "And I wonder *where* she is?"

"I have no idea, I'm sure," said Wilfred. "But I must say, I will not be sorry if she proves to live somewhere warm. I have grown quite tired of being cold."

"Quite so, quite so," said Barnabas. "It will be splendid to leave this cave. Indeed, it will be splendid to leave these nine worlds, indeed."

"Indeed," agreed Wilfred.

"Indeed," whispered the forgotten Sigyn quietly, but the two detectives were too wrapped up in their own thoughts to hear her.

THE END

Fantastic Books
Great Authors

CROOKED CAT

Meet our authors and discover
our exciting range:

- Gripping Thrillers
- Cosy Mysteries
- Romantic Chick-Lit
- Fascinating Historicals
- Exciting Fantasy
- Young Adult and Children's Adventures

Visit us at:
www.crookedcatbooks.com

Join us on facebook:
www.facebook.com/realcrookedcat

Made in the USA
Lexington, KY
31 July 2018